There Goes the Galaxy, Book 3

by JENN THORSON

Waterhouse Press

PITTSBURGH, PENNSYLVANIA

Published by Waterhouse Press. Pittsburgh, Pennsylvania, U.S.A.

This is a work of fiction. Any resemblance to actual persons living or dead is purely coincidental. The Greater Communicating Universe works in mysterious ways.

ISBN: 978-0-9838045-6-7

Cover Art by Dave White

Printed in the United States of America

FOR EACH OF YOU COSMIC PEOPLE
Thanks for joining me on this journey.

The meek do not inherit the earth unless
they are prepared to fight for their meekness.
—H.J. LASKI (1893-1950) ATTRIB.

This is the price I pay for caring about stupid humankind.
—ROSLYN LOUISE MERCER (1989-?)

…There's no place like home.
—JOHN HOWARD PAYNE (1791-1852)
ALSO, THAT DOROTHY CHICK

ACKNOWLEDGMENTS

Flamin' Altair, we made it! *Tryfling Matters* represents the final book in the *There Goes the Galaxy* trilogy and I admit, I shed some sloppy, Joan Wilder-style tears as I typed those last few words of the story onto the page. While I intend the Greater Communicating Universe and its characters to live on in future standalone books, I look back at this time as a wonderful, bewildering adventure of its own.

I owe so much thanks to the people who have been supportive of these books. Your merry embrace of Bertram and company on their mad journey is really what this whole writing thing's about. Thanks for your time, your reviews, recommending it to others … it all has helped the series reach a stellar audience of humorous sci-fi fans. I raise a glass of smorg wine in your honor.

Thanks to Dave White for lending his artistic abilities to yet another ominous, humorous cover. Folks would chuckle at our process; I present him with ill-conceieved sketches and he transforms them into full-blown, colorful Awesome. It is his superpower. Well, that and his ability to eat ghost peppers.

I'd like to thank all of my beta readers who stepped forward to test this book with an eager, "Bring it on." Their sharp eyes and honest opinions were invaluable. And finally, thanks to Betty MacNaughten for lending her brainpower to Ditto's name. She triumphed where quality time with the thesaurus did not.

Thanks again, everyone! And see you around the Greater Communicating Universe, my friends.

1

The landscape wore its lack of hope like a gray, moth-eaten shawl. Snowflakes, dust and road salt churned languidly on the wind.

It was the only movement for miles.

Rozz Mercer shifted in the copilot's seat and Bertram heard her exhale as he guided the Interplanetary Cruise Vessel over I-80 in the Garden State, headed for his parents, headed for home.

It was exactly as he'd feared.

From the moment they'd begun their descent and all down this solemn stretch of highway, the world lay still and silent. Shopping malls sat vacant. Gas stations stood dark. A highway alert sign flickered feebly, a single asterisk its final message to all.

An asterisk: punctuation's official bouncer for sneaky disclaimers.

Bertram Ludlow was braced for the fine print.

"Hey, look!" Rozz strained against her safety harness, waggling a bitten fingernail. "There!"

Bertram saw it, too. Up around the bend, signs of intelligent life shone in the form of red-and-blue flashing lights. The travelers cheered and high-fived.

"That's right," shouted Bertram. "New Jersey state troopers, alive and on the job! I knew it. I *knew* it couldn't be as bad as it looked. I—"

They drew closer. The squad car sat angled, alone on the berm. One headlight beamed bright in the daylight, the other dark, smoky and cold.

Rozz ran a nervous hand over her short, fuchsia hair. "Okay, it's all good, it's fine, it's not slightly creepy or anything," she murmured. "But maybe you should just kinda…"

He did just kinda; Bertram took the cloaked ship in lower, closer to the car, because now they had to see inside it. They had to see the steely gaze and stylishly-shaved head of New Jersey's Finest. They had to know that despite Tryfe — er, Earth— having undergone a serious change of management and a temporary planet-napping, that some things on the Big Blue Marble were still business-as-usual.

They flew in as low as Bertram dared, stirring up clouds of salt along the way. As they glided past the squad car, its lights played around their cockpit walls. Bertram squinted. Rozz craned her neck.

The police cruiser was empty.

"Oh, I knew it," moaned Rozz, slamming a hand against the starboard portal window. "I knew things couldn't Not Suck as much as you were saying."

"Well, look on the bright side…" Bertram adjusted course abruptly to avoid taking out an exit sign. "… There's still power in places. The atmosphere's intact. There's plant life. And look: birds."

He indicated a couple of crows ripping the flesh off a deer carcass in a ditch. "They haven't even mutated."

Rozz stared at him. "Crows without three heads is the baseline bright side for us these days?"

"Work with me, Rozz. Work with me."

Bertram directed the Penumbra Classic away from the highway and it wasn't long before they'd landed the ship in the athletics field next to his old high school. The brick facility was now a boarded-up eyesore, decorated with No Trespassing signs—and signs of trespassers—the latter in faded spray paint along the walls. "RyIt," said one. "Morf," proclaimed another and "Remember to be happy, William," said a third.

At that last one, an unsettled feeling came over Bertram that he wasn't quite sure what to do with. So he double-checked the ship's cloaking settings, though he knew they were still on.

Neither Bertram nor Rozz spoke now. They unlocked their harnesses and left the cockpit for their pile of carefully-chosen supplies in the main cabin. They slung on their weaponry belts, slipped on their coats, donned their gas masks and grabbed their satchels.

"Ready?" asked Bertram.

"Hit it," said Rozz.

And he pushed the button, lowering the ship's ramp to the land of his birth.

They walked down empty residential streets past dark windows, along sleety ground. Cars sat in driveways and along the road, as if parked for a year or since yesterday. Trashbags staggered at the curb like winos, wafting must and decay. In the distance, a dog barked—or at least Bertram hoped it was a dog. Perhaps it was some new alien hybrid, forever changed in the misguided quest to improve on an Earth classic.

"I bet there are still pockets of people somewhere," Bertram suggested, running a finger over the trunk of a car and coming away with frost and grit. "We just need to find out where. I calculated it and we should be able to take at least forty people back in the ship."

"Forty?" An eyebrow shot up behind Rozz's gasmask.

"It'll be a little tight."

The Penumbra was a three bedroom, one bath ICV, and the bath was already populated by a handful of small, rather territorial snail creatures that had come free with purchase. It would be close quarters for all concerned, but Bertram figured the joy of rescue would outweigh any of the more minor inconveniences, like the total lack of privacy or not being able to sit down.

"And what do we do with forty people once we have them?" Rozz asked.

"Rollie said they can stay with him at his library on Ejellan until they get their spacelegs." Given Rolliam Tsmorlood's typical patience with people of any species — something most accurately measured in atoms — Bertram thought this was very generous.

Rozz must have thought so, too, because she didn't press the matter. She paused to pick up a can poking from a trashbin.

"DrinkThis®," said the label, and Bertram recognized the brand from back in the Greater Communicating Universe. It had been a prototype beverage from a company located on the planet Ottofram. That company's CEO, Eudicot T'murp, was the Earth's current owner.

"Manufactured by DiversiDine World, Ltd.," read Rozz. No surprise there; that was some iteration of the Ottoframan firm. "Headquartered in Pittsburgh, Pennsylvania."

At this, Bertram peered over her shoulder for a better look. "DiversiDine's set up shop in Pittsburgh?" He and Rozz had both been going to grad school in Pittsburgh, prior to their respective alien abductions. "That's weird. Isn't that weird?"

"Dude, if you're actually surprised by that? You might want to recalibrate your bright side." Rozz patted his arm and returned the can to the trash.

They continued the journey down Bertram's old street, and he was struck by how little things had changed in his absence. In the cold, damp breeze, the Rosenbergs' wooden porch swing still squeaked on metal hooks. The Jorgensen's sidewalk bowed where the great oak bullied it from its bounds. The Gonzales' house had new siding, but their Colonial stood timeless and proud. And here, Bertram read "The Ludlows" off the now-faded mailbox. Even the basketball hoop hung over the garage like before, its netting long-rotted, but its memories intact.

Bertram motioned Rozz down the front walk to the house.

He grounded himself with a deep breath through his mask and pressed the doorbell.

He could hear the chime through the door, then silence.

"We're being watched," muttered Rozz and she hooked a thumb at the front bay window.

Bertram turned to see the hollow eyes, giant ears, patchy hair and jutting bones of a creature that only the most generous of animal lovers would call "cat."

Rozz flinched as the thing banged and yowled a silent greeting against the window glass.

Bertram rang the bell more persistently now, then pounded on the door.

At the second round of pounding, Rozz clamped down on his arm, stilling it. "Bertram, look: I don't know if you're going to want to go in there. I don't think you're going to like what you see."

"What do you mean?" Bertram reached for the knob. "Someone's in there. They have to be."

"But the cat, it's like an unwrapped mummy. It's beef jerky. It's undead or an evil mutant or something. It's—"

"Oh, that's Mr. Miggins."

This was probably not the response she expected. "Excuse me?"

"Mr. Miggins," Bertram said again. "Mom's cat. He's about nine hundred years old and we've never actually seen him eat. We have this theory he survives on the aroma of cat food alone. The expensive stuff, too. No, he's all right," Bertram assured her. "That's why I know someone's still here."

As if to prove his point, the door swung inward. Bertram and Rozz snapped to attention. And there in a plaid bathrobe, curly hair askew, stood Bertram Ludlow's dad pointing a gun.

On reflex, Bertram and Rozz both drew handlasers and gauged the situation. There were no noticeable signs of plague. No obvious new alien phenotypic attributes. No visible mutations, evil or otherwise. Just one retired dentist who had grown gray around the temples and whose bloodshot eyes squinted in disbelief. "Bertram? Is that you?"

"Larryyyyy," called a voice from inside the darkened home. "Who is it, dear?"

And in trotted Bertram's mom in her yoga outfit. Her perplexed expression mirrored her spouse's. "Bertram?"

"Uh …" Bertram holstered the handlaser and pulled off the gasmask. "Hi, Mom. Dad."

"Bertram," she said again, like the name needed practice. "What are you *doing* here?"

"Well, I just—"

"And what," she surveyed him quizzically, "are you wearing?"

Bertram looked down at the alien military surplus coat and pants and his high-traction spaceboots. It was a little on the badass side for Bertram's taste, frankly, and he probably needed to be taller to really pull it off. But when you plan to save your home planet from the unknown effects of an extra-terrestrial takeover, you come prepared. If there were anything he'd learned from Rollie Tsmorlood, it was that.

"Well, black's very practical," Bertram explained. "It doesn't show bloo—uh, dirt. Dirt."

"Never mind," Mom said, turning on a slippered foot. "I need coffee. Come in."

She retreated down the long, dark hall to the kitchen. Silently, Dad, Rozz and Bertram followed.

The kitchen light popped on and Bertram felt like he'd stepped back in time. Sure, he'd come home a couple of times since first going off to college, but never before had it registered what a tribute to nineties' traditional decor his parents' home truly was. He trailed a hand down the green and burgundy wallpaper border with the fake swags and tassels printed on it. It was like some precious ancient artifact in pre-pasted vinyl. He shook his head at the Tiffany-style fruit lamp still dangling over the table. He marveled at the big brass planters with the ferns in various levels of existential struggle.

"I'm so glad you survived," Bertram told his parents, though he might have been talking to the ferns. "I mean, you guys, you look so healthy. How have you been managing? I see you've got power and—and coffee…"

Mom held up two bags. "French roast or Joltin' Jubilation®?"

"I'm going to need the Jubilation," said Dad blearily.

Mom measured from that bag into the coffeemaker, the same machine they'd always had.

"*Gourmet* coffee," Bertram observed in surprise. "So, uh, things are … livable, then?" It was hard to know how to broach the subject of alien overlords and the decline of human civilization when there was gourmet coffee. And was that … *flavored* creamer?

"Sure, things are livable." His mother raised her voice over the coffeemaker gurgle. "Why wouldn't they be? I mean, my youngest son disappears two years ago—"

Bertram blinked. "*Two* years?" He'd estimated eight months, tops.

"— And we don't hear a word. And to be honest, Bertram, I can understand that." She leaned against the counter. "Your father and I recognize that not everyone is cut out to finish medical school."

"I never started medical school," Bertram said.

"Exactly," Bertram's dad chimed in, pouring sugar substitute into his empty cup.

"You do know I was never studying to be a doctor, right?" Bertram felt his face flush. "I was studying to get my doctorate in—"

"Of course, your brother did so well with it," continued Mom, pouring coffee into Dad's outstretched mug, then her own. "Graduating first in his class at dental school?"

"Just like his old dad," said his old dad proudly.

Mom smiled. "And Archie always did have that natural confidence one needs for the perfect root canal." She held up the pot and looked from Bertram to Rozz. "Would either of you like a cup? And I'm sorry," she turned to Rozz, "I don't believe we've met."

"Mom, this is Rozz Mercer. Rozz, this is—"

But Mom was back to pouring coffee. "It's such a shame,

Bertram." She tucked a mug into his hands. "If only you'd talked to us instead of running away, your father and I could have eased your burden so much sooner."

Bertram's snicker almost shot coffee through his nose. "Oh, really?"

"Sweetie..." She looped her arm through his. "I know what you're thinking, but we aren't disappointed in you."

"You aren't?" This was news.

"Not at all, son." Dad clapped Bertram on the back. "We knew it was a wash way back in preschool. It's okay. We set our expectations."

Mom nodded. "Some children are meant for greatness and others, well, they cause embarrassing missing persons cases."

"It happens." Dad shrugged. "I saw something similar on *Inside Edition*."

Bertram took a moment and closed his eyes. Yes, indeed, this was the good ol' family he knew and largely avoided.

"If only there hadn't been all those questions from the police," Mom sighed wistfully. "Twice they made me late for my book club. But..." She waved her hand, like it was all water under *The Bridge to Terabithia*. "Next time, promise me you'll tell someone before you decide to go find yourself, all right?" But before he could answer, his mother gasped, sloshing coffee onto the no-wax floor. "Oh my goodness! We're missing it! We're missing the pre-show, aren't we?" And she darted into the living room and flipped on the TV.

After getting used to holovision technology, the two-dimensional images on Bertram's parents' screen seemed flat and uninspired. It showed very human announcers in a sunny Earthen spot, fussing over nervous Earthling marching bands prepping to perform backspace showtunes.

Mom dimpled. "Do you remember how much Archie used to love the Tournament of Roses parade as a kid? Well, we started this wonderful tradition. This morning, Archie, Sarah, the kids and Grandma Ludlow will be all here to —"

"Tournament of Roses." Bertram frowned. "This is New Year's Day?"

Dad rubbed his stubbly face. "Boy, is it! We would have been up sooner but those Gonzaleses really know how to throw a party. I'm so glad I prepped the pork roast for the slow cooker before I went to bed. Can you smell it? And I just put in the potatoes."

"I'll snap the green beans after breakfast," Mom said. "Oh, and Bertram: you and … Rose, is it? I have to ask." She leaned in conspiratorially. "Are you an item?"

Bertram should have seen this coming. It was hard to explain that his and Rozz's romantic inclinations had petered out somewhere between changing the fate of the planet Earth and being trapped for six months in a defunct spaceship with waning life support. It was equally hard to explain Xylith, the extra-terrestrial lady he was sort of seeing, but couldn't exactly bring home to Mother.

By this point, Rozz had decided to take things into her own hands. "Are we 'an item'?" She flashed an uncomfortable smile. "Sure, if you mean I'm one item, and Bertram's another completely separate item …" She waited for a laugh, but Bertram could have told her she was playing to a tough crowd. She looked like she wanted to fall through the floor. "I mean, your son's terrific—the best! But these days, we're just friends. And hi," she extended her hand, "I'm Rozz, two Z's. I like computer application development, indiepunk, this coffee and—"

The doorbell rang, and if they'd had beaming technology, the elder Ludlows couldn't have left the room any quicker. Over his mug, Bertram listened to the greetings, peals of laughter, Grandma Ludlow's fussing and electronic game sounds emanating from the entryway. He pondered the difference in the quality of welcome between invited guests and errant secondary sons in gasmasks.

"It is *so* not fair," Rozz whispered, looking drained from her attempt at being personable. "You're famous in the GCU. You're a hero. And you come here and you're …"

Bertram slurped his Jubilation. "Cloaked?"

"Pretty much."

"Yeah." Bertram nodded. "It's what happens when you're the follow-up act on a first-born big headliner. You can be abducted by aliens and no one really notices."

"Unless you make 'em late for their book club." Rozz rolled her eyes.

"Well, *then*. Of course." He took another moment to drink his coffee and tipped the mug to drain the last dribble. How he had missed those beautiful brewed beans. He'd have to stock up on a few bags of the strong, ground stuff when all this World Saving was said and done. And from the looks of things, that might be sooner rather than later. He clunked the mug to an end table.

"You ready?" Rozz asked, nudging him. "You going in?"

Bertram grinned. "Is it wrong I long for evil mutants?"

"Mutants are awesome. Why couldn't we have mutants?" she said. "They're just so laserable. You can't laser family."

"You sure?" asked Bertram. "The day is young."

They moved to greet his brother's throng.

"Wow: triplets," said Bertram. A gaggle of babies wobbled around the living room like a pack of drunks in a Vos Laegos nightclub searching for their lost ICV remotes. These were in addition to the three kids Bertram already knew, who were playing some wrestling game clearly designed to reduce their numbers. "What'd you name them?"

"We wanted something instantly recognizable, yet meaningful," Bertram's sister-in-law Sarah said, tucking long, blond hair behind her ear. "So we named them—"

She said something, but Archie Jr. decided to turn up the TV volume to stadium crowd levels. Bertram cupped a hand to his ear. "What is it?" he shouted.

"… AND HERE WE SEE THE DIVERSIDINE DRINKTHIS FLOAT," screamed the television, "REMINDING US TO 'MAKE EVERY DAY A DIVERSIDINE DANDY DAY.'"

"DID YOU KNOW, TRENT —" Bertram's eardrums buzzed with the announcer's voice. "— THAT EVERY ONE OF THOSE CARBONATED BUBBLES IS MADE FROM OVER A HUNDRED CARNATIONS?"

"I DID NOT KNOW THAT, PEGGY. BUT WHAT'S THIS I SEE UP NEXT? WHY, IT'S THE 'PATTY THE SNACK CAKE' BALLOON, SAILING ABOVE THE CROWD TO SHOW US ALL HOW LIGHT AND FLUFFY DIVERSIDINE PATTYCAKES® ARE."

Bertram's brother A.J. grabbed the remote from his eldest and dipped the volume back to human levels. "Sorry about that." Mom's china cabinet was still vibrating. "So Bertie," he said, with a clap of his skilled dentist hands, "what brings you home after all this time?"

Out of the corner of his eye, Bertram saw Rozz smirk. "Bertie?" she mouthed.

Bertram cleared his throat. "Oh. Well, I just wanted to check in, really. Make sure everyone was all right. And not, y'know, being used as slave labor for creatures from outer space bent on world domination or anything." He'd tossed it out there, figuring it was the most direct way to get his arms around the Tryfe situation. Unfortunately, it was also the most direct way to get everyone in the room to stop talking and stare. He quickly tacked on a laugh.

It came out high and strained. Two of the triplets looked frightened. One began to cry.

"Um, we really should be going," Bertram said, rising.

Rozz rose, too. "Yeah, we've got…something…"

"Oh, but you've come all this way. Stay for dinner, at least," said Mom. Which Bertram thought was pretty kind, considering he'd gone from The Invisible Man to Weird Uncle Bertram in record time. "We have pork roast, potatoes, crescent rolls … There's plenty."

"And apple pie," said Dad. "Your favorite."

Apple pie was A.J.'s favorite. But the food wafting from the kitchen was really starting to smell amazing. It had been ages since either Bertram or Rozz had a meal that didn't involve a

Food Processing Unit or Rollie zapping something with a handlaser. Not that Rollie didn't have a strange flair with meager ingredients and an XJ-37. But it wasn't quite the same.

Bertram and Rozz conferred silently for a moment, then both sat back down on the floral sectional. It was common knowledge that much could be endured for crescent rolls.

Sarah was eyeing them. "So were you guys at some kind of theme party last night?"

"Uh, yeah. Sci-fi thing," said Bertram. He'd forgotten about his battle gear, so he hastily shed his coat and the laser holster onto the loveseat. Underneath was his souvenir t-shirt from Beddsyde Manor. It made him feel a little more like himself.

"We came straight from the party," Rozz said.

Sarah nodded. "And who are you supposed to be?"

"You wouldn't know him," said Bertram.

"Anime character," said Rozz.

"I remember," began Grandma Ludlow now from the wingback chair, "when I was a young thing on New Year's Eve, we didn't do all these crazy themes. No, we'd get dolled up and go dancing. Then we'd wait for the ball to drop in Times Square, sing the wrong words to *Auld Lang Syne*, kiss a total stranger, go home with him and wake up in the morning, skirt up to our necks, girdle on our shoe. Gawd, how I fondly half-remember those days." She whisked a tear from behind her glasses. "But these days, it's different. All the true meaning of the New Year is lost. Like this—" She gestured to the parade. "DiversiDine this, DiversiDine that." She gave it a dismissive wave of the hand and topped it off with a raspberry.

"I'm afraid I have to disagree with you, Lavinia," said Bertram's mom, deftly extracting the TV remote from one triplet's mouth. "I see it as symbolic. DiversiDine's helped create a brand new beginning for us all. It's become such an important part of our culture so quickly, I think it's only right that some traditions change and grow to accommodate it. Think about what a pillar of strength Coach Dandy was for us since The Swirling Times."

"The Swirling Times," everyone murmured reverently.

Bertram and Rozz exchanged glances. For several weeks in the not-so-distant past, Bertram's home planet and a third of the Greater Communicating Universe had been held for ransom, trapped in swirling force fields from which no one could get in or out. Since the Earth was still pretty backspace about the topic of aliens and their activities, Bertram had wondered what the local reaction had been.

"Yeah, so … how was The Swirling Times for you here?" Bertram asked casually. "What's your favorite theory?"

"Well, I agree with NASA," said Dad. "I still think it was some form of natural anomaly. It came. It disintegrated a few robot probes, it kept me from watching *The Chalk Outline Squad* on satellite television and it went."

"No," said Grandma Ludlow. "I keep telling you, Larry, it was a sign from God. It said, 'People, you be good or you get zapped.'"

"But no one got zapped," said Dad. "It just disappeared. How do you explain that?"

She shrugged. "So people got good."

Sarah shook her head in the negative. "I think the government was testing something they don't want us to know about. Spy technology, maybe."

"As you can probably guess, things were a little … tense … around here," said Mom, giving Bertram a you-don't-know-the-half-of-it look. "Lots of people were very concerned about the End of Days, though. The gasoline lines were terrible. And you couldn't get milk, bread, eggs or toilet paper at all."

"Isn't that for a blizzard?" asked Rozz.

Grandma Ludlow said, "People want to go to their Maker with breakfast and clean butts." Holidays were filled with wisdom like this in the Ludlow family.

"I have to admit," Dad mused, "that with all the initial fear and divisiveness that happened around The Swirling Times, Coach Dandy really was excellent for morale. He just leapt in and took charge."

"It's true," said Mom. "No matter what your belief or theory, he gave everyone a reason to come together respectfully, in their own special way."

"Uh, yeah …" said Bertram. This all sounded a little soupy for this crowd, but he supposed sometimes trauma did that to people. "And who's Coach Dandy again?"

But the question disintegrated in the air like those space probes, as A.J. dove across the room to prevent a murder-in-progress.

Yes, poor long-suffering Mr. Miggins was trapped in a headlock courtesy of tiny, yet powerful toddler arms. The cat's growl was low and his sunken eyes, pleading. That much was standard-issue. The startling element was the raspy words hidden within the growl: "Help me."

A chill ran down Bertram's arms, causing the hair to stand on-end.

Help me?

Bertram looked around the room to see everyone else's reactions. But Mom, Dad, Sarah, Grandma Ludlow and all the older kids were just chatting, bystanding or lightly killing each other. Bertram tried to catch Rozz's eye, but she was fixated on A.J. in numb, mute horror while he pried sticky, baby hands off the cat. And Mr. Miggins, well, he turned into a four-legged version of Steve McQueen the instant the escaping was great.

The baby wailed at the loss of its victim, while A.J. moved to comfort this Boston Strangler in training pants. "I know you like the kitty, Delight," he soothed. "But you can like the kitty even more by letting it have continued respiratory function, okay?"

Bertram could not let this pass. "You named the kid 'Delight'?"

"That's what we were telling you," said Sarah. "Delight, Bliss and Jubilation. After our favorite DiversiDine products."

It was Bertram and Rozz's turn to look blank.

"*You* know," Sarah continued, as if everyone in the universe really did know, "like DiversiDelights®, BlissBuns® and Joltin' Jubilation."

"The coffee?" asked Rozz. She peered into her empty mug for validation.

"I know what you're thinking," Sarah said. "Too trendy, right? But like we said, DiversiDine's had such a positive impact on our lives, we had to do it."

"Ah. Yes."

Bertram was thinking he personally liked ramen noodles a lot, too, but he didn't envision naming any future progeny "Maruchan."

"By the way," continued A.J., leaning forward on the sofa, "I don't think I heard; where were you traveling the past two years, Bertie?"

"Oh, around," said Bertram breezily. "Here and there. Hither and yon."

A prickly energy whizzed past Bertram's ear. He turned. One of the triplets had a hold of Bertram's handlaser and had figured out the switch to Level Three Stun.

"G-ah!" Heart pounding, Bertram ripped the thing from its grasp, triggering another fit of infant wailing. "No! No! Not for babies!"

"Aw, he's not hurting your little toy there," said Sarah, moving to comfort the kid and shooting a displeased mother lion look at her brother-in-law. "Jubil's just curious."

"Jubil," Bertram shouted this louder than he'd intended, "almost had the Huggies stunned off him!"

And once again, the family stared in horror at Weird Uncle Bertram.

"We're gonna go," Rozz said, rising. "Definitely go. We're going."

"Er, yeah," Bertram said, buckling the holster and slinging on his coat. The maximum endurance threshold for crescent rolls had officially been reached.

He noticed now that Grandma Ludlow was slumped in the wingback chair, head lolled to the side. It wasn't that she normally didn't end most holidays like this. But it was early and unlike Grandma, a Level Three Stun didn't care about sleep schedules.

"Before you go," said Dad sounding considerably relieved at this upcoming change in cast, "there's a box of your stuff that's been cluttering up the garage. It's under the workbench. You want to take it?"

With no idea what it contained, Bertram said he would.

"Nice meeting you all," Rozz might have said, but she got out the "nice" and a rhythmic mumble as Bertram led her away.

The garage. Plastic tricycles and outdoor equipment were tossed in piles. Nerf launchers spoke of past battles. Grills and bags of charcoal served as evidence of late night shindigs with the Gonzaleses. There was an old couch, cinderblocks, parts of twenty obsolete computers, a dental chair circa nineteen-hundred and a Sit-'N-Spin. There was no room for the car.

Mr. Miggins, Bertram noticed, was sitting on top of the workbench. He eyed Bertram and Rozz with a wary, yellow assessment. On the shelf below him was a dusty shoebox labeled "Bertram," clearly taking up a whole cubic foot of space better-suited for ten more Commodore-64 keyboards and an antique ether machine.

Bertram picked up the box and scratched the cat under the chin. "Take care, Miggsy. Good luck."

But Mr. Miggins looked from Bertram to a roll of wire on the workbench and then, with deliberation, pushed it off the edge.

"For the motherland!" came the strange, raspy voice, followed by an oath ("Aw, hairballs!"), as the object struck the ground and rolled under the charcoal grill.

"Miggsy?" Bertram leaned in closer to the cat.

But Mr. Miggins began to wash.

Bertram turned to Rozz. "Tell me you just heard—"

"I—I don't know," she said. But judging by her pallor, she did.

"Miggsy," Bertram knelt by the cat now. "Miggsy, you said something, didn't you? We heard you. We understood. Say it again."

Bertram had never been able to persuade Mr. Miggins to stay off the counters. He had no idea why he thought he could get him to do a repeat oration now.

It was only after promises of catnip and wet food to sniff—

also to no response — that Bertram rose, tucked the shoebox under his arm and headed to the garage door. He paused. "Bye, Miggsy. Hold down the fort, old man."

Mr. Miggins looked up, paw poised mid-lick. He opened his mouth and for one long moment, Bertram expected him to wish them a fond farewell.

The cat yawned, then returned to his personal hygiene.

2

"I am like water molecules in the stream ... I am like an ergowohm gliding on the wind ... I am like ..." Rolliam Tsmorlood tried to remember. "Like..."

It wasn't coming.

"Aw, frag it, what am I like?" Rollie popped open his eyes and snatched up his copy of *The Guide to Karnaxic Meditation: The Uptight, Stressed-Out Non-Believer's Edition* from the floor next to him. He ruffled through it and dragged one long, scarred finger down the page. "Where are you, ya flamin' slaggard? Son of a Keeltsar, these fraggin' mantras all sound the same." His finger skidded to a stop. "Ah! 'Stardust expanding in space'! Of course!"

He tossed down the book, closed his eyes again and struck Pose of Harmony Four-Hundred-and-Twenty-Seven. "I am like stardust expanding in—"

Bzzp! "Hey, Rollie?"

"I am like stardust expanding in—"

Bzzp! "Rollie, are you there?"

"Stardust fraggin' expanding—"

Bzzp! "I know you're there, Rollie. I can hear you muttering."

Rollie growled, leapt up and stepped to his vis-u.

On the screen was Prinny, projected in 3D. The shapeshifter was in her natural state, a tiered gelatinous form that he understood closely resembled a type of dessert found on the planet Tryfe, the planet its residents called Earth. He hoped she never vacationed there or things could get awkward.

"I'm sorry to bother you, Rollie," she said.

"Just when I was finding my harmonious fraggin' center," he sighed.

"Your what?"

"Skip it." He folded his arms. "What do you need?"

"I need some advice," she said gravely. "I have an opportunity to do a job on the planet Gloftu. Scarvan Regamoid needs someone who can pose as a decoy briefcase in a swap scam, and I don't know if I should do it."

"Then don't." He grinned. *That was easy.* He reached for the off button.

"Usually," she continued and he retracted his hand, "my brother Gleb works with Scarvan's team. But they say his briefcase looks more like a backpack and that's not professional enough for this job. I don't want to step on my brother's base molecules, but..."

Rollie gave an irritated exhale. This was the fifth time she'd vis-ued about stuff like this since their little group had officially left the Intergalactic Underworld Society. "Forget Gleb. What do *you* want to do?"

"Well, I'd like the job. I mean, I do a stellar briefcase, and I've even got this realistic combination lock I've been working on. You want to see? It turns and every—"

Rollie held up a hand before she could start changing forms. "I really don't."

"Aw, but—"

"Take the job, Prinny. Talk to Gleb. Tell him why Scarvan picked you over him."

"But he'll be so—"

"Tell him you'll work with him on his own briefcase for next time. Right? He's a grown, er —" What *was* their species, anyway? "— blob. He'll get over the disappointment."

She looked unsure. "I suppose…"

"Fraggin' straight. Have some confidence, will you? You got talent. Stop second-guessing and do it."

Her face brightened, or at least the goo got brighter at the spot where her face likely was. "Wow! Thanks, Rollie. I really appreciate—"

"And most of all, stop comming *me*." He reached for that off button again.

"Wait, before you go."

He shook his head. *Unbelievable.*

"The guys were wondering what you call it."

He scowled. "Call what?"

"Well, this." She gestured all around her. "You know: our alternative to the Intergalactic Underworld Society. The new organization."

Now this was just too much. "Prinny," he said, enunciating it clearly so there would be no confusion, "how many times must I say it? I am not leading a fraggin' alternate Underworld Society. I am freelance. Independent. There is no new organization."

"Well, sure, not until it has a name. I mean, marketing is so important when you're trying to compete in the cross-space crime niche. So I have some suggestions to run by you." She read notes off a handheld device. "How do you feel about The Lawless League? Or the United Criminal Alliance?

"Bye, Prinny." He gave a Hyphiz Deltan salute.

"Felony Federation! I saved that one for last because it's my fav—"

Rollie flipped off the vis-u and set the device to auto-answer. He dusted off his hands and returned to the clean place he'd made on the floor of the library's office that was also currently doubling as his sleeping quarters. It wasn't fancy, but when you build your own library on a tiny planet you own and that no one ever visits, you can do what you fragging-well please.

He picked up the book on Karnaxic meditation. There was a lot to like about the philosophy of Karnax. For one, Karnax and Rollie shared similar views on self-determination, ongoing learning, a good stew and why trust was so blasted over-rated.

Mainly, the meditation angle was the sticking point. Rollie had thought it might give him more control over his medical condition, the systemic hypermotocerebrostasia that affected a very small percentage of Rollie's species. Hyphiz Deltans were already naturally a rather high-strung and energetic people. But those with Rollie's condition went the one step further, processing far too much information, too fast, with thoughts and stimuli, past and present, all fighting for attention — no lines, no waiting. Left unregulated, it was enough to drive a person mad. In fact, he'd done the round-trip several times.

So for most of his life, Rollie had managed his condition with a rigorous alcohol regimen. Overall, it was quite effective. It slowed the brain down and helped filter the thoughts. That way, his body never reached the ultimate tipping point, where it said, "Hey now, that's enough of this nonsense" and pulled the switch for total shutdown.

Unfortunately, there were times — like when you happened to be exiled to a death planet — that you couldn't just pop off to the local watering hole and have a nice Carsoolian pod liquor or six. He'd hoped meditation would help solve this problem. But he'd been working at it for the past few weeks with little progress.

The other thing he and Karnax differed on was the topic of celibacy, in that Karnax was for it. Rollie wasn't ready for that much personal growth at once.

"I am like water molecules in the stream ... I am like an ergowohm gliding on the wind ... I am —" a clatter echoed from the front of the building, "— a very unfortunate intruder, about to be fragged to bits."

Rollie leapt to his feet, handlaser drawn.

He moved forward quietly, slipping from his office to the darkened main room, eyes searching the dim. Could it be a hexabulon, one of those many-legged monsters with the fine poisonous hairs that reached and wrapped? Shoot 'em, shave 'em, roast 'em, they made a fine dinner. Miss, and you'd never live to regret it. He thought he'd dispatched the last of them some time ago.

He also sometimes was wrong.

But as his eyes adjusted to the darkness, he discovered poisonous pests were the least of his problems. A burly, bipedal figure was poised before the doorway, a satchel across his chest and something in his hands. In a deep, unfamiliar voice, the person called, "Rolliam Tsmorlood? I've got something for you."

Rollie had no doubt that this was true.

No stranger would ever ask for Rollie in this place—no one of pure intentions, certainly. The library was registered to one Dax Q. Phlyjollee, mild-mannered book collector and an alias Rollie had taken great pains to separate from himself. Anyone using the Tsmorlood name here had not made some innocent mistake; they'd set a challenge.

This was an assassin from the original Underworld.

"Captain Tsmorlood? Do you hear me?"

Rollie knew they'd track him down eventually. But two of the most enthusiastic candidates for the task—Jor-Jan Chatta-Chu-Bular Meep-Meep and Rentar Proximetra — recently met rather messy ends themselves and not by Rollie's hand. Meep-Meep had been found in a tree, neck broken, having died in a freak leviboot accident. (Or so the Uninet stories claimed.) Proximetra was discovered deep in an abandoned hovercraft park on the planet Diwaal-1, gnawed to bits by the urban crustaceans called skaggetts. It was the first reported skaggett attack in Diwaal history. And it was made all the more curious since skaggetts are normally vegan.

So while Meep-Meep and Proximetra were gone, that didn't mean someone else hadn't taken up the flag of their cause. Certainly Zenith Skytreg, current Official Leader of the Intergalactic Underworld, was no fan. And he had thousands of members just waiting for the chance to get on his good side.

"Captain Tsmorlood, I know you're here," called the voice again. "I was told to wait until you came. I'm supposed to give this to you in person."

Rollie kept to the darkest shadows and moved soundlessly around the room's perimeter.

"Hello?"

The intruder was just seven kroms away... five now... three kroms ... one ... Rollie slipped around behind his guest. He seized the strap of the humanoid's satchel, yanking it up and across the man's throat. He pulled tight, tighter. He could feel the jolt of surprise in the man's muscles.

"Who are you?" Rollie hissed. "Who sent you? Skytreg? Are you some follower of Proximetra's? Or Meep-Meep's? Speak!"

The lifeform gurgled in response and Rollie recognized the minor disconnect between his method and his goals. So he released the satchel and focused his XJ-37 on the man. "A handlaser is aimed at your head and it's not set to stun. Turn around. Slowly."

The lifeform did so, and light from the window in the front door illuminated this stranger for the first time. It shone on his sweat-beaded cheeks. It shone on his sweat-soaked shirt. It particularly illuminated the emblem on his blue uniform, the one that read "GCUPS."

The Greater Communicating Universe Packaging Service.

By now the courier was shaking clear to his boots. He held out a parcel. That shook, too. "Captain Rolliam Tsmorlood?"

"Aw, blast it all," said Rollie, lowering the laser and flipping on the main library lights. "Sorry, mate."

The courier blinked in the brightness. "Captain Rolliam—?"

"What do you think?" asked Rollie, snatching the package from the man's hands. The return address read "Tsardonee." The handwriting matched the name. The bill of lading was all in Hyphiz Deltan. Rollie let out an exasperated huff. "Tseethe," he grumbled. Rollie's friend Tseethe Tsardonee knew all about his current Phlyjollee alias and several others. If this were a joke, it was a very unfunny one. He set the package aside. "I'll get him for this."

The courier nodded, easily convinced. He held up a retinal scanner. "I–I still need you to...uh..."

"No," said Rollie. "You don't." He didn't sign for anything

under his real name when he was alive. Now that he had officially died on Altair-5, he was hardly about to start giving autographs.

"It's just, see, our policy says every package needs to have a—"

"And my policy," Rollie said quietly, redirecting the XJ-37, "says couriers who don't want to become like water molecules in the stream … like stardust in space … will get one of these." The guy was so busy staring at the weapon, it was easy to hit the fellah with a quick hypo using the other hand. Rollie didn't use this serum often. It was hard to get and expensive. Plus, it never seemed quite fair. But he loved its quick action. The courier's eyes had glazed over and his jaw slackened in no time.

"There ya go," Rollie said gently. "Easy does it, then." He booted open the front door and guided the courier into the late afternoon light. "Go back to your ship, mate. Off to your headquarters with you. On the way there, you're going to mark this entry in your database as an Invalid Address. Then you're going to forget you ever met me. Now, what are you going to do?"

The courier said, "Mark this entry in your database as an Invalid Address. Then forget you ever met me."

"Close enough," Rollie said. "*Paar too*. Fly safe."

"Fly safe," murmured the courier hazily, and he took the moving sidewalk to the library's ICV park, as if in a dream.

Rollie made sure the fellow launched all right (it was a little wobbly), then returned inside and directed his attention to the package sitting on the reference table. He scanned the item for potential explosives and biological weapons, then withdrew a knife from his boot and opened the box. A note in Hyphiz Deltan perched on top. "More where this came from. A LOT more." He lifted the note.

Beneath it lay two bottles of so-very-prime Feegar High Impact Bourbon. Not the standard kind, which was already excellent, but the hundred-year aged stuff. The kind that never, ever was exported, except in important political bribe situations. And even then, begrudgingly.

With Tseethe being neither important, very political, nor prone to sharing, Rollie wondered how he'd managed it.

Then he noticed the writing on the back of the note:

Want in? Meet me...

PLACE: Tsardonea Estate
TIME: Why haven't you left already?

—Tseethe

Rollie smiled. Rollie wanted in.

3

"The Steel City. City of Bridges. The Three Rivers. The Burgh..." As the skyline of glass and steel shimmered into view, Bertram was relieved to see that even under alien management circumstances, some things remained eternal.

There loomed Mount Washington with its breathtaking view of the city, the Point with its fountain shooting ever-skyward, two sports stadiums standing strong and proud, the magical PPG building with its crystalline spires and...

A huge DiversiDine logo on a high-rise shaped like a silver soda-pop can.

Bertram cursed under his breath. How had that thing gotten past Pittsburgh's notoriously-discerning city approvals?

He pulled closer and noticed the building wasn't the only thing that felt off. The PAT busses were rolling today and a crowd of people gathered below. He could only guess what that was about. With everything super-sized these days, maybe the city's New Year's Eve event — First Night — came now with First Morning After.

"So what's the gameplan?" asked Rozz, peering over the landscape like a modern Athena. "I should probably check on the parents. Last I knew, Mom had the house in Shadyside. Dad had a loft in the Strip."

Bertram guided the ICV over the familiar highways and tree-lined neighborhoods. The Penumbra Classic soared over Plus-D'Argent University, where Bertram had spent such happy, ignorant days on a cognitive psychology Ph.D. that he would never receive. From this vantage point, the only thing that had changed was Bertram. "All right, then. Shadyside it is. How about you check on your mom while I hit DiversiDine headquarters downtown? It looks like the busses are running. You meet me at Market Square and then we'll go tackle your dad's."

"Works for me." She seemed riveted by the picturesque Victorian homes, little sloped yards, coffeehouses, restaurants and boutiques below. "Though I don't know where the hell you're going to land."

"I do," he said, and he directed the cloaked ship over the wide, rolling lawn of the Shadyside Institute for Artistic Expression. He'd been practicing his precision touchdowns and he was particularly pleased with how he tucked the craft comfortably between an outdoor sculpture of a stretching monster and a collection of metal shapes doing the tango.

As the ship sighed onto the frosty earth, Rozz said, "Uh, Bertram, you do realize people jog through here, right? You leave this cloaked and someone's morning run is going to start out as cardio and end as a concussion."

"Yup." Bertram grinned. "That's why we're not cloaking it."

"We're not cloaking our *spaceship*." She looked at him like he'd lost all mental bearings somewhere between Sirius and Alpha Centauri.

"Right." He addressed the controls, removed the cloaking field and powered everything down. "See, when I was planning this trip, I asked myself, 'Bertram, what's the best way to hide something large and otherworldly in the middle of a busy, growing city?'" He was so excited; he'd been waiting for the right time to unveil this. He grabbed a bag from underneath the captain's chair and handed it to her.

She raised an eyebrow, then withdrew an item from the bag. It was a metal plaque on a garden spike.

The plaque read:

Interplanetary Cruise Vessel
by Penn Ombré.
Composed of Various Metals
and Super-Thin High Tech Materials

"You call it art and park it in plain sight?" she suggested.

He pointed to her and grinned. "Ding, ding, ding!"

"So what do I win?" They had unlatched their harnesses and were moving into the central lounge.

"Oh, I don't know ..." Bertram peered out the hatch window there. It was still early enough that the traffic outside was thin and sleepy. "Would you settle for peace of mind and a lack of dissection by government agencies?"

"Funny, that's what I always wanted," she told him sincerely. "And so much better than a toaster oven."

Bertram had thought she would like it. They snuck outside and planted the plaque in a prominent spot, then stood back and surveyed the effect.

"You have a fine future ahead of you, Mr. Ombré," Rozz proclaimed.

"Right now, the only thing in my future is a PAT bus headed downtown," said Bertram. "Remember: Market Square. When you're done."

Rozz nodded. "I'll find you."

The Earth bucks Bertram had on him since his abduction were still spendy, and a fraction of them bought him one jouncy trip downtown. This ride was a startling contrast to the post-apocalyptic vision he'd been conjuring all these months. There were no gangs of leather-clad ruffians rolling by on grinding choppers and cobbled-together dune buggies. He spied no human chain gangs with miners' gear, shuffling down Pittsburgh streets being whipped by Ottoframan overseers. He saw no lost souls huddled around burning barrels in the January air, muttering about the good old days before those damned, dirty aliens took over.

Bertram scoured the passing scenery for signs of more subtle concern, but if anything, the streets looked a little cleaner, the shops a little painty-er, the skinny row homes a little homier.

Even the bus driver seemed like a twinklier, finer example of a bus driver. Like there was nothing he wanted more than to drive a PAT bus for Bertram on a major winter holiday. "You from out of town, young man?" he asked.

"Nope. Just got back after some time away," Bertram said.

"Well, welcome back and Happy New Year!" The man gave a bright smile.

"Thank you." Not that friendly bus drivers in Pittsburgh were mythic beings in the way you'd be surprised to see a Yeti manning the local salt truck. But the driver on Bertram's past route had been a case study in what happened to some folks after a lifetime of dealing with the unwashed masses. As for the freshly-laundered masses? That guy didn't much like them, either. Them and their fabric softener smells and smug faces, wanting on and off the bus all the time ... Why couldn't they just leave him alone?

This was a whole new experience. "Quiet today," Bertram observed, looking around the empty bus. "Given it's New Year's, I was surprised you're running at all."

The driver laughed, warm and kindly, like a holiday fire. "Oh, but this is a special day, isn't it? The city was making sure we ran today, of all days. Most everybody's already down there. But an hour or two ago, they were shoulder-to-shoulder in here."

"Yeah?" Bertram frowned. "What's going on?"

"Why, the Kickoff, of course," the driver said. At Bertram's blank look, the driver said, "You're not here for the Kickoff, son?"

"Er, sure, I am," said Bertram. Pittsburgh did love its football and there was nothing more footbally than New Year's

Day. "So who's playing? The University of Pittsburgh?"

"Why, we are, son," he said. "All of us." The bus was at the curb now. "This is as far as this route goes, I'm afraid, on account of the celebration. So you take care now. And have a DiversiDine Dandy Day."

"Uh, you, too," Bertram said and he stepped out onto the curb.

Bertram walked past barricades and detour signs and began to get a sense of just what the bus driver had been talking about.

Thousands of people were milling around downtown, gloves on their hands and smiles above their scarves, wishing each other a happy New Year and wearing their black-and-gold.

Vendors were lined up along the streets offering a variety of treats and also, coincidentally, giving Bertram a richer perspective about the names of his baby relatives.

"Deep-Fried DiversiDelights on a Stick!" said one sign.

"Beer Battered BlissBuns—on a Stick!" another read.

"Joltin' Jubilation Lattes, Espresso and Cappuccino, Hot! Or Frozen! — on a Stick!"

"Stix! —Now in Stick Form!"

Yes, DiversiDine was truly advancing the boundaries of pro-stick cuisine.

Further ahead were souvenir stalls, a visual party in black-and-gold. Bertram thought he might pick up a cheap Pens sweatshirt while he was here, something to represent the hometown in his new interstellar circles. But on closer examination, none of the items was for the city's sports teams.

Instead, there were shirts reading, "I Kicked Off in Dahntahn Pittsburgh!"

Some said, "Have a DiversiDine Dandy Day."

And one read, "Hydrated. Inspired. Unstoppable."

Bertram wasn't sure what to make of it, but people seemed to be buying it by the bagful.

"Excuse me," Bertram asked one of the vendors. "When's kickoff?"

"At six," said the vendor.

Bertram glanced at his old Earth watch. *Seven hours from now.* Pittsburgh's residents did enjoy a good lengthy tailgate. "And who's playing?"

"Playing?"

"Yeah," said Bertram. "Are the Panthers in a bowl? Do the Steelers have a playoff game? Who's playing?" Bowl games weren't even held in the Burgh. Of course, that didn't mean the masses wouldn't turn out for a Jumbotron viewing somewhere.

"Well," the vendor said, rubbing the back of his neck meditatively, "everyone. Everyone's playing."

Bertram recalled the words of the bus driver. "Ah. Of course," said Bertram. "Everyone's playing."

The exchange left Bertram with a vague unsettled feeling. It unsettled him straight through the crowd into the shadow of the DiversiDine building, the newest addition to Pittsburgh's skyline and tucked neatly into a corner of Market Square.

Up close, the building was somewhat less reminiscent of a giant beverage container. With the details visible, Bertram could see how the architecture cleverly merged the industrial past of the city with a modern, hopeful feel.

What Bertram couldn't understand was how DiversiDine not only got the permits to build here, but finished construction and established its presence in the two mere years he'd been gone. It defied everything he knew about bureaucracy and contractors. Not to mention a general public that was vaguely suspicious of anyone who didn't give directions by the landmarks that were there twenty years ago.

Today, the foot of the building was surrounded by walls of DiversiDine vending machines and flanked by a series of cylindrical booths. Based on the length of the lines at the booths, Bertram guessed those were some kind of futuristic port-a-potties. But then, curved across each one, he read, "Get Your Personal Playbook for the New Year—FREE!"

Bertram paused as people with bright eyes and euphoric

faces emerged from these booths, chatting among themselves like they'd just been given hot stock tips or got hugged by their favorite celebrity.

He made a note to check it out, if the lines ever thinned. It looked like the few who weren't waiting for quality cylinder time, appeared to be trailing through Gateway Center, over the tunnel bridge and down to Point State Park, a space normally popular for summer concerts and the city's Fourth of July fireworks. He couldn't imagine what there was to see now.

He'd barely reached the bridge before he noticed yet another one of those cylindrical booths, nestled under some trees and off the beaten path. It was a testament to the importance of location that this one had no line at all.

Bertram was inside in a flash.

Given the booth's slim styling, the guy sitting inside it was something of a surprise. He perched behind a tiny table and wore a black-and-gold DiversiDine sweater. Before him was a slow cooker with something bubbling, a ladle and a stack of tiny cups. "Welcome. I'm Bill, your DiversiDine Dandy Living Assistant Coach today. Please have a seat." He motioned to a tiny chair. "Hot DrinkThis compliments of DiversiDine?" He filled a cup in anticipation.

"Well…" It *was* free and Bertram did like to try new things. Admittedly, in the Greater Communicating Universe, that had gotten him in trouble a few times. But this … he figured this probably wasn't too risky. Plus, it was important to learn as much as he could about DiversiDine and its products, wasn't it? "Since you asked."

He sipped. It was bubbly, sweet and wholly unique. It was gone in no time.

"Now. How can we assist your Kickoff?" asked Bill.

"Oh, uh …" Bertram hadn't realized he was supposed to bring anything of substance to this interaction. "I guess…" he thought fast, "I just wanted to find out who was playing today?"

"Who's playing? Why, we're all playing," said Bill with a wink. "You, me, everyone."

"Yeah, people keep saying that. But I mean at six, for the kickoff."

Bill looked down at a card in his hand. "Do you have questions about: A.) Your past B.) Your present or C.) Your future?"

"Um, really, I'm just trying to find out what's happening at six tonight."

"Say C," whispered the man.

"What?"

The guy looked left. He looked right. And through a gritted smile, he hissed, "That's the future. Say C."

Bertram whispered, too. "Why?"

"I can't go forward in the Playbook unless you choose something. Say C."

"Okay, C."

Bill looked relieved. "You chose C. Your future. Now, do you want a strategy for Offense or Defense?"

"Dude, I don't even know what you're asking me."

"Offense or Defense. One or the other. Look, there's a line waiting."

"Actually, there isn't." Bertram gestured. "You're kinda around the back of—"

Bill's eyes narrowed. "Pick one."

"Fine. Offense."

"You chose an Offensive Strategy for the Future. For this year, you're going to want to keep your eye on that touchdown line with a tight hold of your goals. While you'll be tempted to drive them straight down the middle, you may find the path of least resistance is actually one that involves frequent downs and even some backtracking. Also, don't be afraid to toss play to another member of your Life Team, especially if they're clear and closer to the end zone. Keep your eye on the ball and don't get distracted by what's going on in the sidelines and your upcoming year will be a real winner." The man looked up from his cue card. He pulled a small bag from under the table. "Some samples, compliments of DiversiDine World, *Sponsoring You: in the Game of Life*. Next please!" he shouted.

"But —" Bertram looked from the bag to the man and wobbled to his feet. "Is that it?"

"I said next! Next!"

Bertram Ludlow emerged from the cylinder into the gray January light.

4

"More DrinkThis, darling?"

"No, thank you, darling. But I appreciate your thinking of my potential needs by asking."

"I appreciate your appreciation. I do work to recognize that your needs are important."

"And I recognize that recognition, my love."

Rozz stared from Annette Marie DiAngelo (formerly Mercer) to Stephen Elliot Mercer (unchanged) and did the only thing she could think of when faced with a situation like the one she'd experienced the last half hour ...

She banged her knee off the leg of the wrought iron dining table—and hard.

The jolt of pain jagged its way up from knee to her hip joint and radiated all the way down to her instep where it took a moment to throb.

Yep, she decided, it sure hurt like it was real. It hurt like Rozz was wide awake and truly sitting in her mom's dining room with both of her parents, their world filled with caring, unity and love.

Clearly, the pain was the only part of this scenario that made any sense.

In fact, right this very moment, these same parents were

looking at her with identical expressions of deep, pitying concern. "Are you all right, Rozz? Do you want some ice?" Mom was already out of the chair.

"Dear, I'll get it," offered Dad. "You should rest."

"No, baby." Mom paused at the kitchen door. "You sit. You work hard and deserve a rest as much as I do."

"I tell you what, my Wuvbug…"

Mom blinked dark eyes. "Yes, my Smoochyface?"

"We'll both go get it," Dad said.

"A genius idea. As always."

"We'll be right back," he told Rozz. And they both vanished into the kitchen.

Rozz's head sunk into her hands, her heart beating a million times a minute. What the hell was going on? How was this even possible?

It was like one of those dreams she'd had as a kid where, despite years of witnessing marital battles, emotional injury and mental scars, Young Dumbass Rozz still found herself wishing her two full-time parents, part-time vengeful warriors, would get back together, so they could all be a miserable family-unit again in the way she'd grown accustomed.

Only even then, her dream parents were never this goopy.

Mom and Dad returned to the dining room now with an icepack. They were holding hands, a merry tune emanating from Dad's lips.

He paused his song long enough to extend the item to her. "Here you go, Rozzbud."

Rozzbud? She hadn't been called Rozzbud since she was, like, three. "Now that," she shouted, "is the frozen limit!"

"It's an icepack," explained Dad.

She shoved it away and surged to her feet. "Okay. I tried to overlook it. I did. But this —" she gestured wildly to the clasped hands, the whistling lips, the whole nauseating display, "—must be discussed. What is wrong with you people?"

Mom and Dad turned wide-eyed, innocent faces upon her.

"I come to visit *you*," she addressed her mother, "and I see *your* car is in the drive." She pointed to Dad like the accused in a court case. (He was used to that.) "I think, well, maybe you're picking up some mail that got sent here by mistake that Mom actually didn't set on fire. Or maybe the gigantic alimony payments finally snapped Dad's brain and he came here to whack you, just to make the whole endless, unnecessary cycle of monetary shame stop. No big…"

She paused for breath and continued, "So I ring the bell and hey, here's the first surprise: both of you answer. And even though I've been away for what apparently translates to a little longer than any of us expected, no one's sweating it. No lecture. No 'where have you been?' Nope, you're both just glowingly happy to see me, no questions asked."

"Well, we love you so much, Rozzbud," said Dad.

"We missed you, but we knew you'd stop by when you were ready," said Mom. "You're a sensible adult with your own life. We were sure you had your reasons."

"Okay, maybe," said Rozz, "maybe I can buy that. I remember all the 'just because we hate each other's guts with the fire of a thousand blazing suns doesn't mean we don't still love you, Rozz' crap. But then you two are here today all 'Smoochyface' and 'Wuvbug' and it's weirding me the fuck out."

"I don't understand, Rozzbud," said Dad and he had the nerve to sound sincere about it.

"You," Rozz pointed to Mom. "You hate the way he never let you finish a sentence. You despise how he never asked you about your day, how he obsesses over Steelers football 'like he owns the team,' and the way he plops his napkin on his plate and pushes it to the side when he's finished eating 'like he was Henry friggin' the Eighth.' Do you remember?"

Mom smiled incredulously. "They're just little habits, dear. We all have them."

"And you." She turned on Dad here. "You hate how she pretends to give you choices, but there's always a right and wrong answer. And if you choose the wrong one, she goes totally 'ice queen' on you. You hate the way she laughs when she doesn't feel like addressing an issue. And you loathe the way she says 'to make a long story short,' since it never once has. Which is why you claim you have to interrupt her. There, now isn't something bubbling up inside you? Don't you feel the years of textbook passive-aggression flowing back where it belongs?"

"Sweetheart, people change," said Mom.

"People grow," said Dad.

"Right, and I think I just figured out why …" She leapt up and squeezed her mom's arm, her shoulder, ran hands over her face, lifted up her hair and examined the back of her neck.

"Dear," the woman's voice was hesitant, "what are you doing?"

"I am looking for the flap." Rozz's heart was still beating wildly. Yet the more she searched, the worse it got. She simply could not understand it. The woman's skin had a very natural texture and warmth. There were no seams. There were no manufacturer's marks, no power ports, no…

"Do you have something you'd like to discuss, Rozz?" Mom asked.

She took a step back. "No," Rozz said. "Not now." She needed time to think. She moved to the door.

"Rozzbud, you are coming back, aren't you?" asked Dad. "You were away so long. We both missed you very much. Didn't we, Wuvbug?"

"Indeed we did, Smoochyface," said Mom.

But Rozz was already out of the house, screen door screeching shut behind her.

5

"Next time, fraggin' warn me someone will be stopping by, right?" Rollie said, striding into Tsardonea, Tseethe's expansive home-unit on the planet Bellafar. "Your messenger near ended up in a box of his own."

"Well, hello to you, too, Captain," greeted Tseethe, closing the door behind Rollie. Tseethe was wearing his smoking helmet, a full-head bubble with speaker system and air filtration unit. Required by GCU law, it allowed him to safely be around others and still absorb the toxic fumes his body had mutated to need after decades of smoking. Rollie realized it had been some years since he'd viewed Tseethe's face clearly. There was a sense he was smirking in the smoke now.

"You know, I had to pump your delivery fellah full of MezmerBlot," Rollie told him. "I mean, seriously, mate, using my real name?" He picked up a statue from a side table and turned it over. Rollie wasn't very up on the intergalactic art trade — never took much of an interest, himself — but this piece looked familiar. In fact, it looked like it might be—

"Ancient Hyphiz Deltan," supplied Tseethe, extracting it from him and returning it carefully to the table. "And before you ask, yes, I paid for the statue. Everything here —" he gestured to his collection, which was considerably thicker on the walls and surfaces than it was the last time Rollie visited, "— is legitimately purchased. All items are ones Janix, the progeny and I would have no problem showing to the law, if they popped by for a quick inspection."

"Smart." Rollie poked at a series of crystalline spheres, hovering in formation over a pedestal. They bobbed at his touch. He turned. "And where are you keeping your more … complicated … acquisitions these days, then?"

"Ah, I'm sorry, Rollie, but even friends need to retain a few secrets," Tseethe chuckled.

"What about Janix and the kids? Where are they off to?" It was entirely too quiet. Tseethe's progeny were fine miniature people, but the silence was palpable.

"Recon in Quad Four. A museum show with a few choice pieces. It's a business trip but educational. Like I always say, you're never too young to learn the trade." Tseethe moved to the minibar. "Can I get you a drink?"

"If you're having one," said Rollie, knowing full-well Tseethe was. The man had already brought out his funnel. "Did I mention I had to pump your delivery fellah full of MezmerBlot?"

"Yeah, I believe I heard that somewhere." Tseethe poured Blumdec Aquaflir and Hyphiz Deltan *ootsang* into a shaker.

"MezmerBlot's fraggin' hard to come by, you know," Rollie persisted. "Plus, the risk you took, addressing that package to my real name. You do realize anyone else who done that to me, I'd have lasered by now."

"Aw, quit your belly-aching," said Tseethe as he turned on the centripetal shaker. It hummed cheerfully. "I got your attention, didn't I? Between your print library and running the unofficial Underworld, a guy has to do something to catch your interest these days." Tseethe gestured. "Have a seat."

Rollie dropped down into a chair. "I am not running the unofficial Underworld."

"Oh?" Tseethe turned off the shaker. "And who'd you give assignments to today? Prinny? Backs? Wilbree?" He poured the beverage into glasses.

"People vis-u me with questions and I answer 'em. Being crime's version of Dear Blabby does not an Underworld leader make."

Tseethe handed Rollie a glass. "Hey, two-plus-one or three-plus-zero: it all adds up the same, man."

"Yeah, well …" Tseethe had known Rollie a long time and possibly better than most. Sometimes, it was vaguely annoying. "On to business. Feegar High Impact Bourbon, hundred-year aged. Details."

Tseethe's grin was so broad and bright it was like landing lights in a fog. "You know that's the rare stuff, right?"

"I know that the Feegars aren't big on sharing this particular vintage. That they only export the odd bottle to the Coalition of Planets to make nice, after eating people who disagreed with them."

Tseethe settled into a chair. "Then we're on the same page."

"I also know the majority of the bourbon goes to their Apex, and what he does with it from there, who knows? You'd think anyone brimming with stellar bourbon all the time would be something less than a total slaggard. Yet, by all accounts, he is not. Lastly, I know that you sent two whole bottles of the stuff to me, yet you're still breathing. So something must be amiss."

Tseethe leaned forward in his chair. "What if I told you that a buddy of mine, who's working in conjunction with the Feegars, happens to know the precise details of a whole outgoing shipment of Feegar hundred-year bourbon, just like the two bottles I sent you? And," Tseethe was really on a roll now, "what if I also told you, it's headed out soon and it's ripe for the picking?"

"I'd ask why your friend doesn't pick it himself," Rollie said.

"Simple." Tseethe installed his funnel. "My friend is not in free trade like we are. He's in the information game. He understands it takes timing, technique and a talent for improvisation when it comes to matters of freight raiding. That's why he came to me. And why I came to you."

Rollie couldn't help but stare.

"What?" Tseethe swirled the liquid in his glass, then measured some into the funnel. He slurped this through an in-helmet straw. "You don't like the opportunity?"

"A whole shipment of the finest bourbon ever made in the GCU, which the makers never export? The opportunity's cosmic."

Tseethe might have frowned. "So what's the problem?"

"I like the view out my head, too. Yet, if you recall, the Feegars mucked about with that in some fairly unfriendly ways." Rollie rarely discussed that chapter of his past, but he couldn't imagine why Tseethe didn't remember it. Tseethe had been his second-in-command in the Feegar Rebellion; he'd led Rollie's rescue party from the war camps.

"Oh, is that what this is about? You're scared?" Tseethe sounded relieved that the misgivings were something so trivial. "I didn't think you got spooked over anything, man."

"Not scared," Rollie said firmly. "Reluctant for a second opportunity to be transformed into Feegar cocktail nibbles. There's a difference. One is a chemical reaction. The other is based on life experience and rational misgivings."

"Well, what if I told you that since the Feegars got spanked by the Coalition of Planets over that whole Klimfal mass slaughter shebang, the Feegars have been playing nice?"

Rollie raised a doubtful eyebrow.

"And," Tseethe continued, "what if I told you I have it on good authority that they're using Simulants these days to transport their interplanetary freighters?"

Non-Organic Simulants were androids. They came in varying levels of realism, depending on needs and budget. In recent years, the technology had gotten so good, it convinced itself it was getting a raw deal every time a Simulant was bought, sold or worked long hours for free …

Which, of course, was true.

As a result, many Simulants unionized. Most commonly, they were hired for skilled service jobs, since their programing made them uniquely tolerant of the general public.

"So the Feegars have outsourced, eh?"

"It's a PR initiative," Tseethe said. "To showcase a kinder, gentler Feegar species to the GCU."

Rollie laughed. "What, they only bite your face off every other Moonsday now?"

"Before cake. After the sing-along," said Tseethe.

"Simulants. Hm ..." Rollie considered the possibilities over the last of his drink. But mostly he considered a full freighter of that cosmic bourbon, split two ways. He sighed. "All right — the job: when and where?"

He heard warm laughter echo behind the helmet's smoky glass. "Ah, yes. I knew it," said Tseethe. "I knew you'd want in."

"Well, like the philosopher Karnax says, 'No challenge fails like the one not accepted.'" Rollie set his glass on the table next to the Deltan sculpture.

"Ah, but what does Karnax have to say about theft?" asked Tseethe, leaping up to grab the glass.

Rollie smiled. "Completely silent."

"Karnax: my man!"

6

Earth. Pittsburgh. Market Square. Bertram caught a glimpse of Rozz and her hot pink hair between the DrinkThis slushy stand and the DiversiDogs food cart. He flagged her down and she pressed through the revelers like it was the mosh pit of an Angela's Shark concert.

"Holy introvert's nightmare," she exclaimed, gesturing to the mayhem as broadly as possible without socking someone. "What's the deal? It's like everybody and their grandmother is downtown today. Are they giving away free season tickets? Are we headed to the Superbowl? Is Troy Polamalu dispensing souvenir ringlets dipped in gold?"

"Nope, the locks remain luxurious and intact," said Bertram. "But let's find somewhere we can talk. We have much to discuss."

"Bertram —" She seized his arm desperately, her face wan. "My parents ... It's worse than I'd imagined. The worst."

In the time Bertram and Rozz had been dating and then not-dating, Bertram had seen many sides to the young woman. He'd seen Enthused Rozz and Wryly-Amused Rozz, Ticked-Off Rozz and Fiercely-Determined Rozz — and certainly Stoically-Unimpressed Rozz, who generally ran things. But he'd never seen Openly Sad and Concerned Rozz. So he understood the gravity of this occasion now. "Oh…" He pressed a hand to hers. "I'm really sorry, Rozz."

"Thanks." She nodded solemnly. "It was a shock."

"So what happened? How'd they…" he struggled to choose the word carefully, "… go?"

She blinked. "Go? What 'go'?" He'd left out Perplexed-Yet-Suspecting-You-Might-Be-an-Idiot Rozz, which made its showing now. "They haven't gone anywhere. In fact, they're *staying in* today. Staying in. *Together.* Lord." She stuck out her tongue and shuddered.

Bertram pushed the throbbing place between his eyes. "Start at the beginning."

"Bertram, they're *happy.*" Her face was white, her eyes huge. "My parents are back together *and* they're happy."

Bertram rubbed now at his ear, which perhaps was experiencing a minor audial malfunction. "*Your* parents? The Mercers?"

"Yeah," she said, knowingly. "Something is seriously borked."

"They're not Non-Organic Simulant replacements," she said over a steaming beverage and a hot cinnamon roll at a table outside the coffee shop. "I checked. No hair flap. No brand label on the neck — front or back. No plug. But the behavior? It's totally pod."

Bertram peered across his second cup of coffee. "Pod?"

She huffed a steamy sigh and rolled her eyes. "Body snatchers, Killer Klowns, Stepford… Y'know: pod?"

Of course: pod. Bertram toyed with his coffee stirrer. "Maybe they had counseling or something."

Rozz's bitter laugh made two people turn. "Oh, long ago did my parents experience the wonders of marital counseling. Counselors far and wide began their sessions with Steve and Annette Mercer with stars in their eyes and hope in their hearts. Within a month, these same counselors were begging my parents — begging! — to end the madness and just divorce already. The *S.S. Mercer* was a ship that could not be unsunk. And now, fifteen years after it officially cracked up and settled on the ocean floor, I'm supposed to believe Mom and Dad are all riding the rescue boats called Wuvbug and Smoochyface?"

"Wuvbug and Sm—?"

"I think not." She peeled off a layer of the pastry and tucked it into her mouth. Through it, she said, "So what's with the big tailgate?"

"It's the Kickoff."

"Pitt? Steelers?"

"DiversiDine."

She twitched into a frown. "DiversiDine has a team?"

"As far as I can tell, it's some kind of marketing launch."

She let out another sharp, abrupt laugh. "Dude, even in my cheapest, hungriest college days, I wouldn't have waited out here in the cold for a few free food samples from a marketing launch."

"Same here." And Bertram had always been a devotee of the food freebie. "But they keep talking about some Coach Dandy speaking at six."

"Dandy? Seriously?" She snickered. "And he or she is …?"

"DiversiDine's frontman."

"And he draws this kind of crowd on a holiday." She shook her head.

"I know. I thought Eudicot T'murp would be in charge," said Bertram, "but I asked around and nobody's heard of him."

"Could he be using another name? I mean, 'T'murp' isn't exactly Tryfe-user-friendly. It sounds like stomach problems."

"It does, but I don't think he's Dandy. I picked up this." Bertram tossed a copy of *Twirl* Magazine onto the table. On the cover was a smiling, mustachioed man in a black-and-gold jacket with the DiversiDine logo on it and a whistle around his neck. The caption read, "Coach Dell Dandy. Sponsoring You: in the Game of Life."

Rozz ran a sticky finger over the image. "Dude looks human. I mean, there are ways around that, I guess. Genetic adjustment, holowatch disguise…" Rozz licked her fingers.

"Yeah, or he could just be one of the humanoid species that passes well for Earth people, like Rollie."

Her nose wrinkled. "I'm not getting that vibe."

"Me, neither," admitted Bertram. "And there's always a vibe." It had been his experience that you could take the lifeform out of the GCU, but you couldn't take the GCU out of the lifeform.

Still reading, Rozz pursed her lips. "Well, what's this 'sponsoring you in the game of life' crock?"

"Food's not the only sample they're giving out here today." And Bertram told her about his encounter in the Playbook booth.

"So DiversiDine's in the crappy New Age self-help trade now? Sort of like a talk show psychic with snacks?"

"Seems like it," Bertram said. "But my parents were really supportive of DiversiDine. And it's not like them to fall for hucksters with an agenda. Growing up, Mom practically needed peer-reviewed scientific studies before she'd buy a juice box. Dad made pros and cons charts to choose a Friday night family movie. We Ludlows are not an impulsive people. But you heard them; Mom and Dad couldn't say enough about Coach Dandy. And my nieces and nephew are practically trademark violations."

"My parents are currently violating mutual restraining orders," said Rozz. "Things change."

"And there's another thing that bothers me," Bertram said. "Why here? Why Pittsburgh? Of all the places in the country— in the world—that DiversiDine could put down roots on this planet, it's so coincidental. It feels way too convenient that the company's located here. Nothing's ever that easy."

"We *have* been voted the U.S.'s Most Livable City several times," she said with a smirk.

Bertram tipped back in his café chair. "I'm serious, Rozz. Think. What's here in Pittsburgh that other cities don't have?"

"Um," she said, "other than you?"

He looked at her hard.

"Dude, you were living here and you were The Chosen One," she said. "I mean, me, I got bagged by aliens on a whim, but you? Hand-picked. So if I were Eudicot T'murp and I wanted to open up an Earth branch office, I know where I would break ground first. The only place on the planet I've actually heard of. The hometown of the GCU's most famous Tryfeman: Bertram Ludlow. It's a no brainer."

An awful wave of realization crashed over Bertram. It made him hot and nauseous despite the January air. "So technically, Pittsburgh's extraterrestrial renaissance is...all my fault?"

"Oh, now I wouldn't say that exactly." Rozz reached for another napkin. "Though I will say, if you asked the Pittsburgh Tourism Board for a cut of the action? You probably wouldn't be wrong."

"Thanks. You're a rock of reassurance."

"That's me. Rozzbud Mercer: programmer, intergalactic traveler, rock." Her eyes darted as something beyond her pastry, and behind Bertram, had drawn her attention. She laughed. "Sufferin' Sports Authority, what on Tryfe is she supposed to be?"

Bertram turned to see a young woman wearing a sports uniform or, more accurately, all the uniforms. The complete outfit involved a football jersey, baseball pants and a jaunty hockey helmet. She carried a clipboard. "Join the DiversiDine team!" the woman called out. "New opportunities for driven professionals! Get recruited by DiversiDine and score career satisfaction. Apply today!"

The Earth branch of DiversiDine Entertainment Systems and Aeroponics was hiring? Like, regular human employees? Bertram turned a sudden inspired face to Rozz. "Hey. Are you thinking what I'm thinking?"

Rozz gnawed a thumbnail. "That those cleats were never meant for walking on concrete?"

"Well," he gave this a second look, "now, yes. But also?"

"That there's no better way to get to know a company than from the inside?" A glint shone in her eye.

"She shoots, she scores," he said.

"Bertram, my friend, I do believe it's time to brush up our resumes."

7

"Okay, starboard ... twenty degrees ... ten degrees ... two degrees ... You're almost there ... Almost, almost ... Now! Hit the seal now!" shouted Tseethe.

A ratcheting sound, followed by the gong of metal-on-metal, rattled both of the crafts as the pan-ICV seal covered the hatch of the Simulant freighter and formed a parasitic bond.

Tseethe hooted and clapped. "I take it all back, man," he said, leaning in through the cockpit door. "I take it all back."

Rollie checked the propulsion rate and eased it down. "Just what are you recanting now?"

"The stuff I said earlier about us not using this ship for a raid," he said. "I was talking out of my posterior orifice."

Rollie snickered. "Wish that made a change."

"Don't get me wrong," Tseethe continued, "this Protostar is still lower on the tech scale than that charred goop you find at the bottom of your average household refuse incinerator. But you, my friend, have figured out how to make it do some very-prime moves."

"Yeah, well ..." This was nice to hear after the hour-long argument they'd had about it during the planning stage. "You can celebrate my skill later. Scan for life now, eh? I'm not going in there blind."

"What," said Tseethe, "you don't trust my buddy?"

"I don't trust anyone I haven't met," Rollie said. "And the ones I have are a pretty shady lot, as well. Do the scan."

Out of the corner of his eye, Rollie saw Tseethe salute. "On it, Captain." And he darted into the main cabin.

"And for the last time, drop the 'Captain' excrement, will you?" Rollie called. "We're long past the Feegar Rebellion."

"Ah, but you just hate it so much. Warms the heart."

"Which one?"

"Middle central. That's where I get reflux." Tseethe clunked around in the other room for what seemed like a long moment. Then: "Well, that's weird."

Rollie couldn't see him reflected in the rear-facing mirror. "Is it not working? Sometimes you have to jiggle it."

"Duly jiggled," said Tseethe.

"Did you try turning it on and o——?"

"What am I, new?"

"Hm." Rollie Tsmorlood leapt out of the pilot's seat and joined him at the console.

Tseethe was right. Rollie could see the graphic outline of the ship. He could see the outline of the ship's fixtures, the ship's furniture, the stored shipment... but no signs of life, Simulated or otherwise.

"Ah!" Now it made sense! Rollie ducked around the counter and, wrapping a length of his coattail around the cord, unplugged the connection. The monitor image flickered to life and Tseethe stared at him like he'd just performed magic. "The fraggin' hotplate," Rollie explained. "It's on the same power grid as Tech Scan, and sometimes..."

Tseethe was still staring, but now the magic had turned into that gunk at the bottom of your average household refuse incinerator.

"Aw, don't start with me, mate. This Protostar's a stellar machine. And look." Rollie jabbed a finger at a cluster of red dots on the screen. "Clear as a Blumdec day. One in the cockpit and twenty tech sigs coming from an inner cabin." Rollie frowned at the display. "Odd the bulk of 'em clustered together like that, though. 'Specially once they've been latched. Usually crews go into defense mode during a raid."

"You say 'odd,' I say lucky. How much ya want to bet that's the recharge deck? We got them during naptime, buddy."

Rollie gave a quick assessment of the ship's layout. Cockpit... main cabin ... storage ... engine room ... cargo hold... galley ... Yes. He felt himself breathe easier now. "The recharge deck. Of course."

Tseethe's smoking helmet bobbed an affirmation. "Couldn't have asked for better. We'll crack those Simmis before they're even fifty percent power. No pain, no strain."

Rollie grabbed his surge baton and grinned. "Let's get cracking, then."

Now anyone with even the most rudimentary understanding of freight raiding knew that the key to subduing a freighter with a Non-Organic Simulant crew was to give them a jolt of juice that popped their tech functions. The best way to do that was to hit them with a surge baton on their plug-in port, which was right on the back of the neck.

Barring that, you could perform a Disarm maneuver, which quite literally meant cutting the arms off at the shoulder ball joint. It was a little like carving any of the smaller roasting beasts, only fumier and with sparks.

While Rollie was normally an XJ-37 man, he greatly preferred the XC-series handlasers for this type of job. Sure, they didn't have the fragmentation capabilities of the J series, but their speed and surgical precision were things of beauty. That's why he'd armed himself with four of them, in case he needed a back-up. And a back-up back-up. And something to back-up the back-up of the back-up.

He added an XJ-37 for fun.

Currently, Rollie and Tseethe stood at the Protostar's hatch, lasers drawn and batons at the ready. Rollie opened the first portal and stepped into the connector ramp of the pan-ICV seal. A second later, he'd clamped a Hatch Override onto the freighter door.

They watched in the half-light as the device found the first unlocking number ... the second ... third ... and ... Click! The hatch opened with a puff of air. The ship smelled bitter and metallic.

Rollie looked to Tseethe. Tseethe nodded, aiming his XR-20 (a decent mid-range handlaser) in preparation. Slowly, Rollie swung the hatch wide.

The empty corridor stood bathed in cold, bluish light as the two Hyphiz Deltas stepped inside. Rollie gestured to the cockpit. Tseethe nodded and indicated the first hatch on the right for himself.

The command center, Rollie found, was unlike any he'd ever seen. It was a peculiar nest-like set-up with tiers of semicircular consoles descending to the front control panel. A quick scan of both tiers revealed the cockpit was empty.

He descended further, surveying the systems. Where were the pilot's and co-pilot's charging stations? Where were the inevitable cans of upgrade beverages and supplement bars that Simmis always had on hand? For that matter, where was the fraggin' pilot who'd shown up on the scan just moments before?

It was as he approached the foremost console, he discovered one answer. In the middle of the pilot's seat was a tidily folded garment, some kind of jumpsuit with its own power source, a string of lights pacing ominously across the collar. He grabbed it and held it up. It was designed for a humanoid, but one with excessively long arms.

A cold fear swept over Rollie now, one that sent him scrambling to the nearby refuse incinerator. He fumbled a knife from his boot and pried at the entry panel, but he'd barely heard it pop when his nose got the first assault.

The smell that wafted from the bin was not the scent of discarded snack wrappers courtesy of that Non-Organic Simulant-on-the-go. It was the smell of death and decay, raw meat, half-gorged, discarded and left to sit too long before being purified by flame. Rollie remembered this stench all too well from his time in the Feegar war camps. Only there, it was the smell equivalent of a scream.

Speaking of which, the shouts and clatter resonating from upstairs sent Rollie leaping up the steps two at a time. He burst from the cockpit and started down the corridor as Feegar soldiers flooded from someplace that was Clearly Not a Recharge Deck.

"Why, look what we have here!" one of the Feegars laughed, its voice like congealed grease. "Dinner has arrived."

"Hello, Dinner," another soldier greeted.

Rollie fumbled for the XJ-37 in his mostly-useless arsenal and seized it, fragging three of the soldiers on his highest handlaser setting. When fighting Feegars, you didn't want precision cuts and you certainly didn't want conversation. You wanted distance and total eradication.

But they were still coming and the fleeting reflection in a metal wall panel revealed they were now also sweeping in from behind. Rollie dodged sideways and flattened against the wall, as laser-fire intended for him struck two Feegars surging forward. He jabbed a hatch button with his elbow and continued shooting, taking out two more enemy combatants until he finished the encounter by oozing safely through the hatch at his back.

He'd closed the door and was heaving the wheel for the manual hatch lock, when pain ripped through his shoulder, courtesy of razorblade teeth. It was a familiar sensation, a hardly gentle reminder of the bad old days. But instead of a mouthful of fresh Hyphizite, the Feegar came away with a laser blast for his trouble.

Rollie dodged two other soldiers around a couple of lounge chairs before whacking one with the surge stick and following it up with a pair of laser blasts.

The hatch outside clanged with pry bars and laser-shot. Orders barked in Feegar echoed down the hall, while Rollie caught his breath and surveyed the room. He saw now he had found the source of the original shouting. He saw now he had found Tseethe.

It was an interesting bit of trivia that *The GCU All-Species Handbook*, as available in Rollie's personal library, did not contain a physical description of the Feegars. The Feegars were also not described in *P.K. Flutterbitt's Virtual Encyclopedia of GCU Sentient Species and Their Hobbies*, or *The GCU Journeyperson's Booklet to Who This Is and How Not to Offend Them Spectacularly*. The reason for this wasn't because people hadn't seen the Feegars. It was because there was no real way to convey how hideously chilling they were without sounding petty about it.

Every phrase that came to mind — phrases like "saliva-clotted chins," "transparent exoskeletons," "throbbing visible organs," "long, grasping arms" and even "blood-stained teeth forming eternal ear-to-ear grins" — didn't *quite* convey the cold sense that these creatures existed solely for making others Not.

Because, really, everyone in the GCU could think of at least one species with a saliva-clotted chin. More people than you might expect were biologically predisposed to show-off their inner goodies. And, why, some of those even had massive perma-grins. Yet the great majority of these beings were awfully blasted nice once you got to know them. And even if they didn't end up being the sort who'd water your hydroponic garden and feed your snoogle while you were away, they rarely had plans to serve your entrails with a nice sauce also made of you.

Tseethe, Rollie saw now, was holding off three such Feegars. His current tactic seemed to involve cleverly letting two of them gnaw his arms while the third struggled to make headway, so to speak, with his smoking helmet. Mostly, the guy was just gumming up Tseethe's view.

Rollie picked off the wing-men with a quick blast of the XJ-37 ("Thanks, man!") but the brains of the trio was too fast. That lifeform whirled on Rollie, knocking the laser from his grasp.

It flew across the room and Rollie dove after it, narrowly eluding the Feegar's mighty reach. The gun ended up in a corner, wedged in a channel between a deep, built-in cabinet and the wall.

Dodging laser fire, Rollie scrambled toward it, kicking back his Feegar assailant in the process, sending him floorward and, thankfully, winded—since there was only so much damage you could do to a guy with an exoskeleton.

Bleeding from both arms, Tseethe frantically scanned the area for his own weapon while Rollie struggled to fish his out. The narrow space between wall and cabinet scraped a layer of skin off Rollie's arm, yet his fingertips still brushed short of the piece. Then he remembered—the surge stick!—and in seconds he was using it to extend his reach, trying to maneuver the laser loose.

Unfortunately, delicate tasks easily done under normal circumstances are not so simple where the Feegars roam. By now, the remaining Feegar had gotten his breath and leapt to his feet laughing, grinning his grinniest, ever-grinnable grin. "What a stellar day," purred the Feegar. "All I'd wanted was a little exercise and some Hyphiz Deltan take-out, and the universe has provided."

"Well, lucky, lucky you," Rollie spat. He could see that this Feegar wasn't bothering with lasers now, either, oh no. This fellah was starting that horrible swaying, revving motion that Feegars did right before the screaming and pain began. And sure enough, it was already happening: the Feegar battle cry, the rush forward, the vice-like grip, the great grinning jaws growing wide, wider, widest...

Rollie thrust the surge stick into the Feegar's salivating mouth, propping it open as volts of electricity shot through. The Feegar shrieked and let go of his prey, tongue waggling obscenely to the beat of a sizzling death dance as he tried to remove the wand.

The smell was nauseating, a combination of electricity and fried Feegar. Rollie stood by, watching the lifeform writhe and struggle, feeling a sick sort of fascination. In this moment, he forgot about the handlaser, forgot about the freight. He imagined the philosopher Karnax had something to say about deriving pleasure from other peoples' suffering. (He'd have to look it up.) But, then, he was pretty sure Karnax had never met the Feegars.

It was Tseethe who ultimately took charge of this ethical

dilemma. Cradling his bitten arm with his other bitten arm, he painfully aimed his resurrected XR-20 and did the final honors.

Rollie wasn't sure if he felt disappointed or relieved to see those tiny particles of former Feegar dancing on the air. But he watched them float placidly, while Tseethe lasered up some makeshift bandages from the sofa fabric for himself.

"So how many?" Tseethe asked, attending to the first bandage. "How many'd ya frag?"

This brought Rollie back from his reverie. "Three down the hall, four outside, the slaggard who bit me and the two here playing ring-round-the-sofa. That makes ten. You?"

"Six for me. Well ..." Tseethe nodded to the dissipating cloud, "seven."

"So, seventeen total." Rollie crouched to fish out his laser. The movement made his bitten shoulder throb and he was still bleeding down his sleeve. "Wonder how many more of those slaggards are out there." They'd gone quiet and the silence itself was disturbing.

"Did you see what the Feegars were wearing?" Tseethe asked.

Rollie stopped what he was doing long enough to give him a look. "My interests lie mainly in the bitey and blasty bits."

"Tech suits," explained Tseethe, starting on his second bandage. "Designed to moderate heat signatures and replicate the signal of a Non-Organic Simulant. There were twenty-one of those on our scan screen. So I figure that leaves four Feegars."

"Three," corrected Rollie. "There was an empty suit on the pilot's chair." He came away with his XJ-37, dusted it off and rose. "Which leads me to another point."

"And that is?"

"That your mate set us up."

"No way." Tseethe sounded genuinely hurt and surprised. "MkChi's got no love for the Feegars. I'd call it a ..." And he actually thought about this word before he said it, "miscommunication."

"Miscommunication?" Rollie felt the blood that wasn't

rushing to his wound rush to his face. "And how do you figure that?"

"You know: like an accident. He probably just misspoke."

"Tseethe," Rollie's hands clenched, "miscommunication is saying you'll be there at seven when you mean six. No one accidentally says a freighter will be filled with 'cheerful easy-to-dismantle robot-persons' when they really mean 'ravenous, sociopathic fang-beasts.' It don't fraggin' happen."

"Well ..." Tseethe tugged at his collar uncomfortably.

"What if I hadn't packed this, eh?" Rollie asked, raising the laser. "I'll tell you. I'd have died giving the Feegar army papercuts and you, you'd be saying hello to someone's small intestine." Turning away, Rollie could hear the mantra in his head: *I am like water molecules in the stream ... I am like an ergowohm gliding on the wind ...*

Nope. Wasn't helping. So he moved to the hatch and listened. It was so quiet out there. So uneasily quiet. He eyed Tseethe Tsardonee and his new upholstery armbands. "All right, enough of this. You ready?"

"Hey, we made it this far and we're still kicking," Tseethe said, a pained smile flashing through the smoke.

"Just the way we like it," came a syrupy voice from above them. "The meat tastes so much better if it's carved while you're alive." And a Feegar leapt down from the drop ceiling, laser flaring.

"There *is* a certain succulence when the blood's still pumping," observed a second soldier, making his grand entrance.

"I like mine plain," confessed the third, completing the set. They were all armed to the teeth, besides the teeth, which even Rollie thought seemed excessive.

As the Hyphiz Deltans found cover and returned fire, Rollie knew they had to take action fast. When you're outnumbered by Feegars in a limited space with a single exit that's locked, there really is only one thing you can do. You tell your buddy, "Sorry about this, mate," crank up the knob on his smoking helmet, then yank his intake tube.

Instantly, the room filled with a dense and heady fog and Rollie did not wait to take advantage of it. He shot into the smoke to start things off, then dashed to the hatch and heaved the locking mechanism. Tseethe joined him now and they both moved into the hall, trailing a jet of smoke and laser-fire. But the Feegars were onto them, pressing forward, backing Rollie and Tseethe down the walkway between the two ships.

"You're only doing us a favor by prolonging the inevitable, you know," one Feegar told them. "But go ahead. Fear makes the flesh taste so much better. Please … keep soaking in all those delicious chemical secretions. We recognize that fine food takes time."

"Oh yeah, you're real interstellar fraggin' gourm—" A laser-blast shook the walkway, knocking Tseethe into Rollie and jarring the XJ-37 from Rollie's grasp. The gun went skidding.

"Hyphizites are an excellent source of protein, too," a second Feegar said, switching his settings and aiming at Rollie's gun. The Hyphizite watched his favorite XJ-37 melt into a puddle before him. "Plus, if you marinade," continued the Feegar, "— and you really have to marinade; Hyphizites are *so* stringy — then you get all the health benefits of an extra-lean meat while—"

"Shut it!" shouted Rollie. He darted the ten remaining feet into his ship and felt around for the emergency J-series he'd strapped somewhere under the kitchenette counter. "Just shut it!" He had spent time marinading in the Feegar war camp during the Rebellion and he still had flashbacks about it.

"Yeah, seriously, what is wrong with you slaggards?" asked Tseethe. "The GCU's diverse and delightful tableau of sentient life is not a fraggin' snack bar, people. You know the Coalition of Planets has rules about that sort of stuff."

"It's made it so hard these days to dine out," one of the Feegars admitted, stepping over the threshold of the Protostar.

"But since this is a case of ICV defense…" added the other, laughing.

Rollie felt like he'd been shocked with a surge baton. "What?!"

"Isn't it obvious?" the Feegar asked. "You attacked us. And in that case, the Coalition of Planets says we may legally do what's necessary to eliminate the outsider aggression."

The second Feegar shook his transparent skull sadly. "We can't help it if misinformation reached the wrong people saying we were using, oh...a Simulant crew these days."

"Or that a shipment of hundred-year High Impact Bourbon would be *such* a temptation to unscrupulous characters," the third said. "You Underworld freight raiders are so predictable." And he laughed.

The rest of the Feegars laughed, too. Feegars did not hold back when it came to food preparation or the joys of a healthy taunting. Rollie yanked the XJ-40 from under the counter, flipped the settings and dispatched one comedian into a puff of so-surprised stardust.

Now Tseethe flew into motion, kicking a second Feegar backwards and punching a wall button. The Feegar tumbled into an unused sleeping quarters and instantly Tseethe locked him in for a timeout. The third Feegar, however, let the laser-fire fly, a shooting spree that sent Rollie and Tseethe both ducking behind the counter.

"So many wasted opportunities," sighed the Feegar soldier. "You could have broken latch at any time. You might have even escaped with your lives. But no. You had to have our shipment. Am I right in my theory that the Underworld tends to draw very short-sighted people?"

"We're not Underworld," called Rollie, peering around the counter for a clean shot. He shoved a cord out of his view. "We're independent."

"Interesting. And what do you call yourselves, so I can tell the Coalition of Planets who we had to kill?"

Rollie let out an exasperated huff. Even the *Feegars* wanted to put a fraggin' name to everything these days. You knew the universe was completely zonked when Feegars had started to embrace blatant marketing.

Rollie shifted position, trying to get a better line on his enemy and he growled as he moved that dangling cord once more. This was one of the worst missions he'd ever been on. After decades of work in a robust and entertaining criminal career, this fragging job had to be one of the most ill-formed, waff-headed zlog-ups Rollie ever had the displeasure of—

He stopped.

Cord?

He turned his attention to the thing and, in a sudden quasar light of understanding, realized this object's supreme and beautiful significance. He found himself clasping it in his hands like some hard-won treasure.

The cord. A single laugh escaped him and he released the cable, only to dig frantically into an inner coat pocket. He *knew* he had them in there somewhere... He always tried to keep a pair or two on hand for just such an—

Ah! He fished out the rubber gloves and put them on.

By now Tseethe was looking worried. "What are you doing, man?" came his desperate whisper. "This is a shootout, not an abduction probe."

Rollie Tsmorlood had always viewed the Protostar as utilitarian perfection in spaceship form; it was only a shame so many of them blew up before the official recall. That said, Rollie *had* added a few minor concessions to modern comfort, one of which was the hotplate on the counter above him. Unfortunately, due to the Protostar's unique setup, the appliance wasn't exactly "compatible." Or "fully functional." Or "adhering to minimum safety standards for people who don't appreciate personal injury lawsuits." But as long you wore rubber gloves when you used it, it was cosmic for whipping up a quick home-cooked meal.

Today, that very appliance was about to enjoy an even higher purpose. Rollie seized the cord, plugged it in, then pitched the hotplate straight at the Feegar.

The look of shock on the Feegar's face was rivaled only by the shock of the hotplate on contact. Rollie followed it up with a blast of the XJ-40 and the Feegar was no more.

Rollie thought someone should probably say some appropriate words at a moment like this. So he said, "About fraggin' time." He turned to Tseethe. "You ready?"

"Absolutely!" Tseethe put his smoke intake hose back into place. He'd already gone whole minutes without it. "It is Feegar bourbon o'clock," he said.

"Is that Universal time or Feegar local?" Rollie asked, as they retraced their steps across the connecting ramp.

"Yes," Tseethe chuckled and they turned down the first corridor of the Feegar freighter. "Now you're sure you've got the retinal scan replicator?"

"I am," said Rollie.

"And if they have a keypad — you've got the gizmo for that?"

Rollie patted a pocket. "Right here."

"And what about voice print access? We'd need a modulator and—"

"Tseethe, we went through this list earlier. We're fine, mate." But as they came to the hatch for the cargo hold, Rollie took one look at the security they were up against and started to laugh. "*Really* fine."

Because there was no keypad or voice identification system protecting the goods. No retinal scanner or riddle to solve. Just a simple entry button, like a hundred others on the ship, ready and waiting to be pressed.

And Rollie Tsmorlood was very good at pushing buttons.

As he did so, the automatic lights flipped on and the hatch popped open, illuminating all their hopes and draughts. Silver pressurized crates were stacked from floor to ceiling. Silver pressurized crates stretched from wall to wall. Silver pressurized crates stood waiting to be cracked and their contents consumed, each and every container bearing a Feegar export logo.

"It's beautiful, isn't it? Brings a tear to the eye," said Tseethe reverently. He would have wiped the aforementioned tear, if not for his helmet. He settled for turning on the in-helmet dehumidifier.

Rollie scanned the wall of boxes with satisfaction, until something about that logo grabbed his attention. He looked from one crate to another. He found himself tilting his head ever-so-slightly to the right.

He held out the crooked thumb he'd lost once and sewed back on himself. It bent at an angle he'd found useful in certain visual calculations. He assessed the logo now in reference to the thumb. He frowned. "It's zonky."

"Zonky-cosmic, you mean," said Tseethe, running a hand over one of the crates. "There's enough Feegar bourbon here to last even you a Deltan year. Time to pop one of these babies and celebrate."

"Celebrate later. The logos. They're off. One thirty-seventh of a thumb."

It was good to know he could still surprise Tseethe sometimes. "One thirty-seventh of a—"

"Give or take." Rollie reached out and peeled a logo sticker off a crate. Underneath was another logo that read TrustTChem®.

"Fake?" Tseethe cursed and kicked one of the crates. Glass rattled.

That didn't quite seem to satisfy him, so he moved to kick it again when Rollie pointed out, "Er, maybe we shouldn't jostle the thing, 'til we know what it is, eh?"

Opening a crate proved that they contained bottles all right, but these were not the unmistakable shape of Feegar High Impact Bourbon.

Tseethe grabbed one such bottle and held it to the light. It was an unlabeled eerie green. "Suddenly, I'm not so thirsty anymore." He peered around Rollie. "See any packing data?"

A bill of lading was attached to the inside lid. Rollie leaned in. "No name. Just a product number and a scan code."

Tseethe cursed again. "Look, I'm sorry, man. I never meant for this job to turn out this way."

Rollie shrugged his unbitten shoulder, as he skimmed the rest of the label. "Might not be a total loss if we find out what the stuff is. Surely there's a market somewhere."

"Yeah, well, I'd still like to have a word with my friend about the intelligence he gave us."

"As would I," Rollie murmured. "I'd also like some information on this ship-to address." He tapped it. "Look."

Tseethe wiped a spot of dried Feegar saliva from his helmet with a sleeve and drew closer. "DiversiDine World, Ltd. ..." He looked up sharply. "On Tryfe? In Pittsburgh?"

"On Tryfe," said Rollie. "In Pittsburgh."

"So — what — Eudicot T'murp's buying goods off Feegar middle-men?"

"And having them delivered to Pittsburgh?" Rollie shook his head, uncertain.

"Didn't you say that Bertram kid was heading there to check things out?"

Rollie offered a tight smile. "You start loading this stuff into the Protostar. I need to make a quick comm."

Rollie tried Bertram Ludlow, first at his ICV, then on his pocket vis-u, but to no answer. He decided to try again later.

It was hard to imagine what Ludlow was facing now that he'd arrived home. It was a shame, if Tryfe had been altered in some way. Rollie had rather liked the little backspace planet. He'd only been there a few times but it had some pleasing features like abundant print, interesting people and quaint but compelling music options.

It was with these thoughts that Rollie helped Tseethe load the shipment, and soon they were lowering the last of the crates into the Protostar's hidden freight compartments.

As the final panel closed up tight, Tseethe dusted off his hands and said, "So, what do you say we go have a word with my friend, MkChi?"

"At least one word. Possibly several." Rollie headed to the cockpit and dropped into the pilot's seat. "After that, I'd like to find out exactly what's in those bottles of ours."

Tseethe settled into the co-pilot's chair and pulled down the harness. "I suppose it's stupid to ask whether you installed any chem analysis tech into the Protostar this past year?"

Rollie laughed wearily. There were times he felt no one quite understood him. "Let's just deal with your friend first. I want to know what he knew, when he knew it and where the info went so far fraggin' off-orbit."

8

"Hi," said Bertram. "We're interested in joining the DiversiDine team. Could you tell us what positions are available?"

Bertram and Rozz were sent to the corporate recruitment table, tucked between a refreshment stand and a booth selling the Post-Gazette.

The recruiter powered up a sixty-watt smile at the sight of them. "I'm so glad you stopped by," she said, rising and shaking their hands. "We have a wide range of opportunities for motivated individuals with the drive to make a diff—"

Bzzzp!

It was the vis-u in Bertram's coat pocket. He didn't know he could still receive comms on Earth. Flushing, he clamped a hand over the thing and, thankfully, flipped the silence switch. A moment more and a holographic head would have been shooting out of his coat pocket and into the world. "Er, sorry about that. You were saying?"

"Here's our corporate brochure on careers with DiversiDine." The woman tucked glossy, full-color booklets into their hands. "And if you're interested, I can schedule you for our one-on-one evaluation and personality test. This will help us determine which of the open positions in our

DiversiDine family, if any, would be best-suited to you."

"That sounds great." *It sounds like Scientology*, thought Bertram vaguely.

"All right, then, let me see what's available." The recruiter typed something into her laptop and scrolled down the screen. "I realize tomorrow's Sunday but, because it's Kickoff weekend, a lot of our staff will be in. It looks like our Recruitment Counselors have openings starting at two. Would that work for either of you?"

They told her they could probably manage that.

"Wonderful! Then, I'll just need your names."

Names.

A nerve twinged in Bertram's neck. Depending on how connected the Tryfe branch of DiversiDine was to its GCU headquarters, the name "Bertram Ludlow" could present some serious problems. Not to mention both Bertram and Rozz had been missing for a while. At best, there was a significant gap in their employment records. At worst, their intergalactic infamy would make stealth impossible.

"*My* name …" Bertram's eyes fell on the sign for a nearby bus stop. He read the routes and grinned. "My name's Hill. Troy Hill."

The recruitment officer wrote it down without batting an eye, proving what Bertram already knew: Pittsburghers don't recognize half of the little neighborhoods in their own city.

She turned to Rozz. "And you?"

Rozz was ready for her. "Ada Byron. That's B-Y-R-O-N." This was Rozz's default persona for mailing lists and unwanted admirers. (Ada's phone number, Rozz told Bertram once, was their university library reference desk.)

"Excellent," said the recruiter. "Interviews will be right there in the main DiversiDine building." She indicated the giant soda can. "Just give your names at the front desk. And Troy, Ada…?" She beamed up at them. "We'll see you both tomorrow at two."

With the first phase of DiversiDine infiltration complete, Bertram and Rozz had a few hours to kill before the Kickoff. So they strolled around the city brainstorming next steps, purchased two cheap cell phones and made a quick stop at one of the city's thrift stores.

"We'll need something that says 'young urban professional,'" Bertram suggested, as they headed inside. "Not 'graduate of the Snake Plissken Doomsday Preparatory School.'"

Rozz wholeheartedly agreed.

By the time they left the store, the sun had gone down, the wind had sharpened and it was time they made their way to Point State Park. There, a stage had been erected and the crowd waited, thick and pensive.

Outdoor heaters crackled with life. Glowing light set an anticipatory tone through pylons shaped like DiversiDine cans. A digital clock over the stage ticked down the time left to Kickoff. TV crews had moved into position. A row of community leaders — Big Cheeses packaged in political, religious, academic and press flavors — sat front and center in special folding lawn chairs.

As the timer hit the ten-second mark, the crowd chanted it down. "Ten…nine…eight…"

Cheers rang out as the stage flickered to life, a spotlight revealing a mustached man in black-and-gold winter gear, a large gold book tucked under one arm.

As soon as he took the mic, the crowd went wild. "People of Pittsburgh and the rest of planet Earth…" He tossed a mischievous smile at the cameras that was replicated on the Jumbotron overhead. "I'm Coach Dandy. And welcome to the DiversiDine New Year's Day Kickoff!" The screams of support continued. "For those of you watching at home, it's a cold night here in the Burgh. Are yinz guys cold?" he asked the audience.

"Noooo!" the audience lied and then laughed and cheered

again. But there did seem to be a certain inexplicable heat radiating from the crowd.

"You mean you people are feeling good?" He gasped exaggeratedly.

The crowd "wooooo-ed" and whistled in answer.

"Well, I feel great and I'm so glad to be here with all of you tonight," he said. "We've come a long way from the Swirling Times. You remember those days, don't you?"

Some of the crowd shouted they did. Some laughed, some just booed.

"Back then, we were playing against our biggest, baddest opponent: a talented adversary we call Fear." He nodded sagely at the crowd, and the crowd nodded back. "Now, the thing about playing against Fear is, you can't read up on Fear's power rankings. You can't analyze Fear's weaknesses. Fear doesn't do pre- and post-game interviews. Fear uses the unknown and our differences to pull us apart. It makes us believe that if we take the field, we each take it alone."

An empathetic murmur ran across the crowd.

"So what does Fear do? It taunts us on the sidelines," Dandy said. "Fear stalks us in the bleachers. Fear knocks the DiversiDog out of our hands so it lands mustard face-down every time."

"It does! It really does! Fear's such a jagoff!" shouted a guy near Rozz.

"Fear gets to you and to me," continued Dandy, "to make sure we never step onto that field. Because that's the only way that Fear can win: *if we never step onto that field.*" He shifted the gold book to his other arm. "Yet when our skies swirled with doom, did we let Fear keep us off that field?"

"Noooo!" said the audience.

"When friends and families disagreed, saying 'I don't believe what you believe,' did we let Fear snap us with the wet towel of Giving Up?"

"Noooo!"

"That's right! Today, as I look across this collection of beautiful individuals—" and the camera panned across a sea of bright, buoyant faces, "— I see the strength. I see the hope. And I see we have united against Fear as one unstoppable force. A force I like to call … Team Humanity. So go on, give yourselves a big round of applause, for coming together to keep Team Humanity in the game." And the applause was electric.

Rozz turned to Bertram and made a gagging gesture. Bertram nodded and shrugged. How were people swallowing this load of field manure? Yet it was a good minute before the cheering gave way to silence and Dandy spoke again.

"Tonight I have the supreme honor of welcoming you, Team Humanity, to a new year and a brand new playbook. Fear is gone. It's been sidelined. It's taking a permanent powder. So now we must ask ourselves, 'What's next on the schedule of Life?' Do we simply accept our win, take our trophy and retire from the game, maybe dust it a little on the shelf now and then?"

"Nooo!"

"Do we keep playing using the same old moves we did before? I mean, they were good maneuvers, weren't they? They should still work just fine, if we keep using them over and over and—"

"Nooooo!"

On the Jumbotron, Coach Dandy raised a twenty-five foot, rhetorically-provocative eyebrow and smiled. "Or," he said, "is it time for Team Humanity to assess our strengths, focus on our goals and take our game to the next level?"

Based on the noise, Bertram got the gist it was.

"That's what I like to hear! Which one of you wants to win more happiness? Raise your hand."

Hands shot up all over the field.

"And who here wants to score greater success?"

Hands, so many hands.

"Perfect, because that's the reason we've come tonight." Coach Dandy opened the golden book and held it face-out to the crowd. "Camera people? Zoom in on that, would you?" He tapped the spot. "Right here on page one of the new DiversiDine playbook. Do you see what it says? It says: 'ZOT!'®

Motivational Refreshment Program."

The big screen flashed to a shot of a beverage in a sleek can. The can read ZOT!, where the O looked like a light bulb and the exclamation point was a bolt of lightning.

"Now, you may not know ZOT! yet, but ZOT! knows you," said Dandy. "ZOT! understands each and every one of you. And the more you get to know ZOT!, the better ZOT!'s able to help you reach your personal goals. You start by registering at the ZOT! website. Then, through every ZOT! can, you'll get suggestions tailored to your specific needs, philosophical outlook and belief system. Plus, every can of ZOT! offers the energy you need to tackle those goals. No other product on the market does that."

The young woman they'd seen earlier in the jumble of sports uniforms clomped onto the stage now. "Um — excuse me, Coach Dandy? I have a question. Does this mean ZOT! is like a fortune cookie?" she asked.

"Now that's a great question, Debbie. Isn't that a great question, folks?"

The crowd cheered that it was. Rozz rolled her eyes.

"ZOT! is so much more than a fortune cookie, Debbie. It's a dietary supplement as part of a full Motivational Beverage Program," responded Dandy. "See, fortune cookie messages are random and they're printed in bulk, so lots of people will get the very same message. But the message with every ZOT! can is transmitted with the beverage itself—no paper—and it's specifically designed for the person who drinks it. We use secret space-age technology —" he winked "— to offer each consumer customized inspiration just for them. For entertainment purposes only, of course."

"That's amazing!" said Debbie. "How did DiversiDine do it?"

"DiversiDine uses proprietary software, our unique network of partnerships, breakthrough ingestible technologies and your very own preferences to develop a plan of action just for you. Start the New Year with ZOT! and you'll enjoy hydration, inspiration and action with every can."

"Hydration, inspiration *and* action? I'll believe it when I see it!" said Debbie.

"And see it, you will, Debbie! Because everyone who's braved the cold here tonight gets to try their first can of ZOT! free!"

The crowd cheered. There was nothing a Pittsburgh event crowd liked better than free crap.

"So how do we get our free can of ZOT!?" Debbie asked.

"See those lights shaped like DiversiDine cans?" Dandy pointed into the field. "Each one marks a special ZOT! Station. In a few moments, I'll give the green light to proceed to the station closest to you and our DiversiDine ZOT!Buddies will get you squared away — limit one free can per person. No pushing now, there's enough ZOT! for everyone. And once you try ZOT! and see how it can help you take your game to the next level? Starting tomorrow, you can purchase more ZOT! at all your favorite retailers that sell dietary supplements. That goes for all you folks at home, too," he said, grinning at the cameras.

The cheering was impressive.

"Now remember: we've got music and other festivities coming right up, so once you get your free can of ZOT!, I hope you'll stick around," said Dandy. "Happy New Year, everyone. And have a DiversiDine dandy night! Now go ahead and pick up that free can of ZOT!"

The lights marking the ZOT Stations did, indeed, turn green and Bertram expected a trampling rush of Black Friday proportions. But strangely, there was no pushing, no running, no fights. The crowd reorganized itself into eerily tidy queues.

It wasn't long before Bertram and Rozz were at the head of their line and a smiling ZOT!Buddy greeted Rozz. "Name and email please?" The Buddy poised to type.

Rozz eyed the guy narrowly. "Why do you need my name and email?"

"To register you for the ZOT! Motivational Refreshment Program," said the Buddy. "That's how the product's activated. Then, the more you interact with ZOT! the better ZOT! works to help you win in the game of—"

"Yeah, fine, whatever." This was not the first time Rozz had sacrificed Ada Byron's email to the marketing gods, and it would probably not be the last. She went away with her free can and then it was Bertram's turn. In a moment, they were both squinting at the instructions in the glow of the ZOT! Station light.

"It says to put your thumb and forefinger here as you open the can," Rozz said. And there were two conveniently-located circles on the packaging to make that obvious. She rubbed one of those spots with a fingernail — or, rather, where her fingernail would have been, if she didn't bite them. "Maybe it's like a touch-sensitive Magic Eight Ball or something. Or a mood ring."

"We know it's not a fortune cookie," said Bertram.

"Oh *hell* no. Those cellophane-wrapped slackers? This is ZOT! It cooks and does your taxes and walks the dog and..." With thumb and forefinger in position, she said, "I'm ready. You ready?"

"I think I'll wait and see if your brains liquefy and pour out of your tear ducts first."

"Touching," she said. And she popped the lid.

Bertram leaned in and tried to listen. "Any ... mechanical movement in there?"

She shrugged. "Nothing I can tell." She held it up to her ear, then peered into the can.

"See anything?"

"Besides beverage?"

The outside of the can looked the same, too. There was no message revealed by the heat of her hand or when the pop-top was released. "Maybe it's at the bottom," Bertram suggested.

"Well, here goes," she said and took a sip.

In this moment, Rozz's expression shifted from wariness to surprised pleasure and the sip turned into full-fledged consumption. She'd ingested most of the can's contents before she came up for air. "You know, it's not half bad," she said finally.

"So I gathered. What's it taste like?"

"It tastes like … like …" She inhaled sharply. "*Preparation!*" she breathed.

Bertram frowned. "The hemorrhoid formula?"

But her face had acquired this look of bright-eyed wonder and she shushed him like he'd been talking over her earbuds. In a faraway voice she said, "In order to score employment success, preparing a solid defense must start now. I must anticipate every play and be two steps ahead. The win will come from action, not reaction. The time is now to examine my goals, think through my opponent's potential offense and get my head in the game."

Bertram waited a moment for her to say more, but the lit-from-within look had faded. Then, when she said, "Okay, that was totally weird," he knew that she was back.

"So the message is in the beverage itself," Bertram said.

Her head bobbed affirmation, as if on a spring. "Kind of like when you do infopills or Translachew gum and there's suddenly all this content in your brain that wasn't there before."

"Dandy did say something about 'space age technologies,'" Bertram pointed out.

"So infopill tech, crossed with marketing data associated with our email addresses. Possibly even leveraging our thumbprint smartphone technology."

"Wait, how much tracking are you talking about? That could be very scary stuff."

"Total data consolidation of the individual," she said, "maybe. Hard to say what DiversiDine whipped up while we were gone, but we've been headed there for a while." She shrugged. "The scariest thing is: it's right, you know."

Bertram pulled his coat closer around him. "What's right?"

"The ZOT! If we're going to infiltrate DiversiDine, I'm going to need to focus." Her brown eyes were so wide and sincere, it was like Bambi trying to apply for a home loan. "I mean, these are real interviews happening tomorrow, Bertram, and we still need to make up resumes. And we should probably set up some social media profiles, too. Not to mention, we have job references to fake and cell phones to set up and..."

She was already dragging him from the field.

"Okay, sure, Rozz, I get it." They were almost out of the park now. "But if I could just take one minute and—" Bertram pointed to his unopened ZOT! Now that he saw how it worked, he wanted to know what personalized wisdom the beverage held for him.

But Rozz was on a mission. "You can play with your can later," she told him. "Right now we need to catch a bus back to the ship. There's dumploads to do!"

9

"'The Feegars are trying to make things right,'" squeaked Tseethe, in a mocking, nasal voice an octave too high. "'They're using Simulant crews now for all their shipments. It's the perfect opportunity.'" He scowled through the swirling helmet smoke. "Ha! Tell it to some other froob next time."

ChkChk MkChi was lying flat on the floor with fear, impersonating his own throw rug in his own warm and comfortable tree-top living room on the planet Nobbl. Nucifarians as a species tended to be a jittery people, and at the moment neither Rollie nor Tseethe were feeling particularly sympathetic about stretching those nerves to their limits.

In fact, the only thing Rollie cared about stretching right now was his back because the ceilings were so fraggin' low.

"Really sorry, Tseethe," the throw rug responded, his black eyes blinking sincerely. "I — I had it from a good source, Tseethe. I swear! I—I don't know what happened."

"Oh yeah? Then I'll tell you what happened, Chky. I got bit," said Tseethe, pulling up his sleeve to reveal the marks where the Feegar had gnawed him. It was healing now thanks to a fibroderma accelerator pen, but there were still raised lincs where the wounds had been. "In duo." He yanked up the second sleeve. "My friend here," he hooked a thumb at Rollie, "was also taste tested. And if it hadn't been for the smoking helmet across my jugular, you would only be having this discussion with him." Tseethe leaned down to his informant. "You wouldn't have wanted that. He happens to be a lot less forgiving than I am."

With a slow nod, Rollie pulled back his coat to reveal the new XJ-37 he'd stopped to buy on the way there.

"I, um, I don't believe I've had the pleasure of your acquaintance," said MkChi, voice quavering. He extended a clawed hand from the floor.

Rollie didn't take it. "Rolliam Tsmorlood," he said.

At this, the Nuciferian's eyes went glassy. His breath caught in a single pained hiccup. "The, uh, the leader of that new Intergalactic Underworld? Unofficially?" His pointed ears twitched at the same time as his whiskers, causing what looked like a full-head spasm.

"I am not," Rollie began firmly, "leader of any organization, unofficial or otherwise. I have left the Society. I'm an independent contractor. Do you understand me?"

"Suresure, my mistake!"

"And as such, I require accurate intelligence when I agree to do a job."

"Of course. You're right," said Chky. He licked his quivering whiskers. "Bad info, it's ... inconvenient."

"Inconvenient?!" Rollie felt his face go hot. "Your scab info led to a freighter filled to the brim with blasted Feegars! I'd call that more than a little 'inconvenient.'" He closed his eyes. *I am like water molecules in the stream...*

"Like I said, Captain Tsmorlood," Chky began, "it—it was a mistake. I was fed bad information. I feel terrible. The guy's my upper-brother's semi uncle's war buddy. He's punctual, he pays his debts, he's got six little Nuciferians still in the nest. I had no reason to believe—"

Rollie opened his eyes and stared at MkChi. "You want to make it up?"

And the fellow's nod shook the floorboards.

"Then do this one thing right. Get the word out. Tell

everyone you know not to go after any Feegar freight. No matter how tempting. Especially *if* it's tempting. And do it now. It's the least you can manage. Frag this up and you and I will need to talk further."

MkChi was still nodding. "So, um..." he nodded himself up from the floor and jittered into his Uninet console seat, "there was no hundred-year Feegar High Impact at all, then? The case we got, it was a—what do ya call it? —a ploy? The Feegar ship was empty?"

"No, not empty," said Tseethe. "Instead of Feegar bourbon we got crates of this stuff." Tseethe reached into his bag and clunked a green bottle onto the console table.

MkChi blinked. "No label?"

Rollie said, "Shipping container says it's from TrustTChem."

"Oh." The whiskers turned up. "TrustTChem! Yeah, I know them!" More nodding.

Rollie raised an eyebrow. "Do you?"

"Suresure, they're a Vos Laegon company. Way into environmental exports. Skin exfoliants from desert sands. Moisturizers from ground-up Loombah casings. Stuff like that." And Rollie could see the Nuciferian relax. "Suresure. That makes sense now. I heard something on the Uninet about a TrustTChem freighter vanishing a few weeks back. Guess the Feegars got take-out."

"Explains the smell of their refuse incinerator, anyway," said Rollie.

"Explains why it wasn't a Feegar freighter in the first place," said Tseethe.

"Well, you know what they say: hindsight *is* twenty/two hundred," said MkChi philosophically.

Rollie frowned. "You mean half-blind and wholly unhelpful?"

"Exactly. Nuciferians can't see for crap," MkChi admitted.

Rollie nodded and headed to the exit, trying not to bump his head along the way. Tseethe grabbed the bottle and followed.

"Look, I really am sorry about the Feegar thing," MkChi said at the door. "Glad you still got something for your trouble, though."

"Well, that remains to be seen," said Rollie, trying to stretch without reopening his shoulder wound. "All depends on what's in the bottles. Stuff's got to be tested first."

"Oh!" The Nuciferian brightened, whiskers bolting up. "Hey, why didn't you say so? I have a guy. Real trustworthy, too."

Tseethe laughed. "Trustworthy as your source on the Feegar job?

"Suresure, I—" ChkChk blinked. "Oh."

"Pass," said Rollie and Tseethe.

"But seriously, fellahs, I'd be happy to—"

Rollie put up a hand. "My friend Ditto can handle it. We're heading there now. Just spread the word on the Feegars, would you? I find out you've fragged this up? Me and you, we'll be meeting again."

10

On, off. On, off. Bertram watched the shoe dangle on the end of Rozz's toe, then pop into place again.

Now she tugged at her collar.

Now she tapped on the glossy portfolio folder in her lap.

"Quit it, would you?" whispered Bertram. "You're making me nervous."

"The shoes hurt," she hissed. "And the suit has ..." she sniffed her collar, "... an odor. I didn't notice it when I tried it on. But now..."

Bertram leaned toward her and inhaled. "Ah," he grinned, "a complex, magical blend of mothballs, cough drops and roses."

On, off. On, off. "I call it *Biddy Number Five*."

They watched DiversiDine employees wave their corporate badges at the receptionist and disappear through shiny glass doors.

"She's probably dead," Rozz mused.

"Who?"

"Biddy Number Five. I found this used tissue in the pocket and I swear, it looked like something out of one of those Victorian coughing novels."

Bertram turned to her. "Rozz, if you don't want to do this,

it's okay. I can tackle it myself. I *am* practically unofficial Underworld these days."

He wasn't sure if she laughed or sneezed. "Dude," she said, "I didn't come all this way to just twiddle my thumbs." On, off. On, off.

"So—what? —you think our identities won't fly?" Bertram felt his heart beat faster. They'd spent the better part of twelve hours making Troy Hill and Ada Byron into the perfect job candidates. Their resumes were shining examples of the legitimacy that giant, steaming lies take on when presented in elegant fonts. Their lives were showcased as a rich tapestry of family-friendly wit and wisdom, often in one hundred and forty characters or less. And their online self-expression extended just as far as backdating functionality allowed.

Bertram found it truly mind-blowing what Rozz had accomplished using an alien shipboard computer, a patch-job conduit to the Internet that she'd explained but Bertram had nodded off in the middle of, general hacking skills and the energy of ZOT! Not to mention they'd arrived in the finest interview-wear the ninety-nine cent sale of St. Hubbins Thrift had to offer.

But still Rozz sat there: on, off. On, off.

Bertram told her, "If you have any doubts that we won't make it through a background check, I'd rather know now."

"Our IDs are golden," she said.

He eyed her.

"So, gold plated." She recrossed her legs. "It's solid enough for our needs."

"Then what?"

She mumbled something to her portfolio folder.

Bertram cupped a hand to his ear. "Eh?"

"I *said* I've never interviewed before, okay?"

Bertram blinked. "Never? Not even at Beddsyde Manor?" For weeks on the planet Daglann-Da, she'd worked in the medical facility's IT department, creating workarounds when the number Three went missing. Rozz had skills.

"It was a direct placement. My hoverchair gave me a job

reference." On, off. On, off. "Look, I don't want to talk about it anymore."

"Consider it untalked."

She nodded, satisfied. "While I remember: you tried your ZOT! last night, didn't you? What happened with that?"

He knew she hadn't been paying attention. At the time, she was mumbling to herself about incompatible operating systems and cursing the gods of connectivity. "I think you were onto something when you said ZOT! drew on our email marketing data."

She shifted in her chair. "Go on…"

"I gave them a fake email. And you know what my message was? 'The wise player must trust in his team, as well as himself. Your success depends on opening yourself up to new potential plays. Do not assume that support and guidance will automatically lead to a loss.'"

"So your beverage lectured you on trust issues?" She snickered.

"That was my take away," Bertram said. "And I agree, there's something eerily familiar about the way the message arrives in your brain. It feels like Translachew."

"That *is* a DiversiDine product," she said.

"If that's the case, it's quite a set-up they've got here. I'm also wondering how they got it through the FDA so fast."

She sniffed. "Who knows? It's labeled as a dietary supplement. We know those reviews aren't exactly as involved as for other products. Plus, everybody's so upbeat these days, even the Feds might be slap-happy with their approvals."

"Let's just hope HR's as cheerful with hiring," Bertram said. And he'd hardly gotten it out of his mouth when a grinning young man in gray tweed stepped into reception.

"Mr. Hill? We're ready for you now."

Bertram rose and adjusted his paisley tie. He grabbed his thrifted briefcase and looked to Rozz. She shot him a thumbs-up sign, as he trailed through the glass doors and into DiversiDine's inner sanctum.

✧

"Mr. Hill? Step right in here." Young-n-Tweedy motioned to a small room. The room held a desk, desk chair and a computer terminal. A lone guest chair stood to one side. Bertram moved to the guest chair. "No, Mr. Hill."

"No?" Bertram stopped in mid-sit.

"There." He followed the pointing finger to the computer chair. "Make yourself comfortable."

Comfortable, in this case, meant "sitting awkwardly in a space set-up for a much taller guy and drawing his newly-faked resume from his briefcase."

And what a resume!

Troy Hill's resume looked almost exactly how Bertram Ludlow's might have appeared, if he'd ever entered the workforce. Hill graduated from the same university. He went to the same grad school. Where Bertram Ludlow had failed to get his Ph.D. because of a minor alien abduction issue, Troy Hill had gone on to graduate to a research position in the university that was so cutting edge, he couldn't talk about it. Bertram hoped that would make for a short discussion if they called his main reference, Dr. Phineas Sutton. Dr. Sutton happened to be a cheap cell phone Bertram would be answering in a voice he hadn't settled on yet.

"So what do you want to know about me? My drive to succeed? My thirst for knowledge? My deep devotion to the DiversiDine product catalog?" Bertram asked.

"All of it," said Tweed with an even bigger smile. "Every bit."

"Great! So, I was born in a small town outside of Pittsburgh, with a restlessness that only properly-crunched market data could soothe. In my formative years, I—"

"No, no. Don't tell me," said Tweed.

"No?"

"Tell it." He directed Bertram's attention to the computer terminal.

"It's...lonely...is it?"

Tweed gave the obligatory chuckle. "Mr. Hill, meet the DiversiDine HR4000, an assessment system that helps us determine who's the right fit for our organization. The program runs automatically. You answer the questions and it will lead you through our state-of-the-art personality test. When the process is complete, it will notify me and we can discuss next steps. 'Kay?"

"'Kay," Bertram said. "And, er, you're sure that's all you need?" He waved his resume enticingly.

"Answer the questions honestly, Mr. Hill. That's all we ask."

Funny, Bertram thought, *that's the one thing I can't do.*

- *If you were a DiversiDine product, which one would you be and why?*
- *List your last place of employment and the position held there.*
- *Tell us about your biggest personal weakness and how you overcome it. (Note: weight-training is not a valid answer.)*
- *Have you ever been arrested and was it for anything interesting?*
- *How would you solve a problem like Maria?*
- *If DrinkThis were a staff member who reported to you, what tasks would you assign it?*

Slowly, Bertram Ludlow worked his way through the HR4000's questions, channeling Troy Hill with every step. He detailed his likes, his dislikes and his fictional management of anthropomorphized soft drinks. He had barely hit the "FINISHED" button when young Tweed returned to the tiny room, a stack of papers in his hand. "Now wasn't that fun?"

"A very clever system!" said Bertram. "So unique! I hardly wanted it to end." It was unscientific psychobabble, but Bertram had decided Troy Hill was a suck-up.

"So let's just see what the HR4000 has to say then, shall we?" Tweed turned the first page in his papers and his brows knit together. He stroked his temple. "Now, that *is* something."

"Is it?" Bertram tried to look. "Something?"

The smile now was thin and sly. "It appears someone here has been holding back on us, haven't they?"

"Uh…"

"Someone here hasn't been entirely forthright about certain details of certain things." Tweed flipped a page. "But the HR4000 knows. The HR4000 sees everything."

"Ah." Bertram's eyes flicked to the door and he rose, hoping to slip out before some DiversiDine security guard the size of a walk-in freezer chucked him into the street. "Well, it was nice meeting you." He realized he didn't know the guy's actual name. "Thanks for your time."

Tweed stepped between him and the door, looking concerned. "But where are you going? You can't go." Tweed was trying to usher him back to the desk chair.

"I think I can." Bertram cursed himself for leaving his handlaser in his other clothes. It was one of those things; you get ready for an interview and you're so focused on the resume and tie, you forget the handlaser.

"Oh, but you can't! I mean, yes, simply looking at your employment history, we'd never have known. But clearly, with your hidden talents for customer service—"

Bertram stopped dead. "Excuse me?"

"It says right here." The man shook the paper. "'Based on tactical and empathetic responses, this candidate is ideally suited to the Customer Service: TLC division.'"

"Let me see that." And Bertram took the papers. Sure enough, there in black lettering it said: "Customer Service TLC."

"Congratulations, Mr. Hill!" Tweed shook Bertram's free hand with vigor. "The HR4000 likes you!"

"Great." He wished the HR4000 liked him less. Bertram had chosen cognitive psychology research mainly because he appreciated the humanity in data. He wasn't so big on humanity in actual humans. Especially not in ones you needed to, say, fix.

"The HR4000 has matched your personality to the perfect job within our organization. Isn't that exciting?"

"I'm doing end zone dances but, because I'm a professional, I keep it all inside," he assured the guy. "Now about this customer service... How much wiggle-room is there for—"

"So what I want you to do is, tomorrow, you come in at nine. Go to reception and ask for Assistant Coach Gail Truman. She'll be expecting you. And she'll get you rolling on your new position as a part of the DiversiDine team."

"That's stellar," Bertram said, forgetting for a moment he wasn't still in the GCU. It all seemed so GCUy. "But aren't there other things we should go over first?" he asked. "Like responsibilities? Benefits? Salary?"

"Assistant Coach Truman will make you the official offer and discuss the rest of that tomorrow. But ..."A mischievous smile came over Tweed's face, "... to give you a ballpark, the HR4000 suggests *this* would be an appropriate salary for someone of your skill level." He edged a slip of paper to Bertram.

Bertram took it and blinked. He had no idea working for alien overlords could be so lucrative.

"'Kay?" Tweed yanked back the paper and escorted him to the door.

"'Kay." It was amazing how a good base salary changed a person's perspective, even in a corporate espionage situation. Bertram viewed this as his first important lesson of joining America's workforce.

As they walked down the hall past a number of small offices, Bertram began to wonder which one Rozz was in and how she was faring with the HR4000.

Perhaps she, too, was holding back on a hidden talent for customer service...

Bertram chuckled to himself. *Nah.*

11

Rollie and Tseethe were halfway to the planet Walter and, thus, to Rollie's friend the chemist, when colored lights flashed through the Protostar ICV portals like a star gone supernova. Tseethe craned his neck in his smoking helmet, nearly bouncing it off the portal window, as he struggled to see what the frag was going on.

"What the frag is going on?" asked Tseethe.

"Law," said Rollie. Tseethe found it amazing the guy didn't even bother to verify it in the ship's monitor. This was a fellow who recognized the flash of law enforcement ICVs the second they flickered into view. Tseethe often wondered how someone so good at what he did could still get busted so fragging often. He figured it probably had to do with general percentages.

Then Tseethe moaned as he realized he would be included in this particular bust. "Aw, no way, man! How'd they get on our trail?"

"No clue, unless the Feegars called it in."

Tseethe turned to his friend. "You think the Feegars called the cops before they tried to *eat* us? Crumblin' craters, talk about bad table manners."

"Look, do I know?" The lights had already grown bigger, brighter; the law was closing in fast.

Tseethe unharnessed, leapt up and ran to the side portal for a better view. "This ship isn't still registered under your real name, is it?"

"How many dead men do you know who keep property?" The lights were closer now. So much closer. Tseethe saw Rollie ease down on the propulsion and he could hear the guy muttering: "Nothing to see here … Not trying to get away … Simply out for a pleasure trip in a beloved vintage collectible … Just pass us by … Pass … Pass …"

They weren't passing.

"So what alias *is* the ship under?" Tseethe asked. "Phlyjollee?" Rollie had a few names he'd used over the years, but Dax Q. Phlyjollee seemed to be a favorite.

"Nah, it's a new ID I'm trying out," Rollie said. "Name of Levvyn Moonshot."

Tseethe could read the insignia on the law ICV now, it was so close. "Bargo-2," he said.

"Bargo-2? I've never committed any crimes on Bargo-2," came Rollie's voice.

"Ah, but did you check with Levvyn Moonshot?" asked Tseethe.

"A paragon of innocence and goodwill," Rollie proclaimed. He cut the aft rockets in a final attempt to look like he had nothing to hide and all day to not hide it.

The Bargo-2 Constabulary screamed by, flashing all the way.

Rollie and Tseethe watched it in silence as it zoomed through space and made a left around Treyfab-3.

"Blasted peculiar," said Rollie finally, powering the ship again.

"I wonder where they're off to," said Tseethe, taking a seat once more.

They found out soon enough, as they made their journey deeper into the system. A collection of ships from every law enforcement group in the galaxy was stationed around a small rust-colored planet just on the other side of Treyfab-3.

"I don't know what's more disturbing," Tseethe said of the whirling, blinking collective. "That it looks like some hot constabulary dance party or the fact that planet doesn't even belong there. I'm not losing it, right? That planet was not there before."

"You are correct," said Rollie.

"So where'd it come from?"

"That's Mawdank Roving Confinement Center. It does as it pleases."

"Ahhhh..." Tseethe's helmet bobbed in epiphany. "I heard about that. Rogue planet, right? Moves from system to system picking up offenders along the way. Kinda like a traveling carnival for the criminally-minded."

"That's the one."

"Wonder what the problem is." Tseethe absently stroked his helmet where his chin would be. "Whatever it is, it looks big."

"So long as we're well-clear of it, I do not care," said Rollie. "I have other things to worry about."

Things they would both be dealing with soon enough.

"This? This is where your friend the chemist lives?" Tseethe Tsardonee had never been to Walter. And now he knew why.

Below them was the most boring planet he had ever laid eyes upon. Currently they were flying in low over a prairie of fine, yellow grasses. It was different from the prairie of fine, yellow grasses they'd been looking at for the past twenty thousand kroms by the introduction of one lone tree. Standing there, it gave Tseethe the impression it had gone hiking, lost its way and now held its branches to the heavens, as if asking where its GPS had gone so very wrong.

"What, is your buddy Ditto a social phobic? A survivalist? Hiding from the law?" Tseethe frowned. "Ditto's not actually you, is he?"

Rollie laughed.

"It's a legitimate question."

"Not once you meet Ditto," Rollie said, drawing the ship in closer to Walter's surface. It was only as they dipped down into this topographical yawn-fest that the view began to flicker and change.

The air shimmered around them and momentarily Tseethe saw rows of bright green plants with red knobby fruit. Roads appeared. Hovercrafts and farming equipment roamed below. Buildings dotted the landscape. And as they moved even closer, figures came into sight.

Tseethe started laughing. "Flamin' comets, that boring prairie illusion is the best use of holograph technology I've ever seen," he said.

Rollie offered a tight smile. "Thought you'd like it."

"And the crop, that can't be ..." he looked twice before he dared to say it, " ... gannon berry?"

Rollie gave one curt nod. "It is."

Sap from the gannon berry plant fermented into the GCU's most potent beverage — so potent, it had been banned by the Coalition of Planets ever since the Jarquad Unification in the Way Back era. Tseethe shook his head in wonder. "If the Coalition only knew that there's enough raw materials here to make half the GCU unconscious and leaking through their pores..."

Rollie directed an amused sun-colored gaze Tseethe's way. "They're not going to know, though, are they?"

"My portals are sealed," he said. It never ceased to impress him how long you could be an active part of the Greater Communicating Universe and still learn something new.

"Good." Rollie settled the Protostar down in a clearing next to several large warehouses. "Because if you don't seal 'em, I guarantee Ditto'll seal 'em for you, permanent."

"Just once, I wish you'd introduce me to someone who's a pacifist. Y'know, to mix things up."

The warehouse workers said their boss was out in the east field, and so it was to the eastern field that Rollie and Tseethe trudged. It was unsurprising that the vegetation was much bigger than it looked from the air, but the discrepancy of that size was the real shocker. These were not the average perennials you'd have in pots outside your home-unit but giant succulent trees stretching to the sky. On the trunk of each tree was an apparatus featuring a series of tubes and monitors. This connected to a tap that ran straight into jugs. As each bottle filled, it was whisked away by robot gardeners, and another jug took its place in the blink of an eye.

Tseethe debated asking about free samples, but he wasn't sure what gannon sap would do to the Hyphiz Deltan constitution. Also, he'd left his funnel back on the ship.

Rollie, Tseethe noticed, showed no interest whatsoever in the crops or their processing. Maybe it was because he'd been here before and the novelty was gone, but his manner showed all the signs of an edgy preoccupation. Laser drawn, his gaze scanned between the rows of plants in a tense, methodical way that made Tseethe feel very uncomfortable. It was like they'd stepped into the middle of some battle Rollie hadn't bothered to tell anybody about. Which, knowing Rollie, was a real possibility. Even among his inner circle, the guy tended to keep things pretty close to the astrotogs.

To be on the safe side, Tseethe drew his own laser. "Um, I thought you said Ditto was 'a good friend.'"

"I did," said Rollie.

"And do you always take point when you visit 'good friends'?"

"It's not Ditto I'm worried about." Rollie's jaw was set in a tense, determined way. "It's the original."

At the end of their row, a slim figure stepped into their path. Rollie's eyes narrowed, and he directed his gun on this lifeform. "Dar?"

It was a female of a species Tseethe didn't recognize wearing a steel-gray jumpsuit, a long gray coat, gray complexion and silver hair pulled back in a ponytail. Her goggles glinted in the light as she showed them the barrel of an XJ-90. No one moved a muscle. It was a long moment before Tseethe heard her say: "Rollie?"

The tone was surprised and surprisingly gentle. Rollie's shoulders untensed and his arm dropped to his side. "Aw, thank Karnax! Ditto, good to see you, mate!"

"And you!" she said, coming closer, smiling.

"Dar isn't somewhere round here, though, is she?" Rollie asked with another one of those darting looks.

Ditto gave a sharp laugh. "Not these days. Last I'd heard, she had a job with the Premier of Jarendi."

One of Rollie's eyebrows shot skyward at this. "The Premier of Jarendi hired Dar?"

Ditto blinked. "Did I say 'with'? I meant 'on.'"

"Ah." He nodded, like this explained everything. "Funny, I hadn't heard the ol' Premier had taken a dust-nap."

"I don't know that he has — yet," she said. "But the two main Jarendi political parties can't agree on anything, *except* both of them hired Dar to off the Premier. It's a nice moment for them to share, I think."

Rollie holstered his laser. "I imagine Dar took the yoonies from both groups, though."

"Naturally." She adjusted a bolt on one of the taps. "Dar loves making people happy."

Tseethe pointed out, "Except the Jarendi premier."

"You can't please everyone," Ditto said. "By the way, you are...?"

"Oh." Rollie looked surprised. He never was any good at introductions. "Ditto Balisong, meet my friend Tseethe Tsardonee. Tseethe and me, we're mates way back. Met in Underworld orientation, if you can believe that."

Tseethe said, "Technically, I met him in the ICV lot before orientation. He was breaking into the orientation leader's ship."

"Can't blame a fellah for trying to get a head start." Rollie turned to Ditto. "Talking of Dar, um," he cleared his throat, "she hasn't mentioned me in a while, has she?"

"No. But you know, we don't talk like we used to," Ditto said. "We don't really have that much in common."

At this Rollie actually laughed, full-fledged and with gusto. "Ditto, you're her fraggin' clone!"

"Nurture versus nature, my friend," she said. "I think people don't always understand how important environment can be to the life paths we take. You know Dar; she's got a lot of anger."

"Yeah, I got a sense of that when she tried to murder me in the middle of ..." he chuckled, "never mind. Let's just say it rather put a damper on our relationship."

Tseethe had never heard this story, but he recognized that a person didn't always share every time someone tried to kill him.

Ditto bent to adjust one of the gannon tubes. "Admittedly, the rage is cosmic for the assassination game, but I just never felt it myself. I know it was a disappointment to her at first, but I feel like she's finally come to accept my career decision. So we do lunch now and then. Otherwise, Dar does her thing, I do mine." She paused to prune a dead leaf from one of the trees.

Tseethe asked, "And your thing's niche market horticulture?"

Her smile grew bigger, like now they were on a topic she could get behind. "We've got a stellar crop of gannon this year. And the flavor is out-of-this-world."

Rollie said, "For the two seconds you taste it before you wake up hospitalized."

She laughed and waved it away. "Oh, that was years ago. It's a whole new technology these days. We've completely refined our processes since then."

Rollie looked intrigued. "So it's safer now?"

"Of course. Today, it's a full five minutes before you pass out and begin to leak."

Tseethe shook his head empathetically. "And still it's banned. The Coalition is so closed-minded."

Ditto checked the seal on one of the collection bottles. "So what brings you guys here? Is this a friendly visit or did you come to do some trade? I didn't think this was your assigned quadrant, Rollie. At least it wasn't before you 'died,' anyway."

"You're right, it wasn't," he replied. "But I guess you didn't hear. I left the Underworld. Running my own operations now."

"Self-employed! Congratulations," she said brightly, giving him a hug.

"Actually, Ditto, I came because I got a mystery item here. I was wondering if you could do a chem workup on it for me. Tell me what's involved." Rollie drew the sample bottle from his inner coat pocket.

Her gaze went to the bottle.

"I'll pay," he added quickly.

Ditto gave a little exhale that might have been a laugh. "Oh no. I think this one's on me."

He frowned. "That's hardly necessary."

"Are you kidding? I still feel terrible about leading you on and," she grimaced, "mostly that trying to kill you thing."

"Aw, but you've nothing to do with that. Or any of it," he said. "That was Dar, all the way."

"I know but ..." She wrinkled her nose. "Shared memories. Means we clones get all the knowledge, all the guilt. My therapist says contrition might be healthy for me. You know, acts of open self-differentiation?" Rollie started to protest but she raised a hand. "No. My mind is made up. Anyway, it's not for her. It's for me. This way." And she motioned them from the field.

"So how long's this going to take?" Rollie asked.

They were in the operation's quality control center, as evidenced by the sign overhead and also the stack of test subjects piled unconscious in the corner, dripping.

"Depends on what's in the bottle," said Ditto. She gestured to a door marked Break Room, where a handful of non-robot workers ate lunch in front of a holovision blaring the latest *Heavy Meddler* news. "Make yourselves comfortable. I'll let you know when I have a better estimate."

Tseethe had no problem settling down in one of the empty lounge chairs in front of the holovision, but Rollie was still bristling with energy and busied himself pacing a path in the carpet.

The newscaster on the screen, Tseethe noticed now, was

that cranium-in-a-jar, Pate Maesyn. Tseethe hadn't cared for Maesyn's reporting ever since the presenter won a major journalism award last year. Tseethe felt it went to his head.

Maesyn was saying: "… The prison break was led by this lifeform: Jane Manners of Tryfe." The image cut from Maesyn to the mugshot of a humanoid female looking very young and extremely bewildered in her Mawdank prison uniform. Rollie stopped pacing long enough to stare. "Originally sent to Mawdank Roving Confinement Center on charges of vagrancy, Manners mysteriously eluded the advanced prison system and staged the largest mass escape in GCU law enforcement history. Quadrant One constabulary organizations are currently searching for Manners and the other escaped prisoners."

"Well," said Rollie, "least we know what that hubbub in the Treyfab system was about."

"But she's from Tryfe," murmured Tseethe. "She's not that friend of your buddy Ludlow, is she?"

"Nah, that's Rozz," Rollie told him. "I don't know this one."

Tseethe turned back to the holovision as a no-necked lifeform with intelligent red eyes projected from the screen. The name underneath read, "Warden Wambo F. Kleefer, Mawdawnk."

Kleefer said, "Attention, people of Quad One: we are on an active search for twelve fugitives from the Mawdank Roving Confinement Center. Members of our law enforcement team are scouring every ICV fuel station, space station, home-unit, spacecraft, hovercraft, and craft store in a nine hundred light year radius to find each and every one of these miscreants and ensure the safety of the law abiding citizens of the GCU. These are the escapees."

The mugshots of all twelve lifeforms now appeared on the screen, ranging from the aforementioned Tryfling, to a Marglenian, Hyphizite, Mathekite and something that looked a lot like a cloud of vapor.

But the real surprise came when Tseethe noticed one lifeform in this motley bunch looked precisely like Ditto, who happened to be standing in the door at this very moment, mouth agape.

"Take note," warned Kleefer, "and scan their facial-rec into your home security systems. The data is available on the *Heavy Meddler* Uninet site. If confronted by one of these lifeforms, do not attempt to apprehend them yourselves — unless you have an XJ-296 like this." Kleefer brought out a battle cannon.

"Oh, boy: Mawdank …" Ditto flushed lightly under her pearl-gray skin. "I guess that Jarendi job didn't work out so well after all."

"You could say that, my Other," came a voice from the front door. And there stood Dar Balisong in a Mawdank prison uniform.

"Dar." Ditto's expression bounced between pleasure and apprehension. "Er, what are you doing here?"

"Where better to get a quick change of clothes in this system?" She turned to Rollie with a critical gaze. "Rollie Tsmorlood … I thought I recognized that astro-disaster parked outside. Miss me, did you? Desperate for another glimpse of my face?"

"I don't miss," said Rollie. "Though I recall last time you did."

"Ah, that dry Hyphiz Deltan sense of humor. Or is it just the Underworld Society membership agreement, where witty repartee is mandatory?"

"Wouldn't know," he said.

"He quit the Underworld," explained Ditto. "He's freelancing."

"How nice for you." She went to a closet in the test lab and chose one of several identical gray jumpsuits. She kicked off her soft slippers and began to exchange her prison uniform for the duds with a surprising lack of self-consciousness; this was something Tseethe could respect.

Rollie, however, had other things on his mind. "So how'd your group manage to bust out of Mawdank? That's high security, that is."

"No idea. The plan was not mine." Dar stepped into the

new jumpsuit. "I just happened to be on the right cell-block at the right time and went along for the ride. Speaking of rides," she zipped and turned to Ditto, "they dropped me off. So I'll be taking one of the runabouts."

"Oh you will, will you?" Ditto folded her arms. "I believe we've discussed this sort of thing before."

Dar helped herself to some gardening shoes and gave a disinterested shrug. "Discussed what, my dear?"

"You can't just come in here any time you want, Dar. Yes, we're family and I'll help you when I can. But this is my business. I built it all by myself. And there are boundaries. I expect you to respect them."

"Me, your own mother?" Dar gave her a slow smile.

Ditto stood resolute.

"Me, your very own twin sister?"

Ditto had apparently heard this one before, too.

Dar sighed and offered her clone a sad, lost look, like a snoogle on one of those weepy pet rescue Uninet ads. "May I use one of the runabouts... please?"

Ditto eyed her with a steely gaze and it seemed a long moment... many moments... years... before she finally spoke, "Fine." The word thudded to the ground and lay there.

Dar kissed her cheek. "You couldn't spare any yoonies, either, could you, dear?"

With a scowl, Ditto dipped into her pocket. "One card. That's it."

"That's all I need." Dar pocketed it without even looking. "Unless you can spare a weapon. Doesn't have to be much. Maybe a little XJ-20? A XR-59? A..."

Ditto's face might have been stone.

So Dar turned to Rollie. "Now I know you're a man who's always well-armed. You wouldn't care to do me the littlest favor and—"

"I'm out of here," said Rollie, moving to the door and Tseethe actually had to hustle to catch up. "Ditto, comm me with the test results, yeah?"

"Will do, Rollie," said Ditto.

"You don't think I'd try to take you out right here, do you, Tsmorlood?" Dar called to their backs. "Where's the fun in that?"

But apparently Rollie did. He kept going and Tseethe knew that when Rollie Tsmorlood retreated, a wise man followed his lead.

Tseethe could hear Dar sounding sulky as the warehouse door closed behind them. "Fine. Be that way. I'll pick up something at the Shop-o-Drome."

12

"We're so pleased to have you on the DiversiDine team, Troy," said Assistant Coach Gail Truman, after they'd finalized Bertram Ludlow's paperwork. She was a middle-aged lady with a tight perm, who stood stout and firm in her shoes like gravity had gifted her extra stability, just for the occasion. "You come highly recommended."

"I know," Bertram said. The moment it was out of his mouth, he realized how it sounded. But he *did* know. He'd taken his own reference call around five the night before. Dr. Phineas Sutton, it turned out, was an older gentleman from New England who cleared his throat a lot. "I — I mean, Dr. Sutton was so supportive about being a reference." Dr. Sutton had also been determined to get Bertram switched to anything but Customer Service. Unfortunately, that didn't take.

"So today," continued Truman, "we'll start training as a part of Customer Service TLC. Now at DiversiDine, TLC stands for 'Telephone Life Coach.' It's a very important position, Troy. Particularly now that ZOT! has launched." She held up the beverage she happened to be enjoying right this moment.

"And I'm honored to be a small part of it," Bertram said.

She smiled like he'd just complimented the baby in her office photos. (Or maybe that was a Shar-Pei. From this distance, all he could see was beige rolls of skin, so it could go either way.) She said, "DiversiDine's ongoing mission is to combine our products with general lifestyle support for a holistic approach to customer retention."

Translation: hook 'em, hold 'em, milk 'em.

"Our TLCs," she continued, "are primarily responsible for answering questions about the use of our products. But we set ourselves apart by also providing cogent, yet non-legally-binding wisdom on everyday topics. For entertainment purposes only, of course."

"Of course." Bertram's pocket buzzed.

A fine crease appeared in the middle of Assistant Coach Truman's forehead.

Bertram felt his own face go hot. It was that handheld vis-u again and he was positive he'd turned it off yesterday; he must have bumped it. Here he was with astounding space age technology, but he couldn't keep holographic people from popping out of his pockets. It was shameful.

Fortunately, these were deep pockets. Bertram dug into his coat and searched for the controls. "I apologize." The vis-u was on its second buzz, and an irritated male voice with a foreign accent began cursing out some poor, errant soul named Ludlow just as Bertram flipped the switch.

"Um ..." Bertram offered Truman his warmest, friendliest, most brown-nosiest smile. "So I believe we were at 'cogent, yet non-legally-binding wisdom'...?"

"DiversiDine. My name is Troy. How can I help you take your game to the next level?" Bertram asked into the headset. He adjusted the earpiece. After a morning of supervised calls, his right ear was starting to chafe.

The caller said their can of ZOT! had told them to connect more with their spouse, and she wanted ideas on how to do that.

Bertram might have suggested the caller contact a marriage

counselor instead of a snack company. But that wouldn't have been very holistic of him. So instead he typed the question into the TLC system and read the screen. "In order to strengthen your home game, consider formulating a game plan that you both can live with. No team can survive without a unified schedule. So think how you can make more time for one-on-ones in your game of life."

So far, Bertram had told one guy who was having trouble with the ladies that winning wasn't always about the score. He'd told a woman who was getting unwanted advances from her boss that the best defense was a good offense. And he revealed to an emo teen that the meaning of life was staying in the game.

"Troy, you're doing extremely well," Assistant Coach Truman told him. "You nutshell and categorize their questions very efficiently, and you don't sound like you're reading from a script at all."

Yup, four years of college, plus three on a Ph.D. and Bertram's real talent lay in reading to people.

Truman rose stiffly from her chair at his station and grabbed her beloved dietary supplement. "Why don't you take your lunch break now? Then this afternoon, we'll see how you fly solo. I'll pop by periodically, in case you have any questions."

"That sounds dandy," Bertram heard himself say. Truman patted him on the shoulder and then ambled to her office. He waited until her door squeaked shut, then bolted from his desk, through the cubicle maze and down a long corridor. He looked around furtively, pausing by a set of vending machines. One read "DrinkThis." The other read "ZOT!". On both, the prices had been pasted over with a sticker that read "Compliments of DiversiDine."

Bertram ducked into the corner by the DrinkThis machine, pulled the vis-u from his pocket, made sure no one was coming this way and hit the code for Rollie's ship from his address book. It was only a moment before the Hyphiz Deltan's image projected from the little device.

Fresh wounds stood out brightly on the man's face and neck. He was rapidly running out of places to fit new scars.

"Ah, Ludlow," greeted Rollie. "So you are alive, eh? What the frag has kept you from picking up, mate? I've commed your handheld and the Penumbra and—"

"Hi, Rollie," said Bertram, "I'm fine, how are you?"

Rollie could glare better than anyone Bertram knew. He thought it had to do with the orange eyes. "Look, don't know what you're facing there, but I ran into something on my end that I thought you should know about. Me and Tseethe, we netted ourselves this Feegar freighter—"

"The Feegars? You targeted the *Feegars*? Are you suicidal?" It came out louder than Bertram had expected and he double-checked up and down the hall.

"Look, the Feegars weren't supposed to be —" Rollie growled and changed course. "Blast it. The point is, the shipment we got off 'em was originally going to DiversiDine, a new branch on Tryfe."

"The Feegars have a trade agreement with DiversiDine on this planet? You mean there might be Feegars ... locally?" Bertram looked around almost expecting to be up to his neck in Feegar warriors.

"No, the Feegars don't fraggin' ship to Tryfe. Forget the Feegars. The Feegars don't enter into it." He considered it a second. "Aside from eating the fellahs who were headed there."

"That's comforting."

Rollie ignored this. "The shipment contains bottles from a Vos Laegon company called TrustTChem. We're having the contents analyzed now."

Bertram frowned. "And they were sending that here?"

"To DiversiDine World HQ. And get this: DiversiDine's headquarters for all of Tryfe is located in your city of Pittsburgh."

"That's what I mean. Here," said Bertram, gesturing around him.

Rollie said, "Ah, so you made it to Pittsburgh."

"Better. DiversiDine headquarters."

His surprise was worth it. "Bleedin' Karnax, you work fast!"

Bertram laughed. "Technically, I *work* for DiversiDine."

"What?" Rollie started laughing, too. "How'd you manage that?"

"I'll tell you later. My lunch break's almost up. When do you get the test results?"

"Soon," he said. "Maybe. Well ... depends."

"On?"

"If my chemist gets fragged by her assassin mother-sister."

"Er, yeah." With Rollie, it was always better not to ask. "So you wait for that and... What can I do in the meantime?"

"If it was me, I'd start by talking to the Tryfling who was s'posed to receive the shipment. The name there is —" Something crashed and the holographic Rollie turned to look. "Aw, frag *me*."

Bertram leaned in, as if that would give him a better view. "What?"

Rollie groaned and winced. "Tell me that slaggard hasn't been in there all this time!"

"Wait, what's going on?" asked Bertram.

"Unbelievable! How long's it been? Tseethe," he was calling off-screen now, "you didn't unload the live one before we broke latch?"

"I think the answer to that is obvious," came the voice.

"But how—?"

"I forgot, okay? There was a lot going on; y'know, shipments to load, informants to set straight, other Feegars trying to kill us ..." Tseethe's voice sounded considerably stressed. A spine-tingling shriek echoed from somewhere beyond him. "Kinda like now."

Bertram saw the helmeted Hyphiz Deltan run past in the background, being charged by something that looked a lot like a living, breathing anatomy lesson. It also seemed to be the source of the horrible noise. "A little help here?"

"Rollie," said Bertram, "the contact on the shipment is...?"

But Bertram now heard an eerie, soupy voice say something about retribution and sucking the marrow from bones. And suddenly, Rollie disappeared off-screen.

"Rollie?"

"The contact is …" And he heard Rollie say a name before there was another great bang and a hum that might have been laser fire. Then the picture cut.

"Rollie? … Rollie?!"

Silence.

Bertram stared at the device in his hand. "He'll be all right," said Bertram to no one. "It's Rollie. He's a survivor. He's been through worse." Of course, based on the stories, the worst was the Feegar Rebellion.

Bertram tucked the device back into his pocket. "Okay, Bertram, keep calm. At least we have a contact name: Phil Jones." A pair of young women had stopped to get a beverage and gave him a look, the strange guy lurking in the corner by the DrinkThis machine. They exchanged glances and giggled to each other. They helped themselves to free cans of DrinkThis Diet, giving him the widest berth they could and made their return trip, still laughing.

Phil Jones, Bertram repeated to himself. Then a pang of uncertainty hit him. *Or did he say Bill Stone?*

The second the young women were gone, Bertram re-tried Rollie's vis-u connection.

Bzzp!

Bzzp!

"Pick up, pick up …"

A soothing stock photo spacescape popped on the screen. "You've reached the vis-u for Levvyn Moonshot. Please leave a message and I'll answer your comm as time and inclination permits. Thank you."

Bertram hoped so. He didn't know the name Levvyn Moonshot but the voice was unmistakable. He left his message.

13

Rollie cut short his vis-u to Ludlow and drew his XJ-37 on their stowaway, almost in the same move.

"No! Don't!" shouted Tseethe. And to Rollie's surprise, the man being chased by the horrible, hungry monster dove and knocked the gun out of Rollie's hand. "I'm interrogating him!" Tseethe dodged around a console, the Feegar still in pursuit.

Rollie squinted. "Interrogation in your part of Hyphiz Delta requires a certain amount of running, does it?" Deltan Westerners did have their traditions, but Rollie couldn't see the practicality of this one.

"I found him in the cockpit," Tseethe explained, as he raced the other way. He grabbed a net and went running after the Feegar.

"The cockpit?" Rollie felt anger bubble up within him. "First you left him in the blasted spare cabin, then you let him get to the fraggin' cockpit?"

"Yeah, that's right; it's all my fault." Tseethe and the Feegar were bobbing and weaving around the lounge chairs now. "You saw me lock him in there. Did you double-check? No! Did you hear him in there? No! Because this ship makes so much fraggin' noise, bombs could go off and we'd be asking, 'Did somebody knock?'"

"It is running unusually loud," agreed the Feegar, as he lunged across a low table for Tseethe. "Sounds like your air filtration system."

"Oh, you're weighing in now, too, are you? Cosmic!" snapped Rollie. "Let's everyone have a go."

"Besides," continued Tseethe, trying to spread the net and not trip himself up in the process, "I caught him comming someone. I'm trying to find out who…Who'd you comm?" he shouted at the Feegar.

"Death first, skinsack!" came the answer.

That was it. Karnax himself would not have had the patience for this. Rollie pulled the XJ-40 from his coat, switched the settings and aimed. The Feegar dropped to the floor, a stunned, clattering clutter of limbs—quite audible over the ship noise, Rollie noted.

"Aw, really?" Tseethe stopped short and scowled at the prone form at his feet. "I was right in the middle of—"

"A marathon?" Rollie asked. "I thought we'd do this the easy way. So you don't wear out your shiny new lungs all in one day."

"Yeah, well," grumbled Tseethe, who'd had both sets replaced quite recently, "he was about to tell me everything."

Rollie didn't dignify this with a response. Instead, he crouched by the flat-out Feegar and patted down the soldier's tech suit. From a pocket at the lifeform's thigh, Rollie removed a handheld vis-u. He peeled open the Feegar's eyelid and held the device before the fellow's retina. The handheld unlocked in an instant. "Let's see now…" Rollie perused the screen. "Last comm was to the Feegar Military Command Center for Interspecies Relations."

"Military. Stellar," sighed Tseethe.

"It's all military, though, innit? They're Feegars. They're practically born in a parade rest position," said Rollie, rising. "This just happens to be the PR division."

Tseethe sniffed. "So much for the kinder, gentler face of Feegar. Looks like it's time to go somewhere very far away, very fast."

Rollie nodded. "I'd say. The slaggard shared our coordinates round like they was the vis-u digits of an especially well-programmed pleasure Simulant." He pocketed the device.

"Well, that's it, then." Tseethe drew his handlaser. "We finish this and get on our way." He flipped the settings and aimed at the soldier.

But an amusing idea that had been lurking in Rollie's mind behind three other noisy thoughts took this moment to step to the forefront.

Rollie stayed Tseethe's hand. "Wait."

"Wait?" Tseethe let out an exasperated laugh, but he did wait. "What happened to the guy who wanted to frag our guest two minutes ago? He looked a lot like you."

"Ah, but that guy didn't consider that what we have here is a captive Feegar. And the Feegar culture dictates that capture equals shame. To them, death's the nicest thing we could do for him."

"And the worst?"

Rollie smiled. "Isn't there a Shop-o-Drome round here? I'd like to make a stop."

Inside the space suit, the Feegar screamed epithets that Translachew only lightly addressed. "You skinsacks will regret this. This is a crime against the Feegar species. The Intergalactic Rules of Captivity under the Standing Room Only Communicatives of the Zara Treaty state that any captured Feegars are considered dishonored and thereby must be fragged per the mandates of the Kemfestral Flaginates and—"

"Aw, shut your hatch, you." Rollie put the helmet on over the Feegar's head and locked it into place. He then shoved the bound Feegar backwards into the large pressurized hover container. "You're all very brave, aren't ya, when you're gnawing a fellah's femur? But put ya in a set of astrotogs 'til your lift arrives and you blubber like you're just incubated."

The Feegar couldn't hear but assumed correctly it was

something of a taunting nature. He spit at Rollie, then snarled as the spit ran down his own helmet.

Rollie cackled and closed the lid. He opened the hatch and directed the pressurized container into the airlock gangway. "We there yet?" he called to Tseethe in the cockpit.

"Just about, Captain. Gimme a second."

Rollie took the time to size up the container. It was good— definitely good—but he still felt like something was missing.

"Ah!"

From the Shop-o-Drome bag, he unrolled some festive ribbon, sliced a length using the dagger from his boot and tied it around the container. It ended up being more of a Hyphizite freighterman's knot than a bow, but it served the purpose. Then he grabbed up the handlaser, put it on its lowest setting and engraved a special something on the crate's surface.

Tseethe's voice called, "Okay, we're here. Right at the coordinates that Mr. Bitey sent to his buddies."

"Cosmic! *Paar too*, Mr. Bitey," Rollie said. He saluted the crate then ducked back into his ship, closing the hatch behind him. A second button opened the airlock to free space, and the vacuum did what it did best. A third button retracted the gangway tidily, folding it into the ship.

Rollie observed the free-floating container from the hatch window with some satisfaction.

Tseethe joined him. "The ribbon's a rather twinkly touch," he said approvingly. "And that skull thing…" He pointed to the design Rollie had engraved. "What's that symbol called again?"

"A *jodja*," said Rollie. Historically, it went way back, before the unification of the Underworld Society, when freelance freight raiding was the norm.

"Do they usually have the crossed laser motif?"

"Nah, Meena did that." Rollie's favorite former life-merge partner two times over, Meena Tsoogarkken, was an artist and she'd recently surprised him with the design. The surprise was not that she still kept in touch (in fact, they'd agreed that the touching was pleasant and should happen regularly, as long as it never led to life-merger three). No, the surprise was that in all these years, Meena could do art that actually looked like things. "Now that I'm self-employed, she thought I needed a calling card," Rollie explained. "To establish my own brand."

"It's very you."

Rollie wasn't much for marketing, but he had to agree. The *jodja* had a nice effect. "Think our castaway's colleagues will like it?"

"Like? Well, *like* ..." Tseethe gave the word weight. "Let's just say it'll get their attention. Anyway, it's the thought that counts."

14

Rozz had been in IT for less than a day, but she'd already constructed a substantial monument of empty cans on one side of her desk. Bertram knocked on her cubicle wall and Drinkshenge was shaken but Rozz didn't stir. He reached over and pulled out her earbud. "Hey."

She turned with a glazed expression that transformed quickly into a grin, which was odd, since Rozz wasn't much of a grinner. "Hey 'Troy'!" she greeted with a wink. "Didn't see you in the cafeteria when I went down. Guess you've been busy servicing customers?"

"Could you make that sound less like I'm a gigolo in Mr. Dandy's House of Hot TLC?"

"Could? Absolutely. Will? Not so much."

He offered her a rushed smile. "Look, I've got five minutes before I have to get back to work. Rollie vis-ued."

"Oh, that's cool. How's he doing?"

Bertram blinked. Rollie and Rozz had only met for about three seconds during the early phases of planet-saving. And even then, there weren't exactly formal introductions, what with the running and the laser fire. "Um, he's been better." Bertram leaned in and lowered his voice. "I need you to look something up for me."

"Sure! No problem," she said.

"I don't know if you'll be able to do it."

"Oh, I can do it," she said.

"You don't know what it is yet." But her expression said that was irrelevant. He whispered, "I need you to access the employee database."

"I can do it," she whispered back and grabbed a pen. "Hit me."

"I don't exactly know the person's name. It sounds something like Bill Jones."

She wrote it down. "Gotcha."

"Or Phil Stone."

She wrote that. "Okay."

"Or maybe Al Capone."

Her pen clattered to the desk. "So basically, we want a person with a name."

"I didn't hear it clearly. Rollie got ..." Attacked? Brutally murdered? Picked clean? "... Sidetracked. Can you make a list of potentials? They'd probably be in manufacturing or R&D."

"Consider it done," she said. "You'll have it by end of business day."

"Really?" She was usually more cautious with her time estimates than this. "Great," he said. "This contact was supposed to receive a shipment of chemicals from TrustTChem of Vos Laegos City. So if there's any way to check the past TrustTChem deliveries and who signed for them, that might be the way to go."

"I'll be on the lookout." She took a swig from the can beside her. "Hey, did you see they have free refreshments for the employees?" She waggled the DrinkThis at him. "I mean, I know DiversiDine is probably evil and stuff, but ... Kind of a nice benefit, don't you think?"

"Evil has to have good benefits packages," Bertram told her. "It helps with recruiting. I bet Darth Vader offers a matching 401K." Bertram glanced around and lowered his voice. "Look, Rozz, Rollie's got somebody analyzing the TrustTChem sample right now. He's going to let us know what's in the bottles ... If he's still alive, anyway."

"Um, why wouldn't he still be alive?"

"It's Rollie. So many reasons," said Bertram. "End of day, right?"

"End of day," she promised.

Bertram got the call at 4:32 p.m.

"No Will or Bill Stone or Phil Jones or Al Capone or any combination of the above in either R&D or manufacturing," Rozz told him.

"Shit."

"Ah, but there is a Malone. 'L. Malone.' Lazarus."

"Lazarus?" Now there was a kid who got beat up on the playground. "And I thought 'Bertram' was rough."

"Aw, what's wrong with 'Lazarus'? Old names are popular right now. You never know: Lazarus could make a big a comeback." She laughed. "Speaking of miracles, Lazarus Malone is listed in both R&D *and* Manufacturing."

Yes!" shouted Bertram, then remembered people were sitting three feet away from him on the other side of a half-wall. He lowered his voice. "Rozz, you're awesome."

"It was a simple systems search, really. And if the head of HR hadn't made his password 'password,' it might have taken me a whole hour longer," she replied. "So are you going to be paying Mr. Malone a visit today?"

He looked at the clock. "Thinking about it. But the day is rapidly running out."

"Well, according to the DiversiDine employee newsletter, Malone's team is one of the regional leaders for the company's intramural bowling league. And they practice Mondays at the Cosmic Lanes."

Today happened to be Monday.

"Ah," said Bertram. "You know, it's been a while since I got my strikes on. Feel like joining me for a night under the day-glo star stickers?"

"Mm, how I do love the distinctive fug of boiled hot dogs and rental shoes. Consider me there."

The team groaned as the ball careened down the alley, sending the remaining pins into a split.

"Where's your game tonight, Laz?" smirked a blond woman of about thirty. "You leave it in your other bag?"

Lazarus Malone spun on a bowling-shoed heel and stalked to his seat. He was a lanky guy with lots of black, curly hair and a scowl. His red-and-black bowling shirt read, "R&D-stroyers" on the back in a heavy metal font. The shirt hung loose on his narrow frame. "Remove the gutterball from your own lane, Kelly, before criticizing the seven-ten split in your neighbor's."

"Ooh," said the members who were Not Kelly.

Bertram and Rozz grabbed the lane next to them and Rozz made a production of tying her shoes while Bertram pretended to be engrossed in choosing the right ball. They both took this opportunity to size up the group to their right, and it wasn't long before Bertram spotted his In.

"Hey, guys!" Bertram pointed to someone's satchel, embroidered with a large corporate logo. "You work at DiversiDine, too?"

"Yeah," said the one called Kelly. "Food science."

"We just started this week." Bertram indicated Rozz. "She's IT, I'm Customer Service." Much introductory hubbub ensued, and he was especially pleased they remembered to give their exciting new fake names. Deep down, he'd always known he had a knack for this corporate espionage thing.

Name's Hill, he thought suavely. *Troy Hill.*

Then he realized the brunette woman in the group, Devi, was talking to him. "I'm afraid if you want to join either department's bowling team, you may be out of luck," she was saying. "Both IT and TLC have lineups that appear to be quite entrenched."

"Oh, that's okay. We play for fun," Bertram told her. Now

he had visions of Troy Hill and Ada Byron tearing up the lanes every Saturday night after a nice dinner out. Increasingly, Troy led an exciting life. "So what are you guys in charge of, food-wise?" Bertram asked, giving a particular look to Laz there, slouching in his chair.

"I'm snack chip freshness," said Kelly.

"Flavor development," said a guy named Dan.

"Coatings," volunteered Devi.

Lazarus Malone remained silent, so Rozz stepped in. "And how about you?"

"How *about* me?" Malone eyed her darkly over folded arms. "I don't talk shop while I bowl, sweetheart. So I suggest you confine the chit-chat to your own damned lane."

The team gaped like a school of tuna. Bertram turned to Rozz, expecting her to hit the guy with a bruising retort — or possibly something heavier. But now Rozz was digging around in her bag. Momentarily, she withdrew a can of DrinkThis, popped the top and shrugged languidly. "Whatever, dude."

It was Kelly who still looked mortified. "I am so sorry," she was saying now. "I think he's just being a jerk because the O.K. Kraving Corporation's team is over there." She pointed across the lanes. "They're a big DiversiDine competitor. Last year, they sent one of their players to wheedle some proprietary info out of our friend here. Two more watered down beers and who knows what would have happened? Right, Laz?" She nudged him playfully.

"I don't see her over there this time, buddy," said Dan, eyeballing the competition. "I think you're safe."

"You know what? Screw you." Laz's tone was not merely sulky or sad anymore. It was that of a man teetering on the edge. "All of you... Shouldn't somebody roll?"

Kelly nodded and moved to take her turn.

"Nobody understands what it's like," Laz mumbled to no one in particular. "Of having serious responsibility."

"It can weigh on you," agreed Bertram, who knew a little something about the topic.

"Damn right." And the very moment Bertram thought they

had a chance at real conversation, Lazarus Malone rose and headed to the snack bar.

Bertram watched him lope off like a kicked stray dog in a spaghetti western. "Well, everyone has a bad day sometime."

Dan let out a wheezy laugh. "Day? In case no one's noticed, he's been like that since well before Kickoff."

"It is a lot of pressure, though," Kelly added, as she marked down her strike.

Rozz was trying to get the last dribble of beverage out. Her voice echoed in the can. "What, is he management?"

"He's R&D like us," Kelly said, "but also he sets up the flavorings. You know, before they get combined with water and colorings for mass production? That way manufacturing can just pour them in at the different plants."

"They call him 'The Mixmaster,'" said Dan.

"Technically," Devi began, "Laz calls Laz 'The Mixmaster.' But it's catchy."

Bertram was getting a very interesting picture of the man receiving shipments from outer space. He shifted the bowling ball from one arm to the other. "That's pretty specialized. How many other people do that kind of job?"

"Only two people know the flavoring formulas for the drinks," said Kelly.

"That's how they keep it under wraps," said Dan.

Rozz clunked her empty can to a table. "Who's the other? Coach Dandy?"

Kelly, Dan and Devi enjoyed some spontaneous mirth at this statement.

"What's funny about that?" Rozz asked. "He seems really involved."

Dan turned to his team. "Ah, newbies …"

"Always such grand ideas," Devi grinned.

But Bertram wasn't getting the humor, either. "Well, it's his company. How involved with the products is he?"

"Oh so very," said Devi, who almost doubled over with laughter now. "He and the DiversiDog get together to brainstorm."

"They conference call about it with Patty the Snack Cake," hooted Dan.

Kelly started to add to this when something caught her attention, her head snapping toward the door. The levity vanished in a second. "Is Laz...leaving?"

They turned as a lanky figure in a DiversiDine jacket slipped from the alley. For the second time that evening, Lazarus Malone had split.

With Lazarus Malone temporarily leaving the team down a person, Rozz and Bertram played with the remaining R&D-stroyers. It was midnight before they emerged into the cold night air and made the journey back to their bus stop.

"That was fun, wasn't it?" Rozz's cheeks were almost as pink as her hair. She cracked a beverage and took a long drink.

"Interesting, anyway." Bertram pulled his coat tighter around him. "So Dandy's not as involved in the company as he seems to be...At least, that's what they implied."

"Yeah, but that's no problem," Rozz told him. She seemed to be saying this a lot lately. "It shouldn't be too hard to find out more about the guy. When I get a chance, I'll hit the research. See what I can dig up."

"Certainly getting anything out of Laz Malone was a bust," said Bertram. "Steel wool is less abrasive."

"Aw, have a little empathy, Bertram. He's been burned before. If I had competitors trying to totally Slugworth me out of my Everlasting Gobstoppers, I'd be defensive, too."

"But there are so many questions." Bertram stuffed his hands in his pockets. "Has Lazarus Malone missed his shipment yet? Does he know what the shipment is? Does he know he's got stuff coming in from the planet Vos Laegos? How much does he know about the origins of the company?"

"On the plus side, I think I'm really getting my strike down." Rozz beamed. "Did you see? I was so in the zone by the end and—"

Bertram stopped short and stared at her. "What is wrong with you?"

She blinked doe eyes. "Nothing, I feel great."

"Empathy? Smiling? 'Getting your strike down'?"

"So I enjoyed bowling." She gave that lazy shrug again. "I like a good bowl now and then. What's your damage?"

"You're happy, Rozz," Bertram said.

"Oh," she brushed that to the side. "I wouldn't call it 'happy,' exactly. I'm just feeling good. I'm glad to be here. I'm glad to see the city doesn't suck. So it's enjoying a little renaissance. Maybe I am, too. What's wrong with that?"

"I'll tell you what's wrong with that." He jabbed a finger at the item in her hand. "It's freezing out here and you're having another ice cold DrinkThis."

"I'm hydrating," she said. "Bowling is thirsty work. Plus, the flavor is great. It's all fresh and fruity."

"How many of those have you had today?"

"I don't know. Two or three." She considered it. "Six."

He pictured the cans sitting on the desk of her cubicle and arched an eyebrow.

"So, eight. I mean, hey, we are watching our budgets right now. And at work, it's all free."

"And then you had—what? —two more at the lanes?"

She patted his face. "You're super-nice to worry about me, though." There was that radiant smile again. "It's actually kind of adorbs, but it's totally not necessary."

"Adorbs?" Now he was really worried. Rozz was not very free or talented with compliments. Once she said he reminded her of a "tallish Hobbit" and that was supposed to be a good thing. A couple of times she might have told him he "kinda kicked ass." This was as far as it went, and they were even dating then.

"What I meant is, you're sweet to care. Always thinking of me. Of everybody, really. I mean, I know they put you through a lot of shit, but I think the Seers of Rhobux were so right to choose you to save Life As We Know It, Bertram. You have so many awesome qualities and…"

"You are officially scaring me."

She almost frowned here, then didn't. "I can't say something nice about you every now and then? Tell you I appreciate you?"

"Absolutely not," he said. "You sound like your parents."

"You didn't meet my parents." She brightened. "Would you like to meet my parents, Bertram? They're super-nice, especially now that they're not trying to sue the crap out of each other. You should really meet my parents!"

"Give me that." He grabbed the can of DrinkThis from her and flung it into a bush. "As soon as we can, we're going to find out what's in this stuff."

15

Morning came swiftly inside the artwork formerly known as Bertram Ludlow's Penumbra Classic spaceship. And it started with threats.

"So that's how it's gonna be, huh? We're playing that game? We'll see about that." Bertram Ludlow seized the handle end of the Dental Debris Demolecularization Device (also known as a "deedee") and pulled.

The bathroom snail pulled back.

Bertram's eyes narrowed. These space slugs sure had grown since he first bought the ship. Initially, their infestation was a minor inconvenience. They'd dangled over him during his morning shower or stared while he used the toilet, their unblinking eyestalks waving like some mesmerized studio audience.

Sometimes they grumbled.

Then in recent weeks, the galactic gastropods had doubled in size, sprouted arms and got grabby, fighting him for his towel and toying with the toiletries each time he entered the room. What's more, they were resistant to laser-fire. If anything, they seemed to grow back stronger.

Now that they had moved to stealing his personal hygiene tools, it was entirely too much. Bertram was tired of feeling like an intruder in his own bathroom. He was tired of tipping them, just to use his own towels and soap.

So today he was ready for them, and he had the largest of the creatures right where he wanted it. He reached into his robe pocket and whipped out a container, sending a blizzard of white crystals over the slimy squatter.

"Ha! Say hello to my friend sodium chloride! How do you like the taste of that, pal? You like that? You want some more? That's right! Next, I break out the garlic and butter sauce!"

But the snail wasn't interested in Bertram's culinary aspirations. It showed this first by Not Shriveling to Death, then emphasized it by powering up the deedee and calmly cleaning its teeth.

Bertram stared. "You have *teeth?*" Research. He needed to do a lot more research.

The buzz of the vis-u interrupted any further zoological enlightenment. Bertram darted into the ship's lounge, just as Rollie's head projected from the machine.

"You're alive!" said Bertram, not for the first time since knowing the guy.

"The best state for productive conversation, though some lifeforms don't require it," said Rollie. "Wanted to let you know, my friend the chemist vis-ued with the results of a certain Tryfe shipment." He shook a sample bottle at the screen.

"Great! What have you got?"

Rollie eyed the bottle meditatively. "I think you'll be surprised."

"This is the GCU. Surprise is my default setting," said Bertram. "Spill."

"Well, it appears that what we have here is a bottle of ninety-nine-point-nine percent pure original Vos Laegon jubies." He paused to let that information sink in and smugly waited for the reaction.

"Jubies?" Rozz had emerged from her quarters, hair sticking up and a cloud of sleep still hovering around her head. "The stuff in the air from Vos Laegos? The stuff that makes you go all …" She waved her arms in a floaty, mellow gesture, "'Whoaaa'?"

"If you chose to make that sound," said Rollie, in a tone suggesting he wouldn't.

Bertram rubbed an eye. "Jubies come in liquid?"

"Exactly! News to me as well, Ludlow," said the Hyphizite with some warmth. "The wonders of our cosmos continue to boggle."

Rozz squinted. "But liquid jubies? Here? I guess we could put 'em in a vaporizer. Or use them in a—" The clouds parted and she turned to Bertram with a sharp gasp. "Oh my God, Bertram …" Apparently, she did remember a little something about her behavior the night before. Bertram was glad, because otherwise, he'd have had a hard time getting her to believe she'd told him he was "sweet" and wanted him to meet her parents.

Bertram nodded. "Yep. It would make sense, wouldn't it?"

Rollie frowned from Bertram to Rozz. "Clarify."

"How do we test something for jubies here?" Bertram asked him.

"On Tryfe?" Rollie shook his head. "Dunno. Your Penumbra's not set up for advanced analysis any better than my Protostar. Anyway, you'd need a sample of confirmed liquid jubies to run it against."

Rozz leapt in. "Which your chemist friend still has?"

"Presumably."

Bertram leaned in to the screen. "So if we brought our sample to your friend the chemist, would she test it for us?"

Rollie surveyed them coolly over steepled fingers. "Do you know where her secret lab is located?"

Bertram and Rozz exchanged a look. "Um … no."

"Exactly!" said Rollie. "It's a pretty scab secret if she's got strangers wandering round, asking her to test things. And as you can't go yourselves, that leaves me doing another A-to-B." He leaned back in his chair hard. It made a creaking sound they heard clearly through the vis-u. "You realize I am trying to run my own business here. I'm not just sitting round waiting for to-dos for the Tryfling cause. What is it you want to test?"

Rozz started to answer but Bertram stopped her. "We'll talk about that you once you get here."

There was a pause. A hard look. "Oh, I understand now." Rollie's voice had gone low and quiet; that was never good. "You're enjoying the fact I can't stun you through the vis-u. Is that it?"

Bertram said, "I just figured being the savvy criminal artist you are, you'd appreciate knowing more about the ultimate purpose of your stolen shipment. That it might make it easier for you to offload." Bertram was very pleased with this, considering he had to come up with it fast. "Besides, it's DiversiDine we're talking about: the company ultimately responsible for your little vacation on Altair-5. If you help us find the information we need, we have a much better chance of sticking it to them once and for all. I'd thought that was something you could get behind, but …" He shrugged. "… I guess I was wrong." He wasn't exactly sure how any of that would pan out, but it sure sounded good.

Rollie was sizing him up now like a tiger deciding whether a particular jungle tidbit was even worth the trouble. And it seemed a long moment before he made a sound that was either a laugh, a growl or a sigh. "You've grown canny, Ludlow," he said finally. His tone was not without admiration.

Bertram said, "What time will you be popping by?"

"Consider me on my way."

"Great," said Bertram. "And let me know what—" But light filtered around the edges of the hatch shades, sweeping from one hatch to another. "Uh, we have to go."

"There's not a Feegar loose on your ship, is there?" Rollie asked. "I hear that happens."

But Bertram turned off the vis-u.

Rozz flew to the on-ship sound system and flipped the switch for exterior audio. Bertram never had occasion to use it, but he was so glad they had it now.

"Are you familiar with the artist?" a sing-song voice of indeterminate gender piped into the ship.

"That's one of the mysteries." The second voice was deep and raspy, like the sound of an ice crusher. "There's no one by that name in our records."

"When did it get here?"

"I'm not sure. I drove by the day before yesterday. It wasn't here then. We'll have to ask around."

Bertram raised a portal blind just enough to peer out. Two people stood before the ship, giving it a critical gaze. The man toyed with his beard. The woman's eyebrows had been plucked out and painted on higher than manufacturer's suggested installation. They were perched mid-forehead in interest right now.

"Penn Ombré … It sounds like a pseudonym," rasped Beardy. "Maybe this is a prank by one of the members. Does the style of work look familiar to you?"

"Well, both Meredith and Turbo do industrial," mused Eyebrows. "But Meredith tends to use old kitchen tools and Turbo focuses on car parts. As for pseudonyms, I don't see it. Both of them would be plastering their name all over the thing, if the piece were theirs. This is huge and clearly took a lot of effort."

"I find it reminiscent of Alston Chuckwood's work," continued Beardy. "The structural cohesiveness. The balance between the futuristic and fantastic, yet tangible and practical."

"So right! It's like it's saying: 'I'm real. I'm here. I'm impossible. Embrace me.'"

"Well, it can look for love elsewhere. Contextually, it's the sculptural equivalent of yarn bombing," sniffed the Man of Beard. "I want to find out whether other locations across the city have been hit. We'll need to check with the Carnegie, Phipps, the Warhol…"

"I'm on it," said Eyebrows. "Just as soon as I do this." She drew a phone from her bag.

Beardy frowned. "Who are you calling?"

"The press, of course. A giant mysterious artwork appears in front of the Institute? Think of the PR!"

"The visitors," breathed Beardy.

"The gift shop sales," added Eyebrows.

"Ah ..." Beardy stroked his chin now like a James Bond villain hatching a plan. "You know those paintings Lenore did using toilet bowl cleaner and toothpaste?"

"You mean *Study in Cerulean Blue #1* and *#2*?"

He nodded. "I'm hanging them in the lobby."

Eyebrows twitched with surprise. "I thought you said they were 'embarrassing failures,' with 'neither soul nor depth of meaning, wrapped in a wintergreen stench.'"

"They are," he said, "but the public's coming. You know how the public is. You get enough of them swept up in the moment, offer hors d'oeuvres, maybe a few champagne cocktails, and they'll buy the first garbage they see. We have so much to do!"

"And we," said Rozz to Bertram, "are going to be seriously late to work."

16

"Corporal Scof's coordinates were either wrong or intercepted by The Enemy and altered," said Captain Mau, pilot for the Feegar starship *Delivery*. Mau wasn't sure who The Enemy was in this particular instance. But when you were part of a group who enjoyed all of its fellow lifeforms done tartar, it didn't make you popular. The Enemy was everywhere.

Mau scanned the free space before them for planets, space stations or Interplanetary Cruise Vessels. "I see nothing up ahead," he concluded.

"Then you're a fool," snapped Commander Nom. "What you don't see is because of what you expect to see. You expect to see a ship. Zoom in on the coordinates."

Mau leaned in closer and squinted, then zoomed in on the precise spot using the portal magnification technology. Of course, Commander Nom had been correct. What they had here was not the missing ICV at all, but a small pressurized container wrapped in a turquoise blue ribbon and etched with some sort of symbol. They could never have seen the crate at such a distance.

"Perhaps it's a trap," said Mau. "Like a Hojan Torse."

The Hojans were a people fond of offering their nemeses the sort of giant fancy apology pastries, or "torses," that no one ever ate. This was less due to their baking artistry—which was considerable — than the quantity of Hojan warriors that charged from them before anyone could pass out the plates and napkins.

"The symbol isn't Hojan and the container is too small for their army," said Nom. "I told you to approach. I won't say it again."

"Yes, Commander."

Mau entered the coordinates, and the *Delivery* arrived in thirty minutes or less.

The symbol on the container, Mau saw now, was an engraving of a skull—a general two-eyed, one-nosed humanoid species — and two crossed lasers. "A statement of war?" Mau asked.

"Bring it into the ship," said Commander Nom. And the Feegar crew worked to maneuver the item from its location into the receiving dock.

"Scan it," ordered Nom. "Scan for signs of life, detonation devices and biological residue."

The crew fetched the necessary scanning technologies and, in moments, had gathered the information they needed.

"Biologic inside: one," said Tech Officer Din. "Scanners indicate the species is likely Feegar. Respiratory function is active. There also appears to be some unidentified biological matter inside with no vital signs. No potential detonation devices appear to be present."

Commander Nom nodded. "Open the seal."

One of the crew went to work on the elaborate knot in the ribbon but Nom hastened the task by lasering through it—and nearly through two crew members. (Which was fine, since they were low-level and likely to be eaten later, anyhow.) Then Tech Officer Din pressed the button on the container and the lid opened slowly with a hiss.

Inside was an assortment of colorful vegetables, two bottles of protein pills, a selection of infopill cookbooks on eating meat-free, a confirmation of a donation made in the Feegar peoples' name to the CGU Diversity Society and Corporal

Scarlod Scof, formerly missing in action.

Scof had been provided a space suit, helmet and respiratory apparatus, and he was breathing heavily. Condensation concealed the lower part of his face but his eyes were wild and fearful.

"Kill me," cried Scof, as his helmet was removed. "Kill me now. I have been captured. I have been dishonored."

"Yes, Scof, you have," said Commander Nom.

Scof looked hopeful. "I would make a nice stew. I would braise me first and then slow cook for eight Feegar hours on low. I would go well with some andafran seasoning and garblan spice. I—"

"All in due time," said Nom.

Relief washed over Scof's features and, through his exoskeleton, Mau could see the corporal's heart slow down. "Stellar!"

"But first, we must get a description from you."

"A debriefing. Of course," said Scof eagerly. "I'll share whatever intelligence I can impart, Commander."

The Commander laughed. "Scof ..." His tone would have held pity, if the Feegars were into that sort of thing. "You know that isn't good enough."

Scof's face froze. A vein throbbed at his neck.

"Verbal descriptions are useless to us. They are limited and inaccurate, ruined by bias and weak observation," said Commander Nom. "We have other ways of getting this kind of information. As you are undoubtedly aware."

"Oh no!" said Scof. "No! Not the 'other ways'! NO! NOOOOOOO!"

It took only a moment to secure Scof to the RecoLektron, since their on-ship technology experts were so skilled in this area. Many of them had enjoyed hours of practice hooking up POWs during the Feegar Rebellion, a happy time in Feegar history that was a veritable renaissance in the advancement of torture techniques, medical research and innovative fresh-air dining.

That was when the RecoLektron had been first introduced and, while it had been refined considerably since then, it retained the same basic functions. It drew out and processed the sensory data located in the subject's brain, then translated it and made it available for analysis. The wonderful thing about this was that it was perfectly accurate. It allowed any onlooker to see exactly what the viewer had seen, to hear exactly what the subject had heard. Later models even made it possible to recreate what a subject had felt, including touch, and physiological changes like temperature, heartbeat and more.

Another benefit — perhaps the thing everyone appreciated most—was it hurt more than you could possibly imagine. And when you were a Feegar, imaginations ran quite freely in this particular direction. The more pain, the more fear it caused. And the more fear, the more it stimulated the juices in the body, adding flavor to the meat for later. It was not only useful for military purposes, but it was such a time-saver. Because who really wanted to spend extra time in the galley, when you could multi-task?

The RecoLektron had one final helpful feature. It created a transcription of any dialogue. This was handy to have since it was hard to hear what everyone was saying when the extraction subject was present, screaming his head off.

Why, just the process of adding the connectors proved Scof was going to make a succulent entrée. You could tell by the shrieking, its sharp pitch and enthusiastic duration. Mau felt his stomach rumble in anticipation. The meat would be heady, with a sharp tang to it… So, *so* good! Mau hoped it would be paired with a nice smorg wine, something a little sweet, as an intriguing contrast. But he was always open to alternate ideas.

The extraction and downloading was what took the bulk of time. But soon, a completed file popped up on the screen. And now they were able to experience what Scof had experienced up until the exact moment they pulled him from The Enemy's gift basket.

They had to fast-forward over a series of unrelated activities to get to the good stuff, of course: Scof's sleep and eating habits, Scof's appalling bathroom hygiene and Scof's free time music class, penning fresh and inspiring Feegar battle hymns.

The first thing Scof saw was a ship on the horizon, a lumpy Interplanetary Cruise Vessel that was upon them in a flash. It appeared to be a Protostar 340-K, and if Mau hadn't seen it with Scof's own eyes, he wouldn't have believed it. He had no idea there were any Protostars still operational these days. But there it was, in reasonable working condition and latching on to the Feegars' borrowed freighter, just as they'd hoped. Soon laserfire and jarring movements comprised much of the Scof-eye view. The Commander noted how each Feegar had fallen nobly in the line of duty, and how Scof spent most of several days working to break himself out of a sparsely-furnished guest bedroom.

Yes, the RecoLektron did provide, not the least of which were images of the two lifeforms who raided the freighter and had wrapped up Corporal Scof. They appeared to be Hyphiz Deltan, Quad One lifeforms that were not the tenderest of meat. Most aspiring chefs found them too low-fat to enjoy raw, and too chewy to be prepared using the more popular cooking techniques. Still, a talented culinary artist would know how to prepare them to emphasize the meat's beauty and compensate for its weaknesses.

Mau was just thinking the Deltan called "Captain" looked strangely familiar, when the Commander spoke. "Send this image for facial recognition scanning," he said. "I believe I know this Enemy."

17

Ditto's expression read "perturbed" as it popped up from the vis-u. "What?" came the greeting. Then she realized who was comming, and her face went from dark to dewy. "Oh. Hi, Rollie! What's up?"

"Hate to bother you again, mate, but it looks like I have one more sample for you to analyze," Rollie told her.

"Oh, I'm sorry," she said, eyes gleaming almost silver in this light. "I absolutely wish I could take the time to help. But I am so incredibly busy right now. With the harvest, you know. Ordinarily, I'd be happy to do whatever I could, but today, it's simply impossible." She clasped her hands in front of her. "I'm sure you understand."

Rollie sniffed. "I didn't mean this second, did I? I'm not comming from next door. I won't be beaming over. There's travel involved, woman. Besides, busy ebbs."

She frowned. "Where are you now?"

"Outside Fengdu," he said. "But we got to pick up the test sample from Tryfe first. There's a bit of back-and-forth involved."

Now she looked intrigued. "Tryfe? That little backspace planet?"

"Backspace-ish," he hedged. "Of late."

She leaned in closer to the screen. "The one from the *Real Reality Realtime DocuDrama*?"

"That's the one." He had a hard time seeing where she was headed with this.

She smiled, perfect teeth in a lightly gray complexion. "Pick me up and we'll go to your sample."

Rollie rubbed his neck. "I think I just got whiplash from that U-turn. Did you say you'd run the sample?"

"Sure. We can do it right on Tryfe. I have portable analysis..." she searched for the word, "... stuff."

Rollie raised an eyebrow. "'Stuff'?"

Her face flushed darker grey, like a cloud passed over it. "Are you in the trade? If I told you it was an atomic subdeterminator categoric phenodex, would that mean anything to you?"

"Er..." He hadn't exactly studied up on her particular area of expertise. Given recent days, he realized it probably was a skill worth having.

She folded her arms. "All I'm saying is, if you're outside Fengdu, that's closer to here than Tryfe. There's benefit in an economy of motion, Rollie."

"Yes," he said, trying to sound patient, which he never was very good at, "I recognize that. But what with you being so busy..."

"Well, you're not comming from next door, are you?" She grinned. "You won't be beaming over. There's travel involved. Busy ebbs."

He looked around. "Such an echo."

"So you'll pick me up?"

"If that's the way you want it."

"Stellar," she said. And before he could say another word, her face vanished from the screen, almost like she was the one who'd commed in the first place.

Tseethe, Rollie noticed now, had been leaning in the doorway all this time, dangerously threatening to wrinkle his designer coat. "Just curious," he began, "but did that seem... oh... over-eager... to you at all?"

He already knew it did. Rollie offered him a tight smile and headed for the cockpit.

Tseethe followed. "Why does Ditto want to go to Tryfe so badly? You don't think that her original dragged her into something she's trying to evade, do you?"

"I think it's most definitely something like that." Rollie dropped into the pilot's chair and selected the coordinates for the planet Walter.

"And still we go."

Rollie adjusted the propulsion and watched through the front portal, as their course began to shift. "Look: if you was being manipulated by your assassin father-brother, I'd help you." He double-checked the settings, which were spot-on, and rose. "Now, if you'll 'scuse me, it's time to tell Ludlow there's been a slight change of plans."

He was headed into the ship's lounge when he heard Tseethe say, "ICV model-building."

Rollie turned and frowned, "Eh?"

"That's what my Paternal Archetype's into," said Tseethe. "No cloning. Miniature polymer spacecrafts. He has a few hundred of them."

"Ah," the captain said. Having been sired by people even less tangibly tethered than your average constellation, families were always a little lost on Rollie. He never knew precisely what to do around them and so, generally, avoided the interactions as much as possible. "Well," Rollie searched for surer footing now, "if your dad ever holds you hostage with glue and tiny plastic laser cannons, feel free to comm me for assistance, yeah?" Satisfied with what he felt was a meaningful expression of friendship, Rollie left to contact Ludlow.

"Crap, we're late. So friggin' late," muttered Rozz as she and Bertram hustled down the sidewalk and into the lobby of the DiversiDine building. Beardy and Eyebrows had lingered forever, pacing around the ship while chatting up every press contact they could think of in the tri-state area. Rozz and Bertram only narrowly managed to extract themselves between the departure of two news crews and the arrival of St. Vitus' pre-K fingerpainters, who were seeking to feed their artistic muse before cookie break.

Rozz and Bertram were only on the elevator for a moment when Bertram's pocket buzzed. A familiar male voice called out, "Ludlow. Ludlow, you there?"

Rozz could feel the frowns of their fellow travelers beat down on the back of their heads. Bertram muttered an oath to the metal doors.

The second the elevator popped open, Rozz watched Bertram launch himself from the metal box and she found herself fast on his heels. She had no idea what floor they were on. Fortunately, she spied a closet marked "Supplies."

"Here! In here!" she said, opening the door and shoving Bertram through it. She glanced around, flashed a self-conscious smile at the staring office jockeys and ducked in after Bertram.

"Rollie, hey." Bertram was out of breath. "Weird morning. We're already running behind. What's up?"

"Change of plans," said Rollie. "We're coming to you."

"Who?" Bertram frowned at the holographic figure. "You and your chemist?"

"And me," came a tinny voice in the background.

"And Tseethe," added Rollie. "Where's safe to meet? I understand the equipment's portable."

"Depends." Bertram's face was all suspicion. "How humanoid's your chemist?"

"Aw, she'll blend in well enough. In the right light. With gloves."

"That's reassuring."

"Well, the Penumbra's definitely out," said Rozz, more to Bertram than Rollie. "We were lucky we dodged the news crews as it is."

The alien's bright orange eyes narrowed sharply. "How's that?"

"Oh, it's nothing," said Rozz. Something about that fiery flicker told her it was wise to gloss over any personal challenges they were facing. "Minor snafu."

"Very likely to blow over," agreed Bertram, affirming that tactic.

"Listen," Rollie's voice sounded like the weary host of a children's birthday party — one who didn't like children very much, "I realize you're both new to this game. But typically, news crews are not a sign of successful covert operations. Typically, things don't get bargled straight off the fraggin' launch pad."

"We bargle 'em later," explained Tseethe, leaping into the camera frame. "At more crucial times. Good for the adrenaline."

"Not helping," said Rollie.

"Okay, let's see …" mused Bertram. "Where, across the whole city of Pittsburgh, could we meet three extra-terrestrials toting portable chemistry equipment and no one will really notice or ask any questions?"

The words had barely escaped his lips when Rozz and Bertram both erupted with the answer. "The South Side!"

Rollie frowned. "I thought you were Northern Hemisphere."

"We are," said Bertram. "Pittsburgh's South Side is where you go to get pierced, tatted, fed, sloshed, caffeinated, costumed, entertained or meet three extra-terrestrials toting portable chemistry equipment."

Rozz nodded at the truth of this. If pressed, she would have suggested a good portion of the South Side's population might already be GCU ex-pats. It would explain a lot. "What about Heinrich's Hookah House?" she suggested.

Bertram liked it so much, he high-fived her. "Genius!"

"And that's *what* exactly?" asked Rollie. He looked like he wasn't used to feeling this out-of-the-loop.

"It's a French pastry shop and biergarten," said Bertram.

"It's a coffee bar/hookah den," said Rozz. "It's perfect; their whole business model's practically, 'Overlooking Our

Patrons Weird Shit since 1992.' I guarantee, we'll have no problems there."

This was enough to satisfy Rollie. "Right. Stellar. Heinrich's. I'll comm when we're in your airspace and have a better ETA." And with that, his image disappeared from the supply closet.

Rozz leaned on the shelf of copy paper. "So what's the plan in the meantime?"

"Aside from getting back to the grind before we lose our day jobs?" Bertram tucked the vis-u in his suit pocket. "I want to find out all the ways DiversiDine is interacting with Earth people. I want to know what its corporate pet projects are, how it's positioning them and who's involved. I want to know how much it's done to Tryfe and what we can undo."

"Gotcha."

"I have some ideas about where to start. Also," he said, "I want to find out how much Lazarus Malone knows about where his supplies come from."

Rozz hopped on this one. "That's mine."

"Okay. So meet me for lunch at the DiversiDine cafeteria, one o'clock. We'll work on a plan to get you in to see Malone. Something low key, since the guy already has his guard up."

"Bertram..." She shook her head at him sadly. After all this time, he still had no idea what she did. "I'm IT. Limitless access is practically built into the job description."

"It is?"

She patted his arm. He was kind of cute when he was confused. "We're everywhere. The power is in our hands." She held out open palms and could almost picture the orbs of electricity radiating from them.

Bertram had a more practical vision. "You got that line off one of those two a.m. trade school advertisements, didn't you?"

"I totally did," she said proudly. "And next, we're going to get what we need out of Lazarus Malone. Trust me: the dude will never know what hit him. I'll update you at one." She ruffled around in the supply boxes and helped herself to some items, then swung open the door.

There was, as she'd anticipated, a small crowd of office

workers trying hard to look like they weren't looking. She emerged, holding up a handful of office supplies — "Pens," she explained — but she knew she had given them the ultimate gift: that is, something to gossip about. It would be a fresh, welcome rain to the dry and dusty circle of office life.

Rozz was cool with that. She dashed to the elevator, hit the button for her floor, and left them to it.

"Twenty paces past Jimmy Hoffa, then bear a left at the Ark of the Covenant ..." Rozz Mercer muttered to herself. It was noon by the time she walked down the dim, tiled corridor to Lazarus Malone's lab. A fluorescent light flickered rhythmically above, like a Morse code warning.

It had taken her long enough to find the place. It turned out that unlike every other lab in R&D, Malone's work digs were not reachable via the main elevator. They were only available using some behind-the-scenes freight jobby that careened down to the basement level, then lurched one floor lower for funsies.

She supposed if you were receiving secret shipments from outer space, enjoying a little privacy on an obscure freight route wasn't the worst of ideas.

But Rozz also knew nerds — hell, by all reasonable assessments, she was one. And these days, most people in the Nerd-American community had expectations for their working atmosphere. Things like team interplay, group problem solving and ... oh ... the occasional window. Rozz believed it took a very special person to rock the nine-to-five with only Cthulhu as your lab buddy.

It caused her to wonder exactly how special Lazarus Malone really was.

Currently, the door to the man's research and development fiefdom stood open, propped by a recycling bin filled with empty bottles and cans. She knew he was in there; a shadow played around on the floor, diffused and drawn.

She paused at the door. There was no turning back now.

Rozz drew a deep breath and rapped on the doorframe, hoping it sounded jaunty.

"IT," she called, stepping through the threshold. But the journey came to a quick halt when she discovered "The Mixmaster" was not quite alone.

Rats, she thought.

She didn't mean this in the family-friendly cussing way, since Rozz did enjoy the more piquant options off the verbal menu. No, the fact was a trio of real, yet very dead rodents stood posed in simulated life on a file cabinet right by the door, like the world's most startling and least-helpful store greeters. Once her initial surprise passed, further examination showed this rat pack was simply the opening act for a chorusline of other taxidermy creatures. Bird, lizard, rabbit, cat or monkey ... they perched on top of the desk. They sat grouped on shelves. They looked animate, playful ... And Rozz felt a wave of distaste sweep over her. It beached in her stomach, causing her coffee to clock in at twenty knots with a light chop.

"Um, interesting decor," she managed finally, as Malone revolved in his desk chair to face her, scowling. "I mean, I would have gone more the bobblehead route. But, hey, points to you for originality."

"I remember you," he said, though he still seemed to be trying to place her. "From the bowling alley, right? What do you want?"

She held up her red file folder, the one that she'd filled with random papers from the recycling bin. In her first day on the job, she'd learned that carrying a high-visibility file folder and walking briskly was an important tactic in covert office operations. It virtually guaranteed an undisturbed path anywhere she wanted to go. Of course, much like the fake hall passes of her youth, it was important never to abuse the folder's power. "IT's upgrading to a new mail server," she responded. "We need to update your machine."

He exhaled ranch-flavored chips and impatience. "Can it wait?"

"Sure." She gave a loose shrug. "If you're cool with your

email bouncing like Jell-O salad on a trampoline. I've got a whole list of staff I can upgrade." She tucked the folder under her left arm and turned to go.

"Wait."

She stopped, forcing indifference into her expression, into her limbs and her languid turn.

"Will it take long?"

"Ten minutes max," she said. "You can time me."

"I might." He quickly closed out of the program he'd been using—it was a spreadsheet but she couldn't catch its contents. Then he gestured broadly to his empty chair, like he was offering her the throne of England.

As she took it, he shifted to a nearby lab table. Out of the corner of her eye, she watched him organize the papers and equipment there in a disenfranchised way.

At least it gave her the chance to slip a thumb drive from her pocket into the port. One double-click and the app was rolling. It was fascinating what you could download for free these days tailored to the paranoid employer spyware market.

It wasn't long before she felt his gaze linger in her direction. "Unique hobby," she said quickly.

On the screen, the mail settings dialogue box sprawled like a testament to innocent upgrading. She made sure not to block this view. With one hand casually covering the thumb drive, the other pointed to the parade of wildlife over the desk. "Your fur friends," she clarified. "You do 'em yourself?"

There was a long pause. "Why?"

She gave another boneless shrug. "I don't know. They just look so... extra perky. It's very *Snow White Meets Norman Bates.*" She hoped that sounded like a positive. She suspected it didn't.

He responded with some non-committal noise but his eyes were still fixed on the screen.

She decided to turn things up a notch. "You should totally motorize them," she went on, a little disconcerted how swiftly the idea came to her. "I bet there'd be a huge online market for stuff like that. You know, oddities collectors and ... hey!" She worked a bright excitement into her tone now, one she hadn't used since her cosmic barista days. "If you Steampunked 'em out — with, like, Victorian top hats and bustles and gears and shit? —you could probably even get—"

"Could you please shut up?" Ah, *there* was the healthy repulsion she'd longed for. Dead animals with motorization were one thing, but a man must draw the line at sewing tiny rat bustles. "I'm trying to work here."

He wasn't. But she smiled indulgently. "Sorry." She'd discovered the second rule in covert office operations: annoy the pants off others before they got too curious about you. It bought her a whole extra five minutes of uninterrupted installation and a sly eject of the thumb.

"You're all set!" she announced, rising. "I'll see myself out."

While she hadn't spied anything else during her visit that seemed relevant to shrugging off alien oppression, there *was* a door to the right of the desk that she'd been giving the curious eyeball. It was the only closed door in the lab, and that was what drew her attention in the first place. If her assessment were right, the room beyond it accounted for a significant amount of the space on this floor. You could keep anything in there, of course: lab supplies, safety showers, restrooms … or, say, crates of liquid jubies, fresh off the intergalactic freighter?

Her hopes weren't high, but sometimes you had to grab your opportunities as they came. So instead of turning left to leave, Rozz Mercer took a chance — and a right — flinging the door wide and catching just a glimpse … before the guy wrenched the handle from her grasp and shut it up tighter than a Vos Laegos showbeing's unitard.

"Go." Lazarus Malone's lanky, lab-coated arm pointed out the direction, in case there was any confusion.

"Oh, hey, sorry, dude!" It was still Rozz's barista voice: casual, befuddled, well-meaning. "My bad! This building's a total maze. You know, I've gotten lost more times in the last day than I can—"

The arm was unyielding. "Just go."

She went. Gladly.

Because now she knew where Malone had gotten the source

material for his taxidermy projects. Yessir, all creatures great and small — or, at least, all creatures zoned for U.S. laboratory use — were caged and waiting in that room for the next round of tests. And if they didn't survive these attentions?

Clearly, "Waste not, want not" was Lazarus Malone's motto.

Yet, there was one thing that bothered her. (*One?*). Okay, there were many things that bothered her, but one in particular stood out. In all the noise that erupted from that room the moment the door swung open — the tweeting, squeaking, barking, monkey chatter and rabbits selling cream eggs or whatever the hell they did — one strained and chilling sound stood out. Initially, she wasn't even sure she had heard it. Initially, she was sure that it Could Not Be. But the more she thought about it, the more certain she became.

Someone, somewhere in all that noise had said: "Let meee ouuuut!"

"'Let me out'? Are you sure?" Bertram asked over the tuna salad sandwich he'd grabbed from the DiversiDine cafeteria. They were on a bench in Market Square, thankful for the privacy, if not the wind chill. His eyes darted from a brave pigeon bobbing around their bench to Rozz as she popped the tab on a can of DrinkThis.

"Yes, I'm sure. Of course, I'm sure. Why would you even ask that? And—"

He realized she'd noticed him eyeing the can.

"Oh, don't you give me that face. I hate that face."

"What face?"

"That Concerned Frodo face," she told him. "You do it all the time, but now it's like you just caught me petting the DrinkThis."

Bertram felt that face flush guiltily. She *had* promised him she was quitting the stuff—at least, until they could confirm its ingredients. But here she was, with another one. He wondered if there were a twelve-step program for DrinkThis addiction.

As her friend and a customer service rep, he felt he should probably find out.

"Look, I need this," she persisted, tightening her grip on the can. "Would I need this, if some serious next-level weirdness hadn't gone down today? No." She took a long draught and clunked the can beside her. "So yes, it was 'let me out,' and yes, I'm sure."

"It's not that I don't believe you…"

"Bah!" she said.

"It's just —" Two people he recognized from the office passed them. Bertram lowered his voice. "— Captive human testing? On-site? Who does that?"

"Dude: it's DiversiDine," she whispered back. "They bought our planet. To them we're giant lab rats with… better hygiene and… and…" she seized a word, "yoga pants."

Bertram looked down. "All of us?"

"They're Ottoframans, Bertram. How the hell are we different than anything else they've caged in that room? How is this different than them using you as an entertainment option against your will? Hm?" She nodded at him over a snack chip.

He found himself nodding in unison, though chipless. "Okay. You have a point."

She looked satisfied with that response or maybe that was just the DrinkThis kicking in.

"So they're testing on people." Bertram slurped his hot coffee. "Did you see who it was? Did the voice sound male or female? How old?"

"If I'd actually seen anyone, I would have done something about it while I was there. All I saw were rows of cages. As for the voice, I don't know who it was, but it was strained like it was in pain."

"And you only heard one voice?"

"Only one I noticed. But there was so much noise. Like, half an ark's worth. The room must be sound-proofed. That's why I didn't even realize what I'd heard until the door had already closed. It was all so hard to believe, it took a minute to register."

Bertram popped in the last bite of his sandwich. "And what did Malone say, when you opened the door? I mean, how'd he explain himself? 'Oh, don't mind that, that's just my lab assistant. Doing a little adult role playing. Nothing to see here'?"

"That's what's so strange." Rozz said. "He didn't react."

"Nothing?"

"It was like he never heard. He just closed the door and told me to leave." She toyed with her napkin, giving it a good working over. "You saw him at the Cosmic Lanes. The guy's not socially dexterous. That's part of why it was so confusing. He was irritated, sure. But he didn't look particularly worried or embarrassed or anything. He didn't act like the jig was up."

Bertram gave a short laugh. "Maybe the guy's an alien, after all."

"May be," she said. "And maybe this will shed some light on things." She dropped the napkin and dug into her coat pocket, withdrawing a small device.

Bertram looked from the item in question to Rozz. "You stole the guy's flash drive?"

"The drive's mine," she said. "But thanks to an app on this sweet baby, we will have a complete, real-time account of everything Lazarus Malone does on his computer all day. I set the program up so the data routes automatically to the Penumbra." She looked pleased with herself. So pleased, it forced Bertram to ask his next question.

"Is any of that legal?"

She rolled her eyes. "Businesses do it all the time to track employee productivity, Bertram."

"Yeah, but is it legal?" he asked.

"I thought you were 'practically Intergalactic Underworld' these days." There was no doubt; she definitely snickered about it this time. She returned the drive to her pocket. "Anyway, you won't be complaining when we get the deets on the guy's mysterious little slice of Tryfling oppression."

"Or when he emails his mom on Ottofram?" Bertram grinned.

She reached for another snack chip. "And as for Laz Malone's prisoner, I've been thinking about that a lot. And I know what I'm going to do. It's all about timing, but I need to gather some data first. How's your schedule look in the next couple of days?"

"I've got some research I want to do," he said. These lunch breaks were so short, and his morning had been so packed with calls, he hadn't even gotten a chance to do any digging for Tryfe's cause. It was true what the articles said; it really was hard to achieve work/saving-the-planet balance. "But I can probably slot you in for some Earthling liberation, if that's what you're thinking."

"Cool," said Rozz, rising to throw away her trash. And with her flat tone and distinctly non-French accent she added, "*Vive la revolution.*"

18

"The facial recognition results are in, Commander," Tech Officer Din announced, bursting into the dining room of the Feegar starship *Delivery* and holding aloft the tech in question.

They were winding up a truly inspired meal, Mau thought, one of their cook's tastiest. But Din's entrance brought everything to a halt, stopping Mau and several others, right in the middle of dishing out second helpings.

"Well?" demanded Commander Nom, through what appeared to be a succulent bite of ribs. (Mau hadn't gotten to try those yet.) "What have you learned?"

"One of the Hyphiz Deltan freight raiders has been identified as Tseethe Tsardonee," said Din. "It appears that Tsardonee has a wide-ranging archive of infractions. They include various raids, art theft, public indecency, smoking without a helmet and one particularly tuneless rendition of *Quasar Love* at the Space Bar's Moonsday Sing-Along Night. He's a former member of the Intergalactic Underworld Society and he's believed to have fought on the wrong side of the Feegar Rebellion." Din held out the confirmed image of this suspect for all the diners to see. Tsardonee was an opaquely pink-fleshed lifeform with gold hair — the kind of thick, clinging strands that were such a hassle when food preparation was concerned. You had to shuck it outside or it made a mess of your galley counters, found its way into the food and inevitably became stuck in your teeth.

Commander Nom eyed the image. He finished with a derisive snort or maybe his Scof had just gone down the wrong pipe. "I don't care about that one," he snapped. "What about the other?"

Din was already shaking her head. "The system found no confirmed match for the second subject, Commander. That lifeform's a blank."

"I knew it!" Nom dropped a cleaned bone onto his plate. It made a bell-like clatter. "It's Rolliam Tsmorlood!" He leapt to his feet. "It has to be. The total lack of any identifying data is the giveaway."

"Isn't he from the first season of *There Goes the Galaxy*?" asked Din. "I agree there's a resemblance—in as much as you can tell one non-Feegar from another—but I thought he was exiled and killed on Altair-5."

"That's one theory," said the Commander. "Another is that he escaped and is building his own version of the Intergalactic Underworld. An elite group of hand-picked members for the special purpose of creating GCU unrest. I suspect the symbol carved into the shipping crate we retrieved represents that organization." Here, the Commander's arm shot out and grabbed the last two ribs, then he resumed his seat. This seemed unfair to Mau, because he could clearly see Nom's stomach was almost completely full.

Such were the perks of status.

"The veterans among us may recall Tsmorlood from the Rebellion," Nom continued. "He led one of the outsider troops that interfered in our harvest of Klimfals. He also enjoyed a period of hospitality in our war camp."

A murmur of recognition rippled over the table. "Ah!" someone exclaimed. "I *knew* I recalled him from somewhere. I tortured him once!"

A few others agreed they, too, had spent some pleasant hours performing testing on the Deltan and that they would have recognized him sooner if only he'd been prone, confined, swollen, bruised, cut, bleeding and missing strategic bits.

The Commander's face took on an expression of nostalgic reflection. "Yes, we did have some fascinating sessions while Tsmorlood marinated. Thanks to him, we expanded our medical and culinary knowledge considerably. And while we didn't get to enjoy his company for that final dinner, his time with us was valuable—even lucrative—in many other ways."

Mau noticed Tech Officer Din had pulled up a chair and was assessing the remaining barbecue on the platter. So before she could make her selection, Mau helped himself to a handful of smoked fingers, then flashed her a sorry-not-sorry grin, which came quite naturally when your lips were transparent.

"Commander, I'm concerned," Din said, while giving Mau a dark look. "Tsmorlood and Tsardonee now know all about our latest technique for legalized take-out. If they go to the Coalition of Planets with this information, finding adequate sustenance may become even more difficult for our people."

Mau gasped. He hadn't thought of this. "We could be forced to eat lesser species?"

Din shuddered. "Flavorless, mindless organisms with no fight, raised from birth to the dinner table with no other purpose but food? It would be an insult to our people, our traditions and our entire way of life."

"Fools! We already have been insulted," shouted the Commander now and the table shook slightly. Mau could see the blood pulsing in his neck. "Refusing to dust a prisoner? Knowing our code, yet sending him back to us, alive and shamed? Meat-free recipe infopills? Donations in our name to anti-Feegar causes? … *Vegetables?!*" His voice was a roar. "The Feegar people will not be mocked!"

"Um…" Mau raised a hand.

"— More!" added the Commander quickly. "We will not be mocked more. Yes, there was mockery, but the mockery stops now. There will be no further mockery. From now and into the future, the planet of Feegar and its people will be part of a noble, highly-respected, mock-free zone!"

Quietly, Din asked, "And how will we do that, Commander?"

The Commander pushed his plate aside. "Having been safely presumed dead, Tsmorlood is unlikely to go to the Coalition and reveal himself. It's this new organization and this very personal attack on our ways that concerns me. I would like to stem the flow of information about our new techniques. I would like to honor the loss of our friend and colleague, Scarlod Scof, who we were forced to kill and serve in a savory-sweet sauce with an aromatic blend of herbs and spices." The Commander toyed introspectively with one of the bones. "But most of all, I want this new Underworld organization to understand that Feegar business will never be their business. And if they disrespect our culture or interfere in our methods, they will regret it."

"Yes, Commander Nom!" said everyone at the table, snapping to attention and giving the official three finger salute. Admittedly, Mau managed to do it with four, one being somebody else's finger, but it still counted for something.

At least, the support seemed to give the Commander focus. "Find Tsmorlood," he said. "Find out who his family and friends are. We will set an example that the Hyphizite and his band of intolerant Feegar-mockers will never forget."

"Yes, Commander Nom!"

19

Rollie could see Ditto from the air. She was sitting in the ICV lot, on the larger of two trunks. She leapt to her feet as the Protostar 340-K swept in for landing. The ship's ramp had barely touched down before the lady was already climbing it, her hovercases trailing dutifully after her. "So," she began brightly, from the hatchway. "How was traffic?"

Rollie gave her the once over — from the gray labcoat and jumpsuit to the sleek ponytail. It didn't *look* like Dar, (aside from, of course, the identical face and body and hair and birthmarks), but you never did know. Rollie recognized he wasn't the most observant of lifeforms when it came to the subtleties of personal taste and fashion. Fortunately, Tseethe was. And if bad came to worse, Rollie's XJ-37 didn't care either way. "You've unbusied yourself then, have you?" he asked.

"Who'd have thought?" She stepped aside to let her cases hover past and settle onto the ship lounge floor. "And so, without further ado ..." She turned to the wall panel by the hatch and pressed the ramp retraction button. "... To Tryfe!"

"Aw, now, stall your rockets a parsec, mate." Rollie pushed the button again, causing the ramp to pause and reverse, touching back down onto the surface of Walter. "We've had a journey, haven't we? It'd be nice to take half a moment to breathe some non-recycled air before we pop off to Tryfe."

"Yeah, and refill the di-hydrogen monoxide bottles," agreed Tseethe, grabbing a bag of empties and following Rollie's lead. "What's ten minutes? Besides, it's a beautiful day."

"Oh." Frowning, she fell into step with them as they strode off to the main warehouse. "Sorry. I just got the impression this mission was urgent, that's all. We'll be testing something to determine if it has liquid jubies... Is that right?"

"Potentially." Rollie scanned the landscape before them carefully. He noticed her business operations seemed to be running normally. The same robot gardeners carried raw gannon sap from the fields to processing. The same Walterian artisans moved to and from their shifts. It didn't *look* like a trap, but then good traps so rarely do.

"You can fill your bottles here," Ditto said, indicating several drinking fountains beside the warehouse. "Let me give you a hand." Tseethe had barely unslung the bag from his shoulder when she was extracting bottles to fill.

Once again, it wasn't the helpfulness that seemed off, it was the need for speed. Rollie said, "All right, Ditto. What's going on?"

She looked up at him from her task. "Pardon?"

"Why are you so determined to get out of here all of a sudden? And what's the interest in Tryfe?"

"Oh." Her face took on a nervous, pained expression. She laughed for a moment at herself, then seemed nervous even at her own laughter. "I guess I'm a little worried Dar will come back. I mean, even though she didn't frag you earlier doesn't mean she wouldn't try it at some future encounter and—"

"Ah," he watched her intently. "So all this is because you're worried about my safety. Is that it?"

"Of course." Her face cleared. Relief shone from it, like they'd opened a hatchway in a dark room. "That's exactly it."

Tseethe laughed, capping a bottle. "And if we believe that, she's got some prime black hole real estate to sell us."

"Yeah, let's try this again, shall we?" Rollie said. "What's happened since we left, Ditto? The truth now."

She sighed and set the half-full bottle aside with a frustrated clunk. "Okay, you want to know the truth? Fine." She took a deep breath and met his gaze. "I'm scared for me, Rollie. I'm embarrassed to say it, but this time I'm scared *for me*."

Rollie knew he would never understand the mind-frag it must be living as somebody's clone, particularly when the original was as mind-fraggy as Dar Balisong. But he did appreciate that, despite it all, the ties ran deep. "What's Dar been up to, then?"

"It's not Dar's fault. It's mine." She looked at her hands, as if she searched them hard enough she'd find the words she wanted there. Finally, she said, "Last season was a drought. I had to install a new irrigation system to have any hope of saving the crop. But my cash flow was down and my credit was tapped. So while Dar was in Mawdank, I might have, um …" her voice was almost a whisper now, "…taken out a few small loans under her name."

The Hyphiz Deltans winced.

"Aw, Ditto…" groaned Rollie.

"Not smart," Tseethe was shaking his head. "Not very smart…"

"I know, I *know!*" Her eyes flicked to the field with a hunted expression. "And when she finds that out—which looks like it won't be long, since I kind of was waiting for this season's crop sales to pay everybody back—she will not be a happy woman. I mean, she may be my mother-sister, but she's still a serious force to be reckoned with. She's tenacious and talented. She knows very well she can make more just like me. Or better! Someone more appreciative, who'd be glad to join the family business. Any time now, she is going to come back here and I am going to be no more than a blot of genetic coding on the grass. But on Tryfe, I think I'd be safe. At least, it would give her some time to cool down." And she sighed into silence.

Tseethe and Rollie exchanged glances.

"Well?" she asked. She looked from one to the other with desperation.

"Right. Let's get these bottles filled and hit the skies," said

Rollie. He hoped Ditto's therapist did sessions by vis-u because he had a feeling, she'd need a few.

20

"... So just remember, the first step toward winning is showing up for the game," said Bertram. "Yes, you're welcome, sir. Have a DiversiDine Dandy Day!" Bertram hit the disconnect button and pushed at the bridge of his nose. This was his third hour straight of coaching, and he was fairly sure that if he told one more person you had to play to win, he was going to run screaming into the streets. It seemed like the more obvious and insipid the advice was, the more satisfied people were with it. He flung his headset to his desk and glanced at the clock. Four-forty-five. Not quite quitting time, but if his phone stopped ringing for half a second, maybe he could take care of some Tryfe business he wanted to follow up on.

He minimized his DiversiDine TLC coaching app, pulled up his browser and selected the employee intranet option. This brought up a cheerful page bearing the DiversiDine logo, the phrase "Make Every Day a DiversiDine Dandy Day" and a shot of Coach Dandy surrounded by cartoons of DiversiDine's beloved product characters.

Bertram sized up the navigation before him. There was benefits information (sure enough, they *did* offer a 401K), a collection of DiversiDine news articles, the employee handbook, the corporate branding guide and a number of sales presentations.

Like most company intranets, the busy folks who posted the content there seemed to assume their colleagues knew every bit as much about corporate inner-workings as they did. The result was a business version of *The DaVinci Code*. Pages were littered with mysterious unlabeled links, unexplained industry jargon, obscure internal acronyms and department in-jokes, leaving it up to the audience to unravel its symbolism.

It was a few minutes in this lexiconless labyrinth before Bertram stumbled onto the section he'd wanted: Corporate Outreach. But it didn't take long before he realized that what the corporation appeared to be reaching out with was creepy, green alien hands.

The outreach page itself was a list of events, dates, times and a contact form to sign-up. That was all straightforward enough. It was the events themselves that made Bertram do the double-take.

"'*Neighbor Nosh*? '*Dissecting Minds*? … '*Midnight Invasion and Teen Probe*'?!" He clamped a hand on his mouth, realizing he'd said this aloud. His phone rang. He picked it up, said, "Play to win. Stay in the game. Shoot to score. Dandy bye," and disconnected.

He went back to the screen and reread the initiatives. Yup, his eyes were not deceiving him. It seemed all so cold, so matter-of-fact. Like, "Ho-hum, another day at DiversiDine. Time to taste the people next door and gather up the youth for probing and conversion. Who's with me?"

It *had* to be a mistake. It just had to be. He was missing critical context. He didn't care if it was an alien company — corporate evil couldn't work so blatantly … Could it?

No, evil business was supposed to be insidious. It shook your hand and picked your pocket. It tied your shoelaces together when you were napping. It swapped your shampoo for hair removal crème and laughed its ass off — but suavely, in private, via remote surveillance.

This: this had no nuance. It was alien and in-your-face. It also sounded vaguely like the Feegars might be involved.

He saw the *Neighbor Nosh* was tomorrow night.

Bertram noticed a contact name, phone number and extension on the page. He wasn't going to spend his time wondering; he was going to get to the bottom of this. It was probably nothing, probably his overly-suspicious, one-track, Tryfe-saving mind. He picked up the phone and dialed.

"Hi, is this Martha? My name's Ber—er, Troy. Troy Hill. I wanted to sign up to help out with a few of your community outreach events."

Pleasure filled Martha's voice. "Oh, hi, Troy! That would be wonderful. What can I tell you about our programs?" The woman practically radiated warmth and goodwill.

Bertram felt himself relax a little. "I'm new to DiversiDine," he said, "so I just had a few questions on... on... the *Neighbor Nosh*...tomorrow?"

"I see. Of course! Go ahead."

"Yeah, I was just wondering, uh..." He decided to go for it. "How we explain the missing neighbors to the police after we nosh on 'em?" He added a laugh—a safety laugh, really. That way it walked a fairly balanced line between friendly humor and I-have-been-assimilated.

He was wrong. "Who told you that?" snapped Martha, a cold front overtaking her voice now. "Did someone tell you to say that?

This was not the reaction he expected. "Uh...n-no!"

"Was it Donny? It was Donny, wasn't it?" she said. "Well, you tell Donny, it's high time he lets this go. There is nothing wrong with my program. It's gone successfully for two years now, and no one outside has noticed a thing. So once and for all, he needs to stop bringing this up."

"Look, Martha," said Bertram quickly, "I don't know any Donny. Nobody told me to say anything. I'm sure your programs are ... are great. Like I said, I'm new here. I just wanted to volunteer."

There was a long pause on the end of the line—so long, Bertram wasn't sure if they'd been disconnected. He said, "Hello?"

There was a sigh. "Troy," Martha said, "forgive me. I

misunderstood your intentions. There's just a history with … with Donny's concerns about the program but… Anyway." Her voice brightened. "Okay, let's talk about tomorrow instead, shall we?"

"Uh, sure."

"Now, I'm actually very glad you contacted me about this, because tomorrow night I could really use someone to help with logistics," she said. "Based on this location, we desperately need to control traffic flow. So what I'll be having you do is round our guests up. You'll draw them in from the one entrance and herd them my way. Then my team will take care of the rest."

"The rest? As in…?"

"Dear, you're new. There's no need for you to get involved in all the sordid, messy details. We can see about that for next time, once you get a taste of things. I just don't want any of our guests getting away before we get our hands on them, you know?"

Bertram's brain had glazed over just a bit.

"Mr. Hill?" Her voice was concerned now.

"I'm listening."

"What I'm saying is, it has to be a managed process. Remember: these people really are our raw materials. There would be no products, no DiversiDine, without them. Do you think you'll be able to shepherd them in there for us?"

"Like lambs to the slaughter," Bertram said, trying not to twitch as he said it.

And the woman laughed. She actually *laughed*. Then a beep cut into the conversation. "Oh, I'm sorry! I've got to take this call. Any other questions, feel free to call or email any time. Business casual dress is fine, since things can get untidy. Do you have the location?—" (BEEP!) "— Oh, I really need to go. Anyway, it's on the intranet, along with driving directions. Be there fifteen minutes before start. Ask for me; I'll get you oriented then. See you tomorrow!"

"Um, yeah," said Bertram. And he hung up the phone, not entirely sure what had just happened.

✧

"Logistics?" repeated Rozz later, as they walked down Fifth Avenue toward the Protostar in the evening dim. "She wants you to round people up, send them her way and she's going to, what? Whack 'em, bag 'em, and use 'em in their products? That's nuts."

"Not nuts; maybe snack chips," Bertram said. At the not-amused face she gave him, he added, "I don't know. I'm being oriented tomorrow evening."

"But how do they think they could get away with it?" Rozz blew into her cold hands and rubbed them together. "I mean, Pittsburgh's a city, but everybody knows everybody. If a bunch of people disappear after going to the same event, it doesn't just slip by. It's going to be on the news."

"Yeah, I casually mentioned that."

"You casually mentioned a potential mass murder investigation?"

"Look, I made it funny. I'm awesome like that," he said. "The point is, I inadvertently struck a nerve with Martha."

"I can't imagine why."

"Apparently, some guy named Donny keeps bringing up the risks of this program to her, and she's sick of hearing about it. I want to find out who Donny is and discuss his concerns."

A light snow was coming down and it would have been pretty, if not for all the death, Donny and DiversiDine. Bertram continued, "Anyway, maybe they don't kill everybody at these things. Maybe it's DNA sampling. Maybe they're using the genetic codes for something. Maybe it's mass hypnosis and mind control. I'm just telling you what she said. And it came off kind of...hungry."

Rozz frowned. "This Martha didn't sound Feegar, did she?"

"Rollie said the Feegars weren't involved with those shipments to Tryfe," Bertram reminded her, since he'd already reminded himself of this fact at least once. "Anyway, what's a Feegar sound like?"

Rozz got quiet, since she didn't know, either. And the

silence clung tight as they continued their journey from the bus stop.

It was with some relief Bertram noticed the Penumbra up ahead, still sitting untouched on the lawn of the Shadyside Institute for Artistic Expression. (He'd imagined it being booted or towed.) So he and Rozz approached it like they were two art fans taking a stroll to inspect the city's latest industrial masterpiece.

The Institute's lights were out, Bertram noticed, causing the building to blend into the hillside, eternal, forgotten. A cyclist passed them by without so much as a glance, equally ignoring a red light, several stop signs and narrowly, two SUVs, as the Law of Motion trounced the Laws of Traffic Control with a thumb of its runny nose.

Rozz and Bertram waited for a short line of cars to zip by, then the road stood empty. Rush hour was over and Pittsburgh had settled down to the happy hibernation of a cold January night.

Bertram clicked the remote and the ship's ramp started its descent. It seemed slower than ever as they watched for oncoming headlights through the snow.

They were barely through the hatchway before Rozz began to shed her outerwear. Coat tossed aside, shoes kicked off, suit jacket chucked over a chair, she hit the shipboard computer like a Non-Organic Simulant jonesing for a recharge.

Bertram peered over her shoulder, to see what drove the suddenness of her need. "What are you doing? Trying to find that Donny I was talking about?"

"Yeah, Bertram. It's all about you and your evil outreach." She rolled her eyes. "No. I'm checking to see whether my spyware app's doing its duty on our homey Lazarus Malone."

Bertram leaned in, squinting. "And is it?"

"Yessss!" she said, as an icon popped up on the screen. Until, it was followed by an error box. "Noooo…"

He left her to it, deciding to turn his energies to his old pal ramen noodles and the local paper. There was no better way to find out how much Pittsburgh had changed, than quality time with some op-eds and a cup of chili-lime shrimp.

It must have taken Rozz half the evening to figure out how to get the Tryfling app running properly on a Penumbra system, but Bertram knew when it happened by the cheers. Then the room fell silent again.

The newspaper itself revealed nothing especially unusual, beyond a recap of the Kick-off and ads for DiversiDine products thick within its pages. Some things, though, even an alien invasion would never change. Articles on the city's teams— including the Pirates — showered the sports section with the sort of shining optimism every New Year in Pittsburgh guaranteed. There was something comforting about knowing how, with each approaching spring training, hope for the Pirates sprung anew like some half-mad, eye-patch-wearing, bat-wielding phoenix.

Bertram rubbed his eyes and looked at his watch. Somehow it had become eleven-thirty. He folded the paper, stretched to his feet and joined Rozz at the Penumbra's workstation. "So. What's our friend Lazarus Malone been up to?"

She motioned to the screen. "See for yourself. Looks like he spent the afternoon logging data on this spreadsheet. Not sure what it means, though."

Bertram peered at the list of keystrokes in the spyware report. "'One year', 'Fifteen months', 'Eleven months', 'Two weeks', 'NR'?"

"Yep." She clicked on one of the system's automated screen captures and drew her finger down a numbered column on the spreadsheet graphic. "Maybe subject data? Looks like he has a start date, a percentage, then this stuff he was adding today under the 'R. Dur.' column."

"Results Durability," Bertram pondered. "Report During… Reached Duration…"

"Rolling Durango…"

Bertram grinned. "Rat Duress!" At the look on Rozz's face he added, "Okay, probably not. So how about the guy's emails?" he asked. "Anything there?"

Rozz clicked to a different chart. "Nothing much. One from

the bowling group. They're cancelled for the rest of this week; Devi's sick and Dan has a jammed thumb."

"That was from that spin he kept trying to put on the ball. I warned him." It was amazing how much better Bertram was at bowling when he was nowhere near a ball.

"Malone also got a couple of general inner office memos," Rozz continued. "Oh, and BeakerBuysTheScienceGuys.com is having a sale on pipettes." She leaned back in the chair. "I knew I should have bugged Malone's office, too."

"Well, maybe something will turn up tomorrow." Bertram yawned. This holding down a day job while moonlighting as an undercover anti-alien invasion task force was exhausting. He said goodnight and started off to his cabin.

"I do know the guy clocked out around seven p.m.," he heard her say.

Bertram paused and turned around. "Okay...?"

"I'm taking it as a baseline. I wish we had more time to learn the guy's routine, but I don't think we can wait."

Weary as he was, he knew what this meant. Rozz Mercer had been barista slave labor for Spectra Pollux's personal infopill café back in the GCU. She'd tried to escape three times and eventually was fitted with a fashionable electric shock tiara to keep her from running off. An experience like that was bound to make a person sensitive to certain civil liberties issues. "When are we busting out the prisoner?" he asked.

She didn't look up from the screen. "Tomorrow, after seven p.m."

He hated to say the words. "I'll be at *Neighbor Nosh* tomorrow."

"I know," she said. "I can do this solo."

He had no doubt she could. "But how will you get in? I'm sure Malone locks his office at night."

"Yeah, we use a swipe badge system." She smiled up at him and this one was a doozy. "Guess which department houses the data for the swipe badges?"

"Ah." Bertram got it now. "You're everywhere. The power is in your hands."

"Damn straight."

"Don't stay up all night."

She mumbled something as he headed to his cabin, wondering if he'd actually sleep himself.

21

The next day dragged on, the way it does when you've got a hot date after work, or relatives coming into town, or you're waiting to thwart the plans of alien overlords trying to subjugate your people while wearing the guise of business casual.

The TLC phone line kept Bertram busy, of course. And in-between telling people to shoot to score and play to win, he engaged his anxious brain compiling a list of every Don, Dahn and Donald he could find on the DiversiDine intranet.

He also made time for a little recon.

Neighbor Nosh was being held in the Upper Hilltop high school gymnasium. Bertram dug up a floorplan of the gym online and analyzed its exits. There were three, but only one led directly to the outside, the other two intersecting different hallways of the facility.

If Martha stationed him outside the gym, he could head people off before they ever entered. But if they came in via the main school entrance and down one of the halls, he'd have to guide them smack-dab through the heart of Alien Central. For the first time ever, Bertram wished the sum total of his elite military skill didn't involve a game controller.

He would have to play this one by ear.

When five o'clock finally came around, he picked up the

phone and dialed Rozz's extension. His message was simple. "Good luck," he said.

"Life for Tryfe," she responded.

And that was that. Bertram Ludlow left to catch a bus.

He arrived at the high school forty-five minutes early. *This*, he thought as he stepped from the vehicle, *is why movie heroes don't choose mass transit*. Based on the schedule, he could have arrived now or an hour from now. Being late for a mission was inexcusable; being early ruined the vibe.

He noticed the weight of his overcoat and patted the right pocket, making sure his handlaser was still turned off. For a successful mission, timing and control were everything. And burning a hole through your only suit jacket was a sure-fire way to throw off both.

Bertram surveyed his surroundings. Ten cars were already in the parking lot, empty. No guards were stationed at the doors and most of the school was dark. But a banner spanned the doorway to the gym. "Neighbor Nosh" it proclaimed in red glittering letters and underneath: "Sponsored by DiversiDine World Ltd." The gym doors stood open despite the cold.

Bertram scanned the field beside the school for indentations in the snow, for a fleeting shimmer in the evening dim, a strange bending of light — anything that might connote a cloaked Interplanetary Cruise Vessel. Yet all was dark, smooth and still.

He drew a weighty breath, rested his hand on the grip of the laser in his pocket, then followed the gymnasium's glow.

He'd barely set a foot in the threshold when a piercing sound shrieked and a creature with a too-white face blocked his path. The blood-red smile leered. Bertram leapt back, fumbling in his pocket for the handlaser's safety and —

"Hey, hi, and how yinz doin', Neighbor!" The clown gave a hearty "hyuk" and pressed the air horn again. "Just to let ya know, our event doesn't start for another forty-five minutes." The being looped an arm through one of Bertram's and was ushering him back the way he came. "So we're going to have to ask you to pretty-please-with-DiversiDelights-on-top wait in your car until the big hand says twelve and the little hand says seven and —"

"Dimples, I believe he's one of ours," came a voice and a short, motherly woman approached. "Troy?" She extended a hand to Bertram.

"Martha?" Bertram took it. "How'd you know it was me?" Especially since *he* didn't remember he was Troy half of the time.

She pointed at the DiversiDine employee ID still clipped to his coat.

"Ah."

"Heads up! Excuse us!" At the movement behind them, their group dodged out of the path of two crewpersons with a folding table.

"Put that over there in the Snack section," Martha told the crewmen and turned back to her newest volunteer. "Well?" Her round face was alight, expectant. "What do you think?" She gestured to encompass the room. Dimples mimicked the gesture and, at Martha's glare, slumped off, giant shoes clapping away across the wooden floor.

Bertram finally got a good look around the gym. *Neighbor Nosh* was a very special sort of hell — that could not be denied. But it wasn't the one he'd envisioned.

In one corner wobbled a bouncy house in the shape of the DiversiDine building, all shimmy-and-shake like the set of a nineteen-seventies disaster flick, only perky.

Around the room's perimeter stood various stations featuring trays of snack chips, desserts and chilled beverages, all on daintily-draped tables manned by twenty-year-old women with clipboards.

Dimples the clown had a section set aside for face-painting, balloon animal development and heart attack provocation through strategic horn honkage.

Next to Dimples was a skilled artist, who likely once dreamed of gallery showings and museum displays. He now steeled himself to do large-headed portraits of attendees in permanent marker that would all ultimately look the same.

By the front door, Bertram noticed a coaching booth, just like the one he'd investigated before the Kickoff. A woman from his department stood beside it, waiting for the event to begin. He had some vague sense her name was Carole. As her gaze met his, she waved.

Carole. Carole who sat two cubicles down from him, eight hours a day for the past few days, *had known all about Neighbor Nosh.* He sighed. This is what you got when you had virtually no time for a decent investigation. He suddenly understood Rollie's impassioned and often-shared views on the need for thorough recon.

Scanning the room for any sign of actual threat, Bertram's eyes fell once more on the troop of clipboard-wielding snack hostesses. "So, this is ... market testing?"

"Of course!" said Martha. "We do it once a month over twelve locations across the city." She motioned him to the food tables. "All of these are test products. We wrangle the people in here and then we get opinions on new flavor combinations, different chip shapes and vibrant new packaging on some of our old favorites." She snatched up and waggled a package of Patty Cakes at him. She returned them with a cheerful nod to the girl at the table. "The locals enjoy sampling things and it strengthens their connection with DiversiDine. Plus, there's free fun for the whole family."

A loud honk from face painting punctuated this. Clearly Bertram and Martha enjoyed different definitions of "fun."

"Now, why don't you go hang up your coat in the locker room?" Martha pointed across the gym. "Then when you come back, I'll show you where we'd like you to direct people. We want to make sure nobody sneaks out without us getting their feedback."

"Feedback, sure," Bertram said and trailed off to hit the locker room as requested. Hanging up his coat, he felt disappointment cling almost as heavily as the teenage fug coming from Locker Thirty-Two. Bertram had prepped for battle. He'd braced for the worst. It was strangely difficult to shift his mindset from blood-bath to bouncy castle.

He considered the handlaser in his overcoat pocket. Should he leave it here? Should he carry it with him? Unless things took a seriously nasty turn, he was unlikely to need it at all. And yet...

A whole evening of Dimples and that airhorn...

"Wait here," he whispered to it, petting the pocket. "I may be back." And he closed the locker door.

"I'm back," Rozz announced to no one in the echoing subbasement of DiversiDine World Ltd. headquarters. It was just after seven p.m., and she knew Lazarus Malone had left the building because she'd watched him do it. Some people went home after their shift ended ... Some people went for happy hour with pals ...

Rozz Mercer lurked outside elevators and feigned interest in file folders while she stalked food scientists.

Now, outside Malone's lab, she drew a freshly handmade ID from her pocket. She imagined there were video cameras around. She imagined there was a security guard somewhere, scanning her activity from the comfort of a desk, dining on coffee (Joltin' Jubliation blend, of course) and DiversiDine snack cakes. She imagined it would take more than a few minutes before that dude got off his duff and hauled it all the way down here to the Mines of Moria to investigate. And by that time, she'd already have the prisoner free and clear.

That was the plan, anyway.

Besides — she swiped the card in the reader by the door — her access was totally legit. Who could question the power of the swipe ID? Sure, if they looked at it for more than half a second, they'd see it had no photo. And yeah, if they checked with Lazarus Malone, things were bound to get dicey from there. But by then, the deed would be done. Nothing would be stolen—or at least nothing Laz would want to chat about with Pittsburgh's finest. Rozz would likely be counting herself among her hometown's unemployed, but that was a small price to pay for preserving human rights. Harriet Tubman didn't worry whether the Underground Railroad tracked a little mud in the house.

Inside, Rozz flipped on the lights. She'd originally considered doing this scheme by flashlight but decided that, ultimately, it would be a lot harder to play things off if she got caught. She grimaced a second time at the conga line of creatures cluttering the desk, then made a beeline for the back room. She'd had an inkling it, too, would be locked, and she had come prepared to deal with it. If this had been the GCU, she would have choked down an infopill on the lost art of backspace lock-pickery. But instead, she clanked a purse to the ground that carried the tools she'd swiped from Maintenance.

Fortunately, in her young life, Rozz Mercer had removed her share of doors. One boyfriend had been the type who radiated all things brooding and mysterious. And that had been kind of hot until she realized he also dined on drama and pity like they were chocolate-covered cherries. The smallest thing could set him off and before you could say "borderline personality disorder," he was threatening himself harm and locking the bathroom door. It took her a while to learn the most disturbing thing he'd ever actually planned was leafing through the Precious Moments figurine catalog that the last tenants had left by the toilet. Until then, that bathroom door came unhinged almost as often as he did.

And there was something else she'd learned from that relationship: never assume.

She tried the knob now, and the door opened. The room smelled like a pet store, warm and organic with more than a soupçon o' stink. She felt around the wall for the light switch and came across it, transforming a silent room into a cacophony with one flick. Her eyes had not betrayed her. The room was filled with cages.

Here were cages of mice. There were cages of rats. Here snakes, there rabbits. As she moved further into the room, so moved the room's occupants. Waking, scratching, scrabbling around in the sawdust. Around and around the room she scanned. Dogs, ferrets, cats, frogs and —

"She came back!" said a voice.

Rozz stumbled backwards at the suddenness and proximity of the statement and scanned the shelves of cages frantically.

"She did! I told you she saw!" said another.

"Where are you? Who are you?" She reached above one of the cages and banged on the wall. It didn't sound hollow.

"Here!" said a voice on the left. "I'm Subject Seven."

"Here!" said a voice on the right. "I'm Subject Fifteen."

Scowling, she struggled to focus.

"Come on, lady, we're right here. What are you, blind?"

"I — I must be." She was not seeing a single cage among their ranks large enough to house a person.

"Geez, lady — right here!" A cage rattled and this time Rozz saw the movement within.

Her eyes had not failed her because the origin of the voice was not a human. And it was not a parrot, a myna bird or even a chatty 'keet. A cat's paw shot from between the bars. "Subject Seven. Pleased to meet you." The ears shifted forward. "Now get. Us. Out."

"Well, the cat's out of the bag," breathed Rozz, rushing through the hatch of the Penumbra, a frosty puff of air trailing her. She punched the hatch button, retracting the ramp. "Or, uh, will be, anyway."

Bertram jumped up from his chair in the ship's lounge, heart racing. "So they're on to you? Are the cops coming? Did you free the prisoner?"

"Don't think so ... Don't think so ... And, like I said, about to." Rozz set a small carry-on bag on the floor and unzipped it.

"What's that supposed to mean? Where's —" Bertram saw the yellow-green shine of eyes first. Then one paw emerged and another, until two felines stood blinking in the main cabin of his Penumbra Classic.

"'Cat's out of the bag' ..." Bertram muttered, shaking his

head. "How long were you planning to use that line?"

"Since I caught the bus downtown," she admitted. "It was good, wasn't it?"

"Eh." He waved a hand. "Six of ten."

"Ooh, harsh." Rozz zipped up the bag and folded it.

Bertram assessed the fluffy creatures before him and scratched his chin. "Tell you what: I'll give you another two points if you explain why we're suddenly cat owners."

"Owners!" snapped one of the cats. "I beg your pardon. You're not suggesting our liberation was merely an exercise preceding an alternate form of servitude?" The cat looked from Bertram to Rozz, ears back, eyes narrowed.

"Geez, chill out, Seven," Rozz said. "You've gotta give the guy a chance for a little catch up."

The cat actually seemed to consider this. "You're right. I apologize. It's been a very stressful day." Seven decided to alleviate her discomfort by licking her leg and purring soothingly to herself.

This was all a little more than Bertram had seen coming. "So the cats are …"

"Meet Subject Seven and Subject Fifteen," said Rozz. "Guys, this is my friend Bertram Ludlow."

Seven stopped licking long enough to give him a cordial blink.

Fifteen said, "Charmed."

"So …" Bertram was still trying to jumpstart his brain, "Lazarus Malone isn't working on any human subjects?"

"Not anyone caged in his office, at least," said Rozz.

"But he is working on something that teaches animals to … talk?"

"Teach?" sniffed Fifteen. "I beg your pardon. This is nothing new on our end."

"Whatever it is, it's only related to the cats," said Rozz. "The rabbits, monkeys, rats … all *no comprendo*."

Bertram had a flashback to their visit to his parents' house. "Like Mr. Miggins."

"Exactly like Mr. Miggins," said Rozz.

"So we understand Cat these days," Bertram sunk into a seat.

"I think it's the Translachew." Rozz slipped off her coat and tossed it over the seat of a chair. "It would explain why Malone didn't react much when I heard someone screaming for help. It's the only thing that makes sense."

"Sense, sure," said Bertram. He turned to their guests. "You guys don't happen to be from some other planet, do you?" He felt this would explain a lot about his relationship with Mr. Miggins.

But the cats exchanged glances. "Pittsburgh born and bred," said Seven. "My mother was a bored tabby housecat looking for adventure. My father was a rambling man from the wrong side of the tracks."

"Single motherhood," said Fifteen knowingly.

Rozz said, "I couldn't leave Seven and Fifteen there. In fact, I was trying to figure out how I could free everybody. Get them all to a shelter or something. But with no car, I didn't know how to make it work. And you can't just let a bunch of lizards and monkeys loose downtown on one of the coldest nights of the year. And —"

"It's fine, Rozz."

She looked uncertain, then turned to the cats. "Well, you guys are welcome to stay here," she said. "Or, if you have somewhere else you need to be..."

Seven was already curled up in Bertram's chair. "I'm good."

"Perhaps," said Fifteen. "If the facilities are adequate. I'll need to inspect the ship." And the cat went off to do so.

Rozz, Bertram noticed, was now looking from him to the table of DiversiDine food samples, t-shirts, and logo drink cozies. "I cannot help but notice that you are not covered in battle wounds and also have a pile of stuff before you that looks remarkably like conference swag."

"Yeah," he said. "Tonight was a surprise for both of us."

"No cannibalistic community meet-n-greet then?"

"Er, no."

"No DNA collection or probing?"

"Nope."

"No hypnosis and nefarious mind control?"

"Well, yes. But the amount you'd expect from a corporate marketing campaign," said Bertram.

"Okay, but I'm sure the community was, like, really off-put by the ideas, right? They were resisting and standing their ground?" Rozz looked hopeful.

Bertram said, "There was a line for the bouncy house, and we ran out of Cool Ranch flavor Sleemy Snaps."

"Crap," said Rozz.

"But hey, this was just one initiative. The next on the list is the *Midnight Invasion*. I'm hoping Rollie will be here by then. Because if we have to take on the alien hoards, we're probably going to need a little backup."

22

"So how'd you meet Dar, anyway?" Tseethe asked. Rollie watched him draw his finger over the symbols on the game's screen, swap their order and frown again.

They were halfway to Tryfe and the holographic Pratl® game had been an act of desperation on Rollie's part. Space travel was dead boring when you weren't fighting in-house Feegars, inventorying stolen freight or being chased by the law. He'd already selected his weaponry, packed his gear, fixed a blown fuse, whipped up a batch of Flash Stew and had both tried, and failed, to meditate. Cracking open the game, along with that bottle of Feegar hundred-year old bourbon, was the only way to make the rest of the trip bearable.

"How'd I meet Dar ..." Rollie mused now over his second glass of the aforementioned, which had already started to take the edge off. "Was a small-time neighborhood confinement center on Zarquon-12, as I recall. I'd been Klinkoed for Hovercrafting While Inebriated. Which wouldn't've been so bad, had I not also just robbed their LibLounge branch six blocks away."

Tseethe's smile was a flash in the helmet smoke. "Caught you with the yoonies, huh?"

Rollie laughed. "Yoonies, no. Print, yes."

Ditto laughed, too, pouring herself another bourbon. "Oh, I remember that from Dar's memory files! The whole Zarquon system was going print-free. People thought it was a great deal. Drop your print at your local LibLounge and get free infopill versions for the whole family. Print Liberation Lounges all over the planet were piled high with books waiting for incineration. And that, of course, made it completely irresistible to our collector of lost causes here." She tossed a playful glance to Rollie.

"So there I was, with four bins of the fraggin' contraband in the back of my vehicle, all with 'LibLounge: Designated to Burn' stamped over it." Rollie shook his head and chuckled. "Dar happened to be in the next confinement cube."

"And the rest is history, huh?" Tseethe was still messing with his holo-game chips and Rollie wished he'd get on with it. It had been his play through two blasted solar systems now.

"Dar told me she was in for holding up a used handlaser shop," Rollie went on. "We got to discussing techniques. Seemed we had a lot in common."

Tseethe nodded. "It's hard to find someone who sees the universe from the same orbit."

"Yeah, well … Unfortunately," Rollie leaned back in his chair, "it wasn't to be."

"Because of the whole also wanting to murder you thing," said Tseethe.

Rollie shrugged a shoulder. "Dampens the trust in a relationship, learning you're on your life-merge partner's assassination list." He knocked back the last of his bourbon and refilled the glass. "The whole meeting was a set-up, right from the beginning. And how she did bide her time!"

Here Ditto sighed. "You make it sound like Dar wanted to kill you for fun or something."

Rollie shot her a dubious look.

"Oh, Rollie …" Ditto's gray eyes went all round and sincere, "I know how it must have looked but it really wasn't anything personal." She turned to Tseethe. "Dar had been hired by Blip Flutterbitt, the Underworld member assigned to the Zarquon system at the time. He was upset because Rollie had been stepping on his turf."

"I was only in Zarquon for the print," Rollie insisted. "Blip wasn't even in the illegal print scene, but he got his proboscis all bent about it, just the same. Of course, Dar didn't care; she had no problem accepting the hit."

Ditto snickered. "As a hired assassin, do you really think it was Dar's job to nitpick motivations?"

"It wasn't her job to fraggin'-well cozy up to me at length before pulling the trigger, either. But she did that."

"She was conflicted." Ditto swirled her glass. "Take it as a compliment. If she hadn't found you intriguing, she'd have shot at you much, much sooner. You did have a lot in common."

"Ah!" shouted Tseethe, and with a flick of his hand, his holo-symbols appeared on the main board. "That's ten eclipse points for overlapping your 'pelcrustinate' and five solar flare points for hitting the corners."

Rollie and Ditto both frowned at the board. "*Flarglejemp?*" said Rollie. "You can't use that."

"What's wrong with *flarglejemp?*"

"Other than you completely made it up?"

"What? It's Marglenian," said Tseethe. "It means 'of or having to do with the manufacture of flargle.'"

Ditto shook her head. "That's *flarglejant.*"

"No." But Tseethe sounded unsure. His eyes darted to Rollie.

Rollie nodded. "She's right, mate. *-Jant.*"

Tseethe snarled and swiped at the board. His digital symbols broke apart into tiny dots of light and reappeared on the screen in his hand. "I hate this fragging game. I'm done." He tossed down his screen, rose from the table and turned on the holovision.

Rollie and Ditto split his symbols between them as Tseethe flipped through the channels. Currently, a smiling Calderian was saying, "Who do I trust to chip away my Kreblat barnacles? I go to —" (CLICK!)

"—Your medicine cabinet for headaches during those

uncomfortable cranial mitosis times. Strike back with NogginGon —" (CLICK!)

"—An explosion attributed to a suspect now identified as Jane Manners of the planet Tryfe."

"Hold it," said Rollie, his holo-symbols hanging in mid-air.

On the *Heavy Meddler* news, reporter Zaph Chantseree stood before a blue, goo-covered industrial accident site. A facility sign bore the Translachew gum logo, albeit a sticky, dripping one. "The act of terrorism centered around the Quad One Translachew manufacturing facility you see behind me here in the Denn-Teenn section of the planet Sarulia," said Chantseree. "Footage, as pulled from the factory's security camera, has undergone extensive facial recognition analysis and shows the suspect, Jane Manners, in action."

The image cut from Chantseree to grainy security footage of a blond female lifeform in mismatched clothing, affixing a device to a giant metal drum and fleeing the area. In a moment, the landscape was all shrapnel and sticky blue strings.

The screen went black, and the channel returned to Chantseree on location. "*Heavy Meddler* viewers may recall Manners as the fugitive behind this week's mass escape from Mawdank Roving Confinement Center. GCU law enforcement is still searching for Manners and several other escapees. Meanwhile, maintenance crews have brought in massive quantities of creamy-style squibbly-nut butter, ice, buffers and very large combs as a part of their advanced environmental remediation efforts. Non-Organic Simulant workers present during the explosion will receive in-house counseling."

"Stellar," muttered Tseethe now, turning from the holovision to Rollie. "What is it with these Tryfe people? Are you sure it's even safe for us to go there?"

"Aw, I been there a good handful o' times," said Rollie dismissively. "It's all right. Anyway, you met Ludlow. You know Tryflings aren't all like that." He flung his symbol tiles into play on the board. "There." Satisfied, Rollie leaned back, folded his arms and grinned. "*Tshyamaalyn.*"

It was the Hyphiz Deltan word for "foreshadowing a

pleasurable plot twist that a person never sees coming, unless that one friend everyone has who can't keep his big yap shut ruins it all first."

The Deltans believed in getting quite a lot of value per word.

Rollie pointed to Ditto. "Your go."

23

"Are you going to work or not?" Rozz asked. "Our bus'll be out there in ten minutes." She popped a can of Mountain Dew and slurped greedily (ah, there was nothing in the cosmos like this caffeinated semi-citrus Earth masterpiece!), then grabbed her bagel from the Food Processing Unit. The FPU did not understand the finer points of bagels. She could get them blackened or warm and soggy, but someday — someday — she would figure out the setting to achieve chewy, browned nirvana.

Given the limp, steaming dough-ball in her hand, she recognized that day was not today. She bit into it, anyway. "Bertram, the bus?" she mumbled through it.

He was still in his pajamas, some busy, planet-printed get-up he'd bought in an interstellar tourist trap somewhere. It was part of his modus operandi these days; the more taste-impaired something was, the more it amused him. The GCU had *a lot* to offer in this genre.

"I'm coming," said Bertram now, more to the shipboard computer than her. "I just wanted to check something first."

"You've been 'checking something' for an hour now," she said.

"That was a different something."

Subject Seven twined around Rozz's feet. Rozz scratched the cat's ear and squinted over Bertram's shoulder. "What somethings are they?"

"Research somethings," said Bertram. "Checking out the local news about DiversiDine's outreach programs. The *Neighbor Nosh* event was going on for two years in different locations around the city. So I thought I'd see what I could find on the rest of Martha's events. I started with *Midnight Invasion and Teen Probe.*"

"Sounds nasty," said Seven, who probably knew a little something about probing.

"And when exactly is this invasion?" asked Rozz.

Bertram pulled up a photo of five men in their early twenties staring deeply into the camera. One held up fingers in a hang loose gesture. One had a pout like a mackerel. One guy's hair swept perfectly across an eye and above it perched a hat that read, "UFO: Unbelievably Friggin Outrageous." They were all wearing loose striped ties over tight t-shirts and polyester plaid golf knickers. Rozz thought they looked like they'd fallen into a backstage clothes rack at an old vaudeville show and barely made it out alive. So naturally, they were very sexy. At the bottom of the photo, a logo read "Midnight Invasion," where the "I" looked like a flying saucer beaming someone up.

Rozz raised an eyebrow. "A boy band?"

"Yup. It says here their hit song, *Cosmic Lovin'* is about the chemical reaction of a hot human/extra-terrestrial relationship. A lot of their songs are along that theme. According to the local paper, it's really gotten teen girls interested in sci-fi. There's even a best-selling book series based on these guys."

Rozz rolled her eyes. "Totally educational, I'm sure."

Bertram snickered. "The books are about an awkward high school girl who's rescued from her bullies by these hunky stranded scientists from outer space who also coincidentally sing pop R&B. And as they live in her family's unusually large, messy and unused two-car garage, they teach her about astronomy, chemistry, computer science, self-esteem, love, and —"

"Enough." She put up a hand. "I get it. And so the 'Teen Probe' is, what? Backstage groupie shenanigans?"

"No. DiversiDine hires Midnight Invasion for a concert to get the kids in, then the company uses the attendees for test marketing to reach the teen perspective. There's also apparently a school science fair aspect to it with prizes."

"And no one's gone missing afterwards? No strange behavior?"

Bertram scanned the page. "Looks like a few of the girls have gone on to scholarships in STEM careers," he said.

"Huh." She wiped her hands on a napkin. "Guess we can skip that event, then."

"And all the other ones, too, as far as I can tell. *Dissecting Minds* is about job shadowing for science careers. They also do factory tours. They sponsor a *Keep Our Highways Clean* program. They donate to soup kitchens. They —"

"Hug puppies and feed shut-ins?"

"Oh, you mean the *DiversiDogs Pet Adoption* program and the *Senior Eats-n-Treats* delivery service?"

"Son of a bitch," said Rozz. "What happened to the good old days when Evil Overlords didn't have so many damned layers?"

"I know. It keeps throwing me off my game." Bertram rose and headed into his quarters. She could just hear his voice. "Oh, and I didn't even get to tell you. I talked to my coworker Carole last night about the mysterious Donny. You know the one who was worried about Martha's programs?"

"Yeah?" Rozz grabbed her work ID off the counter and clipped it to her lapel. She realized if this undercover gig kept rolling, soon she was going to need more than one suit.

"It seems Donny was a former marketing guy at one of the big ad agencies. He had a nervous breakdown and now works in the mailroom. He's been poking Martha about her initiative names for years. Says she's not thinking these things through and that they're a PR disaster waiting to happen."

Rozz slipped on her overcoat. "And, what, the guy wants her job?"

"Pretty much." Bertram emerged wearing the one suit he owned and adjusting his tie. "Meanwhile, Martha thinks *Neighbor Nosh* sounds 'cozy.'"

"Cozy … I suppose it does, if you've never heard of the Feegars, or Vernjoolsian Mollusks or …"

Speaking of dead meat, Rozz reached into the ship's fridge and pulled out some Soosian shaved roast they'd picked up from the Shop-o-Drome before they'd left. It was green but then, it was supposed to be. They'd gotten it to go with Samiam eggs. She looked down at the feline at her feet. "I'll see about some cat food and litter for you today. In the meantime, there's this. And I put out a box with some shredded newspaper in it for your, um …" It seemed wrong to talk to a cat about its toilet habits when it could talk back. "That cool, Subject Seven?"

"Very nice, thank you." The cat blinked warmly. "But I would prefer it if you would call me by my given name."

Rozz hadn't realized the cat had a given name. "And that is …?"

The cat sat up stiffly. "I am Cordelia Evangeline Marguerite Beauchat, the Comtesse de Wholey's Fish Market Dumpster Five."

"Yes," said Subject Fifteen, coming out of nowhere and leaping onto the counter. "Let us throw off the shackles of our captivity and regain the independence, strength and dignity due our noble species! I, too, shall henceforth be called by my given name. Let it be known that on this great day, I am once more …" he held his head high, "…Bootsy!"

"Bus," Bertram said quickly, grabbing his coat. "Got to catch a bus."

"Er, yeah. Right behind you," said Rozz. It was way too early in the morning to deal with any sort of feline emancipation ceremony. Rozz would need a lot more caffeine for that.

24

Rollie commed Bertram at a quarter to two in the afternoon saying he was in their airspace and he'd meet them in an hour. Bertram didn't argue; he got on the horn to Rozz. When you're trying to take down an intergalactic corporation from within, you don't worry much about clocking out early.

In Heinrich's Hookah House, the smoke swirled and Bertram coughed. From his place in the booth, he watched the front door through a blue haze. He didn't expect Rollie and his alien pals would ever pass for Pittsburghers. But right now the air was so thick and fragrant, Chewbacca could have bounced in doing a Riverdance and no one would have thought much of it.

Over the years, Heinrich had tried many things to help his small business thrive. The space had been a German brew-house, coffee bar, patisserie, a Mexican cantina, a dim-sum palace and, for one whole week he would not discuss, a hair salon. With each iteration, favorites from the old theme carried forward, while new items were tacked on with gusto. The décor— as evidenced by the painted fans, fake cactus and barber chair shoved in the corner — had followed suit. Heinrich's wore its eclecticism like a glittery Chinese sombrero, and the South Side regulars embraced it.

Bertram had received his double espresso and pork dumplings, and Rozz her German potato salad and bottle of pineapple Jarritos, when the door banged open. Bertram didn't have to look to know who'd arrived. Rollie stood at the door in silhouette. He was in his standard uniform of More Black, rounded out by clunky space boots and a long coat bolted with panels of some lightweight armor. With the light behind him, Bertram couldn't see his face, but he must have seen Bertram's. In a moment, he wove his way to their table for five.

Behind him followed Tseethe, a Hyphiz Deltan about Rollie's age, with finely-tailored clothes and precise hair. Bertram was struck by this, not only because it was so different from Rollie, but because Bertram realized it was the first time he saw Tseethe without his smoking helmet. A carved pipe jutted from between the man's surprisingly white teeth.

Because of Tseethe's entrance, Bertram almost missed the third person in their party, a tall, slim humanoid woman in gray. She carried a square case, in mittened hands.

The trio arrived bringing the cold air with them.

"Ludlow." Rollie nodded at Bertram and thumped into a chair. He squinted across the table. "And Rozz, I take it?"

"I am so stoked to officially meet you in person," she told him.

He twitched a smile and hooked a thumb at his companions. "This is Tseethe Tsardonee. Believe you and Tseethe already are acquainted, yeah, Ludlow?" He didn't wait for Bertram's answer. "And this is our specialist, Ditto Balisong."

"My first time on Tryfe," she said warmly. "Thanks for having me."

Bertram noticed that unlike his last time on Tryfe (er, Earth), Rollie wasn't wearing sunglasses and the man's normally orange eyes had transformed to a strange, inhuman blue. "So what are they, colored contacts? Or did you steal a spice shipment from Arrakis?" Bertram and Rozz both laughed.

Rollie blinked. "Arrakis. What Quadrant's that?"

Bertram shook his head; he didn't know why he even bothered.

"Anyway, it's iris dye," Rollie continued. "It's temporary. Since you was worried about us blending in." He grinned. "What do you think? I did research on Tryfe-human genetic phenotypes."

Bertram looked at him, from the freshly-dyed eyeballs to the erratic white-blond hair, prominent bone structure and overall sense of bad-news-ishness. "Well, I tell ya, Rollie, it makes all the difference."

"Does it?" The grin widened.

"Nope. Not remotely. Dumpling?" Bertram offered the plate.

Grumbling, Rollie declined. Tseethe took one.

Ditto chose to get down to business. "So where is the item to analyze?" she asked.

"Here." Rozz set the can on the table.

"DrinkThis?" Rollie leaned back in his chair and made a derisive sound. "I'd've known that, I could've saved us the journey. Got a bottle o' that back in the Protostar from when Backs raided a shipment."

Rozz said, "Ah, but this is the special made-for-Tryfe version."

"Now with a hundred percent more jubies?" Rollie asked.

"That's the theory."

Nodding, Ditto opened the case before her to reveal a tidy little machine. She removed her mittens and Bertram saw the woman had a surprising excess of fingers. She used them to pop the top on the DrinkThis can and extract an eyedropper from a leather case. She sampled some of the liquid and dropped it into an indentation in the machine. She pressed a few buttons, read the screen, made a notation on a cocktail napkin and then folded her hands before her, creating a disturbing pile-up of digits. "Now we wait."

"How long?" asked Rozz over a sip of soda.

"Until it's done," said Ditto simply.

Tseethe took this moment to examine the tavern, which is to say, he assessed the vague people-shapes and the glow of the electric cactus through the smoke. "I gotta tell ya, this place is stellar." He rose, swung off his coat and folded it neatly over an extra chair, like he planned to stay a while. "What lucky slaggards you Tryfe people are. I mean: smokes! Right out here in the open. For years I've had to wear that fraggin' helmet of mine. And here, you've still got all this, any time you want it. Gotta hand it to you backspace people. You make a guy long for the good old days."

"The days of a marked increase in respiratory-related diseases?" Ditto asked, as she checked the machine.

"Speak for yourself, lady. My body mutated to feed off the stuff; this is a nutrient-packed seven-course dinner for me. So the way I see it: your respiratory disease, your problem."

"Just a quick outsider's view," interrupted Rollie, turning to Bertram and Rozz, "but things didn't look that much different to me on the way here. More vendng machines, maybe. You figure out all that DiversiDine's done to the place?"

"Yes and no," said Bertram.

"Leaning mostly toward the general 'no' side," admitted Rozz.

Rollie smirked. "Give me the infopill summary version, then, would you?"

So Bertram started at the beginning. "See, initially we thought DiversiDine was inviting people to dinner. *As* the dinner."

"Total wash," said Rozz. "Though Bertram did net some very nice swag."

"Then briefly," Bertram continued, "we thought we were being invaded and probed."

"Easy mistake, though … Boy band." Rozz rolled her eyes.

"Then there's Lazarus Malone."

"'L. Malone'? The one getting the shipment of jubies?" asked Rollie.

"We thought he was keeping human slaves in his lab but…" Bertram shook his head.

"On the bright side, we can understand cats now," Rozz said.

Rollie asked, "As a concept?"

"As in totally Doctor Doolittle."

Rollie stared blankly.

"It's this guy and he talks to the animals and ..." Rozz frowned. "You do know what cats are, right?"

Before he could answer, the server appeared. "Can I get you anything from the bar?"

"Absolutely." Rollie's tone was grateful.

"We have DrinkThis daiquiris, rum and DrinkThis, DrinkThis shooters, Vodka and Dr —"

"Surprise me," Rollie told him. "But two things: make sure it has a kick and no blasted DrinkThis." As the server left, Rollie turned to Rozz. "And you, you should come with your own fraggin' version of Translachew, you know that?"

"Look," said Bertram, "what it all comes down to is the fact we know something is wrong here. We can feel it. Everybody's so ... nice. Considerate. Everybody's happy and easy-going."

"Shit, my parents *like* each other," said Rozz, eyes wide with horror.

"And that's ... bad ... then, huh?" said Tseethe, clearly wanting to empathize.

"It's bad, if it's an illusion," said Bertram. "It's bad, if it's all because of the —"

"Jubies." Ditto pointed to the screen, now glowing through the smoky haze. "You were absolutely right. Your sample has a very high jubies content."

"So that's it then," said Bertram. "Now we know for sure. DiversiDine's brainwashing everybody. They're keeping the populace malleable."

"But for what?" asked Rozz. "Eventual assimilation? Easy annihilation? Extra big tax write-offs?"

"Okay ... Here we are." The server set down a martini glass before Rollie. It held a cloudy beige-green liquid.

Rollie peered at it with interest. "What is it?"

The server beamed. "Bacontini. It's bacon-flavored vodka, dry vermouth and —"

"Crisp fried beverage meat!" observed Rollie of the bacon. "Fascinating!" He plucked this garnish from the glass and examined it in his hands like it was a marvelous scientific oddity.

The server, who had undoubtedly seen much in his time while working at Heinrich's, now added this to a list of unexpected customer interactions. In all honestly, it probably didn't rate very high on the list.

"He's from… way out of town." Bertram told the server.

The server said he'd figured as much.

Once they saw Rollie's bacontini, naturally everyone at the table wanted one. By the second round, it was either the -tini or the bacon grease that had thoroughly lubricated their minds regarding the Tryfe problem and its intricacies.

"We should test ZOT! Find out what's in there," said Bertram, somewhat over-loud, even to himself. "And all those snack cake and chip samples back at the Penumbra. We should test those, too! And hey, what else did they give me?"

"T-shirts!" suggested Rozz.

"T-shirts! We should test those and —" Bertram reflected on this and then shook it away. "Okay, not the shirts. But —"

"We should test another bacontini," said Tseethe, motioning for the server.

It was a few hours of brainstorming in this manner before that storm finally petered out, and Bertram and the group drizzled their way beyond the doors of Heinrich's Hookah House.

"All right," said Bertram foggily, surprised to find it was already pitch black outside, "so it's like we agreed: Rozz and I run in to get cat supplies. Then we'll all take Rollie's ICV to the Penumbra to do some additional testing on the DiversiDine products. I have coffee there. Anyone want coffee?"

"Great big sloshy gallons," muttered Rozz, massaging her temples. Rozz didn't drink often and her last bacontini hit hard.

"What's coffee?" asked Ditto with interest.

"I tried coffee once," said Rollie. "You do not want to see a

Hyphiz Deltan with systemic hypermotocerebrostasia on coffee."

Bertram was picturing how much he didn't want to see that when …

"Aliens!" came a voice from behind them.

At first, Bertram wasn't even sure he'd heard right, but his companions' expressions confirmed the truth. Their unspoken consensus: *keep moving.*

They moved.

"It's aliens, I'm telling you!" The voice was closer now. Unsettlingly close.

Bertram winced. He didn't really want to look, but he recognized that some things were better swiftly addressed. And out of a group of two Hyphiz Deltans, one Whatever and Rozz Mercer (never to be crowned the queen of Tact), he was pretty sure he was the best candidate for this.

He turned. Their new admirer was a goateed man of about thirty, wearing a long, blue puffer coat. His hood was pulled up over a tangle of red, curly hair. The coat's tube-like style reminded Bertram of a giant Gortex worm, slowly digesting the guy alive.

If only, thought Bertram now.

"That's your problem, you know?" the guy was saying. "Extra-terrestrials."

"Ah!" Bertram offered the guy his politely indulgent smile, which had been getting a serious workout lately. "So that's it, then. Well, great to know. Thanks a bunch. Take care." Then under his breath, he told the group, "Walk quickly."

"The Coach answers to them," continued the man, keeping pace. "You know Coach Dandy?"

This got Bertram's attention. He stopped abruptly. "You're talking about DiversiDine?"

"Of course. Coach Dandy of DiversiDine. You didn't actually think he was legit, did you? Did you think he was some sort of guru? That he's running the show himself?" A laugh escaped the man like pent up steam. "No way, friend. That guy's a puff of air. A shiny surface. A distraction. He's the big green head in the Emerald City. He's no guru, he sure as hell ain't local, and it's high-time somebody pulled back the curtain."

"Ludlow ..." By now Rollie had backtracked. "You're leaving, right? We're *all leaving*. Remember?" He shot Bertram a weighty look.

"Give me a minute."

"I heard what you guys were saying back there," continued the stranger. "A takeover? Mind control? Absolutely! That's what I've been telling everybody, ever since DiversiDine opened their doors. And think about this —" He leaned in, smelling of Iron City and shisha. "We see the Coach all the time. Events, broadcasts, book signings. Yet the CEO? What do we hear about him? No one's ever seen him in person."

"You mean Dandy's not the CEO?" With Dandy being so front and center, it hadn't even occurred to Bertram there might be someone else in charge.

"And you mean 'never'?" Rozz had joined them. "Like 'never ever'?"

The stranger smoothed the end of his moustache. "Is there another kind?"

"But the CEO," Rozz persisted, "he'd have a board to report to. And investors. There'd be meetings. Status reports. Something."

"Video," the man said. "Never live. Not once. And you want to know why?"

Bertram hazarded a guess. "Because he's ... an alien?"

The guy pressed a gloved finger to the tip of his nose in affirmation, also coincidentally passing part of the sobriety test.

"Interesting!" Rollie said, now that the discussion was clearly not about outing him personally. "And exactly how can you tell he's an alien?"

"Oh, there are signs," the man said.

"Is it a look? A certain look, then? You know what aliens look like?" He was having way too much fun with this and it made Bertram nervous.

But the stranger didn't seem to notice, a smile bristling his goatee. "We know, friend," he murmured. "We know. The proof is out there, people. Just gotta pull back the curtain." He drew something from within the depths of the blue worm. His eyes shifted from Rollie and Rozz to Bertram. He leaned in. "We've already spoken too long here. Contact me. Your codename will be Bacontini." He pressed a card into Bertram's palm and hustled into the night, as fast as his worm coat would let him.

The burnt smell of a mostly-empty carafe of coffee, as cooked in the Food Processing Unit, wafted throughout the Interplanetary Cruise Vessel like a bad college memory. Bertram moved from the table — where he and Ditto were testing all the company's food samples they had on hand — to a wall panel and he turned up the recycled air.

"I am done in," Rozz announced as his movement jarred her to the present. She rubbed her eyes, yanked off her headset and sank back against the seat. "If this dude says 'maximize our growth potential' one more time, I will laser this monitor."

Steps away, Rollie was sprawled in a chair, performing routine maintenance on his handlaser collection. With all the room's surfaces otherwise occupied, the handlasers formed a silvery pile in his lap. He glanced up from one of them now, chuckling. "Rozz, are you suggesting that our colorful conspiracy enthusiast shared nothing of real value with us, then? Who'd've thunk it."

"Hey, just because there's been no big paydirt, doesn't mean it's not progress," said Rozz. "The guy was right on one point. Dandy's not actually honcho-in-charge. According to the website, the CEO's name is James Able. They list some background, work history ..."

"So he's real," said Bertram, feeling more than a little disappointed. Every time he thought they were getting somewhere, another player came into the picture.

"Real as Troy Hill and Ada Byron, at least," she said. "We'll see. Right now I'm checking out the guy's investor videos."

Rollie sniffed. "And what'll they tell you? Expect him to slip up in the middle of quarterly earnings and reminisce about his idyllic childhood playing on the shores of the Crab Nebula?" Rollie twisted an attachment onto a handlaser with a ratcheting sound.

"I just wanted to get a sense of the guy. The way he talks, his mannerisms. Whether it's at all … Earthy."

"And is it?" asked Ditto.

She wrinkled her nose. "Hard to say. Seems to be reading off of a teleprompter."

Rollie sat up straighter. "You don't think he could be Eudicot T'murp, do you? Perhaps in some clever holowatch disguise?" His tone was hopeful. T'murp had not-so-indirectly been the catalyst for Rollie's banishment to the hell planet of Altair-5. Bertram got the sense that even a delayed revenge against the Ottoframan businessman was a pleasing idea.

But Rozz stood up and stretched. "Think? I can't think of anything right now. I'm tired, I'm crabby and I'm going to bed. I'll look into this more tomorrow."

"Rozz," Bertram pointed to the clock they'd set to Tryfe Eastern Standard Time, "it is tomorrow. We've got work soon."

At this, she groaned the groan of the second-shift World Saver. "Have I earned any sick days yet? Please tell me I've earned sick days."

"Doubtful."

"Shit. This is the price I pay for caring about stupid humankind," she grumbled. She paused to peer over Ditto and Bertram's work. "So what's the scoop on DiversiDine's other products?"

Bertram looked up from his inventory checklist. "Everything's jubie-free here so far, except for DrinkThis and Joltin' Jubilation."

Ditto added, "There could be other ingredients we've missed, though. I'd need to set up additional protocols in advance, if we were planning to test for —"

Rozz put up her hand and walked away, mumbling, "Gonna go wash my face."

It was as she headed to the ship's lavatory, the door flew open and Tseethe came flying out. "Nono!" His hands were all a-motion. "Wouldn'tgointhereifIwereyou."

"What?" Rozz tried to peer around him. "Why?"

"Your small furry people."

"The cats?" she asked blearily.

He nodded. "And your sentient pulmonate gastropoids."

"The toilet snails?"

"Yeah." He winced. "There seems to be some kind of gang rivalry turf warfare thing going on in there. I didn't even get to... uh..." He flashed an awkward smile. "I'm just gonna use Rollie's ship." He headed to the exit hatch.

"Okay, that's it!" spat Rozz. "Rollie, hand me one of those." She motioned to the Deltan's array of weapons.

He looked from her to his collection uncertainly. "What do you plan to do with it? Not trying to tell you your business. Just, it makes a difference when —"

"Rollie." Her expression was dark.

"Right." He handed her an XJ-23.

She nodded. "I'm going in."

"You do realize," Rollie called, "handlasers don't work on —"

She marched into the bathroom. The door clanged shut behind her.

"Those fraggin' snails," Rollie mused, "she's just gonna make 'em grumbly."

"She's just gonna make 'em bigger," said Bertram, too tired to do anything about it at this point in the evening. Or morning. Or whatever.

But it was only a moment before the door flew open again, and the prisoners formerly known as Seven and Fifteen came racing out, hot on the trail of a small red dot.

"I've got it!" shouted one.

"No, I've got it!" said the other.

They were followed by Rozz, who was playing the J-series

handlaser along the floor before them.

"It's mine," shouted Cordelia Evangeline Marguerite Beauchat.

"No, mine," insisted Bootsy.

The lavatory door banged closed. "Détente," Rozz said, and with a flip of the "off" switch, she thrust the laser back into Rollie's hands.

The dot disappeared. Cordelia and Bootsy looked surprised.

Rollie shared their expression as he looked from the weapon to Rozz. "Huh," he said. "Always wondered what that setting was for." He pocketed the laser.

"Oh. And by the way ..." He indicated the resident felines, who were now discussing the mysterious presence they had just witnessed. (They debated whether it was a communication from a parallel dimension, a creature with invisibility powers or possibly a group hallucination.) "Their language? Seems to be a great lot of overlap between their dialect and those of the species out in the Jaxin galaxy. Prob'ly a coincidence. But I figure, that with the Translachew's why you understand 'em."

25

"So what's on your to-dos for today?" Bertram asked, as he and Rozz stepped from the bus into the shadow of the DiversiDine building.

Rozz said, "I suppose painting eyeballs on my eyelids and seeing how long I can sleep at my desk with no one noticing is out of the question."

Bertram stopped short as a biker blew by them. "I didn't know you could paint."

"It's eyeballs. It's a little black circle in a bigger brown circle in the biggest white circle. How hard can it be?"

"Yeah, I hear that's how Michaelangelo started." They maneuvered around a double-parked ambulance and paused at a "Don't Walk" sign.

"Now that you mention it," Rozz continued, "I was thinking if I can slip out, I might try to give Coach Dandy and the CEO 'upgrades' the way I did Laz Malone. See what kind of data we can pull from their machines."

"Ambitious," said Bertram. He was not feeling terribly ambitious himself but he was hoping he'd get a second wind. Or, at least, a light breeze. Ditto, he understood, was planning to spend the day doing additional product testing. Rollie had said he wanted to get some supplies. Bertram had no idea what

Tseethe was up to. And Bertram himself was completely out of productive ideas.

He was just about to reach for the lobby door, when the door met him going the other direction. And soon, there came the backside, back and then the more communicative body parts of someone in an EMS uniform. The parade continued with a person on a stretcher and a second EMT. "Coming through!"

Bertram held the door, never expecting he'd recognize the load on the stretcher. "Assistant Coach Truman?" He tried to recall her first name. "Er … Gail?"

"Who's Gail?" Rozz asked.

"My manager," said Bertram. The lady's vacant eyes stared up, unblinking, at the January sky. It looked like rigor mortis had already set in. The woman's arms were rigid, hands akimbo, fingers splayed and mouth open like she'd been put on freeze frame during a particularly animated diatribe. "Oh my God, she's —" Bertram turned to the nearest EMT. "Geez, you people could at least cover her face. Show a little respect."

"Mister, she's alive," said the EMT, in a tone that suggested this wasn't his first discussion about it. "Could you move out of the way?"

"Alive?" Bertram couldn't see how. He and Rozz trailed them to the ambulance. "But what's wrong with her? What happened?"

Their only answer was the resolute clang of the closing ambulance doors.

Inside the DiversiDine lobby, half of TLC appeared to be dispersing, in that very human combination of being concerned enough to see Gail Truman off, while also being totally up in her business. As Bertram and Rozz stepped into the elevator, Bertram's colleague Carole was regaling the group with this morning's excitement. " … Gail was just standing there, all excited about some ideas she said she had for the department. Talking ninety miles an hour about how she was going to increase productivity, improve customer service … How she could see all these new solutions she'd never noticed before and how everything was interconnected. I'd never heard her talk so much. And that's when it happened," Carole said. "She stuck."

Rozz and Bertram exchanged glances.

"What do you mean, stuck?" Rozz asked.

"Froze. Like a mannequin."

"Catatonia?"

"I don't know. It was so weird. The whole time she was talking, I kept wondering if she was on cocaine," continued Carole. "Does that happen when you're on cocaine? Or ... or meth? I mean, Gail didn't seem the type, but you never know. I saw part of this series on cable where this high school teacher got involved in —"

"Bipolar disorder," suggested someone else confidently from the back. "She was probably in the middle of a manic episode."

"I didn't know she had bipolar disorder," said Carole.

"She doesn't," said the voice, "but she might."

By noon, Bertram had discovered the only benefit to his supervisor going all Mount Rushmore on them was that it gave him the freedom he needed to embrace one very windy second-wind idea.

It arrived with his third cup of coffee and a phone call from Rozz.

"I didn't get in," she said.

He frowned and ignored the coaching line ringing in the background. "Where?"

"Anywhere. It was a total lack of In."

"Can you hang on a second?" Bertram disconnected the TLC line. "Go on."

"I started with Coach Dandy's office. I brought the flash drive, my upgrade excuse, even my red file folder. And what did I hear from the Coach's assistant? 'Thank you, dear, but the Coach's machine has already been upgraded.' Upgraded! Can you believe that?" Rozz's voice shot sharply through Bertram's headset. "I told the assistant that this was a brand new version. I even made up a number. Just made it right the hell up. And do you know what she told me?"

Bertram didn't know.

"She said, 'Let me check what the last version was.' She pulled up some crap spreadsheet that probably had her un-reimbursed medical on it or something, and said, 'Yes, that's the number I have here. Someone came by and did it yesterday. We're all upgraded. But thanks!' 'Thanks'?! Stone-cold lying to my face," she spat. "I hate liars."

Given her heat, Bertram figured it wasn't the best time to remind Rozz she'd invented the upgrade in the first place. "And how about what's-his-name? James Able?"

"Oh, Able's people didn't even give me a reason, other than it was 'against policy.' I talked to some assistant and in five minutes, I was wading, like, three assistants deep. I said I wouldn't even bother him. I'd do it when he wasn't in. But the more I pressed, the more flunkies flooded in. Waves of flunkies. It was like the opening credits of *Hawaii Five-0* only I was surfing people in wool suits. I can't believe the whole thing was a total waste of time. "

"You think so?" Bertram grinned to himself, as a tiny glimmer of inspiration began to take shape in his mind. "I think it's been helpful."

"Helpful?" Her voice cracked on the end of the line. "Did you even hear me? The red file folder failed, Bertram. I've got nothing left."

"Ah, but it's given me an idea," he said now. "I'm going to try something. I'll tell you about it after lunch."

The wind knifed through Bertram's secondhand overcoat and burned his ears as he stood on top of the parking garage that squatted diagonally from DiversiDine. On a warmer sunnier day, he imagined it was a nice view of the city. But today he had only one portion of the landscape in his sights.

Bertram flashed a smile at a lady with a briefcase as she emerged from a nearby Audi. At her second glance, he pretended to be searching his pockets for his exit ticket. He did this routine for a moment or two, until he heard the click-click-click of her boots heading to the elevators. Then he stood on the edge of the garage, scanning the corner offices of the neighboring building like some poorly-disguised thrift store Batman.

There, he thought. *This should be it. North side. Corner, top floor.* He squinted in the cold blue afternoon light. He grabbed his cell phone from his pocket and pulled up the camera, setting it to zoom. It was a cheap phone without many advanced features, but the camera was good enough and, with it, he could see straight in to the office of Coach Dandy.

The space reminded Bertram more of a hotel room than an office. It was appointed with lush woodwork and thick carpeting in DiversiDine's corporate colors. There was a mirrored panel on one wall with the logo etched into it. He saw a desk of shiny, dark wood and a glass-and-brass lamp that was currently turned off. The overhead lights, too, were off. The desk was clean — so clean it took a moment before Bertram realized why that seemed so strange.

Bertram scanned the rest of the floor along the building, then dialed Rozz. "Hey, it's me. Can you confirm for me what suite number Able's office is?"

"Give me a second," she said and he waited, his cold, numb fingers having an increasingly hard time holding the phone to his ear against the wind. "Suite fourteen-hundred," she said. "Why?"

"Hang on." Bertram eyed the floor once more through the phone zoom. It made sense that the CEO's digs were located in the other corner office. The blinds were closed. He shook his head. "That's what I thought. But I was hoping…"

"Bertram, where are you?"

"A room with a view. And that view is directly across from Coach Dandy and James Able's offices," Bertram said.

"Cool. Can you see them? Are they working today?"

Bertram laughed. "As far as Dandy goes, I'm pretty sure he's not working any day."

"Well, hell, Bertram, I don't think either of us'll be winning DiversiDine Employee of the Year ourselves," Rozz said.

"You don't get it," said Bertram. "I'd be willing to bet cash money that Coach Dandy has never once used this office." There was a weighty pause, probably because Rozz knew Bertram was innately cheap and did not place bets on anything less than a sure thing. Or at least something that got him a complimentary t-shirt. "You know that computer you wanted to upgrade?"

"Yeah?"

"He doesn't have a computer. His desk is completely clear."

"Well …" He could almost hear her wheels turning, "maybe he's a laptop guy and he takes it with him." But her tone lacked conviction.

"His desk also doesn't have a phone," Bertram said.

"Well, maybe he's a cell phone guy and his assistant takes all his other calls and —"

"Not so much as an intercom."

She sighed. "Okay, yeah. You've got me. It's a little weird."

"I know you've been going through those investor videos," Bertram said. "But is there any chance you could do some research on the Coach? I want to know why the face of DiversiDine has an assistant but doesn't actually use his own office."

"I'll do what I can," said Rozz. "Let's talk after work."

26

Rollie Tsmorlood woke to see, not the ceiling of his cabin on the Protostar 340-K, but the bright and complex patterns of a textile coming closer...

Closer...

Closer.

Hm, he thought groggily, *the elaborate weaving practices of the Lumocytes.* Though it was hard to be certain, what with it so fragging close to his eyeballs.

He sat up abruptly, seizing the item and wrenching it out of its operator's grasp. "Flamin' Altair, what are you up to?"

Ditto's expression shifted from surprise to annoyance to a wan hurt in a matter of seconds. "Well, I thought you might want a pillow." Her tone, too, sounded sad and injured. "I found it in your storage room. You just looked so uncomfortable there on that slab —"

"Deltan bed."

"—Deltan bed," she corrected, "I figured it'd be so much nicer if —"

"That's funny," Rollie eyed her narrowly, treating the cushion in question to a moment of flight, "because I do not now and never have used a pillow in my life. Which you should know, having Dar's memories. Why are you even in here?"

She let out an exasperated huff, like *he* was the problem in this whole breach of protocol. "I wanted to see if you were up. I was heading out. My first visit to Tryfe, and I didn't want to leave without experiencing some of the planet — beyond Heinrich's House of What's-It, of course."

He realized she *was* dressed like she was going out, and her normally gray complexion had been lightened, brightened and Tryfed-up using a pink makeup that probably had some fancy name for pink. With her mittens at the ready, he thought she even had a good chance of being Tryfe-passable. But, then, Ludlow seemed to have different, mysterious standards for these things.

"Okay," Rollie told her, hopping off the bed and flashing her a smile, "let's go."

"Um," she blinked, "what?"

"You said you wanted to see Tryfe," he said. "That's stellar. I've some errands to run, so we'll go together."

"Oh, now," Ditto waved an amply-fingered hand, "that's not necessary. I mean, you haven't even had breakfast. If you're not ready to leave, I'm sure I can —"

"Born ready and, as you can see, already dressed." He gestured to the clothes he'd had on yesterday. When you only slept forty-five minutes a day, it wasn't worth the time required to take your boots off. "Just need my gear." He grabbed his holster from a pile on the floor.

"Well ... uh ... What about Tseethe?" Ditto's gaze flicked to the shared wall between the captain's quarters and the guest cabin. "If we both leave, when Tseethe wakes up, he'll —"

"Tseethe?" Rollie laughed. He was fastening on his holster, then reached for his utility belt. "Tseethe once led a rescue mission to the Feegar war camp. He should be able to figure out how to occupy his own fraggin' self on Tryfe for a day."

"Oh, I'm sure he can, but —"

Belt secured, Rollie swung on his coat, was out of the cabin door and waiting at the main hatch a moment later. "Well?" He tapped his foot and motioned. "Are you coming?"

"When I said I wanted to see Tryfe, this was not what I had in mind," Rollie heard Ditto say. They were standing in the middle of MediaCheep downtown, as she stared uncertainly at the sign twirling over her head. It was a cartoon bird wearing spectacles and holding a volume of print twice its size.

"Ah, but Ditto, don't you see?" Grinning, Rollie gestured to the shelves, racks and bins of fascinating ideas and data of an ever-evolving people, "All of Tryfe is here!"

Her expression remained dubious. "You haven't been drinking enough lately, have you?"

He ignored the comment. "See this?" He motioned her to a case of used movies. "Here you have their faces, mannerisms and ways of living, all to be viewed in two dimensions only."

"So quaint," she said.

"And here …" He moved to a section of used music. "You have their voices, emotions and melodies — the poetry of the people, really — all packaged into stacks of squared circles."

He took a moment to linger over the work of a Tryfling called Johnny Cash. Rollie once bought this same album, along with a squared circle player. And while some of the lyrics were still unclear (he planned to ask Ludlow why "Sue" was such a handicap as a moniker), overall Rollie felt a connection to this Tryfe musicians' way of thinking. He pointed it out. "Tryflings like this fellah prove we're not so different after all."

He saw his companion try to hide a yawn, but that was okay; he'd saved the best for last. He directed her now between the walls of Tryfan books. "And have you ever seen so much print?" He drew a few dusty volumes from a shelf, merely a sampling of the treasures here. "You have their full historic, philosophical, scientific and recreational annals before you. Even Tryfling horticulture; surely that must pique your interest?"

Ditto nodded vaguely, one corner of her mouth turning up. The other couldn't be bothered. Yes, the woman wasn't piqued; she was placating. Realizing he could belabor the point no longer, Rollie tossed a nice assortment of print into a shopping basket and headed toward the register.

"You mean, you actually plan to *pay* for those?" Ditto whispered, a laugh rolling within her words. It was the first genuine amusement she'd displayed since they'd arrived.

"Aw, I've some Tryfe currency left from my last visit," he explained. "Might as well use it."

But the truth was, he didn't much like stealing from backspace people. It seemed unfair somehow. So he paid for his items and even got "change" back. What it had been changed into he didn't know. But then you couldn't go around *knowing* everything all the time, could you? It was one of the things Rollie enjoyed most about space travel. It kept you on your toes and humble.

With the purchases made, Rollie suggested some sightseeing might be more to Ditto's taste. So they emerged onto the city street and hadn't walked far before Ditto saw a sight that, indeed, caught the eye.

It was a parked Tryfe vehicle, sleek and sophisticated, low to the ground, four-wheeled and animalistic. Rollie couldn't recall the name of the creature it reminded him of, but he'd seen it once on a Tryfe program where a boisterous Tryfling male poked at cranky, fanged things.

It made Ditto breathless. "Have you ever piloted a vehicle like that?" she asked now.

Rollie admitted he had not. In fact, he'd never even ridden in what Tryfe people called a "car." And that struck him as both a surprise and a great fragging shame.

Pressing further down the street, Rollie highlighted other points of interest around the city, hoping to engage her. And he was just detailing the Ball of Feet game that was played in one of the stadiums, when a nearby female Tryfling, who'd been speaking rapidly into her phone, stepped to her parked car and stopped.

It was the look on the woman's face that first caught Rollie's attention. For one brief second, he feared it had something to do with them, perhaps shock at their appearance. (Always a concern when you were on a backspace planet.) But after a long, unmoving moment, Rollie saw the expression wasn't surprise. It was dazed and empty. Her remote, used seconds before to open her vehicle, hung frozen in her hand, her arm stuck at a crisp right angle. The arm with the phone remained pressed to her ear. She didn't blink. She didn't appear to breathe.

And when she began to move again, it wasn't the movement of the flexible and lively. It was the movement of the tipping-slowly-backwards-about-to-plummet-into-the-street.

Rollie dropped his bag and scrambled around the vehicle to catch the Tryfe woman, as a large multi-wheeled machine — something like a CosmosCorral for land — barreled straight toward her.

He grabbed the woman up under the arms but was surprised by her lack of bend. He'd expected to maneuver her over a shoulder but her dead weight was straight and stiff, like a Non-Organic Simulant whose joint lubricant system had failed and failed spectacularly. Ditto, he noticed now, had finally moved to action, grabbing the woman's feet. And together they settled the stranger onto the cold, damp sidewalk, just as the rolling machine hissed and stank and rattled by.

Rollie could hear a loud and frightened human voice projecting from the woman's phone. With some effort, he pried the device from the lady's fingers and said into it, "Your friend has had an accident. She's at —" He looked around. He knew Tryfe people liked to label everything so he was fairly certain this place, too, had one somewhere.

Ditto saw it first and pointed. "There."

Flamin' Altair, what language is that? Rollie did the best he could. "She's at Fuht Doo-KWESS-nee BUL-vud and STAHN-wix," he said. "Call the emergency people that do emergency things for your city immediately and send them here."

By now the Tryfe locals who had witnessed what happened were gathering thick around the woman. So Rollie grabbed his dropped bag, and he and Ditto melted out of the crowd. Rollie noticed the Tryflings dialing their phones kept mentioning, "Doo-KAYN Boulevard."

Doo-KAYN? ... He shook his head. There was always something new to learn, wasn't there?

By now, a Tryfe man had put a balled-up garment underneath the fallen lady's head, and a Tryfe woman performed some kind of medical check. Rollie was glad to see this was being successfully addressed by the woman's own people and so he moved to leave.

That was when he noticed the lady's car jarring away from the curb. His eyes shot to the woman's prone form ...

The remote was missing from her hand.

Rollie's touring companion, he noticed, was also suspiciously absent. So the moment the vehicle lurched his way, he dashed to it and leapt into the passenger seat. The car lurched back, then forward ... back, forward ... then jolted further down the road.

"What the frag are you doing?" he hissed at Ditto. With each lurch, his knees slammed into the dashboard.

"I think I got it." Ditto indicated a stick jutting out from between their seats. "D is for 'Do It' and R is 'Retreat.'"

"You cannot steal that woman's ... wheelie vehicle." He was so disturbed at the idea, he'd forgotten the word for "car." "Least not while she's a plank on the side of the road."

"*We* can't steal that woman's wheelie vehicle," Ditto corrected with a grin. "After all, you *are* in the copilot's chair. And since when do you have an issue with theft?"

Rollie scanned behind them to see if anyone saw them go. He couldn't tell, given the gathered crowd and the dramatic arrival of some sort of emergency medical craft. "Look, theft is fine, theft is stellar, made a fraggin' career of it. But I don't make it a habit of stealing from backspace people. And doubly not when they're freshly deadish. It's bad manners."

"Oh yes, you're the first one I look to for manners. Anyway, if she's deadish, she's got other things on her mind." Ditto reconsidered this statement, then shrugged. "Or not. Depending on how that works."

"We're supposed to blend in here," insisted Rollie, suddenly shouting, "Propel left! Left!" as a young Tryfling wearing a headset stepped blindly into the street. They just missed sending the poor youth flying. "If you'd watched any of those flat Tryfe films, you'd know how excited their scientists are to make non-Tryfe people like us all juicy and full of holes. Trust me, I've seen a few, and it never turns out good for our side."

He didn't think she was hearing him. She seemed to be more interested in the center lever panel, the PRND. "Which one of these do you think sends the wheelie vehicle into hover mode?"

"None of 'em," he snapped. "I assure you there's only the one mode." He couldn't believe he was even having this discussion. Mostly, because, there was a part of him that wished he'd thought of it first. "Look, pull over. Let me have a go," he said. "I'll, er, return the car to the lady."

"I can't. I don't know which one does that."

"P," he suggested. "P for 'Pull Over and Let Rollie Have a Go.'"

"What's the red light up there mean?"

"How should I know?" The sound of strain in his own voice surprised him. "I told you I'd never ridden in a car. Why would I even know that?"

"You knew about the Ball of Feet," she said. "Do you think it's a Klinko device? That red means welcome and affirmation?"

"Are you listening at all? Tryfe's backspace. Pretty sure they got no trade agreements with the Klinkos."

The screeching landing gear and sonorous tones coming from the intersecting traffic route suggested red was definitely not a symbol of welcome and affirmation here.

"Well," said Ditto, as they sped off down the road, "now we know that. Isn't that nice?"

"It's not nice to keep me waiting like this," Bertram told Rozz after work. "You said you did the research on Coach Dandy. You said you'd show me back at the ship. Okay, so we're here." He gestured. "What did you find?"

Rozz had already tossed her coat and bellied up to the Penumbra's computer. "You have to see it to believe it, dude."

While she loaded their internet app, Bertram dug into their take-out bag and grabbed his sandwich. A Primantis sandwich, a Pittsburgh classic involving an untidy but tasty combination of meat, cheese, French fries and cole slaw, all on Italian bread. "You want yours?"

She shook her head. "In a minute. Some things are bigger than food."

Either she'd lost all sense of perspective or this was very, *very* big. He removed a curious Cordelia from the counter, and unwrapped his sandwich.

He only got one bite in, before Rozz hit the Return button with a flourish and announced, "Bertram Ludlow? Meet Coach Dandy. Or should I say … Terrence Eugene Crittenden of the First Choice Talent Group?" Her smile blazed of triumph.

The web profile on the screen showed a guy in a number of headshots and full body photos. Some were in casual clothing, some in business attire. There were smoldering over-the-shoulder looks and breezy yet surprised "What's this tennis racquet doing in my hand?" poses. There were varying levels of facial hair. There were one or two rugged glamor shots.

Bertram read aloud: "Terry Crittenden is a photographer's muse, a director's actor, a man's man and a catalog's trouser buttock. He's the ideal host, making ever member of the audience feel like he's talking to them — or, at least, to the guy directly behind them. His versatility has earned him leading roles in the Humbridgetown Little Theater, in JingleSoft Tissue ads (Midwest territory) and in Honk-n-Hungry Drive-thru radio promotions. He's also lead motivational speaker for the *Thousand Shades of Awesome* personal development series."

Bertram wrinkled his nose as he took another look at the photos. "Coach Dandy is a b-list commercial actor?"

"Was," said Rozz, now tucking into her food with gusto. "I'd say he peaked in the mid-nineties."

"What makes you think —"

Mouth full, she pointed. The bottom left-hand photo featured Crittenden sporting an unconvincing middle-aged grunge look.

"Ah. Uni-bomber Chic," Bertram observed.

"I like the extra fur," Bootsy said from the back of Bertram's chair.

"How did you find these?" Bertram asked.

Rozz swallowed quickly. "It was the thirty-fifth page of my search engine image results."

"Thirty-five pages? Geez, no wonder no one knew about this. Don't most people just check the first two or something?"

Rozz wiped her mouth with a napkin. "I'd like to thank the entire pot of coffee I drank today, for my success in this killer research score. Because of its super caffeine jitters, I didn't even need to click the Next button; my hand just vibrated it forward."

CLANG! CLANG-CLANG!

"Though I may have taken it too far; I'm even hearing the vibrations now." Rozz squinted an eye and wiggled a finger in her ear.

"I think you're safe on that point. That sound," Bertram said, "means we have guests." And he leapt up to release the main hatch.

In a moment Rollie and Ditto swept in, causing the cats to scatter.

"I have navigated whole galaxies," the Hyphiz Deltan began, hatch closing behind them. "I have skimmed stars, danced in zero gravity and peered into the maws of massive black holes. I have crossed meteor fields and spanned solar systems. But I can safely assert that I will never, ever comprehend your fraggin' highway system in this Tryfan city." With that, Rollie dropped into a chair.

"What, you mean the Parkway?" Bertram asked. "Aw, that's easy!" Of course, he was lying; it wasn't intuitive at all, but it felt so good to have the home field advantage over Rollie for a change. "I bet I know what happened. You made the mistake of thinking Pittsburgh's on a grid. It's not. It's basically a triangle, see, with all the major highways routing around and — Wait." Bertram realized what the Deltan had said. "*Why* exactly were you guys on the highway?"

Rozz looked horrified. "*How* exactly were you guys on the highway?"

"Well ..." Rollie sighed and clomped his boots onto the built-in coffee table. " ... There was a thing with one of your cars."

"A 'thing,'" said Bertram uneasily.

"Oh, it's fine now. We returned it to where we got it." Rollie considered this further. "General vicinity, anyways."

"Nine hundred kroms, give or take," agreed Ditto, sitting on the arm of a chair. "And really, it wouldn't have even happened if we hadn't stopped to save the life of that Tryfe-human."

"It wouldn't've happened," Rollie corrected, shooting her a look, "if you hadn't six-fingered the remote from the lady while she was deadish." He folded his arms. "Not to say it wasn't an educational and surprisingly exhilarating ride. Least it was, once I got a go. And I must say, there is something satisfying about maneuvering through Tryfe traffic at max speed using only width and depth calculations."

"Okay, hold it right there," said Bertram.

"Deadish?" asked Rozz.

"Car rides?" asked Bootsy, peering from behind the coffee table.

"It's all very simple," said Ditto. "We were walking through your city when a Tryfe female who was getting into her 'car'," she looked proud of her new word usage, "froze up and tipped over in the street. We rescued her before she was squashed flat by one of your giant, multi-wheeled mass transit cars."

"You saved a woman from being hit by a bus and then stole her car?" asked Rozz.

"What do you mean by froze up?" asked Bertram.

"Y'know, stiff and dead-like," Rollie said. "We had to pry her phone from her fingers. Don't think we could've got her arm down, though, without busting it clean off."

Bertram and Rozz exchanged glances.

Rollie frowned. "Does that look mean this isn't a regular feature of being a Tryfling, then?"

"No, this is new," said Bertram. "My boss down at DiversiDine was hauled away this morning with exactly the same problem."

"Son of a Keeltsar," Rollie muttered, clutching at his hair

Rozz looked from Rollie to Ditto. "Could the jubies cause something like this? Say, super-concentrated jubies? Like, mega-jubies?"

"I know nothing of Tryfling physiology," Ditto said, "but that doesn't sound like the jubies."

Rollie nodded. "She's right. A bad reaction to the jubies? Hundreds of species go to Vos Laegos. And they even do parties with the guests breathing hundred percent jubies straight from an aerator. No issues I've heard of. Beyond irrational optimism about the table game odds, anyways."

"Then what about ZOT!?" said Bertram. His eyes went to Ditto. "You'd mentioned you were going to do some additional tests today. Did you learn anything more about ZOT!?"

"I, um, didn't quite get around to that," she said airily.

"It's the timing that makes me wonder," Bertram pressed. "Could you look into it? Analyze all the ingredients? Like ... now?"

"Well, I *could*," she said, "sure, but —"

CLANG, CLANG-CLANG.

Rozz walked her last bite of sandwich to the hatch button and this time Tseethe entered, grinning. "So who else spent the day transforming a few Tryfe coins into a pile at the casino and then blew his winnings in a store dedicated entirely to Tryfan tobacco products?" The grin dropped away as he sized up their tense faces. "What?"

27

There are a number of ways an enterprising lifeform can break into a secured apartment building. But the task becomes fairly straightforward when your entrance strategy involves eating the doorman.

And what an aftertaste! thought Feegar Commander Nom. It was the sign of too many Vos Laegon all-you-can digest buffets. So few lifeforms were properly mindful of how what they ate affected their flavor. In this case, the aromatic oils of flash-fried Klinko cuisine made the meat greasy and rancid. Nom knocked on the apartment door wishing for a nice digestive juice wine to burn that flavor out of his mouth.

But ... duty first.

It had not been easy tracking down anyone truly close to Captain Rolliam Tsmorlood. With so many of his connections having slyly fractured off from the Intergalactic Underworld, Tsmorlood's closest allies were practically ghosts and his genetic relations were strangers. Details beyond that were difficult to confirm. He was rumored to have been life-merged a number of times, but there were no formal records of that. There was no data on any resulting progeny. To that end, Hyphiz Delta kept its citizens' reproduction carefully regulated, with formal government permissions and medical activation procedures required before any little Deltans could be made. There was nothing to indicate Tsmorlood had ever pursued this, but he had also been banned from his home planet many years ago. Even his crimes archive had been compressed and vaulted at death.

Then the Feegar researchers had stumbled on their current target, a Krovlaftian cephalopoid named Fess Sigmin. Sigmin was a part of Tsmorlood's inner circle. He had fought in the Feegar Rebellion. And he had been hiding in plain sight in a comfortable Vos Laegos City high rise. That was his first mistake. The second was opening his door.

"Where is he?" Commander Nom demanded, as he and his team crashed into the home-unit, lasers pointed — teeth pointed, too. "Where is Rolliam Tsmorlood?"

"Dead," Sigmin told him. The cephalopoid's eyes were bright blue globes behind his thick, corrective eyewear. "Exiled to Altair-5. Everybody knows that." In a split second, one tentacle lashed out, whipping a gun from Corporal Gorj's grasp and firing it.

But the shot went wild, as a second team member subdued him from behind with a net.

"Where is Rolliam Tsmorlood?" pressed Commander Nom as Sigmin tumbled to the floor.

"Suck ink, pal!" spat the cephalopoid, along with an explosion of black fluid. It showered everyone and everything in a three krom radius.

Dripping, the Commander clicked his tongue in dismay while Sigmin lay there blinking, surprised, behind spattered spectacles.

Commander Nom laughed and rapped his chest, which made a hard, knocking sound. "You fool! Poison can't be absorbed through our exoskeleton shells. You wasted your neurotoxins. A shame, really. I hear the ink makes a fine sautée." He kicked the net of tentacles on the floor. "Where is Tsmorlood?"

"Go to Altair-5!"

"All right," began Nom, who'd been hoping for this sort of

stubbornness. Like fear, rebellion was a great natural seasoning. "You give us no choice. We know you're a part of the new Underworld regime. And your group has made it very clear how you feel about the Feegar people. If you won't give up Tsmorlood, then we will have to make you our first example. Then perhaps we'll gain your leader's attention." He turned to his new corporal. "Gorj? Go ahead."

At this cue, Gorj moved the net and lasered off one of Sigmin's larger tentacles. The cephalopoid let out a high frequency noise that made the pets cry out in the neighboring apartments. Gorj handed the Commander the tentacle, still dripping.

"Beautiful," said Nom and he brought it to the kitchen counter. "I *could* pop this into the Food Processing Unit," he mused, "but with something so fresh, let's see our other options, shall we?"

He peered into the kitchen's handy food stasis pod, rummaged around and withdrew a few choice ingredients. He looked through storage and found a large pan, then turned on the burner. He dropped in some mootaab butter, diced some bulbs of drem and added those, tossed in some veglimm leaves, sprinkled salt from the seas of Blumdec, then a splash of smorg wine. To this, he added the tentacle.

"Just lightly done on every side. Don't want to overdo," instructed the Commander, as his troop watched carefully. Nom had developed a reputation as a fine chef but he did not often give his subordinates the opportunity to see these talents in action. He plated his latest creation. "Now," he said, sitting before the dish and turning to his locally-sourced main ingredient, "where is Rolliam Tsmorlood?"

"Did ya check the Tarpits? Might find him at the bottom," growled Sigmin. "Look real close."

These Underworld lifeforms, Nom noticed, had a real knack for quick comebacks. He only hoped the same would not be said during digestion. The Commander opened his mouth wide ... wider ... widest and GLOMP!

Gone was the tentacle in one bite. The taste buds Feegars

have all the way down the esophagus informed him that it was delicious.

"Now what else should we make?" mused the Commander, rubbing his hands together. "The possibilities abound."

So they made Fess Sigmin seasoned, breaded and deep fried. They did baked cephalopoid. They did stuffed cephalopoid. They did cephalopoid *au gratin.* They tried cephalopoid chowder and a cephalopoid roll. By the cephalopoid croquettes, there was not much left to interrogate, but still they made the effort. By then, they were asking the location of Rolliam Tsmorlood's home unit.

"He never had one," rasped Fess Sigmin's beak. "He lived on his ship."

Nom was pleased with this bit of information. And it was good that it came when it did. Personally, he was stuffed, and while he could probably force himself to eat the second eyeball, the first one had a texture not worth repeating. "You mean the Protostar?" Commander Nom shook the net. "Do you hear me? He lives on the Protostar 340-K?"

But Fess Sigmin couldn't answer.

Fess Sigmin was gone.

"Should we bag it up and take the rest with us?" asked Captain Mau now.

"No," said Nom. "No take-home bags. I want this new Underworld organization of his to see just what happens when you interfere with the Feegars. Now — back to the ship. And put all troops on alert for that Protostar 340-K. They may think they control the GCU, but we will show them who's truly in charge."

28

"I can't believe it. Nothing!" said Bertram. They sat through sports and feel-good pieces, DiversiDine ads and car commercials. Yet there was not one word on the local evening news about a woman collapsing in the street downtown. Bertram exited Rozz's Tryfe television streaming app and it defaulted back to the *Heavy Meddler* Uninet channel. Bertram sighed into his chair.

"So?" Rollie glanced up from one of his new books — it was on zen gardening — and he shrugged. "The incident didn't make the news. That's a good thing, though, innit?"

Bertram exchanged glances with Rozz, then eyed him narrowly. "What makes you say that?"

"Could mean it turned out to be a bit of nothing and the lady's fine. Plus, *I'm* likely not being tracked down as an accomplice to car theft. So that makes for a pleasant evening." He grinned like a crocodile in a fish hatchery.

"It's bad," explained Bertram, massaging his now throbbing temples, "because it's two cases of the same weird symptoms on the same day — and those are just the ones we know of." Bertram could not understand how an otherwise smart guy could so often miss the truly important things to freak out about.

Apparently, Rozz didn't understand it, either, only she was a lot less subtle about it. "Yeah, seriously, dude, are you living on, like, your own little planet or something?"

Rollie said, "Yes. It's called Ejellan."

"Oh." Her cheeks pinked. "Right." She dodged the foot of a stretching, snoring cat and cleared her throat. "Well, the point is, if these aren't isolated incidents and DiversiDine's behind them, then the shit's already hitting the fan — and we might not have time to duck."

At Rollie's expression, Bertram translated, "We realize Ditto's over there on your ship with Tseethe, working on that ZOT! analysis. But she said she'd have it done by, what, later tonight? Tomorrow at the latest? We're just wondering if that'll be soon enough."

Rollie's face darkened now, his smile melting away. He looked at his hands for a moment. "You know, er, Ludlow," he said quietly, "if I was you, maybe I wouldn't hang all my hopes on these ZOT! results." He looked up, meeting Bertram's gaze with a too-blue concern. "If I was you, maybe instead I'd focus my energies more on —" But his attention had been drawn to the Uninet screen and when Bertram turned, he saw why.

"… And here you can see the presenters formerly known as the Seers of Rhobux being escorted out of the studio on Daglann-Da," the *Heavy Meddler* newscaster was saying. "The explosion occurred during filming of the Seers' popular Uninet program, *ForeCast*, the pre-cognitive talk show where celebrities discuss their most pivotal acting roles that haven't happened yet. Studio damage has temporarily halted show production and minor injuries were reported among the audience and staff. The show's elderly stars have been taken to Beddsyde Manor for observation."

The image showed three ancient bony, glowing lifeforms in white nighties being ushered into the daylight from a smoking building to a small waiting runabout. Their entourage carried sun parasols.

"The explosion was believed to have been set by this lifeform," the newscaster continued, "Jane Manners of Tryfe."

Bertram leapt to his feet. "Tryfe?"

Footage cut to a mugshot of a blond Earth woman with a bewildered expression that Bertram, in many ways, understood. "Manners is wanted for the devastating mass escape from Mawdank Roving Confinement Center, an explosion at a Translachew factory on Sarulia and stealing over five hundred yoonies worth of merchandise from a Shop-o-Drome on Golgi Beta. She was last seen leaving DiversiDine Studios on Daglann-Da and her current location is unknown. If you see Jane Manners, or have information on her whereabouts, please contact —"

Bertram put the station on mute. "Soft drinks with jubies, frozen people and now there's a Tryfe woman on a rampage?"

"Ah. Yes," said Rollie in the same tone one might note the laundry buzzer going off. "Forgot to mention that."

"You forgot to mention there's a woman from Tryfe blowing things up around the GCU," said Bertram.

"Well, been a lot going on, hasn't there? Ah, but you should've seen the Translachew factory footage ..." His voice was filled with admiration. "Half the city's probably still stuck together. Don't suppose she's anyone you know?" He looked hopeful.

"No," said Bertram flatly.

"Sorry," said Rozz. She was under two cats now, both of them stretched out, each with a foot in her face.

Rollie shrugged a shoulder. "Yeah, that's what I told Tseethe," he said. "A bit curious how she got into the GCU, though. Surely the second season of *There Goes the Galaxy* hasn't come round already, has it?"

Bertram Ludlow didn't need to answer.

"Hm," said the Deltan. "Time does fly."

Saturday morning brought promise and plans. Ditto said she'd have the ZOT! results any time now. Rozz wanted to research the product's performance in independent studies.

Rollie shocked everyone, agreeing to sift through Laz Malone's data for new info. Tseethe planned to comm a friend of a friend of a friend at DiversiDine's GCU headquarters about the company's Tryfe branch. And Bertram was determined to get an update on Gail Truman's health.

They would compare notes by three.

By three fifteen, Bertram had learned Gail Truman was still in the hospital, frozen and flummoxing her doctors. Rozz found no independent studies on ZOT, though DiversiDine's own studies pretty much called it the safest, tastiest, mostest cleverest beverage since the Garden of Eden public water fountain. Rollie reported that Laz Malone had sent no fewer than three vague emails to James Able's office requesting a conference call that never took place. And Ditto and Tseethe both begged for more time, with Ditto wanting to run additional tests and Tseethe waiting for a return comm.

Investigation montages are a whole lot more productive in the movies, Bertram thought.

There was, of course, one avenue of investigation that they had not tried, largely because until now, they hadn't been quite that desperate. Bertram dug around in his coat pocket and withdrew a dog-eared business card. The card was made of cheap paper, had obvious perforation marks and had been run through an ink jet printer. It read simply: "Pull back the curtain." There was a phone number underneath.

On impulse, Bertram grabbed his cell phone and dialed.

A recorded male voice on the other end of the line said, "You know what to do."

Bertram waited for the beep. He could feel his team watching him, curiously. "Hi, this is uh … Bacontini. I believe you said we should call if … um …"

There was a clattering sound and for a moment, Bertram thought he might have been disconnected. Then a voice said, "Bacontini? I knew we'd be hearing from you. Are you ready to pull back the curtain?"

"We're ready," Bertram said.

"Good. Then be at the old FanCee Fruits building in the

Strip District at eight tonight. Press the door orange."

"Door orange? What does that —?"

But the man hung up.

✧

Pittsburgh's Strip District is not actually a neighborhood devoted to the art of metal poles and spangly g-string removal — no matter what out-of-towners may expect. For the most part, the area includes a mile of wholesale warehouses perched along the Allegheny River at the edge of downtown. During the day, visitors find bustling marketplaces, unique restaurants, ethnic foods and souvenir couture of the black-and-gold jester hat variety. In the evenings, the area puts out the welcome mat to live music, microbrews, fine dining, and yes, a little something for the pasties-twirling fan.

The old FanCee Fruits building sat beyond this, away from the evening strobe lights and the wafting scent of food, its name written in art deco letters ghosted into the building's brick. Bertram, Rozz and Rollie approached it, swift and silent. Their team was a few people light this evening. Ditto still had tests she wanted to finalize, and Tseethe was just so sure his DiversiDine contact would comm the Protostar any second. Bertram had to admit, he was glad they were otherwise occupied; tonight's meeting would be a lot less risky without them.

He glanced at his watch. "It's eight," he said and moved to the door, because he had this idea that corporate spies should be punctual, as well as stealthy.

The building's exterior looked like it hadn't changed much since its original 1920s construction. This was further evidenced by a bas relief anthropomorphic orange standing in cast iron along the door frame. The company mascot wore spats, carried a cane and sported a jaunty tophat.

"Ah …" murmured Bertram, for sometimes enlightenment came in easy-to-peel sections, "'press the door orange.'" So he did, aiming straight for the fruit's navel. Somewhere a bell rang.

A panel slid open, revealing eyes and part of a nose. "Who is it?"

"Bacontini."

The panel slid shut and the door screeched open.

Bertram recognized their host by the mop of red, curly hair and the goatee. "Welcome!" he said, smiling from Bertram to Rozz to Rollie. "Come in, quickly, come in."

He closed the door swiftly behind them.

Bertram extended his hand. "By the way, my name's Ber —"

The man stopped him. "No real names. It's safer that way. And you," he said, grinning, "can call me Deezle." He motioned. "Let me introduce you around our crib."

The "crib" reminded Bertram of what the Little Rascals clubhouse would have looked like if they'd been thirty-three, tech-savvy, had a little disposable income and were sucked into the twenty-first century by an ill-advised plot device. The tables were all made of salvage. Computer equipment covered most surfaces and a sixty-five-inch widescreen dominated the room's feature wall. Thrift store sofas were staggered like Anglo-Saxon burial mounds. Among these barrows stood two chairs, each shaped like an upheld hand. Lighting involved a range of lava lamps, two repurposed street lamps and one plastic yard Santa with a green alien face. Further ambient light shone from an old IC Light "Beware the Penguins" collectible and an animated Heineken sign where the beer forever poured.

Deezle brought his guests to the folks who were already sprawled cross the furniture. "Bacontini, Pinky, Stretch?" The man was creative on his feet, Bertram had to give him that. "Meet Zoltan, Krestor and Chuck."

Rozz squinted. "Isn't Crestor a drug to treat high cholesterol?"

Krestor, a tall doughy guy in a broad-brimmed leather hat and an oilskin coat said, "Different spelling. Anyway, I had it first. I suspect the pharmaceutical industry has my home bugged."

"Mm." Rozz's indulgent smile came out weak and unconvincing.

"So you all work There do you?" asked Chuck, a young woman in cornrows, a Minecraft sweatshirt and a vintage army jacket three sizes too big for her.

Bertram asked, "You mean Diversi —"

The shushing noise that came from their hosts sounded like a busted water line. "No-no. Remember. No names," said Deezle.

"We call it 'The Company,'" advised Chuck.

"Mm," Rozz said again.

Bertram was starting to wonder how desperate he'd been to contact these people.

But Bertram wasn't the only one questioning the success of this encounter. "Do not like!" piped up Zoltan now. "I do not like it. I feel very uncomfortable." He was a skinny, bearded guy in a seventies paisley dress shirt, with chunky rings featuring skulls and dragons and a nose ring with a chain that wrapped to his ear. "Their learning curve is too great. Abort, abort!"

"Zoltan, cool it," said Deezle. "I heard them at Heinrich's. They're on the level."

Zoltan looked unsure as he toyed with a pewter griffin that had swallowed most of his thumb.

"Have a seat." Deezle motioned his guests into the vacant seating.

Bertram sat gingerly on a bowing couch with a *Dark Side of the Moon* throw over it. He was afraid what might happen if he leaned back.

"Can I offer you some Doritos? Flavor-blasted Goldfish? A Red Bull?" their host asked.

"A red bull?" This was Rollie, puzzled, sitting in one of the hand-shaped chairs. "Is that some sort of ritualistic sacrifice? I read of that once."

"It's a beverage," Bertram said quickly. "One that would exacerbate your medical condition."

"Ah." Rollie smiled tightly. "Pass."

Bertram turned to Deezle. "I called because we want to hear your information on Di — er, The Company. Deezle, you'd said you had evidence the CEO is …" He wasn't sure he was allowed to say this, either.

"An extra-terrestrial?" supplied Deezle eagerly. "Alien? Lifeform from outer space pretending to be one of our own?"

"We call 'em Posers," volunteered Chuck.

"And you see a lot of Posers, do you?" asked Rollie.

"They're everywhere," interjected Krestor, "worming their way into positions of power."

Chuck said, "Usually they're so powerful and so known for their dynamic, aggressive personalities that no one really wants to talk to them directly."

"They work through assistants. Intermediaries," said Deezle. "That's how they stay safely behind the curtain. How they maintain their illusions."

Rollie leaned back in the hand and crossed a leg. "So The Company's CEO is a Poser, too, eh?"

Deezle nodded. "Oh, he's a Poser, all right. The biggest Poser around."

"And your proof?"

"Video evidence." Deezle emphasized this with the crunch of a corn chip.

Rozz Mercer laughed. "You mean like Nessie and Bigfoot?"

The guy's expression clouded. "You doubt our sincerity?"

"Your sincerity I buy," she said. "But, dude, I went through two years worth of videos on The Company's website. If anything were noteworthy there, it'd only be because someone was giving out the Annual Financial-Communications-As-An-Insomnia-Cure awards and this guy was a shoe-in."

"Uh-huh …" Deezle's mustache turned up in a nacho-cheese-dusty smile. "Then clearly, Pinky, you have not seen this." He cued Krestor, who grabbed a remote from the sofa arm and pressed play. The giant television screen came to life and, on it, the image of James Able, large and in charge.

To Bertram it looked like the videos Rozz had studied. The only difference was a "Happy New Year" banner spanning the background.

"Journey with me back in time to January first, one year

ago," said Deezle. "The Company's New Year's address to the city. They claimed it was being broadcast live. Then this happened."

Krestor advanced the video and hit play again. There, Able talked about celebrating corporate milestones, none of which seemed to involve enslaving the population with soft drinks or turning people into unique coat trees or anything. From an alien overlord perspective, it was all pretty dull.

But as soon as the segment finished and the screen went dark, their hosts reacted like they'd just seen an overtime hat trick at the Stanley Cup playoffs. There was clapping, cheering — even a fist-bump involved. A *fist-bump*. It was like something awesome had occurred and Bertram and his group had completely missed it.

Deezle noticed the lack of reaction from his guests with some surprise. "Well?" he said.

"Well," Bertram said, "is that it?"

"Seriously." Rozz gnawed at a fingernail. "What's the big deal? It's a speech. I was hoping for at least some blurry footage of two pie plates glued together on a string."

Rollie was already on his feet, coat swirling around his boots. "Right: I'm out of here." He turned to Bertram and Rozz. "Saw an intriguing little tavern down the street. Anyone care to join me?"

Rozz grabbed her purse and stood. "I'm in."

"Fine," said Deezle with a grand gesture to the door. "Go. Turn your backs on The Truth. Mock the Unseen over a pint of watered-down Weizenbock. We won't stop you. But before you do, let me ask you one question. If you knew you were seconds away from a mind-blowing revelation, from being witness to information that would change how you see your life, your planet, possibly the universe … would you still walk out that door?" And before they could respond, he whirled on Krestor and shouted, "Slow motion replay!"

Krestor resumed the controls and the video rolled until Deezle commanded, "Now! Pause now!"

The time stamp was at thirty-seven seconds and James Able

was frozen on the screen, mouth in mid-sentence. Deezle's eyes shone in the light. "Prepare to be astounded."

Thirty-eight seconds into the film revealed a wavy streak. Bertram had noticed it before. He'd guessed it was a small issue with the digital copy, something wrong with the download. Though the more he looked at it, there was something odd, because the glitch only covered the CEO and not the whole frame.

Then they hit thirty-nine seconds, frame twelve, and everything changed.

Before them was a lifeform not of this Earth. His skin was greenish-gray. He had purple flowers around the temples and green petals projecting like a leafy crown. If Bertram had not been an experienced traveler in the GCU, he would have believed it was spliced footage, some makeup and special effects wheeze designed specifically to delude and defraud. But Bertram Ludlow knew better. He recognized the look, the clothes. This guy was from the planet Ottofram.

And he wasn't Eudicot T'murp.

"Who the frag is that?" asked Rollie, as if reading Bertram's mind. The figure was a lot younger than T'murp and had a moustache that looked like bean sprouts.

Krestor advanced the video to thirty-nine seconds, frame seventeen, and there was James Able looking like a Tryfling again and not like the Giant Eagle supermarket salad bar.

"That, Stretch," Deezle grinned, "is the Poser behind The Company's CEO."

Rozz sank onto the sofa. "Holy shit, how did you come across this?"

First, there was a renewed round of fist-bumping. Then Deezle explained, "We knew The Company was evil. We just didn't have the specifics. Zoltan uncovered it when he was going through the footage for the right screen capture."

"I wanted it for a humorous meme for our *Behind the Curtain* e-newsletter," said Zoltan, noodling with the chain of his nose-ring and looking anywhere but at them. "I find humor to be an important unifier. I have a finely-tuned sense of whimsy."

Deezle said, "We think the entire CEO façade is some kind of computer-animation with a timed overlay that snagged."

That really wasn't too far off. It was a holowatch disguise. But Bertram wasn't going to tell his hosts that.

Chuck said, "It wasn't live very long before The Company caught it and pulled the video from their site. They replaced it with a new one. But," she beamed, "we'd already made a copy."

Krestor turned off the video and flipped over to broadcast programming. On the giant television, several people ran around the woods in the dark, whooping hopefully to the local Sasquatch population.

"So you can see why we've been keeping an eye on The Company," continued Deezle. He grabbed an energy drink for himself from a mini-fridge and passed around another bowl of snacks. "Aliens are among us, friends. For us, it puts a whole new perspective on what happened during the Swirling Times."

Bertram accepted some pretzels and passed the bowl. "And that is …?"

"That they were the beginning of an invasion. An invasion our government didn't want us to know about because they're complicit. They sold us out. And now the aliens are here and the Posers have control."

"Sold you out for what, though?" Rollie asked, forgetting the "you" should have been "us."

Fortunately, Deezle didn't seem to notice. "Medical knowledge. Technology maybe. I mean, 3D printing? Cordless vacuums that never lose suction? The stuffed burger press?" He gave them all a pointed look. "Those can't be ours."

"And this is the only footage you've seen like this?" Bertram asked.

"So far," said Deezle. "We monitor everything now. Everything we can, anyway. It takes time. We've developed some programs to help automate the scanning, but obviously we can't cover it all. We have day jobs. Well …" Deezle looked at Zoltan, "most of us do."

Zoltan reddened and said through his teeth. "I told you, I am looking for a position commensurate with my capabilities."

Chuck added, "We also work with volunteer groups. They report in from various locations around the world, so we have round-the-clock coverage. If anything comes up, we'll be the first to know it."

Rollie leaned against a sofa. "And beyond that, what's your plan?"

"Plan?" Chuck asked.

"Yeah, tactics. You say you know there's been an invasion. You've identified at least one of the invaders. What's your strategy?"

"Well," Deezle looked to the other group members. "Like we said, we have a network..." He thought a moment and his face brightened. "We have the enewsletter."

"Oh, and buttons!" Chuck held up the lapel of her nearby coat. One button was a stereotypical green alien head surrounded by a circle with a line through it. The other said, "Pull Back the Curtain."

"Buttons ..." Rollie grumbled and shook his head. "So no emergency planning. No defense strategy. No end game. And I'm presuming, no military training among the lot of you?" They shifted uncomfortably as a collective.

"My dad was a veteran," volunteered Chuck.

"I have bunions," whispered Zoltan almost inaudibly, looking like he wanted to be eaten alive by the sofa.

"So even if an overt takeover becomes likely," continued Rollie, "you've no means to oust leadership or stage any sort of rebellion."

"Oust? Rebellion?" Deezle's voice came out high and stressed. "Stand down, Slikk Slaughter! You forget: we don't know what they're up to. We thought having some contacts on the inside of The Company would be a start. We could share intelligence. Root out their strategy and plan accordingly. It's just that so far, we haven't had a lot to go on."

Bertram knew the feeling.

"The real question is: now that you've seen our evidence, are you willing to work with us?" asked Deezle.

"We meet Tuesdays," said Krestor.

"And Fridays," added Chuck.

"And Fridays, though that's more of an informal thing."

Chuck laughed. "Oh, Deezle just doesn't want to be home because his mom has friends over for canasta."

"You think it's funny," said Deezle, "but she starts pouring the Mojitos? That shit gets totally cray-zee." And he drew a Z in the air with his finger.

Zoltan nodded with fear in his eyes.

"We usually go over the updates that have happened since Tuesday and then order pizza and watch movies," said Chuck.

"*Day of the Triffids*," said Krestor. "This Friday. You'll come?"

"Uh ..." Rozz's eyes had glazed over.

"We'll consider it," said Bertram. And as he rose to go, Rozz and Rollie were swift on his heels.

"We need you, Bacontini." At the door, Deezle rested a hand on Bertram's shoulder. "You are our only hope."

"You know, about that," began Bertram, "technically, I wasn't even the one who ordered that first bacontini. I —"

"Stretch?" This was Chuck, trailing Rollie out. "I'm curious: where are you from?"

"From?" Rollie's eyebrow twitched. "Er, why do you ask?"

Oh God, Bertram winced. He should have seen this coming. It was so hard to predict what Rollie would do at any given moment, even under normal circumstances. This could get very dangerous, very fast. Bertram was trying to figure out exactly how to intervene, when the answer came to him in the form of the lit Heineken sign. "Hey, have you ever been to Holland?" he asked, stepping between Rollie and Chuck.

"Sadly, no." She shrugged. "On my list, though."

"He's from Holland," Bertram said.

"Oh." She frowned and looked up at Rollie. "That's funny. It's just I'd had a college exchange program in the UK. And the accent sounds really —"

"Yeah, well. I been all over," Rollie said. And he smiled. A nice smile, too, not the one that made you want to bust out the garlic and holy water. "Good night."

And before another word could be said, they'd slipped past the top-hatted orange and into the night.

29

"I'm from Holland," Rollie grumbled as they walked from the bus stop toward the ICVs. He'd been unusually quiet during the ride back to Shadyside. "I'm ... Hollandaise now."

Bertram stifled a laugh. "Wherever you heard that word? Just: no."

"Well, I wouldn't know, would I?" he said, with a twist of his mouth. "It's why I've always kept things vague with Tryfe people. But then you busted in making me Hollandian."

"Dutch," said Bertram. "You'd be Dutch."

"Dutch?" The crease in his forehead was even deeper than the scar there. "How the frag does that work?"

Rozz laughed. "Rollie, that's the beauty of it. Hardly anyone knows. This is the U.S. Not knowing anything about the rest of the world is practically a badge of honor here. You'll be golden."

"Look," Bertram ticked the items off on his fingers, "tulips, windmills, wooden shoes, legalized drugs and prostitution. That's all the average person here knows. It's a non-issue."

"So Holland's like Vos Laegos but with impractical footwear and wind power?" A jagged smile spread across Rollie's face. "Sounds worth a visit."

The Penumbra came into view now. Rollie's Protostar,

however, had been cloaked and tucked further up the slope by the woods. They'd reasoned that two "artworks" suddenly appearing on the Institute's lawn was pushing their luck. And there was less likelihood of its being run into by a groundskeeper or cold-cocking a jogger, if it were somewhat off the beaten path.

As they grew closer, Rollie drew the Protostar's remote from his pocket and hit the access button. But his smile fast faded.

"That's odd …"

He hit the remote again and they all scanned the property. It *was* odd. There was no crack of light. No movement. No hum.

He rattled the remote, the universally-proven technique for fixing all delicate technologies, second only to turning things off and on again. He pressed the button.

His careful ministrations had not worked.

He flashed a worried look to Bertram and Rozz, then dashed up the hill. In a second, he was groping around the area like a mime in a windstorm.

By the time Bertram and Rozz caught up, that's when they heard the groan. About twenty feet from where the ship should have been, Tseethe Tsardonee lay drooped against a tree.

Cursing under his breath, Rollie moved to help, but his friend was covered in a light layer of snow and seemed to be boneless at the moment. His legs wouldn't stand, his arms flopped limp and his head lolled to the side. It looked like a case of a serious stunning.

"Dar," Tseethe rasped. "Can't … believe it … Dar."

"Dar?" Rozz frowned. "What's a dar?"

Rollie made an irritated noise. "Ditto's original."

"Original what?" she asked.

"Can't … believe …" continued Tseethe. "Dar."

"Yeah, well …" Rollie muttered to him.

At this, Tseethe's eyes flew open wide. "You … *knew* …" The tone held betrayal and the rasp of ingested weather. "Knew …"

"Okay, I had some suspicions," Rollie admitted, a flicker of guilt crossing his angular features. "Knew it for sure when she stole the car. Oh — and when she might have tried to smother me in my sleep."

"What?" Bertram and Rozz made this a chorus.

Rollie waved a hand like that was just too much fluff to even bother with. "Point is, after that, I commed Ditto's warehouse on Walter. Guess who was still there, working away in the fields, blissfully unaware her portable analysis gear got six-fingered?" Apparently, the question was rhetorical, because he went on with no pause for breath. "Anyways, Dar did seem to take a fancy to her role as chemist. And I'd figured if she enjoyed her Tryfe holiday enough, she wouldn't do anything rash."

"So much for that," said Bertram.

Rozz frowned. "So, what, Ditto's got a twin?"

"Ditto *is* the twin," said Rollie, hoisting Tseethe to his feet. "Ditto's a clone. Look, it's in the name, Rozz. It's not fancy... Can someone open the Penumbra?"

Bertram watched for traffic, which was minimal at this hour, and he lowered the ramp to his ICV. Moments later they had settled Tseethe into one of the cabins on a cot. Bertram went to get some extra blankets, while Rozz searched their supplies for something to ease Tseethe's post-stun hangover. Both of them remembered their last stunnings vividly and the recovery was always a dilly.

"How well do you even know this Dar?" Bertram called, grabbing two woolen covers from storage.

"Not very," said Rollie. "I mean, there was the life-merger, but ..."

This was a jolt. "Whose?"

"Well, mine," Rollie said plainly.

Bertram stopped short in the hatchway and stared at him. "You were *life-merged* to Ditto's original?"

"For about three parsecs, Ludlow." He was checking Tseethe's vital signs. "In my opinion, it shouldn't even count." Rollie took one of the blankets from Bertram and tossed it over Tseethe.

"Okay, now I *have* to ask." Bertram had been getting

fragments of Rollie's personal life for a while now and most of it was baffling. "How many times have you been life-merged?"

"Uh …" Rollie seemed to do math in his head before he answered. "Sixteen — no, seventeen times. Technically. Since Meena was twice." He grabbed the second blanket and spread it out. "But the point, Ludlow, is not that my past judgment has been lacking. I acknowledge my failures in that area. The point is Dar stunned Tseethe and stole my fraggin' ship."

There was not much more Bertram could say. The man clearly had his priorities.

At this moment, Rozz entered with both the electrolyte anti-stun mixture and their new roommates, the cats. The latter busied themselves inspecting the patient, then got into a debate over whether to employ an advanced regimen of limb-kneading or lying helpfully on Tseethe's head.

A buzz sounded from the other room, because when you're already dealing with one situation, what's one more, really?

Bertram dashed in to see the face of a small, pale man with navy blue hair, sunglasses and a natty beard. He projected sideways from the vis-u. (Bertram kept forgetting to get that thing fixed.) "Hello? Is Rollie there, by any chance? This is Wilbree. Hello?"

"We're here, Wilbree," said Bertram as Rollie joined him before the screen. Wilbree had commed once or twice in the past. He was the only person who consistently introduced himself to people he already knew.

"Hello, how are you? I hope you're all doing well," said Wilbree formally.

"We're not too fraggin' good, mate," said Rollie, "so let's hear why you've commed."

"I have two points of information I wanted to draw to your attention," Wilbree said. "The first is when I commed the Protostar just now, a woman picked up who was probably not you."

"Can't put anything past you, can we?" said Rollie.

"She wasn't very friendly; she disconnected me. It made me think she might have stolen your ship. And so I thought it bore mentioning, if you didn't already know."

"Yes, we know," Rollie's hands were clenched. "We know. And the second thing?"

"Fess has been dismantled."

"What?!" Rollie and Bertram exchanged glances. Bertram had met Fess a couple of times and liked the guy. Bright, brave, loyal ... he was the kind of person you wanted for a right hand — er, tentacle — man.

"Rollie, there's not much left," Wilbree said. "Just a beak, an eye and some brain thingies. Lucky I came by when I did. I gathered what I could and rushed him to Vos Laegos City General in a baggie. They've got him in a tank now, to see if anything can be done. Oh, and there's another thing. So I was wrong. There were three things."

Rollie's whole posture had become tense. "Get on with it."

"All his cooking pots and pans were used, and most of them seemed to have a bit of him in them. I didn't bring those bits to VLC General, though. They were saucy."

Rollie couldn't seem to focus. He ran a shaky hand through his hair.

Bertram asked, "You don't think this was an Underworld hit, do you?" Like Rollie, Fess had left the Society in a rather dramatic fashion.

Rollie shook his head. "No, mate." His voice was very quiet. "Only one species in the GCU does a spread like this."

And before Bertram could ask who he meant, Rozz sneered, "Feegars."

"That's right," said Wilbree. "That's what the note said."

Rollie's head snapped to the vis-u. "What flamin' note?"

"Oh. Four things." Wilbree, pushed up his sunglasses and moved out of the way. On the window of Fess' apartment behind him, written in Fess' own ink, it said:

Rolliam Tsmorlood:
Thanks for the gift basket. It was very useful.
See you soon.
— The Feegars

Rollie winced.

"The Feegars, Rollie?" Bertram's heart picked up pace. "Is this because of that freighter you were talking about?"

"That and ... I might have possibly, slightly made something a bit worse."

Rozz looked pale. "If this is the way they do thank you notes, I'd hate to see what they do for a centerpiece."

"They do this, Rozz. Always so very much more of this." Rollie sounded tired. He took a deep breath, then readdressed the vis-u. "Wilbree, get the word out. Tell everyone you can think of what happened with Fess. Tell 'em to keep their eyes sharp. I don't want anyone else getting hurt."

"I'll do that," said Wilbree.

"Keep me updated on Fess' status, too."

"I will."

"And contact the Coalition of Planets. Tell them what happened to Fess. Take images of the note and send 'em to them."

"Okay," Wilbree frowned, "but won't they wonder?"

"About ...?"

"Why the Feegars are leaving a note for you."

Rollie exhaled. "Fess is in soup, mate! I doubt they'll care about the actual correspondence. It's all about the mode and the murder, innit? There's a signed flamin' note!"

"I mean with that name," said Wilbree. "You're dead, you see. Is it okay if the Coalition knows you're alive?"

Rollie thought about this, groaned and kicked a cabinet.

"Rollie?"

"You're right." His fingers clenched and unclenched. "Absolutely blasted fraggin' right. I'm dead. Stellar. No Coalition. I'll figure another way."

"Okay," said Wilbree. "Just the contacting everybody we know and keeping you updated, then."

And he signed off.

The light had barely faded from the vis-u screen before the Hyphiz Deltan was dialing another number into the communicator's keypad.

"Who are you comming?" asked Bertram.

Rollie's own voice sounded from the speaker system: "You've reached the vis-u for Levvyn Moonshot. Please leave a message and I'll answer your comm as time and inclination permits. Thank you."

"Dar: pick up," said Rollie. "Pick up, Dar. I know you're there."

Dar did not pick up. The device beeped.

"Dar, the Feegars are looking for me, which means they'll be looking for my ship," said Rollie. "I will get the Protostar back, that I promise you. But I'd rather it wasn't decorated with your guts. *Not* because you have not earned the experience. But there are less messy ways to handle the payback you deserve. You'd best hope I find you before the Feegars do. Enjoy it while you can. And *paar too*." It was the first time Bertram heard a Deltan goodbye sound so much like a threat.

And with that, Rollie cut the connection.

30

It was *so* good to be heading back into the GCU, thought Dar Balisong. A little downtime was fine — refreshing, even. But only when there was something interesting on the agenda. Tryfe was *boring* and Dar had no clue why Rollie Tsmorlood — who exhibited a reasonable sense of adventure most of the time — was so fond of the place. Thankfully, her days of architectural tours, backspace history lessons, print and squared circles had drawn to a close. The Universe was filled with bright possibility and she had a shiny, new ship.

Well — she frowned at the smudged cabinets and scuffed floors of the Protostar 340-K — *Not shiny.*

… The antique plumbing, the obsolete appliances …

Or new.

But a ship!

Her eyes lingered now on the hotplate, the rigid furniture and the panel where every other Interplanetary Cruise Vessel in the GCU housed its backup life support. This one contained a mini-bar.

Sort of a ship, she admitted.

But ship enough so she could start where she'd left off before her unfortunate detour to Mawdank.

Speaking of which, she tapped her temple three times and

pulled up her in-eye micro-console. She didn't have much stored in there right now. Just her address book and long overdue To-Do list. She chose the list, then blinked down the bullet points. *Let's see, where were we?*

- Kill the Jarendi Premier.
- Off the High Honcho of Hoorendus-2
- Pick up dry cleaning
- Implement non-fatal stabbing of executive editor of *Dogstar* Unimag
  - Miss heart by hair's breadth.
    - Find out location of heart.
- Get new fake ID
- Rent home-unit in nice solar system
- Assassinate Rolliam Tsmorlood

This last point had been moved around on the list several times in the past Universal decade. It wasn't *precisely* her fault, of course. Things just kept conspiring to keep the man alive, like a slightly skewed laser sight or him waking up the second before a good smothering.

But Dar Balisong made it a policy to never dwell on failure. Instead, she lingered on one item halfway up the list. The dry cleaning. She hoped the molecular cleaners in Vos Laegos City had held that outfit of hers. It was her lucky jumpsuit. She'd had over twenty-five successful jobs in it. Call her sentimental, but she didn't want to see it go.

"Navigate to the planet Vos Laegos," she commanded, "Vos Laegos City." Then she remembered this was a Protostar 340-K. It didn't accept voice commands, you had to set nav the old-fashioned way. She sighed and headed to the control room.

From the lounge, she could hear something coming through the vis-u. It was probably that half-wit Hyphiz Epsilonian friend of Rollie's again. She had no time for his blather. She closed the cockpit hatch and let the comm go to the message system. Whatever he had to say could wait.

31

What a difference a day made.

"…Medical experts are investigating a mysterious malady that may have struck its fourth victim this week," Penny Parson of KDXI confided through the Penumbra's TV streaming app. "Edna Kowalski of East Pittsburgh was taken to Monroeville Medical Center today after she became catatonic during a rousing bingo session here at Our Lady of Perpetual Guilt."

The camera cut to a photo of an elderly lady wearing a black-and-gold "Born to Bingo" sweatshirt and a smile.

"With me now is her friend Agnes Muldovi, age eighty-three, who witnessed the event here in the church rec room. Agnes, tell us what you saw."

Agnes pushed up her green bookie visor and leaned into the mic. "Well, we was just startin' round three of play, with Mary Connolly having won the last round on account of Mary playing thirty-five cards at once and also her bein' amby-dexterous, n'at? And that's when Edna Kowalski, who's normally so quiet you can't hardly hear her … She gets all loud and rootchy in her lucky spot at the back table. So me and Mavis and them says 'What's wrong?' But Edna's dancing around the place sayin' how this amazing bingo strategy just come to her like a bolt from God. Well, we say 'That's nice' and go back to playin' on account of, quite frankly, Edna gets bolts from God every three weeks or so, which ain't never amounted to much beyond her winning five dollars on her scratch-off Lotto. And suddenly she gets all riled up n'at, grabbin' at peoples' cards and insisting 'Yinz guys should play it this way, too.' Then right as we was trying to reason with her, she got this glazed look, froze mid-sentence and topples over stiff as a board. Morty Mortensen, well, he runs over to catch her. But on account of his walker, he don't get there in time. But I tell you, she was still froze like that when the ambulance people come and cart her off. I ain't never seen nothin' like it!"

The reporter patted the lady's arm sympathetically and turned to the camera. "Emergency rescue staff told KDXI that Mrs. Kowalski's symptoms resemble those of three other catatonia-related incidents occurring this past week across the Pittsburgh area. Edna Kowalski's diagnosis is currently unknown but she's in stable condition. A spokesperson for Monroeville Medical Center declined to comment whether the Kowalski case was part of an erupting epidemic. We'll update you right here on KDXI as the news unfolds. Back to you at the studio, Tracy and Patrick!"

"Thanks, Penny!" said Tracy. "Coming up next, Steelers pre-pre-pre-season coverage. Will the new back-up, alternate, retro-futuristic Away Game uniforms give the Steelers the edge they'll need this coming season? Or, once again, will thousands of fans find the team unrecognizable and accidentally cheer for the opposition?"

"Holy shit!" said Rozz, leaping to her feet.

"I know…" rasped Tseethe, who was propped up in a chair. Dar must have hit him with the highest possible stun setting. The man was still practically a liquid. "Your news is so … hard-hitting … compared to our … *Heavy Meddler*."

"Not the news," said Rozz, shifting from foot-to-foot. "In Malone's lab. I just realized: it's not taxidermy!"

Bertram squinted. "Uh, what isn't?" With so much going on, it was getting increasingly difficult to project manage every aspect of World Savery these days.

But Rozz was breathless. "Malone had a bunch of animal statues in his office. Lizards, couple of monkeys, rats, et cetera. I thought they were taxidermy. But Bertram, I think they're his test results." She seized his arm with bruising fervor. "I think they're from ZOT!"

"Of course they're from ZOT!" said Cordelia, causing Rozz's grip to release. The cat hopped up onto the Uninet counter and eyed a pen there. She wiggled her posterior and shouted, "For the motherland!" then pushed the pen over the edge. She watched it tumble to the floor with an ear twitch, a disappointed grumble escaping her throat.

"Cordelia," Rozz met the cat's gaze, "you knew about this?"

Cordelia flopped across the table like gravity was suddenly too much to bear. "Of course we knew. We saw it happen to Four, Six and Thirty," she said. "Each day we were wondering whether our own numbers would be up."

Across the ship's lounge, Rollie groaned. "Not that phrase. Anything but that phrase."

Someone tugged Rozz's pantleg for attention. She looked down. Bootsy said, "The initial tests were fine. The mice, the rats, the rabbits. We thought everything was okay. I think the fur-headed human did, too, since he made the lip-music sound a lot in those days."

Cordelia sighed. "So much lip music."

"But then the lizards and monkeys froze. Oh, and that cat with the gland problem, what was his name?" This last bit was to Cordelia.

"Twenty-Two," said Cordelia.

"That's him." Bootsy toyed with his own tail. "After that we were getting bigger doses more times a day. And we started losing some of the others."

"And nobody thought to share this until now?" asked Rozz of the cats, the room and perhaps the universe as a whole.

"We really do need to work on our inter-team communications," agreed Bertram. Part of the issue, he realized, was a minor prejudice on his part. He'd never thought to expand the team to include members who lick themselves.

Tseethe wheezed, "So you guys … know for a fact … they were giving you … ZOT!?"

Cordelia's tail flicked. "That's what the human male with the excessive head fur said."

Bertram asked, "And did he mention the ingredients?"

"Oh yes!" she said. "He gave us a detailed rundown of all his plans, issued a list of possible side effects and had us sign a legal waiver agreeing to the experimentation before the tests could occur."

Bertram was impressed. "Really?"

"Of course not. We're cats," said Cordelia. "He force-fed us stuff and talked to himself."

Bertram had always suspected cats were sarcastic. Now he knew. "All right, then. Tomorrow morning," he told the group, "we talk to Lazarus Malone."

But Rozz was already shaking her head. "Two problems with that," she said. "One: last time I talked to him, he threw me out of his lab. Two: tomorrow's Sunday. Mr. Malone will not be at the office."

"Ah," said Bertram, grinning, "but who has the power?"

"Um …" she shifted uncertainly in her shoes, "I do?"

"And who's already broken into the HR database once and could just, maybe, kinda, get us Lazarus Malone's home address?" Bertram turned up the wattage on his smile.

He'd forgotten Rozz was immune to that sort of thing. She made a disgusted noise. "He's not going to talk to me."

But Bertram would not be daunted. He had already moved to Dauntless Town, population: one. "That's okay," he said. "I hear I can be pretty persuasive. And if not me — hey, Rollie? You up for a house call tomorrow morning?"

"Always was an early riser," Rollie said with a wink.

It was nine a.m. Based on the car in the driveway and the lights downstairs, they knew Lazarus Malone was finally up and roaming around the Cape Cod he called home. But the doorbell and their knocks both went unanswered. So after five long, patient minutes, Bertram asked Rollie to knock a *little* harder ...

It was nice change to be on the same side of the door that Rollie Tsmorlood kicked in.

"Lazarus Malone?" Bertram said. "We need to talk."

Malone stood in his living room in striped pajamas, cradling a bowl of cereal in one hand, a spoon in the other. The look of wide-eyed horror on his face was not wholly unlike that of the cartoon character on the TV behind him. The cartoon shrieked. Malone took it as a sign. He threw the bowl and spoon at his unwanted guests and started for the stairs.

Bertram shook off the shower of LuckyPufz and found himself dashing in pursuit.

"Ludlow, move!" Rollie shouted and laser energy zinged past Bertram's ear. It missed Malone by the width of a colored marshmallow and dissolved into the stairway as the man ran for higher ground. But Bertram was close, so close now and the power of being the pursuer was heady. Taking a chance, Bertram dove for the guy, catching a handful of Malone's bathrobe and his own chin on the stairs as he dropped onto the floor. Malone continued his frantic journey upward while Bertram scrambled to his feet with only a terrycloth belt and a bruise to show for it.

"Frag it, Ludlow, get out of the way," yelled Rollie, reaching around him for a second shot.

But the slippery scientist had disappeared into a bedroom. Bertram found the guy rummaging around in a drawer and before Bertram could speak, he'd pulled a gun. An actual Earth gun, Bertram noted with some surprise. Something of the Genuinely Planning to Put Holes in You variety.

"Okay. Hold it there." Malone's voice sounded authoritative but his grip was shaky.

Rollie already had the XJ-37 aimed and steady. "Put it down, mate. We just want to talk."

"Talk, sure. Talk ..." Malone's laugh was manic. "I knew this was coming. Oh, I knew. So sorry, but today this," he nodded at the revolver, "will do my talking for me." And with an acute eye on Rollie, Malone stood a little straighter in his slipper socks.

"Well, this," Rollie countered in that quietly calm way that was so much more ominous than any shouting, "is set to Level Two Stun. And I promise you, mate, you'll be chatting up the floorboards before you ever pull that trigger."

"Plus, you're outnumbered," said Bertram, finally getting a chance to draw his own handlaser. Geez, these battle scenes happened so fast. He was going to have to work on his response time. "So you put your gun down and we'll holster ours, and we'll all go downstairs and have a nice, civilized conversation where nobody bleeds, goes numb or explodes into atoms."

Admittedly, it was hard to make a case for affability while covering the guy with scary weapons. And Malone picked up on this. "Give me one reason I should believe you're not here to kill me."

"I find death makes conversation really unwieldy," Bertram said, "how about you?"

Malone didn't answer. His mind was onto other things. "I heard him call you Ludlow," he said, indicating Rollie with the barrel of his gun. "You'd told me your name was Hill. Who are you, really?"

"We're the people who know about ZOT!" said Bertram. "And we want to stop DiversiDine before anyone else gets hurt."

There was a pause, a breath, the slightest hint of a nod. "Okay." Malone's foot jittered nervously. "So maybe we have that in common," he said. "Who do you work for?"

Bertram said, "We're a small, independent operat —"

"I don't mean that. What planet?"

"Uh ..." Bertram glanced at Rollie. They'd moved into somewhat unexpected territory here.

But Malone didn't wait. "The same planet Able's from?" he asked. "You're one of those ... plant people, aren't you? And all that's some kind of projected illusion?"

"What?" Bertram looked down at his clothes. He felt kind

of offended. Sure, the suit was second hand and starting to stink. But he didn't think it was alien-in-disguise material. "No!"

Malone tilted his head, unconvinced.

"Geez, buddy, I'm local," said Bertram.

"I'm Dutch," volunteered Rollie.

"So that's your story, huh? Well, we'll just see about that. And remember: try anything and I shoot." Still covering them, Malone approached them slowly, poked each of them (hesitating slightly when it came to the Dutchman) and stepped back, scratching his head.

"We're working for Earth, pal. We just want to help you," Bertram said. "Help everybody. Look …" And taking a chance he hoped he would not regret, Bertram turned off his handlaser and tucked it back into his coat pocket. "I smell coffee. Did you make coffee?"

Malone nodded, bewildered, over his gun.

"Mind if I get a cup? We were up so early stalking your place. Plus my sleep schedule's totally off these days. There's this fog, right here." He gestured between his eyes. And with that, Bertram turned, praying he wouldn't get shot in the back, and headed downstairs to help himself.

He was in the kitchen, grabbing creamer from the fridge when Malone finally peered around the corner, gun arm hanging limply at his side. He was followed by Rollie, who wore an expression lurking between surprised and highly-entertained.

Bertram poured the creamer, stirred and slurped. "Oh, that's perfect!" It was, too. He pulled out a chair at the kitchen table and sat. "This stuff is magic. I've missed it so much. You have no idea … So." He looked up at Malone and smiled. "When'd you find out your boss is an alien?"

"Oh. Uh …" Malone stepped into his own kitchen hesitantly, confused, disenfranchised. "It's kind of a long story."

Bertram gestured to the coffee pot. "I'm a good listener. Pull up a mug."

Malone looked from Bertram, to the pot, to Bertram again. Then perhaps deciding he'd experienced weirder things while working at DiversiDine than a guy breaking into his house and drinking his coffee, he grabbed himself a mug and poured. Bertram pushed out a chair. Malone directed an uneasy gaze to Rollie who was leaning in the doorway, then an easier one to Bertram enjoying his java. Malone sank into the kitchen chair opposite Bertram in an almost dreamlike fashion.

He cleared his throat. "I guess I always felt something was wrong at DiversiDine," he began, "I just couldn't pinpoint it right away. Some of it was the internal set-up surrounding my role in the company. My job involves a number of tasks, but the big one is mixing up the special flavorings for the manufacturing facilities, so they can use them in their beverage batches. Depending on the task, I work with the heads of R&D or Manufacturing. But I'm also one of only two people in the entire company that knows the complete flavoring formulas for DrinkThis and ZOT!. The other person is James Able. And for that, I report to him and him alone."

Rollie had holstered his gun and took a seat on the floor. It made Bertram think of some intergalactic story-time.

"Initially, my meetings with Able were video conferences," Malone went on. "But like the process at DiversiDine, they were always a little off. In the first one, he gave me the specific instructions for the flavoring mixes, but he also told me to include this special imported ingredient. In the case of ZOT!, he called it *fantasia diaboegis*. He said it was an extract from a rare root only found in Nepal. One of those herbal supplement additives, FDA-loophole-friendly because it's 'natural,' and supposed to increase mental agility. We even put it on the label."

"But I bet it's no root from Nepal," said Bertram.

"And definitely not friendly," said Rollie.

"If pressed, I'd say the ingredient's a hormone," said Malone over his cup, "but it's like nothing I've seen before. In our public test pilot, it did increase alertness and mental dexterity. People connected ideas in unique ways. But we also saw everything from a bright inventiveness and talkativeness to a manic sort of high."

"So you're basically spiking the batches," said Rollie.

"Was," he said. "I stopped including the ingredient in batch mixes as soon as I realized what was happening in the lab. But by then it was too late — the FDA had already approved ZOT! as a dietary supplement. Batches were bottled and headed to market everywhere. So I did the only thing I could."

"You notified Able," said Bertram.

Malone nodded. "At first, I left messages, explaining the results I was getting. He'd conference me back, but always brushing me off. He'd say it was just a few lab subjects, no big deal. That we'd been giving out samples at community events to humans for a year now and nothing had happened. We would proceed as planned."

"Cue the human catatonia," said Bertram.

Malone ran a hand through his forest of hair. "I sent him a couple of panicked meeting requests. And suddenly James Able was in my lab, face-to-face. He said I should just fix the problem. I told him I thought it had something to do with metabolic rates. Some animals, for instance, have a much slower metabolism than others, and that seemed to be a factor. But this isn't my area of expertise. I told him I needed to pull in the whole team. I explained that I'm a food engineer, I couldn't work alone on this. I needed other specialists, medical experts. It's not like I could just pop a pill and know everything instantly myself, but he didn't get that."

Bertram had an idea why.

"And that's when he changed," said Malone. "Literally. He went from a normal-looking middle-aged man to this ... plant thing. He said I needed to understand this project was so much bigger than me and my petty problems. And that this was my planet — *planet* — so I should shut my mouth and make it work before DiversiDine got dragged through the mud. He said quitting was not an option. And going to the press ..." He laughed bitterly. "Who would believe my story?"

"Well," Bertram said, "maybe the *Weekly World News.*"

"Exactly. And this is why, whether investigators tie the victims to ZOT! or Able holds me accountable, I am galactically screwed." His voice trembled with anger. "Yesterday, I even went down to the hospital, lied and said I was family of the first victim so I could check out their medical records, look for a pattern. But the family was already there. That's how I discovered there are a remarkable number of male nurses these days who believe in working the upper body."

"Yours or theirs?" asked Bertram.

"Yes," Laz said, pulling up his pajama shirt to reveal a giant purple area. "And when James Able finds out I haven't been adding his 'Nepalese extract' to the new batch mixes? I have a feeling bruises will be the least of my concerns."

"And that," said Rozz from the kitchen doorway, "is why we're here to help." She turned to Rollie and Bertram. "Sorry, I couldn't wait outside anymore. The neighborhood watch guy was starting to give me the stink-eye."

Bertram noticed Malone's eyes were on her with a similar expression. "You."

"Me," said Rozz pleasantly. "Ooh, coffee!" And she moved to pour herself a cup.

"I knew it." Malone stood and tried to tie his bathrobe, then remembered he was missing his belt. "I knew there was something funny about you. I bet you're the one who stole my lab subjects, too."

"Not stole," Rozz spooned in sugar. "Rescued. Think of it as … Feline Liberation."

"Cat burglary," Rollie suggested.

"Enough," Malone said now. The sight of Rozz seemed to have triggered his old stressed-out self, or perhaps the coffee had just kicked in. "Specifics. I want specifics from you people. How can you possibly help me? What's your plan and how can you ensure my safety? Details."

"Dude," Rozz said between sips, "I get it. I sympathize. I do. You've borne a massive burden for a long time now and you've been handling it all alone. There's a buttload of pressure on you and you've been freaking out ever since your first lizard went stiff." She paused. She blinked. "Poor choice of words. Moving on …" She cleared her throat. "Unlike you, however, our group happens to stand outside of conventional problem-solving constraints. We have connections. Our hands aren't tied with pesky things like confidentiality agreements, traditional resources and … and …"

"Charming yet antiquated defense techniques?" Rollie suggested, leaping to his feet.

Bertram nodded. "Exactly. We offer a unique 'big picture' perspective."

"How big picture?" asked Malone.

Rollie smiled. "As vast as the Greater Communicating Universe, my friend."

Malone, Bertram noticed, took a half-step back. Whether it was the words or Rollie's smile, it was hard to say.

"And like it or not," Rozz said, "we're already on the job. We want ZOT! off the market as badly as you do. So you can either help us, or you can enjoy your Suffering in Silence, Party of One, with house specials featuring guilt, paranoia and impending doom. It's your choice."

There was a long pause. Malone shifted in his slipper socks. "So what do you need from me?"

"Right now, the answer to one question," said Bertram. "Where do the active ingredients get delivered?"

Malone rubbed his face. "I do the flavor mixes out at DiversiDine World Manufacturing. By the airport. They house it for me, but I don't know where they get it."

Bertram said, "Then it's time somebody finds out."

Rozz rested a hand on Malone's shoulder. "Hang in there, Laz," she told him. "We've got your back."

"DiversiDine World Manufacturing," said Bertram on the relatively empty bus back from Malone's place. He scrolled down the address on his phone. "Moon."

"Off-planet," said Rollie, with a nod. "That's brazen, innit?"

"Not *a* moon. Moon," said Bertram. "Moon Township. It's a region. It's north."

"Maybe Malone was on to something," mused Rozz, gnawing a thumbnail. "What if we took a sample of the undiluted active ingredient and leaked it to the press? Think we could take DiversiDine down that way?"

Bertram shifted in his seat. "Possibly. The problem is, while DiversiDine's reputation would take a hit — *maybe* — that doesn't get them off-planet. And they've got a lot of goodwill built up with the public. I don't see the masses turning against them easily, even with an FDA investigation on their doorstep. Not while the jubies are still flowing."

"Also, still sets up Laz Malone as the fall guy," said Rollie. "If we was worried about that." Rollie's tone suggested he wasn't much.

"What if we could stall distribution?" said Bertram. "Or ... or manufacturing? You know, screw with their supply chain? That wouldn't recall the stuff already out there, but it might slow down the chance of more people getting hurt."

"Shame the Penumbra has no laser cannons. We could crater the place." Rollie looked wistful.

Bertram shot him a glare. "Did you hear the part about 'people not getting hurt'? Call me crazy, but I'd prefer not to blow up our former coworkers."

"Oh, that. Yes. Of course," said Rollie.

"Fortunately," Bertram continued, "I think I have an idea how we can tackle this. And since it's Sunday, we may have the whole place to ourselves ..." He grinned. "Y'know, if you guys are okay with a little breaking and entering ..."

Rollie seemed particularly entertained at this. "Might be able to push my morals aside just this once."

Rozz asked, "And if we don't have the place to ourselves?"

"I think I know how to handle that, too," Bertram said. "The only question is how we get out to Moon Township. I'm not sure about the ICV parking situation there, and taking a bus or cab to a corporate sabotage is probably not best practices."

"That problem," Rozz told him, "is one I can solve."

Peering out the window to see where they were, she "ooh-ed," leapt up and pulled the cord. A bell rang. "I think I can get us a car."

Initially, Bertram worried that Rozz's plan for "getting a car" was something along the lines of Rollie's thinking on these matters. But a few hours later, as he looked over the Steelers bobblehead and through the tangle of black-and-gold Mardi Gras beads dangling from the rearview mirror, he put those concerns behind him.

He had all new concerns now. "It's not exactly inconspicuous, is it?"

From her spot behind the wheel, Rozz rolled her eyes. "Dude, are you kidding me? My dad is but one die-hard Steelers fan in the steeliest city in the country. There are hundreds of vehicles out there just like this. We could practically patent this look as a Pittsburgh cloaking device."

In the back seat of the brown Bonneville, Rollie was moving around like a restless, uncomfortable child.

"What are you doing back there?" Bertram asked finally, half-turning around. "Quit it. You're shaking the car."

"I'm sitting on something peculiar and I can't quite — Ah!" He leaned forward brandishing a foam finger. "This," he said, eyeing the item with great interest. "Is it for bathing?"

"Uh, no," said Bertram.

"Hm." He blinked and tossed it aside. "Then this." Rollie held up a Terrible Towel, the famous rally rag of Steelers fans everywhere. "*This* must be for —"

"No."

32

A thousand-yoonie, custom-fit jumpsuit with ample pockets, triple-stitched seams and a built-in utility belt, ideal for the little necessities of the job ... Yet, could the Vos Laegos City cleaners find it?

No.

"When did you bring it in?" they asked Dar. "Oh. Six universal months ago? Well, the redemption ticket *specifically* said garments would not be held after thirty Vos Laegon days. Also, the cleaners can't be responsible for missing, damaged or demolecularized items and ...

"And ...

"And."

So Dar had told them what they could do with their "ands." And she reinforced it with a quick laser shot to her claim ticket. Which *might* have accidentally fallen into their drop-off bin (fashion was *so* flammable these days) and might have somehow caught fire and might have shot flames to the ceiling and sent alarms jangling.

But that was the price you paid for poor customer service in this modern GCU, wasn't it? And here Dar was, doing them the explicit favor of demonstrating why keeping up-to-date on your fire insurance was so very, *very* important.

She was a giver that way.

She could see the building's smoke from the air as she left Vos Laegos City. But even the sight of a whole fleet of conflagration hovercrafts rushing to the scene failed to soothe her saddened heart. So she set her coordinates for the planet Jarendi. She would check her notes and determine where she'd left off with her buddy the Premier. She was sure that would give her spirit the happy little lift it deserved.

She'd need new equipment to complete the job, of course, since her best tools had been confiscated by Mawdank Roving Confinement Center. But that was the benefit of seizing a ship owned by a former card-carrying member of the Intergalactic Underworld. The Protostar would have appropriate gear lurking somewhere.

Unfortunately, with every cabinet she inspected, she was reminded why things had not worked out between Rollie Tsmorlood and herself (attempted murder notwithstanding). The man's whole existence was chaos surging under the thinnest veneer of control. And while that did hold certain short-term attractions, when it came to day-to-day living, the tendencies played out in tedious, backwards and unfathomable ways.

His kitchen utensils, for instance, were found in the same bin as a collection of daggers and throwing stars from the planet Segal-4. In another compartment, she found one holey, bloodied boot, some bandages, a pair of sunglasses and twenty jars of mixed currency. One whole compartment was filled with freeze-dried mootaab cheese, just add water. His liquor cabinet was uniquely organized and impressive, if low on most of everything. And the storage room shelves stood bare. They once had locking doors, but at some point in their history the remote was lost and they had to be pried apart. Their contents now formed a quicksand of objects half-a-krom deep on the floor.

To his credit, the man did have exquisite taste in weaponry, she considered, pulling a smooth ZR-50 long-range handlaser and an elegant PK-5 phaser-bow from the swamp of intergalactic effluvia found there. These, she thought, would come in highly useful when —

The ship shook. And this was another thing. Should she be concerned, or was the machine merely having trouble shifting cycles again? Every now and then, the Protostar jarred like a heart palpitation, the "Service Roto-Rocket Boosters Soon" light flipping on, then flickering off again like it had accidentally entered the wrong hotel room and saw something it shouldn't. But this last jolt seemed … extreme … even for the Protostar. And Dar was deciding what to do about it when she emerged from the storage room and saw the wheel on the Protostar's hatch turning, as if on its own accord.

A second later, the hatch popped open.

With a gasp, Dar dropped the weapons and dashed across the room, determined to slam the hatch shut before being sucked into the vacuum of space. But there was no vacuum because there was no space. Or, rather, there was a small space, a tiny accordion hallway suddenly extending between her hatch and another ship. And in the entrance to this hallway stood a line-up of nightmares come to life.

Dar Balisong had never seen a Feegar in person before and she didn't plan, with any degree of detail, to do so now. She seized the hatch door and shoved as hard as she could, trying to jam it back into place. But the first Feegar was fast and strong. The thing grabbed the door and flung it back at her. The hatch wheel slammed into the metal paneling, creating yet another dent and smudge.

The armed creatures stepped forward.

At a glance, Dar became almost frozen by the lifeforms' impossibility. How could she see all of their inner workings so clearly through their skin? How could she see their sickly huge smiles through their closed mouths?

She had heard Rollie talk about his time in the Feegar Rebellion, speak of this race who purposefully made themselves transparent in a quest to inspire terror in those who would oppose them. But she'd always assumed these tales were tall.

Because the universe was chock-full of liars, wasn't it? And when people weren't lying about their credentials, the beauty of a friend's ugly baby or their plans to attend the Mig-Verlig Assassin College fifty-year reunion, then they were exaggerating about the horrors of the Feegar Rebellion. Lying to everyone about everything made the universe go round. It was comforting; you could count on it.

But as it turned out, the Deltan had been truthful; the Feegars were all he'd described and more. Dar ran to the kitchenette, disillusion running with her, and she flung open a cabinet. She grabbed the first thing she thought of — the daggers from the bin — throwing them one-by-one at her unwanted guests with swift determination.

One-by-one they struck, for Dar Balisong was a certified dead shot with thirty-eight popular GCU weapons. And one-by-one, the daggers bounced off those horrible clear exoskeletons and clattered to the floor.

She went for the throwing stars next — one, two, three, four, five — using all the force she could muster and — PLINK! CLANG! PLUNK! CLONG! CLACK! — the weapons dropped to the tile like shattered meteorites.

In her panic, she'd moved onto a fork and two spoons before remembering she was *so* much better than this. She dove for the ZR-50 and the phaser-bow she'd left by the storage room door.

"This is Rolliam Tsrmorlood's ship," said one of the Feegars through that terrible, impossible smile. "Where is he?"

"Rollie's not able to come to the ICV right now. But if you'd like to leave your name and vis-u number, I'll be happy give him a message." She tried to flip on the ZR-50 but discovered its controls were jammed, melted into place by some previous battle. No wonder the object had been tossed so carelessly into storage; the beautiful weapon was worthless.

"It's foolish to cover up for him," warned the Feegar now.

The absurdity of her ever covering up for Rollie Tsmorlood made her laugh, a full, merry guffaw that surprised even her under the circumstances. "I agree. Why *would* I do that?"

The Feegar jarred ever-so-slightly. "You claim no loyalties?"

"What I claimed was his ship for myself," she said.

The armed Feegars were surrounding her. There were four in total. She brandished the phaser-bow at two, despite the sneaking suspicion it had no more zing than its handlaser companion. "Like I said, he's not here. Don't believe me?" she said. "Check the rooms. Check them all. I'll wait."

The leader nodded to two of his troops and they moved through the various rooms on the Protostar. They tackled the cockpit, engine room and storage first, then the three cabins and the washroom. They returned from each with a shake of their hideous heads.

"We know this is a vehicle for freight raiding," said the Commander when they were done. "We are not fools. Show us the secret storage."

"You had only to ask." She moved to the central counter, balanced the phaser-bow between her knees and pressed a rivet that looked like every other rivet there on the island. Six secret panels opened in the floor. Two peeled away from the walls. And there before them stood a set of bookshelves containing Rollie's latest print acquisitions and the pressurized containers bearing the Feegar export logo.

"See? Like I said." She gave a casual toss of her head. "Tsmorlood's not here. But so your journey's not wasted, why don't you take back your shipment? That's why you're here, right? To retrieve the items he stole from you?"

"Where did you last see Rolliam Tsmorlood?" demanded the Commander.

My, these Feegars certainly were persistent, weren't they? "If I tell you, will you break latch from here without dining?" she asked.

The Commander's great dark eyes seemed to draw in her entire image with a glance. She pried her focus from his gaze and instead assessed a more informative region of his person, his stomach. He'd just had an enormous meal. They all had. It was working its way through the first leg of the Feegar digestive tract. It was the only thing, she thought, that was to her advantage.

Everyone knew the worst impulse shopping happened when you were hungry.

"Tell us where you got this ship," ordered the Feegar.

She directed the phaser-bow at him. "Give me your word that you'll all leave here and spare me." She doubted the Feegar's word was worth much. But then, she thought, neither was hers.

"Fine. You will be spared," said the Commander.

She could see his hand wasn't in the cross-fingered Universal sign of the Syke Loophole. Given the situation, it was the most she could hope for. "Rolliam Tsmorlood is on Tryfe," she said. "A little place in the country called U.S.A. in their city called Pittsburgh."

"Tryfe. U.S.A," the Feegar pronounced it *OOsah*. "Pittsburgh," repeated the Commander.

"Correct."

The Commander nodded. "Normally, we would gain intelligence from you in a more accurate and traditionally-Feegar manner —"

"The kind with the pain and the murder, then?"

"Naturally," and the Feegar looked pleased she'd heard about it. "But our RecoLektron's storage capacity is completely filled. That," he said, "is how many lifeforms we have tortured and interrogated lately."

"Twinkly," she said.

"Yes, instead, we will let you live," continued the Commander with a grand gesture, "to marinade deeply in your own cowardice and shame. Should we meet again, you will receive no such favors from the people of Feegar and when you are prepared and consumed, the flavor will be all the sweeter."

"All righty, then," she said. "Thanks oodles."

And to her surprise, they clattered back down the accordion hallway to their ship. Clearly, they were in a hurry. They didn't even take their crates.

Dar sealed the hatch behind them, tight and fast. "Cowardice, blah, marinade, blah, blah ..." and dusted off her hands. She could see the Feegar ship breaking latch now, leaving the Protostar far, far behind.

And yes, *yes,* perhaps it hadn't been a very "nice" thing to do, telling them where Rollie Tsmorlood was; Dar recognized that. But then it wasn't like Rollie was completely innocent in the matter, either. He *had* stolen their shipment. And if not through her, they almost certainly would have found him some other way, eventually ...

Possibly.

Perhaps.

In some respects, it was a shame to think that soon Rollie would be gone forever. Sure, the man had his pedantic moments. He was far too devoted to ridiculous causes. And his skewed principles would always hold him back from any true greatness. But he also had so much zest for life. He was a pleasing specimen of Hyphiz Deltan phenotypes. And he was so wonderfully off his orbit.

Ah, well. Dar Balisong had learned at a young age that nothing in the GCU lasted for long.

Then a new thought crossed her mind ...

If the Feegars did manage to locate Rollie on Tryfe and settle their score, could Dar finally collect on her unfinished hit? Yes, clients preferred better response time when it came to assassinations and Blip Flutterbitt would never have paid out over the Altair-5 exile — she hadn't even approached him about that. But this... this was practically subcontracting.

It was a twinkly possibility she couldn't quite snuff out. She smiled ...

Yes, suddenly, Dar was feeling much, *much* better.

33

DiversiDine World Manufacturing was located down a winding, tree-lined road that opened abruptly onto a wide, snowy field — a field in which Bertram's team could have easily landed a fleet of ICVs, if they'd only known, and with room to spare. In the center of this field sat a squat, tan factory. And next to it, an equally squat, tan warehouse. Together, they looked like large, suspicious, brown paper packages planted by giants with dark intentions.

Or maybe Bertram Ludlow was simply projecting again.

Rozz directed the Bonneville past the Visitors and Employee Parking signs and headed towards Shipping, ultimately mooring her dad's unwieldy craft into a spot beside the loading docks. Somehow, Bertram wasn't surprised things were business-as-usual at DiversiDine. The loading docks were open and boxes stood in rows, waiting to be loaded.

"All right," said Bertram. "Looks like we're rolling with Option Two."

The Tryflings alighted from the car still wearing their work clothes but with their official DiversiDine badges tacked to their lapels, and Rozz had grabbed her red file folder. A short distance behind them, Rollie followed: purposefully, quietly.

"Get me the manager," Bertram said in a snappy tone.

"Who's the manager here?" He pointed to a uniformed young man bent over a dolly. "Hey! You the manager?"

The kid rose, wide-eyed. "No, sir. The Foreman's Mr. Stevens. He's in there." He pointed in a jerking way to the inner workings of the warehouse.

"Thanks," Bertram said. And he and Rozz clanged up the metal stairs onto the loading dock, trailed by Rollie.

"Hey, hey!" said the kid, stepping in front of them. "Who are you people? You can't just go in there."

Bertram and Rozz flashed their ID badges. "It's okay. We're from Corporate," said Bertram.

The guy looked to Rollie. "And you?"

"He's with us," said Bertram. "And if we can talk to the foreman and get this whole mess straightened out, you won't need to know him."

Rollie offered the guy a tight smile that said you really, *really* didn't want to know him.

It had a nice way of moving things along. "Mr. Stevennnsss …" the kid called inside. "Some people from Corporate are here to —"

But Bertram and Rozz were already moving down the loading dock to the warehouse, inspecting the stacked boxes. There seemed to be two types of loads here, outgoing distribution and incoming shipments. While the former were standard packing boxes, the latter were pressurized crates with the name TrustTChem marked on the side.

"Can I help you?" asked a middle-aged gentleman, and Bertram was struck by how much this man looked like the kid, just twenty years older. He had the same plain features, same beige coloring, the same square jaw. Who knew DiversiDine World Manufacturing was such a happy, family business?

"Mr. Stevens?" Bertram gave him a firm handshake. Stevens' was firmer and almost painful. "I'm from Corporate. We need to know how many cases of the, er, *'fantasia diaboegis'* for ZOT! you have in stock."

"Oh. Well, that's in the stacks. I'd have to check." From the sound of it, Bertram expected Stevens would be stepping away to do this — precisely what Bertram had hoped for. Anything to stall. But the foreman stood there, expressionless and unmoving. Finally he said, "Three hundred and fifty two."

Bertram blinked. "Three hundred and fifty two what?"

"Cases of the active ingredient for ZOT!." said Stevens.

"Okay …?" Bertram shot a look to Rozz.

Rozz pressed a hand to one of the outgoing boxes. "So, what are all these cases here?"

"They're the completed flavor mixes."

"And they're going where?" Bertram scanned the crate for an address label. "Which DiversiDine manufacturing facilities?"

"None. This shipment's for Epiq."

"Ah. Epiq." Bertram infused the word with as much I-know-all-about-Epiq-ness as he could summon. "Sure and … uh … remind me: where is that located again?"

Stevens looked like he didn't know quite how to answer this. "The Outer Moon?"

Bertram smiled and nodded. "Right, right. Outer Moon. And so they're getting the … um … the completed flavor mix shipments at Epiq."

"Both for ZOT and DrinkThis, yes, sir. Just like DiversiDine."

"Great," said Bertram with a clap of his hands. "Excellent. So, then, what we need you to do is to put all of the flavor mix shipments on hold for all other DiversiDine facilities and for … for Epiq … Okay?"

Rozz reached into the folder and withdrew a form. "A copy of this has been emailed to your production manager, as well," she said. It hadn't. It was mocked up by Rozz on the shipboard computer and printed out two hours ago.

Stevens' expression went blank again and for a moment Bertram thought the guy had either gone into shock or had been frozen by a bad reaction to his own products.

It was about the time Bertram considered calling an ambulance that the man jarred to life again. "No," he said, "it hasn't."

"Excuse me?"

"That document hasn't been emailed to the production manager. There's nothing in the system."

"There isn't?" said Rozz with a surprisingly good Surprise Face. "So weird! My email must not have gone through." She consulted her folder. "Now your production manager is Mister ..." She trailed a finger down the page. "... Atherton, right?"

"Brown. Joe Brown."

"Oh, wow. See, I totally have that wrong in my records." She whipped out a pen and made a notation. "I've been emailing Atherton. That explains it. So if you could give me Mr. Brown's email address, I'll just —"

A siren whooped in the background and overhead blue lights rotated on the ceiling, all the way down the corridor. "Unauthorized personnel, Sector Five. Unauthorized personnel, Sector Five!" said an automated voice over the P.A. system.

Mr. Stevens looked at them hard. "Wasn't there another guy with you?"

"Guy?" Bertram blinked innocently. "Oh, him, yeah. Probably just went out front for a smoke or something."

Rozz shouted over the sirens. "So if you would put the flavor mix shipments on hold until you get notice from us at Corporate, that would be so —"

"Unauthorized personnel Sector Four ..." said the P.A. "Unauthorized personnel Sector F — Correction: unauthorized personnel Sector Three ..."

"Is there, uh, something you need to look into?" Bertram asked Stevens. "We can wait."

A rumble reverberated across the building like distant thunder, followed by the sound of doors opening and shutting and many running feet.

"Overflow warning," announced a different electronic voice. "Valve shutoff malfunction in Sector Three. Overflow warning. Value shutoff malfunction in Sector Three."

"Unauthorized personnel Sector Two ... Unauthorized personnel Sector Two ..."

"Overflow warning," argued the second robotic voice. "Valve shutoff mal —"

"Flammable materials hazard," input a third voice to the chorus. "Flammable materials hazard."

Another siren blared now, more like a firehouse whistle. "All non-essential personnel exit the building per protocol 97B! This is not a drill!"

The double doors banged open and workers began streaming out through the loading dock. For a brief moment, Bertram thought he was stuck in a time loop. These men wore uniforms, yes, but all of them had the same neutral facial features. The same beige hair, the same downturned mouth, the same too-square jaw. And they appeared to be of only three different ages: twenty-two, forty-five and sixty. There were small variations here and there, like this one had a prominent mole and that one had brown eyes instead of blue. But it appeared as if the whole factory were staffed by a batch lot of Stevenses.

Stevens the First gestured to two fellow Stevenses and said, "Hold them." And before Bertram and Rozz knew it, their arms were pinned to their sides by a powerful grip.

Stevens then snatched their DiversiDine IDs off their lapels. "I'm calling the police."

"Go ahead," said Bertram. "I'm not sure why you think we're involved in whatever's happening in your operations right now. But we'll talk to the police."

Rozz added, "And boy, are you going to be embarrassed when we go back to Corporate about this shameful treatment."

"Flammable materials hazard! Warning! Evacuate!" shrieked the P.A.

"Valve shutoff malfunction!"

"Unauthorized personnel Sector One ... Unauthorized —"

The double doors blew open again, a cloud of black smoke and dark purple dust issuing forth like the main stage opening of a heavy metal concert. From that cloud flew Rollie, handlaser drawn, coated in purple from hair to boot and sprinting across the warehouse to the loading dock like he was out to break an Olympic track record. He was slightly on fire. He was also followed by a small platoon of purple Security Stevenses.

As Rollie flashed toward them, streaming color, he aimed. Bertram sensed the energy fly from the XJ-37, first at every box and crate he could manage, then: THUNK! THUNK! Bertram felt the grip around his chest loosen and the stench of burnt rubber and metal filled the air. Bertram's personal Mr. Stevens fell sideways onto the concrete, a large hole in the guy's uniform, his innards and wires still sparking. Rozz's Stevens landed on top of him with a thud.

"For fraggin' sake, run, people!" Rollie shouted at them. "Run!"

They ran, dodging laser shots as building security came up hot on their heels. Rozz was already halfway to the car, digging keys from her pocket and hopping into the driver's seat. Rollie patted the flames on his shoulder and dove into the back. Rozz flung open the passenger door and was pulling away, yelling, "Jump! Jump!" when Bertram leapt into the front. A laser skimmed the side of the Bonneville just as the door swung shut.

The sirens seemed louder out here — No, not building sirens. This was a fire truck screaming down the narrow country road headed their direction. Rozz waited until the emergency vehicle rounded the corner into the parking lot, then tore around them, using the truck as a moving shield from laser fire.

As they pulled onto the exit road, two police cruisers came into view. Bertram saw Rollie duck down in the back seat as they whipped past the other way.

Then ... silence.

It was a long moment before anyone said anything.

"So, Rollie ..." said Bertram finally. "You, what, skipped over general equipment sabotage and went straight for the 'blow shit up' angle?"

"You'd be surprised how one leads rather naturally to the other," Rollie told him with a shaky yet exhilarated grin.

"I can't believe there's a whole factory of Non-Organic Simulants," murmured Rozz, "right here in Western Pennsylvania."

"Well, it's perfect, innit?" Rollie wiped his purple face on the Terrible Towel. "No hiring problems. No questions. Saw a room filled with power hookups in there, just for the workers. It's like one big robot dormitory. The whole lot of them stay at the plant, rent-free, and management gets the maximum hours out of 'em between charge-ups." The towel was now purple. "Flamin' Altair, this stuff stinks."

"You're not kidding." Rozz powered down the windows, despite the cold.

"I wonder where Epiq is located in Moon." Bertram scanned the roadside, as if he looked hard enough, he might actually spy an Epiq logo right now on a building next to the Hoss's or the Super Panda Buffet.

"Epiq?" asked Rollie. "What's that about, then?"

"Oh, you missed that." Bertram turned in his seat. "They had a whole shipment of the flavor mixes prepped to send somewhere that wasn't DiversiDine. Some company called Epiq. It's in Outer Moon somewhere."

"Ludlow ..." Rollie's iris dye job was wearing off. He blinked orange-blue eyes in a sea of purple. "Epiq isn't *in* Moon. It's *a* moon. A populated moon. Third moon for the planet Boss, in the Quad One perimeter. It's backspace, but a stellar place to visit. Picked up some print there. Unique philosophy, they have."

"DiversiDine World is exporting from here to another planet?"

"Another backspace planet," said Rozz. She made the turn onto the Parkway West. "Think they're having the same problems that we're having here?"

"I think it's an excellent time to find out," said Bertram.

"Okay. But before we do," said Rozz, "we have to make a little stop."

34

DrinkThis was some seriously kickass stuff. Rozz gained additional insight into this point, when they went to drop off her dad's newly purpled, freshly-lasered car.

He sat there on his futon with KDXI burbling away in the background, a mug of warmed DrinkThis in his hand, and he listened intently to Rozz's tidily-wrapped tale of B.S.

She'd been braced for the same red-faced righteousness he'd demonstrated over past First World horrors like a C in English, flavored coffee or people who don't use turn signals. But new Jubies-Saturated Dad was all chuckles, offers to use his washroom and "Kids will be kids" about the thing. Never mind Rozz and Bertram had been adult material for years and Rollie Tsmorlood technically could have served in World War II.

Rozz hoped her Paternal Archetype would be half so jubies-jolly if the cops came around wondering why the Bonneville had been spotted at the DiversiDine plant during one of the biggest production sabotages in manufacturing history. She found it to be an interesting coincidence that a news segment on that very sabotage was wrapping up right now on KDXI. If "interesting" were defined as "having a moment of desperate panic to keep the man's attention engaged elsewhere, anywhere, during the three minute spot."

Which, traditionally, it isn't.

Fortunately, the newscaster moved on to a new topic before Steve Mercer was once again drawn to the boob tube's alluring glow.

"… They're calling it Action Figure Syndrome, and the Pittsburgh Department of Public Health and Human Safety has confirmed their sixth case locally," said Penny Parsons, with an efficient and flirty forty-five degree turn to camera two. "Symptoms include rapid speech, excessive movement and an influx of unrealistic, impulsive ideas that ultimately escalate to a statue-like catatonia."

Rollie chuckled. "Story of my life." At the sharp look from Rozz's dad, he added, "Medical condition. I'm used to it."

"Medical experts report that while some symptoms do resemble those of bipolar disorder or schizophrenia, none of the patients under evaluation to-date have been previously diagnosed with those illnesses. Common viral and environmental factors between the patients are being examined."

And how much do you want to bet that each and every one of them was sucking down ZOT!? thought Rozz.

"Pittsburgh DPH cautions there is no evidence that Action Figure Syndrome is contagious," Penny Parsons went on. "It is also believed to be unrelated to Stiff Person Syndrome, a rare disease of the nervous system; Stone Man Syndrome, a disease affecting the connective tissue; or Robot Syndrome, the irresistible compulsion to dance The Robot at weddings. Coming up next … "

By this point, Rozz was thoroughly invading her dad's kitchen cupboards. It was a quick job, since even before he'd spent much time at her mom's, Dad was a follower of the Mother Hubbard style of food shopping. A peek in his refrigerator revealed the items she'd been looking for. She pushed aside the old mayo jar and the hairy Tupperware and emerged with two bottles of DrinkThis and an unopened pack of ZOT! She brought it to her father. "We're gonna go," she said, "and we're gonna take this with us, okay?"

"Sure, Rozzbud!" he said. "Whatever you need."

"I don't know how soon you'll see me again," she continued, an unexpected sadness coming over her. "Just ... don't buy any more of this crap. And don't let Mom buy it, either. It's terrible for your blood sugar and your heart ... and ... and other things. Promise me?"

"Aw, my princess cares about her old dad, doesn't she?" He leapt from his seat and threw his arms around her. It could never be said that Rozz Mercer was terribly pro-hug — she generally distrusted its level of captivity   but there was something about this moment ... this Dad ... She didn't dodge this one. Dad smelled like DrinkThis and those handmade lavender soaps Mom liked.

She patted his back with the two bottles in her hand and tried to imprint it all in her mind. To call it up for those times when she thought of Earth. "We've got to go," she said finally.

"Take care, sweetheart. See you soon. Maybe you and your mother and I can do brunch." He looked so bright, so hopeful.

"Sure. Brunch," she said, knowing that if he really did stay off the DrinkThis, family brunch would be less likely than an Oasis reunion. Suddenly, the air around her felt colder, the light through the skylight, grayer. As they left the loft and she tossed the DiversiDine products into the dumpster outside his building, she wondered at the irony of finally getting what you wanted.

Of course, when you're bent on saving your planet, there's no time to dwell. As soon as they got back to the ICV, they cranked up the Penumbra and began their journey to Epiq, the third moon of Boss.

Rozz watched through the ship's lounge portal as they left the Earth's atmosphere. It was a view that never got old. "How surprised do you think the Institute for Artistic Expression peeps will be, when they notice their mystery sculpture's gone poof?"

Coming in from the cockpit, Bertram laughed. "I'm wondering what our departments will think when they notice we're not at work. Depends, I guess, on how quickly they trace the factory job to us."

"About that," began Tseethe. He'd improved greatly over the last day. He could hold up his head, move his limbs a little and even speak without wheezy pauses. He folded his arms now. "You guys blew up the DiversiDine factory and I missed all the fun."

"Aw, not blown up precisely," said Rollie over a glass of something he'd poured from a flask. "Whole roofs didn't come down. Beams didn't melt. Nothing imploded. This was just spillage, chemistry and a couple of tiny walls of fire."

"Practically a normal day," said Bertram, flopping into his favorite chair.

"Won't stop their operations permanent, o' course," Rollie continued, swirling his ice, "but should've bought us some time. Anyway, Tseethe, I'm sure when the next massive destruction of private property job pops up, you'll be right there helping to make it happen."

Inside his smoking helmet, Tseethe grinned. "Thanks, man." And he drew on the intake pipe in a contented way.

"What can you tell us about Epiq?" asked Bertram.

Rollie considered it and offered a vague shrug. "Nice library. Acceptable libations. Clean confinement center."

"Confinement center?" Bertram didn't know why he was surprised anymore.

"Well," Rollie said, "it *was* a three-day weekend."

"What about the populace?" asked Rozz. "Are they going to take one look at us and freak?"

"Nah, they're humanoid like us. Two eyes, the one nose and so on." He stroked his chin. "We'll need to manage a few pair of antennae, though …"

Bertram drew his handheld Uninet from a pocket and Rozz could see him typing, "Get craft supplies."

"Anybody know where DiversiDine has the biggest presence on Epiq?" asked Tseethe.

Nobody did, so Bertram consulted the handheld for that, too. "Nothing about it on the DiversiDine site."

"Then I'd say we head to Blef," said Rollie. "Major city, known for manufacturing. If DiversiDine's on Epiq and they've done their research, they'll be there."

"Blef it is." Bertram was on his way to the cockpit, when a familiar buzz stopped him in his tracks.

Wilbree's face projected sideways into the room. "Hello, everyone! This is Wilbree here comming you from the vis-u."

Rollie stepped forward. "You have news? What's happened? Is anyone else hurt?"

But Wilbree didn't answer. He squinted at Rollie and started fussing with the controls before him.

"Wilbree?" Rollie banged the vis-u's microphone to get his attention. "Ay, Wilbree!"

"I'm sorry. My color's off. You're coming in a bit purply."

Tseethe laughed. "Should've seen him a few hours ago."

"Never mind that," snapped Rollie, "how's Fess?"

"He's been examined by the medical staff. They're trying to induce cell division," Wilbree said. "They think if they can get his bits replicating, he might have a chance."

Rollie's voice went airy. "Oh, thank the stars … That's cosmic news."

"Semi-cosmic," corrected Wilbree. "They're not so worried about the arms, since Fess' people redo those up nicely. But he'll have to regenerate most of his brain. That's more complex, you know." He leaned into the camera. "Not to say Fess is fortunate, as this is a terrible thing what's happened. But I just keep thinking, what if it'd been me? Hyphiz Epsilonian brains are a one-shot deal."

"I wouldn't dwell," Rollie said.

Wilbree polished his sunglasses. Bertram realized it was the first time he'd really seen Wilbree's eyes. They looked puffy and bloodshot. "You think he'll be the same fellow, then? If they grow him a new brain?"

Rollie twitched slightly and looked down, then murmured, "I … I don't really know."

"I hope so. I rather liked Fess as he was."

"We all did, mate."

"Do you think he'll still beat me at Pratl?"

"Not a doubt," said Rollie.

Tseethe nodded. "Even with just that little bit of brain, buddy."

Wilbree looked somewhat cheered by this. "Good. I'd like that. I'll keep in touch." And he cut from the screen.

"Hand me that bag of pom-poms?" Rollie asked. If, months ago, someone had told Bertram Ludlow that someday he'd be sitting around, doing arts-and-crafts with his alien kidnapper, Bertram would have been in danger of a concussion from laughing himself off his chair.

Now, he just passed the bag of pom-poms.

"How long to Blef?" asked Rozz.

Bertram leapt up and strode to the cockpit. He checked the ETA gauge on the console. "Not long now. Hour maybe," he called and returned to the counter.

"Think we'll be done with these in time?" Rozz held up the item she'd assembled so far. Their handmade antennae were being rigged from a combination of audio headsets, flexible metal tubing, polymer clay, spray paint and the aforementioned bobbles. She wrinkled her nose at her work. "It looks ridiculous. The people of Epiq might be backspace, but that doesn't mean they're total tools. They'll never fall for this."

"Aw, that's coming along fine," said Rollie warmly, assessing the item in her hand. "Needs a bit more clay, is al —" He went to grab one of the pom-poms from the bag, but Bootsy was on the counter now, between him and it. "Hey, now …"

"For the motherland!" Bootsy shouted and purposefully pushed the bag off the counter. He watched it plummet. He groaned. "Aw … hairballs!"

"Okay, enough!" Bertram whirled on the cat. "What *is* that? The 'for the motherland'? Even Mom's cat, Mr. Miggins, was doing it."

"Oh." Bootsy's ears went to attention. "You mean the prophecy?"

Rozz snickered. "Cats have prophecies?"

Bootsy's whiskers twitched. "Hello — worshipped in Egypt! Of course we have prophecies. It's part of a fine oral tradition," he said. "Our ancient prophet, Felidius, predicted that one day, the Earth would be invaded by ancient creatures from another dimension. And foretelling the arrival of those sent to enslave us, the barrier between our worlds would grow thin." He licked a paw and stroked his brow. "We like to keep an eye out for that."

Bertram choked back a laugh. "By chucking small objects off tabletops?" He tried to maintain a respectfully neutral expression, but it was hard.

"'Where down is up and earth and sky become as one ...'" came Cordelia's voice from a chair. "'When the veil grows thin between worlds and the tiny objects, they do slip under the Great Sofa of the Universe ... The invaders will rise and the noble race of Cat will fight tooth and claw to defend its motherland.'"

"And, uh," Bertram scratched Bootsy under the chin, "just where do humans fit into all this?"

Bootsy and Cordelia exchanged glances. The ship was silent a long moment.

"Um, you're ..." Bootsy looked away, tail twitching, "... there. Somewhere. I imagine."

"Surrrrre," Cordelia purred sweetly. "You know how prophets are. They're not detail-oriented. They only hit the high points." She hopped to the counter and patted Bertram's arm with a paw. "I mean, I've never heard it specifically addressed, but I'm sure you're right there behind us, trying to help. Feeding the troops or something."

"Great," said Bertram flatly. "Thanks." Yep, didn't matter the civilization or the species, some guys never got the glory. He leaned down and picked up the package of pom-poms. "Enough talking. Let's get this done."

35

They swept in cloaked over the city of Blef and soon Bertram
settled the Penumbra in a clearing along the Bleftern River.
Things had certainly changed since Bertram Ludlow was first
abducted from Earth. He'd left home sure his sanity had failed
him. Now here he was, an intergalactic adventurer, pilot of his
own ship and the alien invading someone else's backspace
home.

Which reminded him … He popped in a refresher ball of
Translachew (novelty edition) that they'd picked up on a pit-
stop when they'd grabbed their craft supplies. In addition to its
normal repertoire, the gum included three billion archaic or
otherwise "backspace" languages. Originally, it had been meant
for historians and anthropologists. But once *There Goes the
Galaxy* hit the Uninet, it suddenly became trendy to converse in
languages no one could understand. Since DiversiDine
manufactured Translachew, Bertram wasn't very surprised the
languages of Epiq were included in the gum's capabilities.

The flavor, he noted, had also improved from the earlier
prototype version. Its tangy essence of hamster cage and nine-
volt battery had been replaced by a healthful mix of alien veg.
Strange for an Earth gum, yes, but considerably more palatable
than metallic poo.

He adjusted his homemade antennae and held up a metal tray to catch his reflection. "Rollie, I still don't know about this…"

Rollie was attending to his own headgear. It added an extra eight inches to his height. With his black garb, freshly scrubbed purple-pink face and blond-lavender hair, Bertram was reminded of a demonic Easter bunny. He flashed Bertram a grin that did not dispel this image. "I like it. We'll blend in perfect." And he motioned to the group. "Let's go."

Blef was like no interstellar city Bertram had ever seen. Most cities in his travels had employed a uniformity of architecture, or at least an overarching tone. But not Blef. Here was a towering skyscraper. There was a yert. This business was out of the back of a carnival wagon. This one was an elaborately constructed temple to art.

And Rollie had been right. It was easy enough to blend in here, since everyone was a humanoid wearing completely different styles of clothing. It was like all points in the planet's history had converged into the here and now. So lifeforms in armor chatted with beings in bathrobes. Vendors in head-to-toe knitwear served customers in lavish fabrics and feathers. There was only one thing they had in common …

"Good call on the antennae," Bertram said. It killed him to admit this, but their craft project really wasn't that far off.

Rollie just shrugged like it was no big deal, or he knew it all the time, or both. Most likely, both.

"Excuse me …" Tseethe, who had left his smoking helmet back at the ship, stepped in the path of a passing woman who wore a wimple, "could you tell us where DiversiDine is?"

She shook her head in the negative, the wimple going along for the ride. "Sorry."

"Okay, thanks … Pardon me, sir?" He stopped an old man before the guy could pretend not to see him. "DiversiDine? Is it around here?" Tseethe asked.

The old man cupped a hand to his ear. "DiversiWhat?"

"Dine."

"Couple of restaurants, that way." The man pointed.

"Son of a ..." He let the man go, scanning the street for his next target. "Hey kid," he motioned to a little girl selling cups of beverage at a stand, "you know where DiversiDine is?"

"Yep." She eyed Tseethe calculatingly from under a giant plumed hat. There were holes for each antenna to peep through. "How thirsty are you?"

"No cash on me, kid."

"I take credit." She pulled out a small machine to prove it.

He chuckled and puffed his pipe. "Funny. What are you: seven, eight?"

"I'm two-thousand five-hundred and ninety-four days."

"Well, I'm looking for a purely free informational transaction. Do you know where DiversiDine is, or not?"

"I said I did, didn't I?" She pointed to the front of her stand. They looked at the blank paneled wood.

She peered over the counter, too, then growled and rose. She marched around the front, crouched and picked up a large piece of white cardboard that Bertram had originally thought was a homemade welcome mat. She mashed the slightly-gravely tape back onto the front of the stand. It read:

Dversidine Custum Bevergiz
Wet! Cold!
10 Flavurs to Chose Frum!
74 brasseses a Cup

"I have their Blue one," she said, bringing out a can that looked suspiciously like DrinkThis without the label. "And I can add any of our custom flavors." She thrust a slightly crumpled leaflet at them. "Here's my list."

The optional flavorings ranged from spicy breakfast meats, mellow fruit blends and aromatic baked goods all the way to Epiq soil, bugs and wood.

"Wow, that's, uh, really some variety ya got there," said

Bertram. He handed the leaflet back to her since she only seemed to have one copy.

"Soon, I'll have a new Purple type. And I think that will really jumpstart my sales." She leaned in confidentially, toying with one of the strings of beads around her neck. "Lorto on 25th Street has to attend summer school, so he's closed half the day. I offer a signibigant advantage because I have more flavor options and more convenient hours of operation."

"So there are other booths like this?" Rozz asked.

She looked like she was sorry she'd even mentioned it. "*Not* like this. That's what I said. My local competitors offer inveerior service and selection."

"Where do you get your supplies?" asked Bertram.

"From the franchise office." She eyed them suspiciously now. "You're not interested in your own booth, are you? You're *old*. DiversiDine is about youthful energy and indooziasm."

"No," said Bertram. "We just want to learn more about the company."

"Oh," she sighed. "Like that strange lady yesterday."

"Strange lady?" asked Tseethe.

She sighed again, this time with an extra infusion of drama. "Look, I'm running a business here. If you're not going to buy anything, I'll have to ask you to leave."

"Kid, I told you," began Tseethe, "we don't have any local currency and I doubt our credit's good here."

"Well, then ..." She pulled out a long spoon and began to swat at their legs. "Go! Go! Bye-bye. Bye-bye now!" Her technique was surprisingly effective. "Bye-bye!"

"Ow! So much for customer service!" said Tseethe, backing off.

"Shit, it's like being back in Catholic school," said Rozz, leaping backward. "Geez, kid, Sister Agnes has nothing on you."

"Happy day and goodly byes to you!" the little girl called.

Bertram knew how to take a hint. They were clearly going to have to track down the franchise office themselves. It couldn't be that far, could it? Because how much free-range did a two-thousand five-hundred and ninety-four day-old kid get on Epiq?

But he noticed Rozz had paused to dig around in her satchel. In a moment, she'd emerged with a smug look and a handful of something. She set the latter on the kid's counter and backed away before she got the spoon again.

It was six colorful, shiny rocks, two large chromatophore scales shed from a Biblucian and a carved, wooden alien bug.

The little girl's eyes grew wide with wonder.

"Would that buy us some information?" Rozz asked.

The kid had picked up one of the scales and was tilting it in the light, watching it change colors with its environment.

The kid spent another mesmerized moment. Then she cleared her throat, slid the collection of treasures into a drawer, locked it and folded her hands before her on the counter. "I believe we might be able to do business."

And that was Bertram's cue. "The strange lady asking about DiversiDine. Strange how?"

"She was in a hurry. She had no cash, like you guys. And she had *no feelers*. Just none." The little girl tugged on one of her own antenna. She looked at all of them with another narrow assessment, focusing feeler-ward. Her mouth slid slightly to one side, lips pursed in this examination. She let go of her antenna and it boinged back into place.

"And did you tell her where the franchise office was?" asked Bertram.

She sniffed. "No." She rolled her eyes. "*Lorto* told her." There was weighted disgust on her competitor's name. "For free. He walked her there."

"Could you show us?" asked Bertram.

She eyed them, looked at the locked drawer, looked at them again, heaved a great sigh, came around the front and closed the main doors on her booth, locking the whole thing tight like a wardrobe cabinet. "This way," she motioned.

They followed her through Blef's warehouse district and Bertram was drawn to the signs.

Moderately discounted goods!

Reduced profit margins today!

Questionably-made garments but at low prices!

Food! Heated and combats hunger!

Swimwear! Six colors plus white,
which turns translucent when wet
because it's not lined!

"Geez, it's so … truthy," said Rozz, sounding both surprised and a little uncomfortable.

"Facts are important," said the kid. "How else would you decide whether you wanted to go there?"

Greddie's Bar
Meet people and get drunk!
Unremarkable snacks available.

"We're almost there," the girl said. "It's just down at the end of this block."

And they were halfway down that block when Bertram noticed the barricades and signs at the end of the street.

"Ohhhh," said the kid stopping short. "That's new."

What had recently been a building was now a pile of still-smoldering rubble.

"Wasn't me," said Rollie quickly.

The signs read:

No Trespassing!
You Could Be Injured Upon Entering!

We Cannot Legally be Sued if You're Stupid Enough
To Ignore Clearly Posted Warnings!

"That's our only franchise office," sighed the girl. "How will I get my Purple now?"

"Excuse me," Tseethe motioned to a barber standing outside his shop. His sign read:

Uncreative but Adequate Hair Cutting.

Tseethe gestured to the building. "When did this happen?"

"Yesterday," said the barber. "At first I thought it was thunder, then an earthquake, then I saw the smoke and dust rolling down the street."

"What caused it?" Bertram asked.

"Some kind of bomb. They believe they have the perpetrator in custody. I've never seen anything like it. She didn't even try to run when our RulesRegulators came. She stood there waiting for them. She let them take her away."

"She *wanted* to be arrested?" One of Rollie's newly lavendered eyebrows shot skyward. "Who does that?"

"Some people think she's not mentally right." The barber motioned to the brain area of his uncreative yet adequately-trimmed head. "She had no feelers. It's been suggested that she might have purposefully cut them off." He snipped at the air with his shears and shuddered. "Of course, there are other potential explanations for this, as well. Like being born without them or losing them in an accident. Time will tell the facts," he said assuredly. "Unless it doesn't."

Tseethe thanked him for his help.

"We should have more information soon," he continued. "Her trial starts tomorrow morning."

"They haven't identified her, have they?" Bertram asked.

"Yeah. Manners. Jane Manners," said the barber. "It's pretty offensive, isn't it? People with manners tend not to do stuff like that. It's false advertising."

The next day, Bertram, Rozz, Rollie and Tseethe filtered into the courtroom, which was standing room only. Up front and through the crowd, Bertram spied the defendant, Jane Manners, perched on a platform for all to see. She looked different from her Uninet mugshot. Now she wore a prim hat and under it, her straight blond hair hung lankly on either side of her long, un-made-up face. She wore a long skirt and a sweater embroidered with various Epiq motifs. At her throat was a metal choker with a yellow star shaped centerpiece, like a very ugly cameo. Her hands were folded tidily in front of her. Her feet were crossed at the ankles.

Also up front was a young man with a bushy beard down to his waist. He wore what might have been a ceremonial robe but, given Epiq fashion, it was hard to be sure. "We've taken roll," said the young man, eyeing a clipboard, "and cross-checked against District Fourteen registration. And I understand Velmar Dimspung isn't with us? Velmar?"

"Velmar's got a stomach bug, Your Supervisorness," came a voice. "He can't leave for the yakking, but said to send you his regrets."

The Supervisor nodded and made a note. His finger trailed down the page. "And Meglan Mardiblar? Meglan, you here?"

"My wife Meglan died last night," someone called out. "She lived to the ripe old age of one hundred and twelve. This is the first trial she's missed since she was Voteworthy! It's a sad day for our family."

"Well, that's a real shame," said the Supervisor with a solemn nod.

"After the trial, we're having a cremation and barbeque," added the grieving widower. "Separate fires, of course."

"Of course."

"You all are welcome," Mr. Mardiblar announced to the crowd, "so long as you bring a covered dish."

A warm, reverential murmur came over the group.

"I appreciate the update," said the Supervisor. "I'll take her off the list then." He marked that down, reexamined the list and stroked his beard. "Last, I see I'm missing Lula Trubludgett. Lula?"

"I'm here," came a high voice from the door. It was the girl from the DiversiDine stand. "Sorry I'm late. My sib isn't Voteworthy. I had to take him to the minder."

"Glad you made it, Lula."

"Thank you." As she scanned the room for a place to sit, she noticed Bertram's group in the back. She flashed an uncertain smile, but Bertram waved her over and, in a moment, had boosted her onto an unused podium, so she could see.

"Now," said the Supervisor, "we are here today for the trial of one Jane Manners. Defendant Manners has been charged with burning down a District Fourteen building for the company called DiversiDine World Manufacturing and Imports. So we must decide: what are the facts of the case?" The Supervisor turned on an overhead projector. "Fact: the DiversiDine building has become rubble." He showed a photo of the crumbled DiversiDine building.

"Fact: it was not rubble as of the day before yesterday at hour fifteen." The image showed the DiversiDine building upright and strong.

"Fact: District Fourteen RulesRegulators found Defendant Manners standing outside the rubble at hour fifteen-point-five. Fact: one RulesRegger Merl Lampicrav was a witness. Is that a fact, Merl?"

A man in plaid stood up. "Yes, that's correct."

"And how did you find Defendant Manners?"

"I found Defendant Manners standing before the building with a bomb detonator in her hand and bomb-making equipment in a sack."

"And was this detonator connected to the destruction of the DiversiDine building?"

"Yes, our experts connected that detonator to matching residue in the building."

"Does anything else connect Defendant Manners to the building?"

"Yes, sir. Defendant Manners confessed she blew up the DiversiDine building."

The Supervisor turned to Jane Manners. "Did you admit you blew up the building?"

"Yes," she said. "I did."

"And would you please tell us why you blew up the DiversiDine building?"

"I thought I'd do you a favor on my way to Tryfe," she said.

He inhaled sharply. "You destroyed public property as a benefit to District Fourteen?"

"To your whole city. Your whole planet," she said.

"And Tryfe is?"

"My home planet."

A murmur swayed over the crowd.

"You claim you're not from Epiq?" The Supervisor seemed like he was trying very hard to control the skepticism in his voice.

"That's correct. I'm from Mystic, Connecticut, in the United States, on a planet the Greater Communicating Universe calls Tryfe."

"And what do you do there?"

"I teach five year olds."

"You teach them bomb building?"

"Mostly the alphabet, numbers and why paste is not an *aperitif.*"

The man scratched his beard pensively. "And can you prove that you're from another planet?"

"Well …" She removed her hat.

The people in the room gasped. "She's got no feelers!" someone shouted.

"Yes!" She stood, parting her hair on each side to show her smooth scalp. "That's right! I am Tryfling and I am feeler-free!"

This caused quite a sensation, and eventually several doctors were summoned to inspect and officially verify that the woman's antennae did not appear to have been surgically removed.

By now, the Supervisor looked considerably ruffled. "Do

you have any other evidence to prove that you're an alien from another planet?" he asked the defendant.

"Yes," she said. "I have a spaceship."

Nervous laughter rustled across the crowd.

"And where is this spaceship?" asked the Supervisor.

"Outside the city, in a park."

Bertram was starting to feel a sort of kinship with Jane Manners.

"And did you mention this spaceship and its location to the RulesReggers yesterday?" the Supervisor asked.

"Yes, I did."

"And did the RulesReggers find this 'spaceship'?" The Supervisor turned to the officer.

"We found a large unidentified item in that location." A worried murmur crossed the crowd now. "Its technology appears highly sophisticated. It is of a size that could possibly transport passengers. Consulting engineers are examining it."

And at this, Jane Manners leapt to her feet. Security moved forward, poised for something more. "I came here in that ship to destroy DiversiDine on your planet and send a message to their corporate office," she proclaimed. "DiversiDine has been using both your planet and mine as test beds for its products and as playthings for its own entertainment." She tugged at the ugly yellow choker. "They're here now, with us, via this small camera. The camera your own officers tried to remove but couldn't."

Bertram nodded knowingly. Oh yes, he'd had a Yellow Thing of his own during season one of *There Goes the Galaxy*. But his, at least, was not an implant. Clearly, Yellow Thing technology had come a long way in a short period of time.

Jane Manners went on, "They abducted me from my planet and tossed me into their prison system to see what I'd do. Well, I hope they've enjoyed the journey, because I know I *loved* watching their building come down." Her face lit with a crazed passion. "If you keep me here, my own planet will never know the truth. And I understand the people of Epiq value the truth above everything else. Thank you." She sat, with finality.

Another murmur swept the crowd.

"We do value the truth here," said the Supervisor, trying to digest all this. "However, I can't personally say DiversiDine's products have felt particularly invasive to my life. Can anyone here say so?"

A murmur of no rippled from every corner. Bertram noticed Lula's "no" was emphatic.

Jane's face went a furious red. "That's because they're using different tactics here," she spat. "They know their audience. They're going with your culture. It's only a matter of time that it will grow, slowly, until you don't even know who you are anymore, and —"

"It is a fact that I can't fault a company for what it has not yet done," said the Supervisor. "And it is equally a fact that the unwanted demolition of any private property in District Fourteen is against the law. Now I understand that within the building itself, there were no casualties?" The Supervisor looked to Merl.

"That's correct. We found no bodies in the rubble that could be called bodies. We did find some parts of rather strange people-shaped mechanical devices that we believe operated the manufacturing."

The Supervisor nodded and pushed a button. The overhead presentation showed an image of various parts of Non-Organic Simulants, faces identical to those of the Stevenses from the Moon factory, except these had antennae.

"So in summary," began the Supervisor with another comforting stroke of his own beard, "Defendant Manners makes many claims. We've heard them today. Yet it is the job of Blef District Fourteen *not* to judge the validity of her actions, but determine whether she is guilty of destroying public property. And, if so, the appropriate level of sentence.

"Options include: community service, community service and a set monetary restitution, one to five years imprisonment, five to ten years imprisonment, eleven to thirty years imprisonment, thirty-one to fifty years imprisonment, or life in prison. Everyone please cast your vote."

Suddenly, it seemed everyone was holding a small, screened device, including Lula.

"Don't do it, Lula," Bertram whispered, as he saw her finger heading for the down arrow toward Guilty. "There's so much more to this you don't even know."

Lula scowled at him from under the brim of her hat. "It doesn't matter. She said she did it. That's a fact."

Lula chose "Guilty" and Bertram felt his heart sink to his stomach. As he watched the citizens cast their votes, that anxiety swelled within him, prickling the nerves and making him fidget. This anxiety didn't lessen as he noticed Rollie was perfectly still and sizing up the room like a vaguely-purple predatory bird.

Bertram glanced back at Lula's screen. He couldn't quite read what she'd ultimately entered for punishment. But based on her scrolling, it was way past community service.

"Last minute to make your decisions," announced the Supervisor.

"We can't let Jane Manners go down for this," whispered Bertram to Rozz.

"I know, I know!"

"No problem," said Rollie. His hand slipped beneath his coat and settled where one of his holsters normally hid. "Zap, zap. We bust her out. Done and done."

"Rollie, handlasers are not the answer to every problem," growled Bertram.

The Deltan looked genuinely surprised at this. "Are you being funny? Most people benefit from a good stunning."

Tseethe nodded enthusiastically. "Does wonders for settling family arguments at the Hy-Holidays, let me tell ya."

"But these people, they're ..." Bertram searched for a word, "us. Better informed and slightly less knee-jerk ..."

"More logical and procedural," Rozz added, "totally."

"But they're in the same position we are. You can't just barge in with —" Bertram's words broke off with a little caw.

"Barge in with what?" asked Rozz.

But he waved her away unable to find his words under the

white-hot flash of a sudden, blinding idea.

"Five seconds," said the Supervisor. "Four ... three ... two ... one ... Voting has ended. It will take a moment to tabulate the results."

"Dude, if you have a plan," said Rozz to Bertram, "time to piss or get off the pot. Otherwise I'm totes rolling with Rollie's jailbreak fu."

"Didn't get half what she said," Rollie hooked a thumb at Rozz, "but I agree."

"Just shut up for a minute, both of you." Bertram's idea was coming clearer now. He almost had it. His next move all depended on what that computer said at the front of the room. "I've got it. Leave it to me."

They didn't press him and he was glad. He didn't want to have to say his idea aloud, he just wanted to Do. It was about ten minutes of pre-Do waiting, before the Supervisor looked at the screen and began nodding. "The results are in." There was no hint of smile behind the grizzly beard. "Defendant Manners, you have been voted Guilty of the willful destruction of the DiversiDine building. Due to the danger of the situation, your admitted pleasure at your actions and the potential for a recurring crime of this nature, you have been issued thirty-one to fifty years imprisonment this day in the Fourteenth District of the city of Blef."

Applause broke out in the room. Justice had been served.

Tseethe said, "Oh, well, that's not *too* bad, then ..."

But Rozz's eyes shot darts. "'Not too bad'? When your species' average life span is seventy-five?"

"Oh." He grimaced. "That's fragged up."

"Thank you," said the Supervisor to the people. "Thanks to each and every one of you who came today for —"

Bertram stepped forward and called down the aisle. "What if I could show you all, with your own eyes, what DiversiDine could do to your society?"

The crowd turned and stared. Jane Manners looked astonished.

"What if I could prove to you beyond a shadow of a doubt

that Jane Manners' actions, while seemingly radical, were in the best interest of District Fourteen and specifically targeted to DiversiDine alone? What if I could prove that she poses no harm to non-DiversiDine entities? Would you consider reducing her sentence?"

"I don't believe we've met." The Supervisor squinted at him. "Are you from this District?"

"The fact is I'm not."

"Well, then, I'm afraid —"

"Do you let polling stations determine your truth?" Bertram snapped. "The facts say Jane Manners did this. She says it herself. I don't dispute the Guilty verdict. But what if there are facts that additionally support the view that Jane Manners merits a lower sentence? Would you be open to investigating that information?"

"Well, I —"

"Or are you the kind of person who turns your back on the truth in the interest of speed and efficiency?"

"Of course I believe in truth, mister. Sure, I'd be open to it."

"Great."

"But what I think doesn't matter. I can't make that call alone. We'd have to vote to undertake that vote," said the Supervisor. "So everyone come back … Back in here please, we're not quite done for the day." He grabbed his handheld device and everybody who had been leaving filtered back into their seats with some moaning — particularly the people who were going home to that cremation and barbeque.

"The issue that has been posed to the people of District Fourteen is: would you consider new information that could reduce the defendant's sentence, with, um, a second vote?" The guy almost looked embarrassed. "It's sort of a two-tiered thing."

Bertram sighed. It wasn't quite what he'd been looking for, but it was in the right direction, and at least they didn't take roll again.

In a minute, the votes were cast and in another ten, they had the results.

"You," the Supervisor pointed at Bertram, "the answer to your question is a sixty-one percent vote in favor of voting on new information."

"Stellar," said Bertram, but he knew he couldn't relax yet. "Then I suppose I'd better start with this." And he removed his set of antennae.

A man shouted, "They're everywhere!" and fainted. A woman screamed. A little child started crying. Lula's eyes were big as satellite dishes.

"Like Jane Manners, I am not from Epiq. I'm from Tryfe and my name is Bertram Ludlow."

Jane Manners' face looked almost illuminated at the sound of his name. A hand went to her forehead and she started laughing uncontrollably.

"This is my friend Rozz Mercer," Bertram continued, sweeping a hand to Rozz. "She's from Tryfe, too."

Rozz whipped off her antennae and rubbed at the part where the headband had been pressing into her head. Bertram imagined that might have been causing some flashbacks for her, anyway.

"With us," Bertram pressed on, "are a couple of friends from another planet, Hyphiz Delta."

Tseethe saluted with his pipe. Rollie stood tense and alert, like he was still waiting for the bit where he could stun everyone.

"Epiq is but one inhabited planet out of thousands all over space," Bertram explained. "These planets have unified into what they call the Greater Communicating Universe. The GCU. But my home planet's like yours. It doesn't even know about the GCU. It has no idea the head of DiversiDine owns the whole property and can develop it however he wants. And now on Tryfe, DiversiDine's products have started to make some people sick. The company has created an atmosphere where the people have become dependent on their products, even against their own health and best interest. This is what Jane Manners was worried about for you. I would like you to see this firsthand." And he went in for the kicker. "I propose

District Fourteen takes a field trip with me to Tryfe."

Bertram grinned as the commotion in the room reached Epiq proportions.

"Listen, listen!" He whistled sharply over the crowd and that got their attention again, "If I'm just crazy, my spaceship won't work and you'll have nothing to worry about. You leave here, fire up Grandma, then get the burgers going for a big family evening. Nothing will have changed. But if I'm telling the truth, you all are missing out on some very big facts. And I get the impression you folks don't want to live that way."

They'd calmed down a bit now, but there was still a lot of discussion.

"This is madness!" said someone.

"Why are we even listening to him?" asked someone else.

"We don't have to listen to him. Let's go."

"Thing is," called Bertram, "you did vote in favor of receiving evidence in the Manners case. And that evidence is only available on Tryfe."

"We did vote," the Supervisor said frowning.

"We did," they muttered, wringing their hands. "We did vote, didn't we?"

"When would we go?" asked the Supervisor.

"As soon as possible," said Bertram. "Things on my planet were dicey enough when we left."

"Um, Bertram?" Rozz tugged on his shirt sleeve. "Among other issues with this plan? I think you're forgetting something kinda important. There are, like, three hundred people here. We have one small ship."

"Two ships," called Jane.

"Two ships," said Rozz.

"Ah." She was right; Bertram hadn't thought of that. This was what happened when he got impulsive.

Fortunately, Rollie had a Ph.D. in impulsive. "I could call in some favors," he said. "See who's in the neighborhood working Quad One right now. Let 'em do a bit of humanoid transport for a change. Maybe bring us a load of that novelty Translachew, too. We'll need it. And Karnax knows, my mates owe me for all the free advice I've given 'em lately."

Bertram felt hopeful. "How soon could they get here?"

Rollie considered it. "Roughly two Universal days. For this planet, that would be ..." He seemed to be doing some mathematic calculations, muttered, " ... carry the seven ..." Suddenly, he looked surprised. "Er, still two days, actually."

"Do it," Bertram said. "It would be great if we could get twenty, thirty ships."

"Bertram," pressed Rozz, "I want you to think this through some more."

"We could leave in two days," announced Bertram to the crowd. "That will give everybody enough time to pack and to, um, reschedule any dental appointments. Anyone who'd like to see one of the ships we'll be going in, follow us."

Across the room, a cuffed Jane Manners was being led into custody, put away for safe-keeping. Over her shoulder, she gave Bertram a bright smile and a nod.

Bertram nodded back.

"Bertram —" Rozz was still trying to get his attention.

"Thank you, all of you, for your votes," the Supervisor shouted, though everyone was already leaving without officially being dismissed. "We'll reconvene here. Two days. Same time!"

They flooded out the doors, some dispersing to their homes and businesses while the majority of them trailed after Bertram's group, curious to see this vehicle from space.

"Dude, you are being a dumbass," Rozz told Bertram in hushed tones at the head of this parade. "There is so much wrong with this plan."

"How can you say that?" Bertram could not stop smiling. "It's perfect! It was the cats that gave me the idea, you know."

She emitted a pained exhale. "Tell me you're not taking advice from creatures who poop in a box."

"I meant their prophecy. How do you get a backspace planet that's living a lie to see it's living a lie? You bring the undeniable, unvarnished truth straight to the people."

"Depends on who you're trying to convince: the people of Epiq or the people of Tryfe?"

"Well, either, really. But don't you see?" He put a reassuring arm around her shoulders. "This solves all of Tryfe's problems."

"Us coming with an alien invasion?" She shot him an unimpressed look and shrugged off his arm.

"No-no. Not an *invasion* —"

"But your cat friends said —"

"A diplomatic *mission*," Bertram corrected. "A friendly collection of alien buddies popping by for a little come-to-Jesus discussion."

Rollie added, "Though completely non-specific to your various fascinating Tryfe religions."

"Exactly," Bertram said. "Good diplomacy doesn't discriminate."

A "bah!" escaped Rozz's lips for the second time of late.

"'Bah' you say now," said Bertram. "But you'll backpedal that 'bah' later. Think about it, Rozz. Eudicot T'murp chose Tryfe because it was backspace, because it was completely different in its approach to marketing than Epiq — the perfect control planet for product user testing."

"I know that, Bertram, but —"

"But if the Tryflings and the, er — Epiqites? Epiqers? Epiqurians? —" He looked to Rollie and Tseethe who had no clue. " — People of Epiq all know they're being used, there can't be any more blind testing. If the subjects rebel, the project's a wash."

"Right," Rozz said. "So T'murp won't need us anymore."

"Exactly!"

"So he could just sell us to somebody else. Or blow us up. That is, if our 'alien buddies' even get to chit-chat with the Tryflings before our own people get totally freaked and blow us out of the sky."

Bertram said, "I notice you're stuck on a theme."

"Recent days set a tone," Rozz told him.

"Did you see the thing around Jane Manners neck? That is one of those cameras, like that Yellow Thing that DiversiDine had set me up with."

"I noticed. I kinda have a thing about accessories that are built directly into your body." She shuddered.

"We take Jane Manners with us and DiversiDine will be filming everything — and T'murp will be watching all of it. We'll rip the blindfold off his double-blind testing right in front of him. Plus, I have an idea or two to give us some extra leverage."

"Well …" Her tone suggested he was winning her over. "Our own government could still blow us up, though."

Bertram shrugged. "Minor detail. We'll work on it."

Bertram had to admit, he was impressed. The people of District Fourteen didn't just say they were open to new information, they walked the walk. He found his credibility solidified with the locals quickly once Bertram uncloaked the Penumbra and they looked inside his gently-used, lightly-renovated, personal UFO. They gasped when the ramp lowered. They oohed over the lounge, ahhed over the cockpit and kinda screamed a lot when they met the gang of toilet snails, who were four feet tall now and communicating to each other in staccato hums.

It was probably this last encounter that really drove the aliens concept home. All three hundred curious locals evaluated the ICV like they were part of some innovative neighborhood home tour. And most of them went away saying they'd have to think about what they saw but that they were eager to learn more.

Twenty stayed to ask further questions while Rollie started comming all his buds who owned their own ships. The people of Epiq looked on in wide-eyed wonder as beings that resembled gelatin desserts, or large bugs or had two faces popped up on the screen. Bertram knew a few of these folks from previous Intergalactic Underworld events. One of them he knew a bit more intimately. Most of them said they could get there shortly. Some said they were already on their way.

Finished with the task at hand, Tseethe and Rollie took turns showing the people of Epiq GCU weaponry and Rozz demonstrated the Uninet. Eventually, Bertram popped some snacks in the Food Processing Unit, Rozz cracked open some FizzyYum and Rollie lasered up a quick one-pot Deltan creation from things sitting around the supply cupboard. They put on music and the talk turned to Tryfe and Epiq, print and possibilities. They even discussed their planets' shared experience of the Swirling Times. And Bertram felt, for the first time in forever, that he had finally found the right path.

36

They would have reached their destination so much sooner, Feegar Commander Nom considered, were it not for the strikingly unoriginal naming conventions of Tryfe's inhabitants.

Did no one take note that there were multiple places on the very same planet with the same name? Did no one track this data and reject mindless repetition for the good of clarity and the enrichment of Tryfling culture as a whole?

Obviously, not!

Vital time was wasted in brief stops in Pittsburgs found in the lands of Alabama, California and Ohio (all within the unified realm of Usa) until Captain Mau finally found the correct Burgh of Pitts in the land of "P.A."

Further research showed that this "P.A." territory was also not named in celebration of Paternal Archetypes and the manifest propagation of the species. No, the ship's Uninet source dubbed it an abbreviation for "Pennsylvania," so-named for an archaic writing utensil these "Pennsylvanians" worshipped. The Commander was curious to examine one of these *pennsyls* and see what all the fuss was about.

Nom observed this particular backspace city was quite densely composed, narrow at its center and not efficiently structured to park Interplanetary Cruise Vessels at length. So he ordered the cloaked Feegar ship to settle in a wide green space, where the realm's rivers met.

"We shall keep the ship cloaked, to ensure the secrecy of our mission," Commander Nom said as he presented a large, black box to his troops. "Within this box is opportunity. A chance to become one with these backspace bipedal livestock. We shall blend in, follow their customs. We will present the face of innocence. That will be our advantage." He opened the box to reveal forty-one shiny new holowatches.

He took a watch for himself, then passed the box to Captain Mau for distribution.

"Put on the holowatches. Scan yourselves carefully. Leave no part unscanned. Our facades must be flawless. There must be no suspicion of our true motives. I will show you how." Nom demonstrated the proper scanning technique, then paced authoritatively before the now-scanning crew.

"You may find your transformation shocking, even hideous." It was always important to set expectations. "Do not let it daunt you. You are warriors. You are survivors. And you will do what is required to complete our mission."

"Yes, Commander Nom!" they shouted. As each Feegar completed the task, that Warrior-Survivor-Doer stood to attention and waited.

After a moment, Nom surveyed the crew. "We are ready? Good! Fire up your holowatches!"

Forty Feegar warriors powered up their holowatch disguises. And forty Feegar warriors vanished, replaced by a crowd of opaque humanoid fleshbags in ignoble garments.

It was repellant, unworthy and degrading to the Feegar species, and Commander Nom saw the loathing overtake the troops as they laid eyes upon each other. Tech Officer Din now appeared aged and male, with skin folds upon its face, neck and hands. It wore leg and abdomen coverings up to its sternum. It wore chest coverings buttoned up to its larynx. Its footwear and belt were white.

Captain Mau appeared female. But not like Feegar females, who could be recognized swiftly by their visible internal sex organs, thus avoiding any time-consuming uncertainties during mating season. This one was clad in a fabric tube. It had that disgusting hair many species tended to have, formed and frozen into some yellow protective helmet. Its face had been covered in the ceremonial battle paint that seemed to designate a high-ranking warrior.

Corporal Gorj had been transformed into skinsack progeny, its cheeks and nose spattered with red constellations. It wore blue short pants and a blue chest covering trimmed in embellishments. Its hair was reminiscent of the shape of a bowl better used for containing the blood of one's enemies.

Yes, overall, this group was grotesque, yet the disguises were perfect for their quest. Commander Nom pressed the button on his holowatch and gave a satisfied nod to the troops before him. The specific form of his own transformation did not concern him. Leadership was about doing what was necessary despite personal inconvenience. But, while they said not a word, the troops' expressions and the way they immediately looked to the ground hinted that the Commander's visage was perhaps the most loathsome of them all.

"It is time," said Nom.

And so, as new beings, they exited the starship onto the cold, backspace land.

They had split into twenty groups of two, with Commander Nom joining one of them to form the only group of three. The planet was quite different from expectations. Being an uncivilized land, Nom had anticipated that the communities would be quite rural and sparsely populated, making finding a single Hyphiz Deltan among them an easy task. Yet the Burgh of Pitt teemed with life. Finding Tsmorlood in this crowd would be a challenge.

They approached a Tryfe man carrying a handled rectangle and wearing a fabric noose. Captain Mau held out an image of their quarry that they'd printed directly from the late Corporal

Scof's brain. "Have you seen this lifeform?" Mau asked.

With shake of the head, the Tryfe man had walked away.

"You, there — have you seen this lifeform?"

But the people of the land either responded in the negative, with barely a glance, or they didn't answer at all. It was problematic. And there were far too many of them to take aside for torture; that would just be inefficient.

Perhaps Feegar tactics were the problem. "Stop," said Commander Nom to his soldiers. "We must observe and do as they do. Follow their rules of socialization." And he paused to watch the Tryfe people and the way they interacted. Their first subjects were three young females who emerged from a building carrying cups of steaming liquid. They walked closely together, making a sound of merriment and conspiracy.

"That," said Commander Nom. "That is our first example."

Or there, across the street, trooping down the walkway, a group of males in identical colors — part of some platoon, perhaps — chanting, "Let's go, Pens! Let's go, Pens!"

"What does it *mean*, Commander?" asked Captain Mau with wonder. "'Let's go, Pens'?"

"More worship of ancient writing implements," the Commander explained.

"Ahhh …" the soldiers nodded.

Then there were those two Tryfe people in black fabric coverings standing on chairs. "The Swirling Times have COME and GAW-unn!" shouted one of them, holding up a book of print in one hand and perpendicular crossed sticks in another. "But the Swirling Times WEE-ull come again, if you have NOT turned your life a-ROUND! YOU, sir —" The Tryfe man pointed a bony finger at someone walking by. "Do you have a moment to talk about what the Swirling Times meant to you? Have you turned your life a-ROUND? Have you LOOKED at yourself and your WAYS of EE-vil? Go ahead! Take a good look! The Swirling Times were the MEE-ruh of the SOW-ull and we ALLLL have to face ourselves someday!" The other held a mirror aloft, catching the light and flashing it into the eyes of the Tryflings as they passed.

It was very informative. "Do you understand what we must do now?" Commander Nom asked his troops. They nodded.

And the timing was right. A male and female lifeform emerged from the very same building that the three young females had, also with steaming beverages. The Commander urged Mau forward. Mau approached the couple, held up the image of Tsmorlood and mimicked the high, jovial noise they'd heard earlier. "Do you have a MO-ment to talk about the image on this paper?" he asked. "In exchange for infor-MAY-tion, we would be willing to pro-VIIIDE to you the beautiful writing implements that we ALLLL do covet."

At first, the female of the duo made that high jovial sound in return, and the Commander was pleased that headway had been made. But then she turned to the male and rolled her eyes in a manner suggesting she was having some kind of neurological problem. "I *told* you all the weirdos were drawn to me," she said and made the sound again. And like all the other Tryflings, the pair walked off.

"Skinsack!" the Commander shouted. It was indeed a blow to Feegar honor.

Commander Nom's group scoured the city in silence for a while, the Commander regretting his brief loss of authority in the face of emotion.

They were not far from their ship now, Nom realized. He paused to examine a Tryfling male who stood behind a small, metal cart. "All-beef hot dogs! Delicious! Homemade kielbasa! Just like your *babcia* made! Fresh kraut! Good luck for your New Year! Best in the Burgh! Get your hot dogs and hot sausage here!"

The smell wafting from the cart was intriguing. Nom approached it. He tried the high-pitched sound of merriment again to show his goodwill. "This is food from here?"

The vendor looked around and then peered over the cart. He blinked in surprise, then addressed his words instead to Mau. "A hundred percent local. Homemade hotdogs, made from grass-fed, farm-fresh beef," he said. "Or if sausage is your thing, I can do you a nice kielbasa and kraut combo for five bucks."

Nom sniffed the air. "I smell … intestines," he said with some delight.

"Natural casings," said the vendor to Mau. "That's right." He peered over the cart again, curiously. "Is this some kind of ventriloquist act?"

"Such juicy belly meat," said Nom. He eyed the vendor's round waist.

"In every one," the vendor said, frowning. "Seriously, you're good. I don't see you moving the baby's mouth or nothin'. How are you even —"

"Sweet lips and succulent feet …"

"Geez, you have some nose on ya, too." The vendor withdrew a steaming food product from the cart. "So what do you say? Yinz guys interested in a little bite? I can even do you a plate for the 'infant'…" He laughed nervously.

"Yes," said Nom, finding himself salivating now. "Oh, yesssss. A bite. A very big bite."

"A very, very big bite," agreed the troops.

37

By the time Rollie's friends started arriving, the people of Blef District Fourteen were completely on board.

Literally: they split themselves up into groups and boarded the ships, carry-on luggage in tow, without so much as an "I have a peanut allergy." To that end, they even brought their own food and beverages. It was an impressive example of organization, understanding and calm.

Bertram was equally impressed by the number of Rollie's friends who actually showed up. It turned out organized crime really was. A total of twenty ships arrived to support the cause, twenty former members of the Intergalactic Underworld ready to lend a hand. And when a finger of one such hand lightly tapped Bertram on the shoulder, he turned to spy two faces he was always pleased to see.

"Xylith!" Her long dark hair was swept into an elaborate braid. She wore a layered jumpsuit in metallic cobalt blue. A pair of lasers hung from the holster at her hip. Her boots matched the blue ensemble and hinted at the vaguely fin-like feet Bertram admitted he found strangely alluring. She gave Bertram an enthusiastic right-faced kiss that almost made him forget why they were there.

As she pulled away, her left face dimpled. "Now, Bertram

Ludlow, you didn't think I'd promise to come and then fail you?" she asked in her lilting drawl. "You're staging an invasion of your own planet. How could I possibly miss such an event? And I always did want to see Tryfe."

"Diplomatic mission," Bertram corrected, as he remembered to breathe. "No invasion: mission."

"A mission, of course …" Her indulgent tone said invasion or mission, it was all just piddly details. "Perhaps when you're done with being diplomatic on your planet, you and I could spend a little time … enhancing our own interspecies relations." Both smiles were insidious.

"Barring being shot, blown up, or captured by my government and squirreled away in Area Fifty-One for testing, my schedule should be completely free." He winked.

"Stellar …" The word lingered on the Epiq air.

"Stellar," he said, unable to make his words do that.

As she sauntered back to her ICV with a little wave over her shoulder, Rollie snickered. "Who'd've thunk it? It's still all systems go between you and Xylith, eh?"

"The universe can be a pretty wonderful place sometimes, Rollie," Bertram said, clapping him on the shoulder. "Of course, because of this, I'll probably die in some stupid, disappointing way. But hey," he motioned, "let's get prepped."

Once the full team arrived, Bertram passed out Translachew to everyone, then took the pilots aside and gave them his strategic run-down. He'd been working on this for the better part of a day now, with input from Rollie and Tseethe. And as he stood with the bulk of the Underworld's defectors around him, Bertram realized how oddly right this leadership position felt. It was almost like everything since his abduction had been building up to this one point in some bizarrely-plotted story arc.

Of course that was ridiculous, even for the GCU.

But the journey to Tryfe was not exactly a luxury cruise. If things had been overly-cozy with five humanoids and two cats, now the Penumbra Classic was downright snug. To his pre-existing passengers, Bertram had added Blef's Supervisor, Jane Manners, six RulesReg officers, Lula, Lula's baby brother and ten other Blefians of varying sizes, shapes and aromas. Augment this with a gang of fun-loving toilet snails tall enough to shop in Misses Petites, and Bertram considered spending the trip nestled safely away in his pilot's chair. At least in the cockpit, he wouldn't get stabbed by rogue antennae or hummed at by space mollusks looking for love.

The challenge with having an admitted terrorist on board, however, was that even among the open-minded folks of Epiq, Jane Manners would never be popular. And since the whole ship's lounge was packed like the CosmosCorral on two-for-one Tuesdays, avoiding her became complex. It wasn't long before the District Fourteen Supervisor rapped on the cockpit hatch and asked if they could move her to somewhere — anywhere — more solitary.

Bertram wasn't sure where that would be. There were people hanging out in the storage room. There were people in the bunks. There were cats in the air ducts, struggling to retain some sense of upper management status.

"Bring her in here," said Bertram, indicating the copilot's chair.

The Supervisor looked uncertain.

"She's cuffed, right?" Bertram asked.

He nodded.

"Send her in." Bertram had changed into his best space duds for this journey and he patted the laser holster at his thigh. "I have this," he said confidently, "in case she gives me any trouble."

From the ship's lounge, he heard the officers arguing about it. But a moment later, Jane Manners stepped through the hatch in her prison uniform.

"Have a seat." Bertram motioned.

She smiled as she took the chair, perching uneasily with her hands cuffed behind her. "I never imagined ... Bertram Ludlow," she said, a strange reverence in her voice. Strange because it was about him. "When I first heard your name in court, I didn't believe it. I thought it had to be a DiversiDine plant for the show. Some ..." she considered her word choice, "... look-alike ... a Vos Laegos impersonator maybe."

The idea that there might be a Bertram Ludlow-themed Vos Laegos act had never crossed his mind. He hoped vaguely that their Bertram didn't sing. "So I guess you know about the show *There Goes the Galaxy.*"

"It explained so much." Her freckled face gained a far-away expression. "Those weird old people who gave me the necklace ... The trumped up charges that sent me to Mawdank ... Why the guard kept smiling at my neck, offering me his good side ... Why my confinement cube was the only one that suddenly malfunctioned and popped open ..."

"Oh, that's how you got out!" Having been to Mawdank once, Bertram knew it was no slipshod operation. The only thing that opened doors there was bail money — and lots of it. "So it was all a part of the script."

"Yes," she began, a wry smile on her lips, "I was the Mawdank exemption."

Bertram nodded. He clearly recalled how Eudicot T'murp's people helped things along when they got a little dull. "So then the other prisoners who escaped in that jailbreak, they got out because of —"

"Me," she said simply. "I used it as a cheap distraction technique for the guards, and it worked. I should have realized then that something was up. But on the way out, one of the inmates heard I was from Tryfe. She made a joke about how the whole thing was just like this *There Goes the Galaxy* show. Well, as soon as I got a chance, I looked it up. It was as clear as day. I was being used. And I saw red." Her eyes narrowed like that red might return along with the memories. Her freckles had blended into her burning cheeks. "I was so angry, it was like I stepped outside myself. And that moment I decided: if they wanted a show, I'd give it to them." She sighed. "Unfortunately, I never did get to take down DiversiDine on Earth."

"Uh, yeah, well ..." Bertram grinned, picturing the cloud of colorants as it rolled down the DiversiDine loading dock. "We might have lent a hand in that direction, anyway."

She gave him an arch look. "What does that mean?"

"Talk to my friend Rollie." Bertram hooked a thumb to the lounge behind them. "You can compare notes on detonation devices and laser discharges. He'd like that."

But Jane seemed to find no pleasure in the idea. She just sat there, studying her knees. "I'd like to help. I would. But I'm not so sure I understand where you're going with this trip," she said at last.

"I know," he said, "and I'd tell you everything. But who's going to watch, if they already know the ending? And we, Ms. Manners, have company." Bertram's eyes flicked to the Yellow Thing in her neck. "Just trust me on this. The season two finale? It'll be worth the wait."

The starship had reentered the Earth's atmosphere, making its approach over the U.S. And Bertram Ludlow was ready. "Hey," he dragged one of the Blefian guards to the cockpit, "can you watch her a minute?" he asked, indicating the prisoner. Then he darted into the bathroom, locking the door behind him. He drew his cell phone and a dog-eared business card from his pocket. He dialed.

"Deezle," Bertram said. "It's, um," — he'd resigned himself to it — "Bacontini."

Deezle's voice brightened. "Hey, Bacos, man! How are you? You didn't show up Tuesday so I thought we might have scared you off."

"No, we've just been busy." Bertram switched the phone to his other ear. "Look, we've got something big in the works.

Something you're going to want to see. We're going to be downtown near the, er, The Company building soon. Can you get there?"

"Sure. I mean, I'm at work but — Ow! Ow! Ow!"

Bertram twitched. "What's wrong? You okay?"

"Feels like a sudden toothache," laughed Deezle. "I'll have to leave work early."

"Ah," Bertram untensed. "Attaboy."

"So what's the deal, anyway, 'Tini? What's the scoop on The Company?"

"No time to go into it. But believe me: you'll know it when you see it. One thing …"

"Anything."

"I need you to film everything that happens, okay? As many of you as possible. And upload it to as many places as you can when it's done. We've got to make this thing go viral."

"Wow, mysterious …" he said approvingly.

"Can I count on you?"

"Absolutely, Bacontini! We're all over it! I'll call the troops."

"Thanks, Deezle. We'll be in touch."

It was as Bertram ended the call, he heard rustling behind him. One of the toilet snails had pulled back the shower curtain. It wore a shower cap. It said, "Am I going to need to release my stinging spray for this endeavor?"

Bertram blinked. They had stinging spray? "Er, we'll let you know."

The creature nodded.

There was something about suddenly being able to understand the snail that made Bertram feel really uncomfortable. His past snail-centric history flashed before his eyes. "And, uh … hey, sorry about lasering you guys and stuff."

The snail shrugged. "It's forgotten. It was another me, another time." It pointed. "Hand me that towel?"

With the Golden Triangle up ahead, Bertram hit the comm to his mini-fleet. "This is ICV-One. Everybody stay cloaked until I give the word. You copy?"

"ICV-Two, affirmative," came Xylith's voice.

"ICV-Three, I read ya, son," Rollie's friend Backs responded.

"ICV-Four, copy," said Prinny and they went down the line until all the ships were accounted for.

Bertram surveyed the landscape ahead. "ICVs Sixteen to Twenty, see the two stadiums? Time to pick your team and do a little tailgating," he said, and the group confirmed.

"ICVs Eleven to Fifteen? You're going to land smack-dab in the middle of Liberty and Fifth Avenues. Try not to flatten anybody. Use your turn signals. Show 'em how it's done."

A chorus of voices said they understood.

"ICVs Eight to Ten: you hover low over the rivers. Make it dramatic. Churn up the water a little. Give them something for their money." Bertram felt really good about this Being In-Charge thing.

"ICV Seven, you cover The Point. That's the, er, pointy place where the rivers all meet. Hover like you mean it." ICV Seven swept off into position.

"ICVs Five and Six, you land on that east highway, Boulevard of the Allies. Again, no squishing the locals. It makes the whole friendly alien shtick a harder sell." Bertram waited for confirmation.

"And ICVs Two to Four, you come with me. We're going to take these babies camping on DiversiDine's doorstep!" He felt a laugh escape him, giddy and manic. From the co-pilot's chair, Jane Manners looked concerned. "Don't judge me, lady. You blew up buildings." And before she could answer he'd squeezed the comm again. "This is ICV-One. Okay, everyone heading to position? ... Uncloak!"

The fleet of interstellar machines revealed themselves in a fine example of technological burlesque. Down below, people pointed, cars screeched to the berm and faces pressed to the windows of the skyscrapers, wide-eyed and slack-jawed.

As the ships approached the ground, locals dodged out of the way. Piles of snow melted instantly. The Penumbra settled with a hiss of satisfaction and steam. Bertram spied Deezle now, along with the rest of his team. They were filming, using everything from smartphones to professional camera equipment. Even at a distance, he recognized the logo and writing on the side of the main camera. "Property of Plus-D'Argent University," Bertram's alma mater. Clearly, Deezle had connections.

"ICVs Two to Twenty: remain in your ships. I repeat, *remain in your ships* until I give alternate instructions," Bertram ordered. He searched for the exterior P.A. switch and grabbed the mic. He'd never used it before. He'd never had an occasion.

He pressed the communicator and said: "PEOPLE OF PITTSBURGH, EARTH, (ALSO KNOWN AS THE PLANET TRYFE): WE COME IN PEACE." He'd always wanted to say that. But really, who hadn't? "MY NAME IS BERTRAM LUDLOW. YOU MAY HAVE HEARD OF ME. I LIVED IN THIS CITY, UNTIL I WAS ABDUCTED BY ALIENS. I'VE RETURNED TO TELL YOU THAT THE PEOPLE OF EARTH ARE LIVING A LIE. WE DO NOT OWN THIS PLANET. REPEAT: THE PEOPLE OF EARTH DO NOT OWN THIS PLANET. THE PROPERTY IS OWNED BY THE CEO OF AN INTERGALACTIC CORPORATION WITH ITS EARTH HEADQUARTERS IN PITTSBURGH. YOU KNOW IT AS DIVERSIDINE. AND EVERY PRODUCT YOU BUY FROM THEM AND EVERY TIME YOU LET THEM INTO YOUR LIVES, YOU ARE AN UNWITTING PARTICIPANT IN A MARKETING EXPERIMENT THAT SPANS GALAXIES."

Bertram could see squad cars screeching onto the scene and police emerge, initially gung-ho but then losing momentum because academy training didn't cover UFO situations. Most of them decided pulling their guns and covering the spacecraft entrances seemed like a good idea, so they settled on that.

"INITIALLY DIVERSIDINE MIGHT HAVE MADE LIFE SEEM BETTER FOR YOU AND YOUR FAMILY," Bertram persisted. "IT MIGHT HAVE MADE YOU FEEL HAPPIER OR MORE PRODUCTIVE. THEIR PRODUCTS WERE DESIGNED TO DO THAT. BUT IT COMES AT A PRICE. DIVERSIDINE HAS BEEN ADDING SECRET INGREDIENTS — ALIEN CHEMICALS WITH DANGEROUS SIDE EFFECTS. ZOT! HAS THEM. IT'S CAUSED THE ACTION FIGURE SYNDROME YOU'VE SEEN IN THE NEWS. AND THE COMPANY WANTS TO COVER IT UP."

Reporters from a downtown news station were hustling across the street, equipment in tow, and Bertram also noticed a few vehicles from the local FBI branch had arrived. The agents leapt from their cars, saw the cops with the drawn guns, conferred, thought the approach was pretty groovy and followed suit.

Bertram decided he'd better introduce his main act before the National Guard dropped by. "YET WE, THE PEOPLE OF EARTH, ARE NOT THE ONLY ONES BEING MANIPULATED BY DIVERSIDINE," he proceeded. "THE PEOPLE OF THE PLANET EPIQ HAVE SHARED OUR FATE. THEY'RE HERE WITH ME TODAY TO MEET YOU AND SEE HOW DIVERSIDINE HAS TAKEN OVER OUR LIVES."

People from the DiversiDine building, Bertram noticed, had begun to flood onto the street like it was an evacuation drill. Or maybe it was. After what happened to the Moon Township plant, who could blame the managers for being jumpy? These were employees who couldn't be remolded.

"I WILL NOW LOWER THE RAMP TO THIS SHIP," Bertram explained. "AND WE WILL COME OUT SLOWLY TO MEET WITH YOU. WHILE I DO, MY FRIEND ROZZ MERCER, ALSO FROM PITTSBURGH, WILL TAKE THE COMM."

He motioned Rozz up front and she looked surprised, then fought her way to the mic. "HEY, YINZ GUYS," she said.

"UM, HOW 'BOUT THOSE STEELERS?"

"Steelers didn't make the playoffs," Bertram called as he pressed onward to the hatch.

" — PENS ... HOW 'BOUT THOSE PENS?"

Eudicot T'murp, CEO of DiversiDine Entertainment Systems and Aeroponics had started following *There Goes the Galaxy* season two production more closely right after Jane Manners blew up the Translachew factory on Sarulia. Prior to this, he'd been content with status updates from his production team — useful snippets of information like: "It seems the Tryfe woman escaped from Mawdank but also released a cell block of dangerous prisoners."

Or: "The Tryfe woman has almost severed the arteries in her neck trying to remove the camera."

Or even: "Sir, we understand the Tryfe woman now seems to have stolen a collection of detonation devices... Also, lunch."

By the time she'd made her strike on the Seers of Rhobux, T'murp started to wonder whether things had gotten a *teensy* bit out of hand. Once she'd reached Epiq, his misgivings were many.

Epiq was backspace and T'murp had liked it that way. He appreciated the people for their individuality and fact-driven natures and he'd learned a lot over the past few years about reaching their market. Unlike their Tryfe cousins, mass messaging didn't work on Epiq because Epiqites didn't get swayed by peer pressure and trends. All product claims had to be observably honest or they were completely ignored. He told the branch CEO there, "Customized is the way to go. Make it all low pressure and tailored to personal taste. It's the only way to get a response."

That's how they came up with the child-run beverage stands. What could be less threatening than a kid trying to make some cash? Sure, DiversiDine would never gain huge sales, but that wasn't the point. This was about finding out how to reach the most diverse population with the most universally-marketable products. The data was the value.

Then Jane Manners blew up the Epiq distribution center and T'murp considered kiboshing the whole initiative. But how could he, with a big juicy trial on the horizon? It was perfect for season two, a real Uninet ratings grabber. And when Bertram Ludlow and his friends showed up to speak on Manners' behalf? Well, that was more supernova than anything T'murp could have imagined. There was nothing Uninet audiences loved more than cameo appearances by their favorite Uninet personalities. The Hyphiz Deltan criminal, in particular, had tested well during season one. Getting him for season two was a sensation, especially considering his death.

But now Eudicot T'murp had let things go too far, and they were unraveling so swiftly he wasn't sure he could catch the strands. Bertram Ludlow, for instance, had grown surprisingly dynamic since T'murp first had him plucked, fresh from his home planet. The proof was in the live footage on the screen before him: Ludlow was on Tryfe, serving up DiversiDine's behind-the-scenes details to everyone within earshot.

Some of those details were a surprise even to T'murp.

"What's this about ZOT! side effects?" he asked his head of the Putting Things Out There department. "Are Tryfe people really having some kind of reaction to the product?"

"I don't know, sir. I hadn't seen anything about that in the progress reports," said the executive.

"Neither have I ..." T'murp absently scratched a frond. "Last I'd heard, it had passed all safety standards. And what's this stuff?" He indicated a Coaching booth on the screen. "Some kind of system of self-help philosophy? Fortune-telling? I don't recall that being a part of the original marketing model."

"I don't recall that, either, sir," said the executive.

"Contact what's-his-name. The branch CEO."

"You mean your nephew Bud?" asked the head of Putting Things Out There.

T'murp cringed. He didn't realize that was common

knowledge. Bud was his sisters' seedling. She'd assured T'murp that the young man was perfect for the job and initially, that appeared to be true. Bud had an advanced degree from one of Ottofram's most prestigious business schools and received glowing recommendations from all his professors. He'd digested all the best infopills on marketing management, had work experience in several DiversiDine branches and his interviews brimmed with knowledge and confidence. Plus, his reports had always been clear and concise.

Too concise, T'murp now saw.

"Yes, I mean my nephew Bud," T'murp said. "Get him in a meeting. I want answers and I want them now."

As Bertram Ludlow lowered the Penumbra's ramp to Earth, anticipation hung heavily. He paused at the top of the hatch, trying to get a feel for this crowd before introducing his extra-terrestrial pals. He knew he couldn't expect the kind of reception they'd had on Epiq. Most Earth folks were decent enough, but they'd never *quite* gotten over the fact that the entire universe didn't revolve around their planet. It was like a college kid coming home to find his room suddenly turned into a gym and his parents happier than they'd been in years, tanned and taking up salsa dancing. It was a jolt and a sore spot in human history. Painful truths made Bertram's job that much harder.

But Bertram gave a last scan of Market Square and everything seemed in control. He took a deep breath and started down the ramp as Jane Manners and the people of District Fourteen followed.

Rozz's voice echoed over the ship's public address system. "BERTRAM LUDLOW AND HIS INTERSTELLAR AMBASSADORS ARE NOW EXITING THE SPACECRAFT. THIS IS A HISTORIC PAN-PLANETARY INFORMATION-SHARING AND GOODWILL MISSION — SO DON'T BE A JERK AND SHOOT ANYONE. THANK YOU."

The police and FBI exchanged narrow glances at particular members — there were always a few in every bunch—but overall the situation looked good. News crews were filming. Local citizens waited expectantly, enraptured. Rollie and Tseethe, he noticed, stood guard at the top of the ramp, just in case someone decided not to follow Rozz's sage advice.

Bertram vis-ued the Penumbra. "Hey, could you send down some toilet snails? Volunteer toilet snails to the ramp, please!"

There was a pause. Then: "THEY SAY THEY PREFER TO BE CALLED AQUAPHILIC HOUSE GASTROPOIDS," responded Rozz over the P.A.

Bertram pushed at the sudden pain between his eyes. "Look, I'll call them whatever they want," he said. "Just ask them to come out here." He'd seen these guys demonstrate the "space aliens are real" side of things. He was beyond clinging to semantics.

Luckily, whatever Rozz told them, it did the trick because now several pairs of eyestalks peered around the hatchway.

Bertram waved forward these interplanetary guests. They emerged onto the scene in full, causing gasps and even applause from the locals. "Welcome to Tryfe, locally called Earth," Bertram told the snails. He figured when you'd spent the better part of your life in a spaceship lavatory, some more formalized orientation might be required. "You're in my hometown of Pittsburgh, as featured briefly in the popular entertainment program, *There Goes the Galaxy* season one. Thanks to my fellow Tryfling Jane Manners and her convenient on-person camera system —" he indicated that lady, " — you will likely be seen in *There Goes the Galaxy* season two. You will want to hire an interstellar lawyer to connect with DiversiDine about video permissions to use your image. Also remember the words 'financial compensation.' You'll thank me later." Bertram grinned. He had a feeling that, somewhere, a shiver had just rippled up Eudicot T'murp's stem.

"Now," Bertram turned to his alien entourage, "before us is DiversiDine's downtown headquarters. Note the architecture, its subliminal messaging and its giant wall of vending machines." He gestured to the items mounted at the foot of the building. "Additional machines are conveniently located across the city every two hundred feet ...

"Also, note the billboards around our fair city," he continued, indicating these, "all featuring DiversiDine's products and sponsored events."

At this, the Blefians were especially baffled. "But the signage is covered in unproven claims!" someone said.

"It's brazen self-interest in the guise of community!" said someone else.

Bertram smiled to himself. *Now they were getting it.*

He led them further around the building, "If you're looking for support for any of your daily life dilemmas, pop inside a DiversiDine coaching booth. During special events, these booths are manned by DiversiDine Life Coaches. But on regular days, you can pick up the receiver here — or call their toll-free number from your own phone — and a live DiversiDine employee like Carole over there —" he waved at his former colleague from the group of DiversiDine evacuees, "— will offer you vapid advice that encourages more DiversiDine product purchases."

He could hear Carole say, "Isn't that Troy Hill?" to the colleague standing next to her.

"And here we have our local law enforcement," Bertram said, leading the group to Pittsburgh's Finest, who seemed unsure whether they should holster their guns or make with the firepower. "Officers, right here we have cops from the planet Epiq, District Fourteen of the city Blef. You guys should swap stories. But right now, tell me: what's your favorite drink to have on duty? You." Bertram pointed.

"Um ..." The cop looked at his gun, wondering whether he was still supposed to be pointing it and at whom. "Well ... I like a big mug of Joltin' Jubilation in the morning and then, pretty much, it's DrinkThis all day."

Bertram turned to the Blefians. "Joltin' Jubilation is a popular Tryfe wake-up beverage called 'coffee' with special DiversiDine mood-enhancement additives," he explained.

"Ohhhh," the Blefians said, wide-eyed.

Bertram asked the cop, "And how do you feel when you drink these products?"

"Uh…" The officer looked like he wished he could copy someone else's answers for this quiz. "Really good, I guess. You know, kind of relaxed and happy? Like it's going to be a dandy day of law enforcement here in Pittsburgh."

The other officers murmured affirmation and patted him on the back. "Good answer, good answer," they chanted.

"And how did you feel before you had DiversiDine's products?" Bertram asked.

"Well …" He almost frowned, "I guess I used to feel kind of worried about stuff. Like I might get killed in the line of duty. But," his expression cleared, "that was a long time ago. I don't worry about anything like that anymore. And most people are pretty okay, I guess."

"Fascinating," breathed one of the Blefians. "DiversiDine has created an entire chemically-controlled contentment lifestyle."

"The streets may be safer," mused another, "but at what price? I'd like to see an independent cost-benefit analysis of this."

"Now," Bertram was gearing up for the big finish and he turned to the FBI, cops, press and the regular citizens of Pittsburgh, "is there anything you'd like to ask the people of Blef? Or our Aquaphilic House Gastropoids? They have translational gum."

Someone in the crowd shouted, "How come you have to walk down some lame ramp? Don't you have beaming technology? They have beaming technology in *Star Trek*."

"Ah," Bertram said. He'd expected this, but he thought it might come a little later in the Q-and-A. "I'll take this question. Beaming technology was just discovered in the Greater Communicating Universe, and it hasn't quite trickled down to the spaceship manufacturers yet. Next? Any more questions? Questions for our outer space friends?"

"Who gets the blame for The Swirling Times?"

"Are any of you Jedis? And if so, are you taking applications?"

"So what are those antenna made of, anyway? I'd like to replicate them for cosplay."

"Cheese planets," someone shouted. "Where and what flavors?"

38

The Feegars' time on Tryfe had been more belly-filling than directly successful. Search as they did, they had not found Rolliam Tsmorlood and it was only after some effort — and a snack or two along the way — that they discovered a shop owner who remembered selling the Hyphiz Deltan some print.

Commander Nom had guessed one thing correctly. In his arrogance, Tsmorlood had not bothered to wear a holowatch disguise. He'd foolishly assumed that his opaque skin and the correct number of visible appendages made him unobtrusive on this planet. It was this simple misconception that cost the vendor his life, for Feegars rarely left witnesses and never so close to mealtime.

Unfortunately, all the encounter proved was that Tsmorlood had been on Tryfe as described. Perhaps the local news would reveal more. Tsmorlood was notorious for his criminal activity. Surely, he would find it difficult to be law-abiding for long. Further investigation showed that in this city, the latest crimes were detailed in stacks of print, available from a machine on the street. Captain Mau was busy lasering open one such machine when Commander Nom raised a hand.

"Stop! Listen," said the Commander, his face tilting skyward.

They did as ordered.

"Interplanetary Cruise Vessels?" Mau asked, frowning and scanning the heavens.

The Tryfan sky appeared clear, but the hum was unmistakable. Ten or twenty ships were coming in—and fast.

Then a ray of sunlight hit at just the right angle and Commander Nom's trained eyes detected a familiar outline in the sky. Yes, it was an oncoming fleet and, since Feegars never waited for a battle to come to them, he and his troop drew closer.

But when the ships uncloaked, Nom experienced a most rare emotion: surprise. He'd expected it would be the Coalition of Planets, the Vos Laegos City RightGuides or some other law group that had gotten wind of the Feegars' new grocery shopping tactics.

But this... this was no organized armada.

Secure in their holowatch disguises, the Feegars joined the Tryfling crowd that surrounded the collection of motley interstellar transport. And when the arriving lifeforms emerged from their ships into the Tryfan city, Nom noticed who was among them. The Commander could not help but smile. This new upstart Underworld would learn who truly controlled the GCU.

From his position at the top of the Penumbra's ramp, Rollie Tsmorlood had an excellent view of the festivities. Ludlow was hosting some sort of Q-and-A between the Blefians and the locals. And while that wasn't the direction he would have personally chosen (his own Q-and-As were usually at laserpoint), he respected Ludlow's open diplomacy and determination. This was Ludlow's home planet, after all, and his show to run. Like the philosopher Karnax once said, "A skilled lifeform knows when to seize the helm; a wise one recognizes when others must take the wheel."

Rollie felt he owed Ludlow that, at least — what with

kidnapping him from Tryfe in the first place. The abduction had been a sticky point in Rollie's mind ever since he'd gotten to know the fellah. At the time, there hadn't been much choice. But he still felt that rare, guilty pang…

Life, he thought now, *would be so much easier if I didn't have this fraggin' conscience*. He often wondered where he'd picked it up so he could return it. It was glitchy and kept him from getting more done.

The crowd certainly looked engrossed in Ludlow's goings-on, their expressions ranging all the way from awe and amusement to intrigued trepidation. Even the planet's law enforcement seemed to be engaged.

Then Rollie spied the group of beings gathered in the back.

There were about forty of them, of varying ages and races, male and female. They paid no attention to Ludlow, the Blefians or the gang of lavatory snails. Rollie had spent enough time on Tryfe to know that a meet-n-greet with extra-terrestrials — particularly five-foot-tall gastropoids — should have something of a wow factor. But this particular collection of Tryflings spoke quietly among themselves like bored wallflowers at an unpopular Hyphiz Deltan dance club.

They did not stare and yet Rollie had the strangest feeling that they were all looking his way.

"How paranoid am I?" Rollie asked Tseethe, who stood opposite him on the Penumbra's ramp.

"Very," Tseethe said, without one moment's hesitation. "Always have been."

"And how often am I right?" Rollie asked.

This took longer. "Less than you think, but more often than I can mock ya for."

Rollie nodded. "That's honest." He'd always liked that about Tseethe. No nonsense; you knew where you stood. Rollie called into the ship, "Rozz: come here, would you?"

She arrived at the portal wearing purse-lipped amusement. "You realize I don't work for you, right?"

"There's a group of Tryflings at the back left," he said. "Look but don't be obvious." He gave her a moment to do so.

"By Tryfe standards, are they odd?" It had always been hard to tell what was odd and what wasn't on Tryfe, when so much Tryfe fashion involved willingly impeding your own mobility.

"Now you mention it," her nose wrinkled, "that kid's got a serious case of Gainsborough's Blue Boy going on that would get his ass kicked at school. And Grandpa there is rocking the kind of white boots I haven't seen outside of a Nancy Sinatra video."

Once again, Rollie wasn't sure of her specifics, but he got the gist.

She continued, "If they were alone, then: whatever..." she shrugged. "But together they're all a little too ... *something*. What do you think their deal is?"

"I don't know," he murmured, "but I don't think they want to deal." He drew an XJ-25 from his inner coat pocket and stuffed it into her hand. "Stay here. Cover me."

"I still don't work for you," she told him with a smirk.

"Whatever." He flashed her a tense smile and thumped down the ramp.

He skirted around Bertram's little tour group. "Good morning," he said in his most pleasant tone. They watched him uneasily, which was how most people watched Rollie, anyway.

"Morning," he greeted the law enforcement persons and the FBI, as he navigated around them, too.

"Afternoon?" one suggested, though still covering him.

"Ah, so it is!" said Rollie, noting the angle of the sun. "Afternoon!" And Rollie made his way to the wallflowers at the back.

It was there he stopped. "And a stellar afternoon to you," he announced. "Couldn't help but notice you all the way back here. Do you not want to meet the fine people of Epiq?"

They exchanged glances, almost as one.

"What would we say to them?" asked the old man in the white boots, in a voice that did not sound male or old.

"You could ask them about their planet." Rollie watched for sudden movements. "Find out what their families are like. Ask about space travel."

"What else?" asked the child that Rozz had called Blue Boy, in a voice that did not sound young.

"You could ask about their schools and what they learn," Rollie suggested, surveying the boy's empty hands suspiciously.

"And me. What could I ask them?" A woman stepped forward with hair like a helmet and a voice like a kachunkettball Lower Lobber. "Could I ask them about what the food is like on their planet?"

"You could." Rollie eyed the woman closely.

"And how the people of their planet taste?" A sinister amusement touched her eyes. "Because if it's anything like the flavor of your friend the cephalopoid, Rolliam Tsmorlood, I think we'd all be excited to try a Blefian banquet."

Rollie had his XJ-37 on the disguised Feegar in an instant, but the Tryfling law had already turned their barrels on Rollie.

"Put your weapon down and step away from that woman," ordered a Tryfling lawman.

Rollie had been expecting this and a slow smile broke over his face. "Put *your* weapon down and *my* friends —" he nodded toward Rozz and Tseethe, " — won't stun you rubbery."

"I repeat," said the officer, "step back from the woman. Put the weapon down."

"Did you not hear it threaten me?" Rollie asked. "That is not a Tryfe person. That is a dangerous alien — a Feegar in a fraggin' holowatch disguise. And while it might be female, unless you're another Feegar, I guarantee it don't matter much."

"Put the weapon on the ground and—"

With a sigh and a sudden educated guess, Rollie switched his laser to his left hand, dove and shot the hair-helmet woman sideways. Bullets flew where he'd stood a second before. The woman fell, flickering, and a Feegar was in her place, pierced cross-ways and holowatch steaming.

The lawmen's gunfire practically drizzled out when they saw that. "What the —?"

Rollie scrambled to his feet. "Why does nobody fraggin' listen?"

By now the Feegars surged forward, the Blefians scrambled to the ships and the people of Tryfe dispersed to the sidelines like amazed fans getting front row seats.

Rollie examined the downed Feegar. He'd purposefully set his laser to a low frag setting so he could see who he was dealing with, instead of sifting through dust. He checked for the military rank that Feegars liked to etch into their exoskeletons. With the older ones, their bodies practically read like resumes. But this one — he cursed: it wasn't the Feegar Commander. It was their fragging pilot.

None of this was over yet.

Bertram Ludlow didn't know what started the shootout but he had a pretty good idea who. The diplomacy had been going so well, why was he even surprised it was interrupted by gunfire, running and screaming? That was just the Tsmorlood way.

And sure enough, there was Rollie, laser drawn, standing over a limp body while mayhem crashed down all around him. But a second glance proved that the limp body was not a local.

The Feegars were here.

His first thought was to get the Blefians out of harm's way, but the Blefians were already on top of that. So he drew his laser and decided to help Rollie. Only Rollie seemed to be shooting a group of angry, aggressive Tryflings.

"What are you doing?" Bertram shouted. "Where are the Feegars?"

"These *are* the Feegars," Rollie said, lasering what looked like a skinny teen in a style of sports uniform that Bertram couldn't identify.

"Holowatch disguises?" Bertram asked.

"What do you think?"

"But how would the Feegars know you're here? Fess?" Bertram picked off an armed elderly woman who came running toward them like the wind.

"Doubtful. Duck!"

Bertram dropped down, as energy whizzed over his head. He noticed the group of real Tryfe people, including the cops and the local FBI, had gathered over to the side. They oohed and clapped as the beam hit a DrinkThis machine and it exploded into foam.

Bertram saw now Xylith had joined the battle. She asked, "And just why are we fighting half the populace?" She took down a young guy careening toward them in a lumberjack shirt.

Rollie said, "Feegars with holowatches. Pass it on."

"And how do you tell the real Tryflings from the disguised Feegars?" she asked.

"Oh, I dunno, the real Tryflings aren't trying to kill us?" Rollie snapped. "Just cover the Tryfe people, would you? Keep 'em out of the fraggin' way."

"They're doing a fine job of that themselves. There's Tryfe law over there. Are they normally so hands-off?"

"Not in my experience," said Bertram, who recalled once getting a ticket for jaywalking. Something was definitely up.

But there was no time to ponder it. A guy in a bathrobe hoisted a cannon-like weapon that seemed to come out of nowhere. Xylith and Bertram both aimed and the Feegar dodged at the last second, a tree behind him catching fire.

"Ahhhh!" said the crowd approvingly. There was another round of applause.

"Hey, Rollie, what if we got — Rollie?" Bertram turned to the person beside him and came eye to eyestalk with one of the house gastropoids. The snail looked at Bertram, nodded, then turned and let loose a string of shots from a handlaser he picked up somewhere. The snail had serious skills.

Bertram looked to see where Rollie had gone, but there was no sign of the Hyphiz Deltan. So Bertram did the only thing he could do; he upped the settings on his laser from Wound to Seriously Frag and leapt into the fray.

✧

It could never be said that Rollie Tsmorlood had much experience with babies of any species. But he was fairly sure Tryflings of the infant persuasion were more into Toe Discovery and Disproportionate Head Management than they were combat rolls behind park benches.

It was this last movement that caught his eye.

And while he wondered what the proper age *was* for Tryfe progeny to begin combat training, the miniature menace in question broke from his hiding place at a very un-infant run.

What is that baby aiming to do?

He watched it skirt past clots of Tryfe people and skim shrubbery, circumnavigating the scene on what appeared to be a sly trajectory for the Penumbra.

Rollie moved swiftly and had just intercepted the kid at the ICV ramp (*Wonder if Ludlow has a net ...*), when it ricocheted away from the ship and into another crowd.

People shrieked as they were flung aside by something that was far bigger than advertised. Rollie followed the motion and soon had the creature cornered at a bank of DiversiDine vending machines. Its back was to him. The baby's inconsistently large shadow explained so much.

"Settle down now, Commander, it's naptime," Rollie said, aiming his XJ-37.

The baby whirled, smiling up with a toothless malevolence not often found in those of the babble-and-burp demographic. The mouth was borrowed. The smile was chillingly familiar. The baby was also well-armed. The real laser looked bulbous and strange in its tiny holographic hand. "Ah, your battle tactics have not changed, Rolliam Tsmorlood. As always, I lead and you foolishly follow."

"Well, children shouldn't be left unattended. Figured someone should keep an eye," Rollie said.

"Speaking of eyes," sniggered the Commander, "I thought we'd relieved you of yours some time ago."

"Oh, these old things? I got these after we met. Lab regrown. Like 'em?" His POW days of the Feegar Rebellion were not a time he particularly cared to relive (bouts of PTSD to the contrary), but at least it sounded bold.

The baby directed a chubby thumb to a vending machine. "Then tell me," it rasped, "what does that say?"

Rollie couldn't imagine where this was leading. He frowned. "What, ZOT!?"

The kid's smile grew. "Have you tried it, Tsmorlood?"

"Nah, and you shouldn't either. Stunts your growth."

"I'm curious what the effect would be if you drank it," the baby mused. "Its whole impetus is thanks to you, after all."

"Funny, I don't recall working for DiversiDine," Rollie said.

"I know you recall the war camps," said the baby. "How much do you remember about our little experiments? The time you spent in marinade? It was quite precious to us. Without it, we would never have gained such an in-depth understanding of Hyphiz Deltan physiology — or the right cooking methods for your people. And your unique medical condition was quite the revelation."

"Yes, I rated that trip a one-star on VoyageAdvisor. The accommodations were terrible and the staff was too hands-on."

"Did you know we were able to replicate your systemic hypermotocerebrostasia? It was surprisingly easy," said the baby.

"Makes a great gift," said Rollie.

"On that, we agree," said the Feegar warmly. "Did you know that in a diluted form it bolsters mental dexterity and productivity in non-Deltans?"

Rollie's gaze shifted from the Feegar to the ZOT! machine. "I suspect I'm starting to."

"So many benefits. We knew when we uncovered it, we had something big. And TrustTChem knew it, too, when we approached them about the development rights. They paid us generously."

"And DiversiDine paid them," said Rollie as it all came into focus. "So that's what this is about, eh? The side effects aren't *like* systemic hypermotocerebrostasia: that's the stuff. And you couldn't just fight me. You had to be an obnoxious chatty slaggard and taunt me about my role in ZOT!." Ever since Zenith Skytreg became Official Leader of the Intergalactic Underworld Society and started the trend, nobody ever wanted to just shoot each other anymore. It was all brag, brag, brag ...

"I thought you'd enjoy knowing your time with us spawned something beyond your rather species-ist disdain for Feegars."

"Show me a Feegar who don't try to torture me, eat me or bore me to death, and I'll reconsider my position. Until then..." Rollie was out of patience. He fired the laser and...

A Tryfe woman screamed and sprayed something in his face. "You leave that poor defenseless baby alone!"

Rollie's most recent pair of eyes was suddenly on fire and his reconstructed tear ducts turned on the pressure hoses. Through the streams he tried to make out where the Commander had gone. He could tell that at least one shot had hit; he smelled burnt Feegar and could hear the sound of retreating feet.

"Are you zonked, lady?" he shouted. "Did you not see the stand-off going on here? That's one of the head baddies from the fraggin' planet Feegar!"

"That sweet innocent child?"

"With a giant weapon?"

"So it was raised in a household of violence. End the cycle!"

"I was about to end his cycle! Then you fraggin' sprayed me." He wiped his face on his coat sleeve. "Where is he?"

"I will not be a party to —"

"Where'd the slippery slaggard go?" The world was still a blur and the light caused stabbing pain. Unfortunately, Rollie soon learned where the Commander had gone, as a laser shot through his neck.

The pain seared and the world wobbled. Clamping a hand to the wound, Rollie squinted in the direction of the beam and saw the baby struggling with the settings on his handlaser, trying to bump it up higher. Rollie realized the only reason he wasn't dust was because the WK-90 was notorious for jamming on lower settings.

Thank the stars the Feegars are fine medical researchers but rotten judges of quality tech, he thought miserably.

Yet even now, the stupid Tryfe woman was trying to help the "baby."

"Oh, you poor thing, so small, so alone ... My, you're very young to be walking already. Where are your parents? You shouldn't be allowed to play with nasty things like this." She reached to take the gun away from it and instead must have grabbed the Feegar Commander's well-disguised lower leg. She blinked, confused.

Rollie gritted his teeth. He knew what came next and it could only benefit the Tryfling gene pool. But nonetheless, the Hyphiz Deltan found himself yanking her away, as that too-large shadow fell over the space she'd occupied and jaws snapped on empty air.

"De-FENSE!" chanted the crowd. "De-FENSE!"

Bertram Ludlow scanned Market Square to see how many Feegars were left. Xylith and Tseethe currently combated two at a café, Prinny trapped one in a Coaching booth and Jane Manners, Backs and someone Bertram didn't know were dealing with several Feegars in a Whack-a-Mole situation. Most of the invaders, however, had moved to the soda machines at the base of DiversiDine to support what appeared to be an infant in a shootout situation with Rollie Tsmorlood.

A Tryfe woman screamed past Bertram as he rushed to join them: "That's not a baby! That's *not* a baby!"

All around, piles of dust and physical casualties lay from both sides, but there was no time to think about it. There were more immediate concerns. Like the orange-red fluid running thick down Rollie's neck and into his collar.

Rozz, Bertram saw, was already in the melee. "Give it up, Cabbage Patch!" she shouted, laser drawn. "Nobody makes a buffet out of my Burgh."

The baby pressed something unseen at its chubby wrist and

the child vanished, revealing the Feegar Commander underneath. The crowd of locals gasped. With one long arm that extended even longer, the Feegar seized a nearby gastropoid who'd been holding his own in battle using advanced martial arts techniques. (Bertram had never seen such a flawless pinwheel kick performed by someone with no legs.) It was inspired. Sadly, it was not enough.

The Commander called out, "Territorial negotiations are now open between the brave and noble people of the planet Feegar and the pathetic, puny, cowardly, skinsack traitors in the secondary and significantly lesser Underworld."

"Long as you're approaching it with such an open mind." Rollie peered coolly over the barrel of his XJ-37. "What are your terms?"

The Commander's hand tightened around the snail's neck. "We the Feegar people will continue to obtain nourishment across the GCU Quadrants with no interference from your organization, nor any interaction between your people and the Coalition of Planets about our tactics."

Rollie sniffed. "Cosmic for you. What do we get out of it?"

"In return," continued the Commander, "we will not dine lavishly upon you, those you love and anyone we happen to find on your SpaceLog buddies list. We will officially scrub away the public shame that you, Rolliam Tsmorlood, singlehandedly brought to one of the finest warriors with whom we ever had the privilege to rampage. And we will generously overlook your past mockery of our unique and beautiful cultural traditions."

The Tryfling crowd looked curiously at Rollie now.

"He sent them a vegan gift basket," explained Tseethe.

"Ohhhh," groaned the crowd.

"Aw, c'mon," Rollie snapped. "That was funny." His words were strong but he was looking increasingly pale and unfocused.

"Agree to these terms," said the Commander, "or we will make it our business to systematically reduce your team to a pile of hair, bones and those chewy cartilage bits that no one really likes so you have to spit them into a napkin but no one's sure about the etiquette for that and so it's tricky — and we will start right here." Commander Nom's hand squeezed even more tightly around his captive's neck.

"Don't do it!" rasped the snail. "He'll never keep to any agreement! The needs of the many outweigh the needs of the one Aquaphilic House Gastropoid. No one should live in fear! Don't hide in your shells! Stand proud against those who would suppress and sauté you! Life for Tryfe! Life for Tryfe!"

"Life for Tryfe! Life for Tryfe!" the crowd began to chant along with him.

And before anybody could say anything more, a determined look crossed the gastropoid's eyestalks and he let loose with a well-aimed poison dart. Poison dripped down the Feegar Commander's face and onto its chest.

The locals cheered even louder now. "Life for Tryfe! Life for Tryfe!"

Bertram cheered, too, expecting the Commander to seize up or begin to have convulsions. But the Feegar only wiped his face and grinned. "Stupid snail," he sneered. "You thought your silly poison defense would subdue us, the mighty Feegars?" And with that, the Commander ran a claw across the unfortunate gastropoid's throat. A rich blue liquid, the tropical shade of toilet bowl cleanser, oozed from the wound.

The gastropoid's eyes grew wide, then gained a faraway expression. "Don't ... hide ... in your shells ..." he murmured and fell forward onto the sidewalk.

People in the crowd screamed. Aliens and Tryflings alike wept.

"Who's next?" asked the Commander.

"You," shouted Bertram Ludlow stepping forward, his laser drawn. "At a Coalition of Planets tribunal for murder and violation of ... uh," he looked to the Hyphiz Deltan, "what's it called again, Rollie?"

Rollie blinked glassy eyes. Bertram could see the man had lost an awful lot of blood and was trying hard to hold it together.

"*You* know ..." Bertram pressed him, "the thing the Coalition of Planets put the Feegars on because of the Feegar Rebellion?"

"Probation?" Rollie muttered vaguely.

"Probation!" Bertram said. "Your kinder, gentler PR campaign is done, Commander."

The Commander laughed. "You have no evidence we've broken probation," he said. "Just the word some backspace lifeforms, some disgruntled criminals and one freelance freight raider I can't kill since he technically isn't alive." The Feegar Commander thought that was really funny. "We cannot be stopped. We have thought of everything. We are ten steps ahead of anything you skinsack sub-creatures could think up and as soon as you recognize the Feegar superiority in these and all other th—"

"You do realize this is being filmed as a part of *There Goes the Galaxy* season two," said Bertram.

"Er, what?" asked the Commander.

"Yup." Bertram gestured to Jane Manners. "Ms. Manners here has been filming the entire incident with her neck thingy."

She nodded, giving a Vanna-like flourish to the thingy of neck in question.

"The footage is all going back to DiversiDine where the whole marketing department is probably watching it right now, live feed. And if it shows, say, a violation of lifeform rights, well ... not only will it be great evidence for the Coalition of Planets, but the Uninet series is gonna have one helluva season two ratings bump when it airs."

"Chew on that!" shouted Rozz.

This exchange even gave Rollie a brief second wind. "You might be able to claim self-defense in the freight raiding incident," he told the Commander, "but it's going to be pretty fraggin' hard to build a case for your mended ways when you came to a backspace planet, preyed on the locals, interrupted a peace-keeping mission and murdered innocents on camera."

"Wooooooo!" cheered the crowd. "De-FENSE! De-FENSE!"

"So …" Bertram turned to the police and FBI, "anybody here have handcuffs?"

Considering their rather bizarre, laid-back approach to the whole extra-terrestrial shootout, Bertram was surprised how fast the local law leapt into action now.

Of course, the Feegars weren't about to take this sort of treatment lying down. After all, they were a superior species who could not be stopped. They were mighty. They were righteous. They were still a little snacky. Bertram knew all this, because they told everyone over desperate bursts of renewed laser fire.

So it must have been something of a letdown when they discovered that even the most mighty and righteous foodie-warrior was ultimately no match for a group of highly annoyed Underworld ex-pats with worn-out listening ears and their handlasers set to stun.

Yes, like it or not, it wasn't long before the Feegars took it lying down in a very literal way. And Bertram found it satisfying to see how efficiently these soldiers moved from "Never give up, never surrender!" to "Please frag me per the ways of my people" as mumbled through stunned lips.

"We'll put these slaggards on their own ship," suggested Tseethe, while the exo-skeletoned warriors were being dragged off before the cameras. "I'll fly it to the Coalition of Planets home office in Quad Two. They'll know what to do. It's about time these guys feel what it's like to be prisoners of war."

"I'll go with you," offered Xylith. "With this group, you're going to need backup. I'll get someone else to fly my ship back to Epiq." She whirled on Bertram with a double-smile. "And don't worry: I'll catch up with you later."

"No, let me handle this." Rollie's face was pained but determined. "It's my fault the Feegars came here. My job to make it right."

Bertram, Rozz, Tseethe and Xylith exchanged glances and laughed.

"What?" The Deltan frowned. "What's even remotely funny about that?"

Bertram turned to him, "First of all, you've got a hole straight through your neck."

"And you look like Carrie on prom night," added Rozz.

Rollie shrugged away these minor concerns. "Got some reinforced super-stick tape back in my satchel. Slap that on, it'll be fine."

"Secondly," continued Bertram, "anyone who trusts you to bring the Feegars back alive anywhere would have to have a hole in *his* head."

Rollie's eyes, which had fully-returned to their normal orange, scowled. It looked like it took all his energy to do this, but he managed it.

"I promise, man," said Tseethe, "We'll keep all these slaggards completely restrained, pumped with DrinkThis and propped in front of the Uninet."

Xylith said, "I'm sure we can find some vegan cooking shows to keep them entertained in-flight."

Rollie never did utter the word "fine," but he made a grumble that might have been acquiescence. Bertram estimated that blood loss saved them about an hour of debate.

So with the logistics settled, Tseethe and Xylith left to take care of the Feegars, while Bertram, Rozz, Rollie and Jane joined Deezle and his team, who had been waiting patiently in the wings.

"Hey," Bertram greeted them, "how about you guys? How does total vindication feel?" He offered fist-bumps all around.

But Deezle didn't fist-bump and didn't look vindicated. In fact, he looked more like he'd just learned *The X-Files* was cancelled. "I've uploaded forty minutes of footage so far. We've already gotten a few hundred comments."

"That's great news!" Bertram said.

"Amazing!" said Jane.

"Social media kicking butt," said Rozz.

Deezle snorted. "Not if they think it's 'shopped."

"What?" said Bertram's group.

Chuck nodded. She pulled out a smartphone and read from her screen. "'Alien version of *Blair Witch* but cinematography too unbelievable' … 'Signs was better.' … 'Pink-haired chick could be hotter.'"

"Hey," said Rozz.

Chuck continued scrolling. " … 'Special effects so Old School.' … 'Trying too hard.' … 'Why do so many aliens in sci-fi have British accents?'" She grimaced. "That's just a sample."

"Excuse me," said one of the Earth cops now, stepping forward to shake hands with Bertram, Rozz and the rest of the team. "My partner and I think what you've done is great. We're proud to have such creative films like yours made in this city."

The partner chimed in, "No kidding! I mean, we would have liked a little heads-up about the filming today. Between you, me and the lamp post, you guys are going to have to do some serious backtracking with the city permits office on this. But we recognize it would have ruined the spontaneity. Totally changed the feel of the thing. Also, sorry about that initial gunfire."

"What we're saying is," continued the first cop, "we'd be happy to put in a good word for you with the city, if it'd help."

"Wait a minute," said Bertram, "you people don't seriously believe that this whole thing was just—"

"Yeah, thank DiversiDine for us for sponsoring the show, will you?" one of the FBI agents interjected, also coming to shake Bertram's hand. "I normally don't go for such obvious product placement in movies, but you guys made it work."

"Oh, come on now. You're kidding me, right? No one believes this is real?" Bertram pushed at the bridge of his nose again. A headache was coming on and it promised to be a whopper.

"Real fun, for sure," said the one cop. "I like the costuming. The clear exoskeletons? So scary."

"But—But—" Bertram was still trying to find words. The crowd was dispersing swiftly at this point, since no one ever wanted to help with the less glamorous aspects of event breakdown. "Guys, there was weapons fire!" he shouted. "At least ten different kinds of alien life! There are spaceships! Look at all the spaceships!" He gestured. "How do you explain the fucking spaceships?"

The FBI agent grinned, "Amazing, isn't it? You never know what those kids from the Plus-D'Argent Entertainment Technology group will come up with. Remember when they did special effects for that *KnightMan* film? And *Detective Widget?* We're so lucky to have so much talent in this city."

And the law enforcement personnel agreed they were very, very lucky, as they trickled away to wrangle the last of the onlookers and ultimately return to their stations and their normal Tryfe routines.

Bertram watched them go in a cold, numb sort of disbelief.

"I'm sorry, Bacontini," said Deezle, patting his shoulder now.

"Yeah, it really sucks," said Krestor.

"Grim is reality," sighed Zoltan, toying with a ring. "But still we abide."

It was no consolation, no consolation at all. Bertram's mission had triggered the biggest Tryfling-Feegar-Hyphizite-Gastropoid-Whatnot battle the planet had ever seen. Bertram Ludlow had brought genuine extra-terrestrial life to his planet. And nobody bought it.

After so much effort, it was hard to simply let it go. "You can tour the ship!" Bertram called suddenly to anyone within earshot. "Would you like to see the ship?" A ship tour had done the trick with the people of Blef. Why couldn't it work here?

"*I'd* like to see the ship, Bacontini," Deezle told him. But the regular locals all said they had to get back to their shifts. They'd already been on break too long as it was. Bertram could hear the news crews over in one corner of Market Square talking about potential fines for the film company for tying up traffic and failing to get permits. They said the Mayor had gotten out of a meeting and was on his way to have a serious chat with the filmmakers in charge.

"We'd better get out of here," Rozz said.

"Yeah, in that case, I'll take a raincheck on that ship tour. Check you later, Bacontini," said Deezle, grabbing their equipment. "Fight the good fight, man. I'll keep you posted."

And in a moment, they, too, were gone.

Bertram started directing the Blefians and their respective pilots back to their ICVs for take-off, and helped deal with the non-dusted dead and injured along the way. Rollie even took a moment to say some words in honor of his fallen comrades. Bertram wondered how anyone could believe that wasn't real.

Bertram was checking his own passenger list when a voice said, "Mr. Hill, er, Ludlow?" He turned. It was Carole from DiversiDine TLC. "I just received a request from James Able's office. He says he and a Mr. Eudicot T'murp would like to meet with you and your crew. He's out at our Moon location. He sent some escorts and a shuttle. He would like you to join them now."

Bertram noticed a dozen men emerge from DiversiDine headquarters that looked like Mr. Stevens from the Moon manufacturing facility. There was a certain no-nonsense tone about being confronted with a troop of Stevenses. Especially after his last encounter with them.

"Good," said Bertram. "We've been wanting a few words with James Able and Eudicot T'murp, too."

Bertram noticed a fierce look come over Jane Manners' freckled face. "The sooner, the better."

39

"You don't think they've loaded us to up to whack us, do you? Or they're bringing us out here so the Moon Township cops can arrest us for sabotage? Or— what are you doing?" On the DiversiDine shuttle, Rozz peered over Bertram's shoulder, onto the Uninet device in his hand.

"Just an idea," he said. "I'm curious whether—"

But then one of the gastropoids got carsick. And Lula had questions about the ethics of billboard advertising. Jane was arguing with the Blefian cops about the indignity of handcuffs. And Rollie decided to sew up his own neck with stuff he had in his pockets. So Bertram and Rozz never did finish their discussion.

Fortunately, Rozz's earlier concerns about being nabbed and slabbed were put to rest once the shuttle hit the DiversiDine Moon Township campus; there were no cop cars waiting to collar them and no trenches dug for swift execution. There were only ICV-shaped indentations in the field behind the plant and one more Stevens there to greet them. This Stevens wore a suit and tie—an Executive Stevens—and he led them into the plant, down a vaguely purple hall and into a conference room.

The room already felt crowded and, considering Bertram's recent intergalactic travel situation, that was saying something.

The whole shuttle group was escorted to seats at a huge table across from a variety of non-Stevens executives, largely Ottoframan in species. At the head of the table sat Eudicot T'murp and at T'murp's right hand was the CEO of DiversiDine World, James Able. Bertram recognized him, sans-holowatch disguise, courtesy of Deezle's decoded video.

"Thank you for coming," said T'murp once everyone was settled. "I believe many of us have met before. But for those who haven't, I'm Eudicot T'murp and I run DiversiDine Entertainment Systems and Aeroponics for the overall GCU." He smiled warmly at everyone around the table, like this was a welcome reunion and not a brief, post-shootout détente. "This," he gestured to the younger man at his right, "is my nephew. You may know him as James Able, but his Ottoframan name is Bud C'nara. He's been running DiversiDine's Tryfe operations."

Bud's expression, and even the leaves around his neck, seemed tense.

"I've called you here because I'm reevaluating DiversiDine's Tryfe situation and Bud has something he'd like to say," said T'murp. He elbowed him. "Bud?"

Bud glanced stiffly at his uncle, then turned to the group. "First of all, it's a pleasure to have all of you here today. We at DiversiDine believe that communication is a two-way flight path between our corporation and the stellar individuals in the communities we serve."

Eudicot T'murp looked pleased with this, his temples flowering a lovely purple at his nephew's words.

"Uncle Eudi believes I owe you, the people of Tryfe, an apology," continued Bud. "Something deeply personal and from the heart. I know, because he gave it to me on infopill as written by his Making Things Up department." Bud tossed his uncle a tight, sarcastic smile. "See, my Uncle Eudicot knows that as long as you apologize on camera and say you've changed, lifeforms will forgive anything: adultery, military invasions, Stella Cygnus' last movie … and any little changes a company might have made to somebody's planet."

"Bud…" There was warning in T'murp's tone.

But Bud went on, "You see, what I've been trying to explain to my uncle for the past few days is that I couldn't be more proud of my work on Tryfe. And I think if we all look at this objectively, we'll agree that the plusses of DiversiDine on this planet far outweigh any little minuses you people happen to experience along the way."

Commotion broke out around the room, with DiversiDine execs worried about corporate damage control, Earth people issuing protests, gastropoids threatening stinging spray and Blefians calling for a vote on something, anything. But Bud C'nara would not be daunted. He continued, "The simple fact is, DiversiDine came to Tryfe and we made it a better place. That cannot be denied. Communities are thriving. People have direction. And individual life satisfaction ratings are at an all-time high."

Bertram couldn't believe his ears. "You call statues happy?" he asked.

"Oh, cut the drama, Mr. Ludlow," sighed C'nara. "So a miniscule percentage of Tryflings are now enjoying a slower pace and more Me time. Who wouldn't want that? Yes," he addressed the group as a whole, "it's true that DrinkThis and ZOT! were originally supposed to be contained to small pilot programs. The intent was never to intrude on Tryfe culture…" Then Bud leaned in confidentially. "And what a huge missed opportunity that would have been!"

T'murp's face had become a darkened green. "Bud, I think that's enough."

"Oh, but it wasn't enough," Bud said, flashing his relative a look. "Not nearly enough. Yes, we knew what the products could do. But we needed to see how far they could go with the right marketing. A whole society based on beverage consumption and motivation! And, as I predicted, it was an enormous success! People who drank our jubies-infused products got along with others better. They made more time for each other. They trusted each other more, gave each other greater opportunities. They took more pride in their families, homes and in their neighborhoods. Their enthusiasm is infectious. It's even spread to non-users. DiversiDine has helped make Tryfe a veritable paradise."

"Dude, it's a lifestyle built on DrinkThis and delusions," said Rozz.

"Well," Bud laughed, a surprised, exasperated guffaw, "delusion, *of course*. I mean, it's marketing. You can't have happiness *and* truth—everyone knows that. Most species spend their whole lives lying to themselves about a thousand different things just to get through the day. How is this any different?"

"Bud," said T'murp through gritted teeth, "if you don't mind, I'll take it from here."

"You took it nowhere, Uncle Eudi," Bud snapped. "Nowhere! Where were you when, after the Swirling Times, the people of Tryfe cried out for cohesion? You had a whole planet, scared, unsettled, fractured. They wanted something that people of all countries, races and creeds could get behind."

"Lousy sports metaphors?" asked Bertram.

"Exactly!" said Bud, eyes bright. "Generic, comforting, personalized advice in an easily digestible format. Not threatening to any existing status quo. Universally-compatible. Adaptable. See, I learned that from Epiq. You have to work with what the people want. And the people wanted this. Don't you understand?"

"I do," said T'murp, nodding. "I really do understand." And with that, Eudicot T'murp rose, pulled a handlaser, aimed at his nephew and let it fly.

Surprise lit Bud C'nara's eyes for a fleeting moment, then he fell limp. As the young man's forehead bounced off the conference room table, T'murp and the rest of the group winced.

"It's all right. It's stun-level one," T'murp said, though somewhat uncertain. "I only hope someday my sister forgives me."

He tucked away the gun and cleared his throat. "Moving on. To my original purpose for this meeting ... What Bud was supposed to relay to you—*and* the audience of *There Goes the*

Galaxy season two —" he grinned in the direction of Jane Manners' neck, " — is this: Tryfe and Epiq were designed to test market on two unique and disparate backspace cultures. Both operations have now been tainted. Based on what I've seen, Epiq is likely to someday join the Greater Communicating Universe. And Tryfe is, uh, well…" T'murp frowned, "I'm not sure how that's going to shake out. Anyway, my point is I can't get anything done with you people. So DiversiDine is cutting its losses and I will be putting up both planets for sale."

"Aw, crap," moaned Rozz, head in her hands. "Not this again."

"Fraggin' nepotism," sighed Rollie. "Eventually, it hurts everyone."

"So what'll it be?" Bertram asked. "Sell to the highest bidder?"

Rozz suggested, "Or the ol' Whoever Has the Flashiest Business Plan?"

Lula raised her hand. "Could we vote on it?"

Her district Supervisor and all of Bertram's passengers from District Fourteen expressed some enthusiasm for this particular idea.

"I'm sorry, young lady," said T'murp, "this is not a voting type situation. This is a—"

Bertram asked, "Will you sell the planets before or after you compensate us for our roles in *There Goes the Galaxy*?"

One of T'murp's fronds cupped around his ear. "Excuse me?"

"Compensation," said Bertram. "Recently, it occurred to me that you filmed and distributed *There Goes the Galaxy* using us, our names and our images without our permission. So I did a little digging on the way here. And I discovered you also issue some pretty twinkly merchandise associated with the series." He pulled up his pocket Uninet and held it for all to see. "Look, there's official Bertram Ludlow *There Goes the Galaxy* t-shirts, Rozz has her own branded shade of fuchsia genetic hair color…"

She scratched her head. "I do?"

"...There are Rollie Tsmorlood handlasers," Bertram turned to Rollie, "Kind of low-impact, though. No XJ-37s. Purely stun guns."

Rollie shook his head and glared at the executives across the table. "Lazy research," he told them.

Bertram said, "Plus, there's Bertram Ludlow Tryfe-themed snacks and Rozz Mercer infopill organizers. All distributed through DiversiDine Entertainment Systems and Aeroponics. And that's just the stuff I found on the ride over here."

Eudicot T'murp tugged at his collar. "Ah...Well..."

"I know I didn't give any permission for it. And I certainly didn't receive compensation," said Bertram, turning to his friends. "How about you, Rozz? Rollie?"

Rozz and Rollie said, no, they hadn't seen one single yoonie.

By this time, T'murp was motioning to his executives. "Um, can someone cut the neck video feed? Who's in charge of that? Ms. Manners' neck feed?"

"Hey, what about you, Jane?" Rozz asked the schoolteacher. "Anybody approach you about the rights to use your image for *There Goes the Galaxy* season two?"

"Not that I recall." Jane frowned. "But I've been kinda busy."

Rozz nodded. "And have you experienced emotional distress during this journey?"

Jane let out a bitter laugh. "If by 'journey' you mean being abducted and erroneously sent to an intergalactic prison?" She tucked a lock of hair behind her ear. "It was no cookie break."

"Mental anguish," said Rozz. "Bertram and Rollie, too, could build reasonable cases for mental anguish compensation, all because DiversiDine purposefully put them in stressful, risky situations for entertainment value." It was nice to see Rozz finally getting to use those GCU law infopills she'd digested, back when she was barista slave labor.

By now, Eudicot T'murp's voice held a strained tone as he scanned his staff, "C'mon, no one here worked on the Yellow Thing neck feed?" His executives all shrugged, exchanged glances.

"Mental anguish, Mr. T'murp," Rozz said again. "And I'm willing to bet there are lawyers all across the GCU who'd be jazzed to take our case. So we can either discuss this in the Greater Communicating Universe legal system…"

T'murp turned to her: "There's no need to be hasty, Ms. Mercer."

"Or," Bertram leapt in now, "we could make it simple. Transfer Tryfe and Epiq to us and District Fourteen as part of a sensible compensation package, and we can avoid all that messy legal stuff."

"You want me to give you Tryfe," said Eudicot T'murp.

"Oh!" said Rozz and she actually smiled. "Hey, there's an idea!"

"An entire planet?" said T'murp.

"Two planets," said Lula.

"You did say they were worthless to you now," Rollie pointed out.

"I meant for test marketing," said T'murp with a glare. "And about all this compensation you think I owe you. I might remind you, you did blow up several of my operations."

"The cost of ground-breaking entertainment," Jane Manners explained, tapping the Yellow Thing.

"She totally broke ground," agreed Rozz. "Also other things."

"Look, T'murp," said Bertram. "I get it. No deal's good unless both parties feel like they've sacrificed something. So I tell you what I'll do…" He began dumping out the contents of his pockets onto the conference table. It included a few Tryfe dollars, two yoonie cards, a fake ID, his DiversiDine employee card, his cell phone, the handheld Uninet, the Penumbra remote, three Starlight mints and an emergency package of ramen noodles.

He slapped down the yoonie cards before T'murp. "I've got fourteen yoonies total on those." He wished he'd dipped into his money stash back on the ship but, really, a person could only pre-plan so much.

Rozz was already rummaging in her pockets and tossed her

yoonie card onto the table. "I've got about ten on here." She looked to Rollie.

He shrugged. "Sorry. My yoonies were in my Protostar."

Jane Manners held out empty hands. "I just stole stuff."

The Blefians apologized for not being involved sooner in any sort of unified currency situation.

The gastropoids didn't have pockets.

"So twenty-four yoonies," announced Bertram.

"Oh!" exclaimed Lula, like she'd just realized she needed to use the restroom. "And these!" She removed her necklace and put that in the pile.

"Twenty-four yoonies and some beads," said Bertram.

T'murp eyed the items before him.

"It's a great ending to your season," Bertram reminded him. "Picture the headlines: Heroic Business Mogul Completes Landmark Entertainment Project — Sells Property Back to Its Inhabitants."

Rollie said, "And truly, mate, the Tryfling-in-space theme? Been done to death. People see it coming."

Jane Manners nodded vigorously. "It's why my season worked out the way it did."

Rozz suggested, "But why don't you think of this as a kick-ass opportunity to branch out? Like, how about a show where you film Ottoframan law enforcement on-the job? You could call it ..." It took her only a moment. " ... *Law and Orbit*. It could have a catchy theme song and everything."

Bertram noticed excitement beginning to stir the execs from the Putting Things Out There department.

One of the gastropoids piped up, "Or how about a series about the birth, attempted extermination, growth and eventual Vos Laegos stand-up comedy career of an Aquaphilic House Gastropoid? Who doesn't love a good snail-against-the-odds story?"

"I've got it!" Bertram shouted and pointed to their host. "Why don't you star in one, Mr. T'murp?"

"Me?" T'murp's expression went from surprise to a vague, quiet pleasure.

"Why, I can't believe we didn't think of this sooner!" Bertram continued. "Look at that face! Those fronds! Those dashingly flowering temples!" Yes, Bertram was laying it on a little thick. You did what you had to in the name of Saving the Planet. "I can see it now. A show where lifeforms across the galaxy present you with their most marketable food product ideas and the winning item gets included in DiversiDine's snack line."

Jane said, "Genius! It's fun, it gets people involved and it practically cuts the creative work right out of the process."

"Uh," said someone in the Making Things Up department, "let's not be hasty."

But the momentum was already there. Bertram pushed the yoonie cards and beads to the CEO. "Think about it, Mr. T'murp ..." He grinned. " ... *Eudi* ..." He knew he was stretching it with that, but sometimes you had to test the boundaries. "You won't get a better offer. And I'll tell you something else: we'll even let you quote us in a press release saying how you helped underdeveloped planets gain their independence. It's a supernova deal."

T'murp looked at the little pile of Universal currency cards before him. He looked at the Yellow Thing in Jane's neck. He looked down at his nephew who had gained some motor control but was still drooling lightly on the conference table. "Bud," he said, "we're repositioning. Time to shift our efforts from Tryfe and Epiq to exciting new horizons."

Bertram felt his heart lift, while Bud responded with a series of gurgled consonants.

T'murp bent down to listen. "Er, what's that, Bud? I can't *quite* make that out. I—"

Rollie said, "He's saying, 'You're not really going to give in to these people, are you? This is blackmail.'"

Everyone around the table looked at Rollie.

"What? So I've had to decipher my share of stunnings. Move along."

"Ah," said T'murp, rising and patting his nephew's head. "It would seem my young relative has confused blackmail with

DiversiDine's ongoing corporate mission to lend a supportive hand to our backspace brethren in times of need." Bertram was impressed how fast T'murp had embraced the positioning on this. "And don't you worry, Bud. Though you conclude your tenure here at DiversiDine World, Tryfe branch, I haven't forgotten all you've done for us. In fact, I have a brand new career opportunity that's opened up and it's perfect for your skill set."

Bud tried the vowels this time.

"That's right," T'murp went on, "you will be DiversiDine's new Vice President of Loam-Centric Agricultural Enhancement: Compost division. Isn't that cosmic?"

Bud burbled some words onto the table, along with a skosh more drool.

Rollie explained, "He says, 'But DiversiDine's an aeroponics company. We don't use soil.'"

"Glad you're as excited about it as I am, Bud," T'murp said quickly. He pointed to one of his executives. "Could you please pull up two property transfer forms? I'll need one for Tryfe in the amount of twenty-four yoonies, and one for Epiq in exchange for some, er—" He picked up the necklace.

Lula said, "Handcrafted jewelry featuring semi-precious stones?"

"What she said," T'murp told them. "List it as payment in full rendered, in exchange for name and image usage rights for *There Goes the Galaxy* series one and two, and one quote per person for an upcoming press release. Make the first document out to Bertram Ludlow, Rozz Mercer and Jane Manners."

He turned to Bertram, Rozz and Jane with a broad, very fake smile. Through his teeth he said, "Sign this, and you must never approach me again for any additional form of compensation. Are we clear on that?"

"Crystalline," said Bertram.

"And no reunion shows," added Rozz.

T'murp hesitated. "Come on. Not even a little anniversary special? A cameo maybe?"

Bertram said, "She's right. No reunions or we walk."

It felt like a long moment. Then T'murp sighed. "Fine. No reunion specials. Got it." He turned to the executive. "Add that to the contract." The words sounded like they hurt. "And make up another contract for the child here—"

"Lula Trubludgett," said Lula, "and all the residents of Blef District Fourteen."

"And Blef District Fourteen," said T'murp.

"And when you've finished with that," Rollie said, "I wonder if you and I might have a private moment…"

The crowd on Bertram's ship toasted, as the Penumbra Classic took off on a trajectory for Epiq.

"Here's to planetary ownership," Bertram said, clinking glasses with all the lifeforms surrounding him. The beverage was a small keg of a limited-run oomloo berry flavored Carsoolian Pod Liquor he'd been hiding in his quarters for a special occasion. He'd heard that oomloo berry tasted a lot like candied yams with marshmallows. So naturally he had to try it. "Cheers!"

"*Tsu nae fra-gra nee!*" said Rollie, which Translachew roughly translated to, "May you never need your backup liver."

"To everybody for being awesome!" said Rozz, clinking.

"To insight, truth and a bright future!" said the Superintendent of District Fourteen.

"To the motherland!" came a voice from the floor. It was Cordelia the cat. She wasn't imbibing.

"And to all those who sacrificed to help get us here today," Jane said. She said this with a specific eye on the gastropoids, but they were already chugging their drinks and going back for seconds. It was apparently a big improvement over shower water.

Bertram mused over his glass. "You know, I feel kind of bad …"

Rollie's laugh was incredulous. "One sip? You *are* a lightweight, Ludlow."

Bertram smirked. "You gonna let me finish? I was about to say, I feel kind of bad because you didn't get anything out of this, Rollie. I mean, they screwed you over as much as us. More maybe. You got stuck on Altair-5."

"Aw, Altair's not so bad." A slow, disturbing smile spread over his face. "Anyways, I got what I wanted."

Bertram raised an eyebrow. Then he recalled Rollie *was* late on the return shuttle, wasn't he, having lagged behind in a talk with DiversiDine's CEO? "You didn't frag T'murp, did you?"

"What?" Rollie sniffed. "Why is that always the first thing everyone thinks of? I do have other areas of interest."

Bertram just smiled patiently at him, waiting for a real answer.

And it came with a growl, "No, I did not frag, T'murp." Rollie polished off his drink and poured himself another. "T'murp's done me a favor, actually. As you know, this *There Goes the Galaxy* season two footage contains some pretty hefty evidence of the Feegars' crimes against society. So T'murp's had his Sending Bits of Video department, or whatever he calls it, pack-up certain Feegar-related pre-release footage to the Coalition of Planets, to be used as evidence. The Coalition received the files one Universal hour ago, so they'll be well-informed by the time Tseethe and Xylith get there with the prisoners." There was an expression of dark pleasure on his face. "I don't think the Feegars are coming back from this one."

"And Fess?" asked Rozz quietly, like she almost hated to bring it up.

"Ah," Rollie said, "been so busy putting things to rights, I didn't realize we hadn't heard from Wilbree lately. Let's give him a shout, eh?" Lifeforms dodged out of his way as Rollie moved to the vis-u.

He entered some numbers into the keypad. After a moment, Wilbree's sideways face showed up.

"Hello, this is Wilbree here on the vis-u," he said. "Oh!" He pushed up his sunglasses and grinned. "Rollie! You've not been eaten! Why, that's a sunny thing, isn't it?"

"I like to think so," said Rollie. "We're wondering about Fess."

"Ah!" he said. "Stellar timing. I'm here at Vos Laegos City General, so see for yourself." He moved the handheld vis-u to showcase what appeared to be a large tank next to him. There was a little something floating in the water, but it was hard to tell what it was.

"Right ..." Rollie squinted. "And what do we make from that?"

"He's regrowing!" said Wilbree.

"He is?" Rollie tilted his head. "All I see's maybe a beak, an eyeball and a blob of other stuff fanning round in fluid."

"Exactly!" Wilbree brightened even more. "And that blob of other stuff is a much bigger blob than it was yesterday. And an even bigger blob than the day before."

Bertram leaned closer to the screen and wrinkled his nose. "It is?"

"By next Moonsday, who knows?" said Wilbree. "That blob might get to be a nodule or even a full-fledged knob." He nodded enthusiastically, adding, "It's also brain."

"So that's ... good," Rollie sounded uncertain.

"Hopefully hopeful, I was told."

"The doctors said that?" asked Rolllie with a frown.

"Er, not precisely ..." Wilbree toyed with his beard. "They said words I didn't really understand. But the cleaning robot was in at the time and then it explained it to me."

"Thank the stars for the medical insight of cleaning robots," said Rollie heartily.

"We're playing Pratl right now, Fess and I. I have to choose the moves for both of us, but Fess is winning."

"I'm sure he is," said Rollie.

"Anything you want me to tell him, if his ear bits start regrowing?"

Bertram wondered where the "ear bits" were located in Fess' species since, as far as he recalled, Fess didn't have ears.

Rollie said, "Tell him the Coalition of Planets is about to receive a shipload of his Feegar assailants. And tell him the

Coalition will be glad to hear his testimony, when he's up and ready."

"I'll do that," said Wilbree.

"Also," Rollie's voice was quiet now, "tell him I owe him one, would you?"

"Of course." And Wilbree blipped off.

40

When am I ever going to learn that in the GCU, optimism is for suckers?

Bertram had thought, when he reached Blef, that he was simply dropping off his District Fourteen passengers and they'd go on their merry way. He imagined there'd be good-byes, wishes for a safe journey, some tears and, of course, profuse thanks for helping them achieve planetary independence.

Y'know, same old, same old.

But filing down the ramp, Bertram distinctly heard the Supervisor call to the group: "Don't forget, everyone — we have one open item that requires a vote. We'll need to gather all District Voteworthies and decide whether or not to reduce Defendant Manners' sentence."

Even Rollie, a GCU veteran, looked astonished by this. "Reduce?" His voice cracked. "This is something that actually requires mulling over, is it? After all that's happened? Flamin' Altair!" He shook his head to the heavens. "This is why I hate the fraggin' law."

"It's okay, Rollie," Jane said quietly, the Blefian guards surrounding her. "We did what we set out to do. And you all were more than fair about helping me. I own thirty-three percent of Tryfe—er, Earth. The planet is safe. I will serve my sentence now, whatever may come." Her face was full of peace and light, almost like she'd been hitting the DrinkThis.

Rollie was still muttering about the whole thing being "fraggin' absurd," sharing dark words with Rozz of revolution, as Bertram's group trailed Jane and the guards to the courthouse. It wasn't long before the whole of District Fourteen had joined them.

The Supervisor didn't waste any time, either. "Now I know everyone's tired from the trip, eager to be home and reflect on what we've learned. But we do have this one last order of business, so let's get to it." He clasped his hands before him. "District Fourteen was tasked to experience the planet Tryfe and DiversiDine's effect on it. Today we must use that information to decide whether Defendant Manners' actions — when she endangered the public and blew up private property — were in the best interests of Epiq. Today we must ask ourselves: can we safely reduce the Defendant's sentence?"

The Blefians nodded, grateful for the recap, since so much had happened over such a short time.

The Supervisor said, "In the interest of speed — and also on account of no one's had a chance to unpack yet — I think we can skip roll call today. So does everyone have their voting devices?"

He waited and surveyed the room as the people of Blef raised their voting machines in affirmation. "Excellent!" he said. "As before, you will see a number of available sentences on your screen. Please select one and submit your vote." Everyone busied themselves choosing options. Bertram tried to see how Lula was voting, but her hat was in the way.

"Lula," Bertram whispered. "Lula, reduced sentence, reduced sentence…"

"Shhhh, Mr. Ludlow… My vote will not be influenced…" And she waved him away.

The votes began trickling in and Bertram felt the tension within him build as they waited for the tally. It all seemed to be taking an incredibly long time.

Rozz apparently agreed. "Why is this taking so long? And look at Jane up there." She drew their attention to the Tryfe woman. "I hope she's okay. Am I wrong or does she have this weird kind of Joan of Arc vibe going on?"

She was, indeed, sitting in the defendant's box with this odd, contented calm.

Rollie turned to the Tryfe-people, intrigued. "Joan of Arc: is she a mathematician?"

"No, why?" asked Rozz suspiciously.

"Just curious. We had a Dree of Secant back on Hyphiz Delta. A bit zonked, that one. Always going off on tangents."

Bertram was about to explain that Ms. of Arc was more about mass than math, when a shout erupted from the front of the room.

"It's in!" the Supervisor announced, leaping to his feet. "The results are in! And what an overwhelming response there's been!" He stared at the screen, tears glistening in his eyes. "My friends, never in Blef history have we had such a consensus as this. With ninety-eight percent of the votes, it has been decreed by District Fourteen of Blef on the planet of Epiq, that Defendant Jane Manners' sentence has been altered. She shall now go to the Gallows and—"

"What?! The gallows?" shouted Bertram. "That's insane!" He hadn't even known death was an option on the list. Had it been an option earlier? He didn't think so.

"This is a total joke!" shouted Rozz. "A travesty of justice! This so has to be a mistake!"

"It is a far, far better thing I do than I have ever done before," said Jane Manners. "It is a better place I go to than—"

"Hold it! Hold it!" The Supervisor looked at them like they were all a few bricks short of a building. "What's the problem now?"

Bertram, Rozz and Rollie had all pulled handlasers. Bertram said, "You think after all we've been through, we would stand here and allow you to send this woman to the gallows?" He motioned to the prisoner. "Come on, Jane. This time we are busting you out."

Jane blinked in a glassy daze.

"I don't get it," the Supervisor scratched his beard. "I've

never had anyone object before."

"Well, it's hella time someone did, mister," said Rozz. She covered the Supervisor while Rollie covered the guards and Bertram maneuvered Jane toward the door.

"But they're regarded throughout the District as responsible, kind and fair-minded people," the Supervisor said.

"Who is?" Rollie spat.

"Our community service managers, Glerbert and Bajumbi Gallows." He gestured to an elderly couple, hair like cotton candy, that Bertram saw in the Blefian tour group but had never spoken to.

"Hi!" They waved.

"Glerbert and Bajumbi Gaaa …" Bertram stopped in his tracks. "Ah."

Rozz's face was as hot pink as her hair. She started to return the wave, then realized she still held a gun. She hid it behind her back and waved with the other hand.

"Uh, momentary confusion," Bertram said, as he and Jane returned awkwardly to the courtroom and resumed their respective seats, which somehow seemed to take way too much time. Bertram tugged at his collar. It was suddenly very warm in there. He motioned. "Carry on."

"Er, yeah. Sorry," said Rollie. "Sorry." He filed back into his aisle looking slightly disappointed that a jailbreak was not, in fact, meant to be. He'd been deprived of this twice now.

The Supervisor waited until he was sure the group was fully committed to staying, then cleared his throat. "Jane Manners, these are the terms of your community service: for one week you will help clean up the area around the property you blew to smithereens. This includes helping repair any broken windows in the neighboring buildings and moving bricks to recycling. You will stay with the Gallows at their halfway house. You will not be required to wear tracking technology, unless you fail to report there during the assigned hours. The Gallows will provide your meals during this time. There are rumors of homemade sweet rolls that may prove true. Do you understand?"

She smiled. A normal person smile, too, not that "I will bravely endure the flames at my feet" sort of smile. "I understand," she said.

"At the end of that week," continued the Supervisor, "you will be free to go, provided you don't detonate anything within that timeframe. Do you think you can manage that?"

"I believe I now have an excellent chance of being detonation-free, sir," she said.

"Good. Then report to the Gallows immediately," said the Supervisor. "Everyone else, you are dismissed."

District Fourteen cheered and began to disperse. The guards unlocked Jane's cuffs and released her into the custody of the Gallows. And as the trio was leaving, Bertram approached them, tucking his portable Uninet into Jane Manners' grasp. "At the end of your week, call me on that. My ship number's in the address book. I can either swing by and pick you up, or get someone to do it."

"Ohhh," there was teary gratitude in her eyes, "thank you so much, Bertram. You've been so kind to me. But —" She pressed the device back into his hands. "I've been thinking, I might stay here on Epiq for a while."

Rozz blinked, incredulous. "Seriously?"

"You know, I have no one back on Earth," Jane said. "Nobody special. And my introduction to outer space was a little ..." she gave a sharp laugh, "intense. The people of Epiq will be getting ready to make contact with the GCU. They've taken the first step. So I think I'd enjoy easing into this new normal along with them."

Bertram recalled his own introduction into the GCU — and Rozz's. They were both on the abrupt side. "I think I can understand that." He reached out and shook her hand. "So I guess this is goodbye. And good luck, Jane."

"Thanks for your help," she said, smiling from Bertram to Rozz to Rollie. "All of you."

"Looks like you're in good hands," Rozz said, indicating the elderly couple. "I mean, you just know these two are a laugh riot."

"Oh, we are, dear?" asked Mrs. Gallows, flushing prettily.

"Sure," said Rozz. "Gallows humor."

Bertram cringed. "We've gotta go."

"Aw, you'd be laughing your ass off, if you'd thought of it."

"And once again," said Rollie, trailing them out, "I know I am missing some Tryfan cultural reference."

"We'll get you a book next time we're on Tryfe," said Bertram.

"You keep saying that. I'm going to need a lot of books."

The Hydrophilic House Gastropoids wanted to go to Vos Laegos. One of them heard that snail racing was big in certain Underworld betting facilities, and she thought her sleek physique could earn her some big yoonies in the sport. Another wanted to check out a few of the clubs, since the nightlife as found in a Penumbra Classic bathroom was, admittedly, fairly limited. Then there was the gastropoid who'd pitched the Uninet series to T'murp. His name was Zib and he really did want to be the GCU's first gastropoid stand-up comic. He understood it would be a tough gig, but he felt certain he had the hard shell and the determination to follow his dreams.

Feeling strangely like a parent who'd been looking forward to the peace and quiet of his golden years, Bertram Ludlow didn't question these ideas. He was willing to do whatever it took to get the grown kids out of the house.

So he set the course for Vos Laegos City with hope buoying his spirit and plans for his own future resurfacing in his mind. "First thing I'm going to do when we get there is hit the Klinko Buffet Nice No-Kill-You All-You-Can-Digest Buffet," he said, adjusting the ship's thrusters. He'd seen ads for the place and had to find out what it was like. "Then, if I can still walk, I'll stop at a travel agency and reschedule my tour."

Some time ago, when the Earth was trapped in the Number Three virus and Bertram Ludlow had found himself with unexpected time on his hands, he'd planned to do a little intergalactic sightseeing. Ultimately, this trip was pushed aside for more immediate concerns, but he still longed to experience the Rings of Ragul-Sfera, check out the Ice Caves of Arcalogia and, of course, stare in awe at the universe's largest herd animal sculpture made entirely of toenails. Because a good vacation wasn't just about fun, it was about culture, too.

He told Rozz and Rollie, "You guys are both welcome to join me, of course ..." He'd been thinking of inviting Xylith, actually. But when you've spent so much time saving Life As You Know It with people, you don't want to look like you're simply shoving them out the hatch.

Fortunately, from the copilot's seat, Rollie shook his head in the negative. "Nah, Ludlow, I'm not really a Universe's Largest Toenail Thingy kind of fellah. I'm thinking I'll check in on Fess at VLC General, then see what the city's got up to by way of career opportunities and personal diversions." He gave an ironic laugh. "I seem to be running some sort of alternate Underworld organization; it's probably time I work out the details."

"And love ya, mean it, Bertram," said Rozz from the hatchway. "But we've already spent entirely too much quality time together in the past few bazillion light years."

Bertram grinned. "I didn't want to say it ..."

"I figure there's got to be someone out there who needs an awesome programmer with diverse skills," said Rozz. "Someone who appreciates my sublime ability to organize crap through masterpieces of database gorgeousness. Or who needs someone who can hack into a secured system." She shrugged. "Either one."

Rollie gained a thoughtful look. "You don't know anything about creating electronic library catalogs do you?"

"I don't work for you." Bertram could see her reflected in the ship's front portal. She almost seemed on the verge of smiling.

"Ah," Rollie said, "not yet, perhaps, but—" Something had caught his eye in the blackness of space on the starboard side. He tried peering around the corner of the portal window, then leapt from the chair and ran into the lounge for a better view.

"What? What's going on?" asked Bertram. He noticed the cats had come running to see, too.

From the lounge, Rollie cackled madly. "Unbe-fraggin'-lievable!" His smile was broad and manic, his eyes practically lit from within, though Bertram was pretty sure Deltans couldn't literally do that. "Karnax always said, 'What goes around comes around' —"

"I wasn't aware that was his work," said Bertram.

"— And flamin' supernova," Rollie continued, "if it hasn't come round and bit her right where it hurts."

It was only now, peering around Rollie's shoulder, that Bertram saw what the fuss was about. Off to the right, floating dark, was a Protostar 340-K Interplanetary Cruise Vessel. "Dar?" breathed Bertram.

"Dar," Rollie laughed pitilessly.

A sudden thought crossed Bertram's mind. "But the lights are off. Your Protostar's pretty distinctive. You don't think, when the Feegars were looking for you, they might have … er…" Bertram had visions.

"Serves her fraggin' right if they did," Rollie said. But Bertram could tell, the Hyphizite's vehemence was starting to flag. He moved to the cockpit and scanned the controls. "Frag it, you got no latch ramp on here, Ludlow. This ship is completely useless for any in-nav transfers."

"If you'll recall, I wasn't exactly planning on doing any freight raiding when I bought it," Bertram reminded him.

But Rollie just mumbled something in Hyphiz Deltan that didn't translate, and he dropped down into the pilot's seat as if Bertram, the ship's captain, wasn't even there. He gave his options a second quick assessment and grumbled, "Guess the winch will have to do."

It was only a few minutes before Rollie had the ships aligned and connected. Soon both the Penumbra and the Protostar were trekking along to Vos Laegos City.

Gray dust swirled in the desert around the popular tourist destination as they approached the grounded Protostar. A creature the basic color and shape of the rocky terrain scrambled across Bertram's boot, causing the Tryfeman to nearly jump out of his own skin.

Rozz rolled her eyes and turned to Rollie. "How are you getting in there, if Dar has control of your ship?"

Rollie drew a large, clumsy ship remote from his pocket. "She never got this. Didn't need it. If you're already inside, you can still work everything." He tried the device now and, as with the last time he'd done so, no hatch opened. No ramp appeared.

"Systems dead," he murmured. "Looks like we'll have to do this the hard way."

"What's the hard way?" asked Bertram.

Rollie never answered, but sighed like the weight of the universe was suddenly upon him. "Forgive me, *na tseenee*." His tone was unusually gentle and Bertram wasn't quite sure who he was speaking to.

Then he drew the XJ-37 and blasted open the Protostar's hatch.

As the hatch steamed, all was still and dark within. They waited. They listened.

A second later, Rollie unveiled that grappling hook he always carried around with him and had it secured to the ship with a clang. "Cover me."

Bertram and Rozz both drew their handlasers, focusing on the hatch and the darkness, looking for any sign of movement. Rollie shimmied up the side of the ship and scrambled inside. Bertram watched him press the button by the hatchway. Once … twice … But the ramp didn't descend.

He turned his attention to other things. "Dar?" Rollie called. "Dar?" and disappeared into the dim.

Bertram heard a distant thumping.

"Dar?"

They heard a muffled female voice. "Who else would it be? Get me out of here."

"Back. Get back from the door."

There was a blast. Then a voice, louder now. "Oh, it is *so* good to be out of there! Three days. *Three days* I was stuck in there."

"And what did you do to my ship?" Rollie's voice was like ice.

"What did *I* do? Nothing!" Bertram could hear Dar clearly now. "This ship is a time bomb. I plugged in the hotplate, thinking I'd heat up one of those containers of flargle soup I saw in the storeroom. I went to grab it, then the vis-u came on and half the electrics fried. It was pure luck it didn't wipe out the life support and on-board gravity field, too, or the GCU would have lost a very special person that day."

Bertram could see them now, headed toward the exit.

Dar seized the rope and began a rather graceful descent while Rollie took that moment to sniff derisively. "You were running the Uninet, too, weren't you?"

She looked up. "So?"

"Flamin' comets, woman! You can have the hotplate and Uninet, or hotplate and vis-u, but not all three at once. As always, Dar Balisong, you got fraggin' greedy."

"So this is my fault." The ice had shifted.

"As a start." He climbed down the rope and thumped to the earth.

She appealed now to Bertram and Rozz. "Any other ship ... *any* other ship, being trapped in the storage room? No big deal. But not in this pile of interstellar floating excrement. The shelves don't secure anything. So do you know what happens to all that junk in the storeroom when you descend? It's like being shrunk down and stuck in an Emperor's G'napps machine — all these playing pieces come flying at your head. I could have died." She massaged an angry red knot on her forehead as evidence.

"I don't care about your contusions," Rollie said. "I'm unmoved by your death of a thousand head injuries. I'm not here for you. I'm here for my ship. So, on your way." He aimed his XJ-37 as some encouragement in that direction.

Her tone was injured now. "You're simply stranding me here?" She squinted at the scenery. "I don't even know where 'here' is."

Rozz snapped, "Oh, for cryin' out loud, lady, you're outside Vos Laegos City. It's hardly an exile planet. You'll get by."

Rollie said, "And if I ever see you again, Dar, I will not be so kind as I am this moment."

Dar shrugged and started off in the direction of the City. "As if you've never stolen anyone's ship before…"

"You sent the blasted Feegars after me," Rollie shouted. "The *Feegars*. Innocent people were killed on Tryfe."

She turned, her expression sour. "And yet somehow you're still alive."

Truthfully, she hadn't gotten the full "-live" out before Rollie discharged the XJ-37 and Dar Balisong dropped to the ground.

Bertram wasn't sure what setting it was, but her skin was a paler gray than usual, not wholly unlike the Vos Laegon earth below her.

"Did you —?" Bertram hated to ask.

"Should have done." Rollie gave Dar's prone form a narrow furious look, clenched and unclenched a hand. "Might still."

But instead of upping his settings and finishing the job, Bertram was surprised to see Rollie Tsmorlood sit down on the ground cross-legged, close his eyes and take a few deep breaths. He muttered, "I am like the water molecules in the stream… I am like an ergowohm gliding on the wind … I am like … Like …"

"A Hyphiz Deltan with systemic hypermotocerebrostasia who really could use a few Feegar bourbons and a decent ICV parts store?" Bertram suggested hopefully.

Rollie's eyes popped open. "I could be like that. Yeah," he said and got to his feet. He clapped Bertram on the shoulder. "Maybe not Feegar bourbon."

"No Feegar bourbon," Bertram said. "Got it."

The Rings of Ragul-Sfera made Bertram Ludlow think of music. Or maybe that's because of the music playing in his rented touring pod, an inspiring alien instrumental specifically orchestrated and timed for optimal ring-viewing.

Xylith said, "It was simply cosmic how receptive the Coalition of Planets was to Tseethe and I once we arrived." She brushed a lock of dark hair from an eye. "You should have seen it. Why, they just swept those Feegars out of our possession, saying they'd take it from here, ma'am, and done was done. All because they received some very enlightening video footage of our Feegar friends in action."

"Well, you can thank Rollie for that," Bertram told her, adding quickly. "Not now, though, if you don't mind." It was hard to retain a certain mood when you're talking about Rollie and the Feegars.

But she nodded and sipped her thimble of wine. "And I hear Eudicot T'murp's almost completely packed up from your Tryfe, his buildings as empty as his life-coaching advice ever was."

"I heard that, too," said Bertram. Deezle had been keeping him looped in to things. "On Tryfe, they think it's because DiversiDine's trying to dodge a potential personal injury lawsuit for Action Figure Syndrome."

She peered over the thimble with interest. "Is that right?"

"I guess investigators discovered the two things all the victims had in common were unusually slow metabolisms and a few too many cans of ZOT! I don't think they've figured out the rest yet, but it may not matter much now, anyway." The pod turned to offer a different, equally stunning view of the rings.

"And did I hear correctly that one of those victims actually came out of it?"

Bertram gave an indecisive sort of nod. "One of the earlier victims — and sort of. They've regained a little movement, nothing huge, but at least there's improvement."

They felt silent and he was glad, because he was tired of talking about work and worry. He'd spent too much energy on that in the past. It was time for something new.

So Bertram pointed to one of the gleaming platters of food on his portal-side table. All of the items displayed there, he'd noticed, were cleverly ring-themed. "Try one of those crystalline purple hoop things," he said. "They're delicious."

"Ah." Xylith, reached for one of the hors d'ouevres and held it aloft, like some rare gem. It matched both sets of her eyes. "Why, it's cross-sectioned candied hearts of favinath! Such a daring culinary choice."

Bertram raised an eyebrow. *Hearts? In an actual organ-y sense?*

He adjusted the belt of his beautifully-embroidered Ragul-Sfera souvenir bathrobe and decided then and there, it did not matter. You didn't end up owning one third of your home planet by playing it safe. You didn't come this far, with the wonders of the universe stretched before you, hoping all of your destinations would be just like where you've been.

Yep, Bertram thought, *home is where the heart is.* And sometimes, that heart must wend its way through your digestive tract, wherever your course is currently taking you.

Bertram Ludlow helped himself to another purple ring.

ABOUT THE AUTHOR

Jenn Thorson is a marketing writer by day and an author by night — so sort of like Batgirl, but with less crime fighting and more carpal tunnel. She lives in Bertram Ludlow's hometown of Pittsburgh, PA, but is definitely mostly sure she's never met extra-terrestrials there. Her stories have been published in the *Humor Press*, the journal for the *Lewis Carroll Society of North America*, *The Timber Creek Review* and *Romantic Homes* magazine.

IF YOU ENJOYED THIS BOOK...

Tryfling Matters (There Goes the Galaxy, Book Three) is an independently published novel. So if you enjoyed this book, the author would be delighted if you'd tell a friend about it.

One way to help is by reviewing the book on **Amazon.com**. Amazon ranks its books, in part, by the number of customer reviews a book receives. So you can help *Tryfling Matters* reach *even more* eyeballs by going to Amazon.com, searching for the book and creating your own review.

Other ways to share *Tryfling Matters* with fellow Earthlings are:

- "Like" the *There Goes the Galaxy* trilogy on **Facebook**, for book and author updates, plus lots of spacey fun, at: **Facebook.com/ThereGoestheGalaxy**

- Visit **ThereGoesTheGalaxy.com** to check out *TGTG* themed goodies.

- Follow the author, Jenn Thorson, on **Twitter** at **Twitter.com/Jenn_Thorson**

www.ingramcontent.com/pod-product-compliance
Lightning Source LLC
Chambersburg PA
CBHW031425240626
47154CB00001B/208